PAR ANGUSTA

AD AUGUSTA

Through Trial to Triumph

By Philip Scholz

Contents

Chapter 1

Jefferson Thomas glanced up When he heard the ding.

"Ladies and gentlemen," the flight attendant said over the PA system, "as we prepare for landing, we would like to remind you to make sure your seatbelts are buckled and your seatbacks and tray tables are in their upright and locked positions. Flight attendants will do a final check of the cabin. If you have anything you wish to dispose of, this is the time to do so. We thank you for choosing Delta Airlines and welcome you to Berlin."

Jefferson sighed and ignored the flight attendant as she or a colleague repeated the announcement in German. He would give anything to be on the ground, but back in the United States. This was a trip he never wanted to take.

Things were already bad when he had to make the reservations. They didn't improve when he had to persuade the airline to make an exception to their rule about receiving paperwork for his guide dog forty-eight hours in advance.

"I can't wait forty-eight hours," he'd protested. "I need to get to Germany as soon as possible."

True, he could have left Presley at home. He had enough colleagues whom he could trust to watch her. Any of them would be thrilled to take on the assignment. But he didn't want to rely on stranger after stranger to navigate this foreign country. Plus, he had to admit he needed the innate comfort the dog exuded. This trip wouldn't be long or easy.

Fortune smiled when the State Department stepped in to impress the urgency of the situation. Delta Airlines relented upon receiving Presley's paperwork. The dog, not concerned about the grim cause of this sudden adventure nor the complicated logistics surrounding it, was currently curled up by Jefferson's legs. She'd tucked her butt underneath the seat in front of them while her head rested against his shin. She could afford to be content.

* * *

Delta Airlines flight 46 landed at the Berlin Tegel Airport at 10:30 in the morning. Passengers could soon to unbuckle their seatbelts and the usual scramble for stowed carry-on luggage ensued. Next came the traditional jostling and impatience to deplane.

Keeping a curious Presley in check, Jefferson rose and made his way out of his row of seats. His only blessing on this flight had been that the couple seated next to him were too self-absorbed in their iPads to suck him into a lengthy conversation. They now merged into the stream of deplaning passengers with just a quick goodbye, meant more for Presley than Jefferson.

"She's so cute," the woman remarked for the twentieth time as she disappeared.

Jefferson too joined the line of passengers heading towards the plane's door. Forced to stay behind him due to how narrow the aisle was, Presley peeked around his legs whenever possible, looking for a way to take the lead again.

The pair was stopped by a woman inside the jet bridge.

"I believe I'm to escort you," she said with an accent in her voice.

Having flown often enough for conferences and similar affairs, Jefferson figured this woman was a Delta customer service representative. He had requested an escort when he checked in at JFK.

"Guess I'm the one you're looking for," he said.

"What would be the best way for me to help you?" the woman asked.

"Mind if I take your elbow?"

Sure, Presley could follow someone on command, but Jefferson's limited flying experiences were frequent enough for him to know airports were crowded. Presley was just as skilled at navigating crowds as anywhere else, but her line of sight was at people's knees. There was a fair chance she'd lose whoever she was supposed to follow, and she might then tail a different person by mistake.

"Sure," the woman said. "I've got my arm out for you here. Where are you heading?"

* * *

8

Even though Jefferson brought everything he'd need in an overnight bag he'd carried onto the plane alongside his briefcase, he directed the customer service representative to take him to the baggage claim belts. It wasn't long before he heard his name.

"Mr. Thomas! Mr. Thomas!"

He and the customer service representative stopped. Presley looked around, seeming curious about who was calling out like this.

"Hello," another woman said, approaching the group. "Jefferson Thomas?"

"Yes," Jefferson replied.

"Hello. I'm Cassandra Kingman with the U.S. Embassy here in Berlin. I'm the one who will guide you through everything that needs to happen."

"Nice to meet you," Jefferson said, not caring that his hands were full. "This is Presley."

The dog, who had been staring at something on the carpet only she seemed to see, looked up at Cassandra, her tail wagging while the tension Jefferson felt in her harness lessened as she straightened out at the sound of her name.

"Nice to meet you," Cassandra said. "I'm sorry it's under these circumstances."

"Do you need any further assistance?" the customer service representative inquired.

"Oh, sorry," Jefferson said, releasing the woman's elbow. "Yeah, I'm fine here. Thank you."

The customer service representative gave him back his briefcase, which she'd been carrying, and left.

"Are you all set?" Cassandra asked. "I'm not parked far away."

"Let's go then," Jefferson insisted.

* * *

"Oh," Cassandra said as they walked through the parking garage. "I've got a Golf. It's small ..."

Jefferson knew where this was headed. He'd had this conversation many times.

"I guess she could ride on the backseat," Cassandra suggested.

"Don't worry," Jefferson said with a wave of his briefcase-holding hand. "Presley can ride in the front passenger wheel well."

"Excuse me?"

"It's something they train the dogs to do. Makes it easy to take them into just about any car. Do you mind if I stick my stuff in the trunk? Like you said, it's a small car."

Cassandra obliged with a silence that suggested bewilderment. Jefferson didn't speak either as they kept walking.

"Here we are," she finally said, fumbling with her jingling keys. "It's to the left."

She opened the Golf's trunk and Jefferson put his briefcase and overnight bag inside.

"Hey," he admonished as Presley moved forward to sniff the trunk space. "You're not riding in there, so get your nose out."

He and the dog had been matched up four years ago. Their partnership was so strong, he no longer needed to strictly adhere to the commands she'd learned. The tone in his voice made the meaning of his comments clear. Presley stepped back from the trunk and Cassandra closed it.

Jefferson trailed the side of the Golf with his fingers and found the passenger door. He got in, keeping one leg outside as he unbuckled and removed Presley's guide dog harness.

"Inside," he encouraged. "Inside."

Presley moved forward and sniffed the wheel well. Before Jefferson needed to remind her, she stepped into the car and curled up in the space, her head leaning against his knee. Jefferson brought his other leg in, double-checked that Presley's tail was tucked in, and shut his door as Cassandra entered behind the wheel.

"She's compact," she remarked.

Jefferson managed a slight chuckle as Presley rummaged on the floor, trying to arrange herself to lie just right.

* * *

They drove in silence for a few minutes while the airport fell behind them in the distance.

"We're going to the embassy, right?" Jefferson finally asked, staring out the window and imagining the buildings going by. Thinking of what there might be to see made doing all this a little easier, if that was possible.

"Yes," Cassandra replied.

"Are the kids going to be there?" Jefferson queried, feeling anxious now. He turned to look in Cassandra's direction, inadvertently moving his foot. Presley, who had again been using the appendage as a pillow, groaned in protest.

"No," Cassandra said. "They're at my house. We'll see them later."

Jefferson leaned back in his seat, both glad and frustrated that he wouldn't see the kids yet.

* * *

The ride lasted roughly another fifteen minutes before Cassandra pulled up to the front gate of a reinforced fence which enclosed the American Embassy. She gave her ID to the guard on duty and, after another guard conducted a quick sweep of the car, was granted access. She parked and led the way into the building.

"It's been tough on all of us here," she said. "We never saw it coming. They were good people."

"That's good to hear," Jefferson said, managing a slight smile. He could still be proud of his brother.

* * *

In her office, Cassandra's desk was almost buried with the many forms Jefferson needed to fill out and sign.

"I'm not much of a legal mind," she admitted as they sat. "Someone from the legal department should be here soon to help us."

Jefferson nodded as Presley selected a portion of the carpet that seemed to meet her standards … for what, no one could be sure. She settled down on it and fell asleep in just a few seconds.

The lawyer arrived ten minutes later, and they set to work. Despite being a lawyer himself, Jefferson felt overwhelmed by the complexity before him. There were forms for the funeral home in Berlin, paperwork for what would be done with his brother's property and affects, arrangements for transporting the bodies, establishing temporary guardianship of the kids so he could get them back to New York without being charged with kidnapping and related felonies … the paperwork never seemed to shrink. Jefferson had a friend back in New York who specialized in Family Law, but Eric's briefing the day before only covered a fraction of what he now had to organize.

At some point, someone dropped off lunch consisting of multiple containers from a local restaurant. Jefferson selected the egg noodles and pork strips, soon forgetting the German name Cassandra and the lawyer had called the dish.

"You and my brother worked together?" he asked as they took a break and ate.

Cassandra nodded.

"We were Foreign Service construction engineers," she explained. "We don't actually build anything. Instead, we oversee bids and contracts related to construction and renovation of U.S. properties throughout Germany. I majored in Architecture at Boston University and learned about this job through a friend. My first station was in Muscat in Oman, then Lima in Peru and Santiago in Chile, and now I'm here."

The lawyer sat in the corner, eating his food without a word.

"Did you know Stan and Maggie before you were posted here?" Jefferson asked.

"No, but I wish I did," Cassandra said. "I didn't know them long enough."

Jefferson realized he too had not had enough time with his brother and his family.

* * *

They completed the enormous task around 4:00 in the afternoon. The lawyer headed back to his office after offering his condolences and packing up his leftovers.

Cassandra finished packing the remaining forms in a cardboard box to be shipped to Jefferson's home in Manhattan. They'd already faxed most of them to the people, departments, and agencies who needed them, but a few had to be submitted by Jefferson himself when he was back in the United States. Having learned this ahead of time, he had already recruited Eric to help file the paperwork with the courts.

For now, they were in a manila folder being held shut by two rubber bands and placed in Jefferson's briefcase.

"Okay," Cassandra said, taping the box shut and pasting a shipping label on it. "Now for the hard part."

* * *

The room was quiet to the point of feeling eerie. the florescent lights above were only adding to the spooky ambiance. Various instruments lined the walls, and a few gurneys stood nearby.

Cassandra and Jefferson stood by two gurneys in the center of the room, looking down at the bodies. Cassandra described everything in a soft voice that felt anything but comforting.

On the right lay a woman with red hair who wore a simple blue dress. Her hair had been washed and styled, and someone had applied fresh make-up to her face. The sandals on her feet matched her dress. Her simple gold earrings likewise matched the necklace around her neck.

On the left lay a man whose features somewhat resembled Jefferson's, including the dark brown hair. He wore a suit, complete with a tie and dress shoes. His hair had also been neatly groomed and there was some make-up on his face.

Both bodies' eyelids were sewn shut and their arms lay crossed over their chests, their wedding bands visible on their fingers.

Though he couldn't see them, Jefferson stared down at the bodies of his brother, Stanley Allan Thomas, and his sister-in-law, Margret Bailer-Thomas. Presley lay by his feet, looking up at the gurneys. She seemed to sense something was amiss, but she'd have no clue about what her role here was. Even Jefferson didn't know what exactly she ought to do in a moment like this. He did appreciate the warmth of her leaning against his leg.

According to Cassandra's description, the bodies showed no signs of the accident. The funeral home seemed to have made sure of that. Another co-worker of Stanley's made the official identification a few days earlier.

"What happened?" Jefferson asked in a shaky voice. "I've only heard snippets about it."

Cassandra took a deep breath and sniffled.

"Four days ago, Stan and Maggie went out to dinner with some friends of theirs," she explained, her voice also shaking. "They were driving home when they came up to the intersection … the light was green, but then, out of nowhere, this other car smashed into them … The police said the driver was drunk … The coroner determined they were both killed instantly. Not even the airbags helped,"

Jefferson nodded. He couldn't think of anything to say. His brother and sister-in-law were dead because of some random moron. What could he possibly say about that?

"Did they catch the guy?" he asked, his tone taking on a bitter edge.

"Yes," Cassandra said, wiping her eyes. "He's in jail, awaiting his trial. They're not going easy on him because of the alcohol. It was a nineteen-year-old kid. He took a bump to the head and got some cuts on his arms, but he walked away from it …"

She looked at the two bodies, unable to finish the sentence. She didn't have to. Jefferson had heard all he needed to hear for a lifetime.

A man with graying hair stepped into the room. He motioned to Cassandra. As he began speaking, Jefferson wasn't sure if he couldn't understand because the guy was speaking German or because he was mumbling.

In just a few seconds, Cassandra turned back to Jefferson.

"He wants to know if you'd like a minute alone before they seal the caskets," she explained.

Jefferson nodded. Cassandra and the man quietly left the room. Alone, he looked back at the bodies, unsure of what to say. Finally, he took a deep breath.

"I'll take good care of them," he promised, his voice shaking as a few tears ran down his cheeks.

* * *

As Cassandra explained earlier, the kids had been staying at her house for the past few days. Right now, her teenaged daughter was babysitting them.

"Taylor's been taking it pretty hard," Cassandra described as she drove through the suburbs outside Berlin. "She had a really close bond with Maggie. Abigail … well, let's just say there are times when she's there and then when she isn't. As for Matthew, I'm not sure how much of all this he is understanding right now. He's just very quiet."

Jefferson nodded, thinking. Though he made frequent phone calls and always sent cards for Christmas and birthdays, he hadn't seen his brother and the family in about five years. It wasn't really that surprising, despite them having grown up together on Staten Island and both attending Columbia University. Stanley was working for the State Department as a foreign service officer and therefore moved around a lot. Jefferson was a professor at New York University School of Law and therefore stayed put in Manhattan for most of his life. He hadn't seen his nieces since they were two and he never even had a face-to-face meeting with his nephew. In fact, Maggie had found out she was pregnant a few weeks after the last time they saw each other.

Now, Jefferson would take these kids back to the United States to live with him, all because some idiot decided to have a few drinks and then drove on the streets anyway, killing two people in the process. The whole thing made no sense.

* * *

They pulled into the driveway of Cassandra's home and got out. As she led the way to the front door, Cassandra commented that her husband was already home from work.

"He hasn't been staying late," she added. "Not now."

"What does he do anyway?" Jefferson asked, trying to sound casual.

"He's a computer technician. It's somewhat difficult for him to keep a job because we move every few years when I get reassigned, so he works freelance. Right now, he's working remotely for a school district in Arkansas. He's also done some contract work for the Embassy."

They entered the house and were met by Cassandra's husband, Darren. Cassandra introduced Jefferson and asked about the kids.

"The girls are watching television," Darren replied. "I think Matthew's upstairs."

With that, he went to find the little boy.

Jefferson paused to consider how real this suddenly became. He was now in the same house as the kids. When he'd leave tomorrow, they'd be going with him. That was less than twenty-four hours from now.

Cassandra led Jefferson through the house, introducing him to her sixteen-year-old daughter, Tiffany, along the way. They came into the living room, where a pair of identical twin seven-year-old girls were sitting on the couch, watching some sort of cartoon. Jefferson could hear the cacophony of weird sounds which seemed to be standard for such shows.

The girls had red hair and blue eyes which matched their mother's. Their skin was fair like their father's. Maggie once told Jefferson that, hard as she tried, she never found a physical characteristic to distinguish the girls.

"They're both perfect," the proud mother had declared on more than one occasion.

The twins looked at the newcomers as Cassandra announced herself.

"Hi, girls," she said. "This is your uncle Jefferson. Do you remember him at all?"

"Hey girls," Jefferson added, nudging the couch they were sitting on with his foot to get a sense of where they were. They had yet to speak. The noise from the television was helping a little bit, but it didn't quite pinpoint their positions.

15

"Hello," Abigail said, but her sister, Taylor, remained silent.

At least one of them spoke, Jefferson thought, feeling certain the other twin wasn't far from the source of the voice. He was also fairly certain both girls recognized his voice from their many telephone conversations over the years, but the sight of him was probably strange to them. What a way to start.

"Your uncle came to pick you up," Cassandra continued. "Remember what we talked about? You're going to go and live with him in New York."

Abigail nodded but Taylor seemed to be choosing not to respond. Jefferson stood there, waiting for his next cue.

"Are we leaving now?" Abigail asked, unsure about if she should run upstairs to get her things.

"No," Cassandra said. "You're going to spend one more night here and then you all will fly back to New York tomorrow."

This time, neither of the girls responded. Jefferson figured Abigail had just switched to acting like her sister, as Cassandra had described earlier.

"Found him," Darren announced, coming up behind the group with a four-year-old boy in tow.

Matthew Thomas looked a lot like his father and uncle and had the dark brown hair and eyes to prove it.

"Matthew," Cassandra said, turning to face him as she crouched down to his height, "this is your uncle Jefferson."

"Hey there, little man," Jefferson said, holding out his hand. "How are you?"

Matthew reached up and shook the hand, but he didn't say anything. Figuring they weren't needed anymore, the girls turned their attention back to their cartoon.

"How long until dinner's ready?" Matthew asked, looking up at Darren.

"About ten minutes," Darren replied. "We'll call you."

With that, Matthew hurried off to some other part of the house.

"Give them time," Cassandra advised.

Jefferson nodded. This wasn't much easier on his end.

"Hey," Darren interjected. "How about you and I have a beer before dinner?"

"Sure," Jefferson replied, thinking a beer or six would do him good right now. "Thank you."

* * *

At Cassandra and Darren's insistence, Jefferson stayed to have dinner with the temporarily extended family. It was a simple meal, consisting of macaroni and cheese. The Kingmans had not been sure of what Abigail, Taylor, and Matthew liked to eat and, as Cassandra privately told Jefferson, Abigail was notorious for her picky eating habits.

"She's got a list," Cassandra elaborated. "Believe me. She's got a list."

So, for the time being, macaroni and cheese was deemed a safe bet. Abigail didn't voice any objections.

During the meal, Jefferson told the kids what they could expect about their new lives in Manhattan, trying to put a somewhat positive spin on the situation. But only Abigail showed some interest. Matthew seemed to be too shy, and Taylor just wasn't talking. Eventually, Jefferson switched his approach and tried to get them to tell him about themselves, but again, only Abigail participated.

After dinner and another beer with Darren, Jefferson accepted a ride from Cassandra to the nearby Hilton. He and Presley would sleep for a few hours before their second and last hectic day in Germany began.

Despite his long flight and the subsequent long day, Jefferson couldn't sleep. He soon gave up and opened his laptop, logging onto the hotel's Wi-Fi, and charging twenty-four hours of access time to his room. He'd swallow the otherwise outrageous price, which converted to over twenty-three dollars.

He opened his e-mail and scrolled through his new messages. Word was trickling through the law school and he saw many condolences from colleagues and students. He found nothing important and switched to Google.

But he didn't know what he wanted to search for. Should he research how death affected children? Should he look up something about being a parent? He didn't know where to start and he didn't have much time.

Chapter 2

The alarm rang and Monique Vasquez wearily opened her eyes. Usually, she was a morning person, but even a morning person had some rough days.

Waving her arm around wildly, she was finally able to find her alarm clock on the nightstand and turned it off. She lay there, her eyes still half-closed.

It wasn't long before she could hear footsteps outside her bedroom. She turned and her eyes met those of a woman who was a bit older than her and wearing a white nurse's uniform.

"Morning," Monique said.

"One of these days I'm gonna get here before that alarm wakes you," The nurse, Joan Anderson, replied.

"We'll see."

Monique was still too tired to add a grin to that retort.

"You need a man," Joan muttered as she came towards the bed.

Monique rolled her eyes. The comment was well-worn.

The morning began as usual, with Joan looking Monique over to make sure she didn't have any injuries like skin tears or pressure sores. She took Monique's temperature and blood pressure and used a stethoscope to check her lungs and heart.

Once she was satisfied her patient was healthy, Joan allowed Monique to use a remote on her nightstand to raise her bed's head-end so she was sitting up. Joan didn't look it, but she was strong. Of average height and build, she used her wiry strength to lift Monique out of the bed and into a wheelchair.

Using a touchpad to control the chair with one finger, Monique maneuvered herself into the bathroom and over to the shower stall. There Joan helped her strip and get into a stationary chair that was bolted down directly beneath the stream of water.

"Holler when you're done," Joan instructed before sliding the door shut.

It took Monique a little while to get her arms to work right, but she finally managed to grab hold of the shower knob and turned the water on. As usual, the initial burst was freezing cold. Seconds seemed to pass by at a snail's pace until the temperature reached humane degrees.

Monique hummed to herself as she took her shower, glad she couldn't be heard. she didn't believe she could keep a good rhythm. When she was done, she reached out and turned the knob back. But her arm wasn't cooperating, and she could not turn it all the way. Monique devoted a moment to cursing out the stubborn thing.

"Joan!" she called.

The nurse slid open the stall's door and turned the knob the rest of the way.

"You know I don't actually mean you should 'holler', right?" she asked, pulling a large towel off the nearby rack. "The door isn't soundproof."

She wrapped the towel around Monique's shoulders and torso.

"You wanna shave today?" she asked, glancing at Monique's legs.

Monique took a moment to run her hand along her thigh. The hairs didn't feel that long.

"Maybe tomorrow," she concluded. Shaving was an arduous task and she liked to only do it when absolutely necessary.

"You need a man," Joan remarked again. "You'd be asking for a razor every day."

"I doubt that," Monique replied. "Sex isn't really a priority for me."

She paused, considering whether Joan's statement or her own words carried more truth in them.

"Just you wait," Joan said, grabbing a smaller towel to dry Monique's hair. She didn't seem to have noticed Monique's brief hesitation, or maybe she was being kind and not commenting on it.

When Monique was dry, Joan helped her out of the shower stall and back into the wheelchair.

"Anything special you want to wear today?" she asked as Monique moved towards the sink.

"No," Monique said. "Just something casual that still says that I am capable of living my life at a professional level."

This was her normal response to the daily question.

"You need a man. You wouldn't be so 'casual' about what you wear then."

Monique rolled her eyes as Joan left the bathroom and shut the door. The nurse had made such comments every day since she first began helping her eight years ago. Three times was usually the max. But Joan would always be adamant, and Monique would simply let her continue saying what she was thinking.

With the large towel still draped around her shoulders and torso to keep her warm, Monique began brushing her teeth, taming her hair, and generally grooming herself. When she finished, she looked in the mirror, where a thirtyish-year old woman with brown hair and hazel eyes looked back at her, the wheelchair partially visible in the background.

Monique believed that, while she didn't belong in the fashion magazines, she was still an attractive woman. Maybe she could lose five pounds and her eyebrows were too bushy, but not too bad. Monique was sure that, under different circumstances, she could have snagged a man by now.

But, in the real world, many men were put off by her lifestyle, of which her chair was a clear indicator. True, she did date on occasion, but those relationships never lasted. Friends of hers sometimes set her up on blind dates, but those never went well. Monique had been stood up more than once and she was sure that, when the person came and saw her from a distance, they simply turned around and left without a word.

Despite her bad luck with the opposite gender, Monique knew she couldn't complain. She had her health, she had her friends, and she had her store. Despite the large chains and the internet providing tough competition, she had her store and was making a decent living. No, her life was pretty good.

Using the wheelchair's armrests to support herself, Monique slid over onto the toilet to take care of that business. While she did need help getting out of bed and in and out of the shower, this was something she was able to do on her own. Knowing many people in her position didn't even have control of their bowels or bladders, this always gave her some solace. She wasn't completely dependent.

With the hygienic tasks accomplished, Monique returned to her bedroom, where Joan had laid out her clothes. The nurse pulled the towel away and began helping Monique get dressed. Once she was ready to go, Monique was moved into a larger, more elaborate, red and gray wheelchair, where Joan strapped her in at her chest, waist, and thighs. She put shoes on her patient's feet and strapped her ankles in so they didn't slip out of the chair's footholds. Overall, this chair was designed so Monique could sit in it comfortably for hours on end and the straps prevented her from falling out. It was complete with a padded headrest, which Monique sometimes put to good use if she wanted to take a quick nap. It wasn't like she could crawl into a Nap pod.

When she was settled in the chair, Monique used the joystick to steer herself out of the bedroom and into the kitchen of her apartment. Joan had already put out a bowl of cereal. As Monique dug in, Joan prepared some coffee in a plastic tumbler, which she attached to the chair for Monique to drink through a straw.

While Monique ate, Joan went to make the bed, collect any dirty laundry, and straighten out the bathroom. She came back just as Monique was finishing up and put the dishes in the dishwasher.

"I think that's everything," she said, attaching a clean tumbler and straw to the chair for Monique to use later.

Monique nodded in agreement. they wished each other a good day before Joan left via the exit and the exterior stairs beyond.

Now on her own and fine with that, Monique steered her wheelchair over to a set of elevator doors. Using a remote control attached to the armrest of her chair, she got them open and wheeled herself inside. As soon as the doors slid shut, the elevator began moving, taking Monique one floor down. No buttons needed to be pushed, the pressure pad on the floor taking care of indicating she was aboard. There were only two floors to choose from … it was either up or down.

Monique emerged in the backroom of her bookstore and wheeled herself through it, stopping for a moment to unlock the door to the back office. she unlocked another door and emerged in the bookstore itself.

The store wasn't a large one, but its tall shelves were filled with books of every conceivable genre. Monique inherited it after her mother retired and left Manhattan. it was a fixture in Greenwich Village for as long as anyone cared to remember. It's status as a staple of the community was the only reason Monique was able to continue living and working there, keeping her head above the sea of competition.

As she maneuvered through the store towards the front door, Monique looked around, making sure everything was in order. So far, nothing seemed to be wrong, but she'd have one of her ambulatory employees check things out more thoroughly before they opened for the day.

Entering two codes on a keypad beneath the front counter, Monique disengaged the alarm and unlocked the front door. She pulled open the door, hearing that familiar chime. It sounded as it always did the dozens of times she heard it every day, announcing the entry or exit of a customer for the past thirty-plus years.

A florist who was setting up an outdoor display across the street waved. Monique was somewhat able to raise her hand wave back, though she couldn't recall this particular man's name at the moment. Though that store had been a neighboring establishment for at least fifty years, it had changed hands at least a dozen times. Somehow, it was still called "Carmen's Flowers".

"Good morning!" Monique called.

"Morning!" the florist returned.

Monique smiled. Overall, her life wasn't so bad.

* * *

The store's two employees, Kathy and Frank, soon arrived to help Monique set up for the day.

Kathy Quigley was in her early seventies who had worked at the store for about as long as it had been there. Her short white hair was in its usual bob. Her smile was inviting with the caveat that she would not tolerate anyone trying to deceive or insult her or anyone she cared about.

Frank Norris was a man in his early forties who had been an employee for about seven years, holding a second, part-time job as a custodian for the New York City School District. He'd been married and divorced twice and didn't seem to be hurrying to find wife number three. His black hair was short, he wore frameless glasses, and was in good shape thanks to his routine manual labor.

Frank and Kathy both conducted a more thorough inspection of the store, but as Monique suspected, everything was in order. They helped her finish setting up and, like any other day, they were open for business by 8:30 a.m. With no one waiting to come to shop or browse, the three chatted amongst themselves.

The topic of discussion that day was the open position, recently vacated by Finley Matheson, a college graduate who had worked at the store for three years while he lived with his parents in Chelsea. He had accepted a job offer somewhere in Silicon Valley and they were now a man short.

"You've got an interview scheduled for 9:00 today," Kathy said, consulting a day planner by the register.

Monique nodded and headed back to her office in the back room. She couldn't recall why she'd insisted a day planner be kept by the register, but she also didn't care to remember why at that moment.

While her mother had always wanted to keep the store old-fashioned, Monique had added a few 21st Century touches. These included an up-to-date cash register which had left Kathy stumped for a month, a newer telephone, and an up-to-date computer with appropriate software to better track the inventory and manage the finances. Since she did not have full control of her arms, Monique was cursed with a horrific script and preferred to use a keyboard.

22

Though she had poor control of her arms, Monique did have almost perfect control over her hands and fingers, allowing her to type quickly and efficiently. All she had to do was rest her arms in specially designed cushions mounted on her desk. Like the ones on her wheelchair's armrests, these cushions were grooved to keep her arms from flaying around while she used her hands for various tasks, such as typing and controlling her chair.

While waiting for her computer to wake up, Monique put on a headset which enabled her to verbally control the cursor on the screen. When everything was booted up, she pulled up the application for the prospective employee who was coming in for his interview. She also confirmed the appointment on Outlook, her mind again straying to the question of why a physical day planner was even needed anymore.

The applicant's name was Samuel Bridges. He'd majored in Business at Fordham University, graduating the previous spring. He seemed to have trouble finding a job and was taking this position to make some money for the time being, a fact Monique could infer from the information in the application. What fresh college graduate would want to spend a lot of time working at a bookstore for sixteen dollars an hour?

Samuel Bridges did possess retail experience, having worked in a couple of different stores and boutiques during his high school and college years. Monique thought his resume looked good, but she would wait to meet the person.

When she'd posted the position on various job boards, she hadn't written "Note: The owner is quadriplegic and uses a wheelchair. Don't shy away from the job because of this." People generally learned about this fact when they came in for their interviews. But unfortunately, not unlike Monique's luck with men, people tended to slink away from the job after meeting her.

When she first took over the store, Frank, who had been working there for a year, seriously considered quitting. A stern lecture from Kathy kept him around. Finley Matheson had been the nephew of a friend of Monique's mother, which was the main reason he got the job … that, and because he didn't look at Monique with pity or like she had three heads.

Monique knew she would have to look in the real world for employees from time to time, but this had not been an easy quest. Still, she pushed herself to remain optimistic. Her experience told her that, if she found someone who would take the job, she could get them to treat her more like a human being later.

At precisely 9:00, there was a knock on the office door.

"Come in," Monique said just loud enough to be heard.

A young man dressed in a blue button-down shirt, beige pants, and a yellow and blue tie stepped in. He had been wearing a jacket earlier, but it was now draped over one arm while his hand held what seemed to be a copy of his resume.

Samuel Bridges stopped in surprise when he saw Monique, like so many before him. His eyes seemed momentarily transfixed on her chair, headset, and arm cushions. Behind him, Frank slipped away without a word.

"Good morning," Monique said, trying to get the young man to focus on his reason for being there.

"Oh … yeah … good morning," Samuel Bridges said, seeming surprised to discover she was capable of human speech.

Deciding to move things forward, Monique raised her hand across the desk to shake his. It took the young man a second or so, but he finally seemed to decide that, despite the fact her arm was shaking slightly, she wasn't carrying some deadly virus. He stepped forward and shook her hand.

"Have a seat," Monique invited, taking the copy of his resume.

Samuel Bridges sat across the desk from her and set his jacket on his lap.

"I'll just be blunt," Monique said. "What makes you a good choice to work here in this bookstore?"

"Well," Samuel Bridges said, still clearly nervous about being there, "I've worked in a lot of different stores and I've met a lot of different people. I generally get along with everyone and my bosses always liked me. And … if you'd let me, I'd be able to share some ideas. I've done that at some of my other jobs and, well, some of them worked."

He fell silent, probably wondering if he had offended her.

Monique was also silent. She wasn't offended. This young man had just assumed she ran the store and therefore considered her to be his potential boss. Not many came to that conclusion, assuming she was just HR at best. Flattered, Monique couldn't hide a slight smile.

"Well," she said, focusing again. "We'll see about that. For now, let's get this out of the way. Did you leave all of these jobs for academic obligations?"

She gestured at the resume.

Chapter 3

At 6:30 the next morning, Jefferson met Cassandra outside of the Hilton. She drove him back to her house, where Darren and Tiffany were already getting Abigail, Taylor, and Matthew out of bed. None of the kids were happy about this early wake-up call, but they grudgingly cooperated.

They ate some breakfast while the adults finished packing their things. Each child had two large duffel bags for the trip along with one backpack as their carry-on item. By 8:00, the luggage was stuffed into every available space of Darren's Audi station wagon. Cassandra, Tiffany, Taylor, and Matthew rode in Cassandra's Golf while Darren, Jefferson, Presley, and Abigail rode with the bags.

"How can she do that?" Abigail asked, peering over the luggage next to her on the backseat to watch Presley curl up in the wheel well by Jefferson's feet. Unlike her siblings, she seemed interested in this trip.

"She learned how to do it," Jefferson explained as Darren began driving. "They taught her that at guide dog school so she could ride in anyone's car."

Abigail seemed momentarily captivated by this information. but soon, her attention was taken over by the passing scenery. She remained silent for the rest of the ride, watching everything fly past the car with great interest. She seemed to find someone to wave at every time they stopped at a red light.

* * *

The ride to the airport wasn't long. It lasted maybe twenty minutes. But that was enough time for Taylor to decide she didn't want to go any further. She sat in the Golf, refusing to get out despite Jefferson's pleas.

"I don't want to go!" she wailed. "I want to stay here. I want my mom and dad!"

Thankfully, no one was close enough to hear it. Jefferson and Cassandra didn't have to explain how they weren't trying to abduct this child. They could instead focus on convincing Taylor to come along.

"Come on," Abigail said before anyone else could speak. "It'll be fun. We're gonna see New York."

"You're so stupid!" Taylor snapped. "We're not gonna see it. We're gonna live there. We're never coming back."

She crossed her arms in defiance and turned to look out the Golf's far window, facing away from the group.

Abigail had seemed to have been aware of this fact but had chosen to forget it for the time being. That time period seemed to be concluding.

"Come with me," Darren encouraged, taking her over to where Tiffany was heaving bags onto luggage carts. Matthew stood by one cart, watching the airplanes fly by overhead. Cassandra and Jefferson, the latter now understanding why they were here so early for a flight scheduled to depart at 12:30, stayed with Taylor.

"I want my mom and dad," The girl whined. "I wanna go home."

Jefferson was not yet sure about how to deal with this, so he let Cassandra take the lead.

"Sweetie," the woman said, bending down to stick her head in through the open car door. "You're going to go to a new home with your uncle Jefferson. Remember how we talked about this?"

Taylor squeezed her eyes shut and tightened her crossed arms against her chest.

"All right," Cassandra said, shrugging her shoulders. "If that's the way you feel, we have to go and get on the plane. You'll have to stay here all alone."

She straightened up and turned towards Jefferson.

"Let's go," she said in an authoritative tone, taking his arm.

"Wait," Jefferson said, startled. "We're not gonna leave her here by herself, are we?"

At that moment, the fact she wasn't properly leading him away from the Golf couldn't reach the forefront of his mind. The thought of just abandoning Taylor seemed ludicrous.

"Yep," Cassandra replied. "That's what she wants."

Jefferson opened his mouth to object.

"Come on," Cassandra insisted, taking his arm again before he had a chance to speak.

They kept walking towards the others, Jefferson wondering how this was supposed to help the situation. For one thing, a seven-year-old was being left alone in an unlocked car parked at an international airport.

A few seconds later, a voice called, "Wait for me!"

Everyone turned to see Taylor had gotten out of the car and was running to catch up, one hand clutching her backpack.

Her plan having worked, Cassandra smiled as she went back to lock up the Golf. Jefferson released a sigh of relief as Taylor reached him, taking her backpack and placing it on the luggage carts standing next to him.

"Okay," Cassandra said, rejoining the group. "Let's go."

"You weren't really going to leave her behind, were you?" Jefferson asked under his breath as they began walking again.

"No," Cassandra admitted. "Sometimes, you have to bluff with kids. It works, but sometimes they may call it."

Jefferson nodded. He still had a lot to learn. He wondered what Cassandra would have done if Taylor had called this bluff.

"Nice response by the way," Cassandra said. "Played very well, despite you having no clue what I was up to."

"My performance felt very genuine," Jefferson replied. "You have quite the poker face. You ever do any gambling?"

"I lived in Vegas for a while. I worked as a blackjack dealer during graduate school."

Jefferson nodded.

With everything set, the group headed across the parking lot towards the terminal building. While Taylor wanted to walk, Abigail, who had seemingly forgotten the earlier confrontation with her sister, was fascinated by the luggage carts.

"Can I ride it?" she asked.

Darren Obligingly set her on top of one of the large duffel bags, where she seemed to act like a lookout in a ship's crow's nest. Matthew was riding in the basket of the other cart, which Cassandra and her daughter took turns pushing.

Jefferson thought the group must be a sight as they entered the terminal and got in line at the check-in desk. Abigail was busy trying to see everything at once while Taylor was keeping her eyes fixed on the three adults, wondering exactly what would happen next. In the basket, Matthew was playing with his fingers.

Thankfully, Presley found them all very interesting, making it easy to keep her mind on the group so she'd follow them through the terminal. It also made getting through the ribbon-line maze easier. These sorts of things didn't go well with guide dogs, the latter not seeing the ribbons and consequently assuming there was no required guideline to follow. This sort of thing had caused problems before at places like Jefferson's bank, where Presley would simply walk him right into the ribbons because she saw it as a quicker and easier way than what everyone else was doing. Unlike this airport, she'd gotten used to their procedure at the bank and no longer made this mistake. But she did not know this airport.

Though the line was long, it moved pretty steadily. Soon, the group was up. Cassandra stepped aside and Jefferson took the lead with the check-in agent.

"Four for the 12:33 flight to JFK," he said after confirming the woman spoke English. He slid the tickets across the counter.

Since the kids were not traveling with a parent, it quickly got a little confusing, but eventually, Jefferson and Cassandra managed to quietly explain the situation while Darren and Tiffany kept the kids occupied. After reviewing the notarized documents that authorized all this, the agent finally checked the six pieces of luggage and handed over the group's boarding passes. Thankfully, Presley's presence didn't cause a problem, as there had been times when people didn't understand that guide dogs were allowed a lot more access than regular pet dogs, including being allowed to fly in the cabin of an airplane instead of underneath despite their size. After all, they were needed to help their handlers.

"Do you have any health records for the dog?" the agent asked.

Jefferson produced these, along with documentation affirming Presley's status as a certified guide dog. Everything was soon in order.

"I'll take a gate pass to accompany them," Cassandra said, presenting her driver's license.

With that and the group's boarding passes in hand and the large duffel bags checked and heading for the plane's underbelly, it was time for Darren and Tiffany to say "goodbye." The three kids all hugged the pair

"Say 'thank you'," Jefferson encouraged, thinking the phrase wasn't enough.

miraculously, the kids all repeated the words. Jefferson thanked Darren and Tiffany as well.

"Next time you're in New York, look me up," he said to Darren. "Then the beers are on me. I got a buddy who knows all the best brews."

Darren smiled and promised to hold Jefferson and his "buddy" to that. Jefferson thanked Tiffany and wished her well. She gave him her condolences and left with her father, turning back to wave to the three kids one last time.

"Do we have to walk now?" Abigail asked, eyeing the spot where the two luggage carts had stood before an airline employee took them away.

"Yep," Jefferson said, handing his niece her backpack, "and you have to carry this now."

Abigail made a face.

"He can't see you do that," Cassandra reminded her. "Don't bother."

They headed for the security checkpoint, which fascinated Abigail. She intended to run back and forth through the metal detector but was quickly stopped by Cassandra.

"You go through once and stay on the other side," she reminded the little girl. "Come on. You've done this before."

As Jefferson knew from experience, the metal in Presley's guide dog harness set off the metal detector when she walked through it and the two of them had to be taken aside and patted down. This was standard procedure and he found relief in the German authorities' consistency with the process he knew. Thankfully, Cassandra was around to take charge of Abigail, Taylor, and Matthew, leaving Jefferson to briefly wonder how he'd handle this situation on his own in the future.

Cassandra led the kids to get their bags as they came out of the x-ray machine while Jefferson followed a security official. The pat down procedure was identical to the one he went through in the U.S., including right before yesterday's flight to Berlin. His hands were checked for chemical residue and he was then cleared to rejoin the others.

By the time Jefferson was done, the group had their bags, shoes, and jackets again. All he had to do was grab his overnight bag and briefcase.

After they left the security checkpoint, all three kids complained about being hungry. This wasn't surprising since breakfast hadn't been that substantial. The group found a McDonald's and headed there, with Abigail constantly repeating she wanted a hamburger with no pickles.

"Surprisingly, that's the only topping she's opposed to," Cassandra whispered as they entered the restaurant.

After settling the kids in a booth, Jefferson and Cassandra went to get three kids' meals, two with hamburgers for the girls and one with chicken nuggets for Matthew. Jefferson also got a burger and fries for himself while Cassandra got a salad.

"Does my burger have pickles in it?" Abigail asked as soon as they returned with the food. "I don't like pickles."

"I'll just check on that," Cassandra said after handing the much less picky Taylor her food and drink. "You can eat these fries while you wait."

She handed Abigail the French fries from her meal and, while the girl was distracted, quickly unwrapped her burger, removed the pickles, and re-wrapped it.

"Here you go," she said, handing Abigail the burger. "All clear."

While the girl inspected it herself for any signs of the pickles, Cassandra quietly explained to Jefferson what she had done.

"You just have to remember to destroy the evidence," she finished.

Jefferson heard a crunching sound, surmising she was eating the pickles herself.

"You are deceitful," he commented while Abigail dug into her burger, satisfied the "evil pickles" had been vanquished.

"I learned with my own daughter," Cassandra explained. "It's just a phase. She'll grow out of it soon enough."

"What was it with your daughter?"

"The worst was lettuce. Now, she's almost a vegetarian. Like I said, it's just a phase."

This was good news in Jefferson's mind.

Just then, Taylor, who had been quietly eating and wasn't paying attention to anything else, spoke.

"Are you coming to New York with us, Mrs. Kingman?" she queried.

"No," Cassandra replied, speaking slowly and pausing to choose her words. "I'm just gonna make sure that you all get on your plane safely. But your uncle will take good care of you, I promise."

Taylor nodded and returned to her food. Jefferson wondered if she would get upset again like earlier in the car. He could hear other people around them and prayed there wouldn't be a scene. But for now, Taylor seemed to be okay.

Then Matthew asked, "What's New Fork?"

"That's New York, dummy," Taylor shot back. "Not New Fork."

"Taylor," Cassandra admonished. "Be nice to your little brother."

Taylor stayed quiet as she continued to eat.

"What is it?" Matthew asked, ignoring his food. He was apparently undeterred by his sister's put-down.

Cassandra nudged Jefferson with her elbow so he would take this. He lived there. She didn't.

"It's a big city where I live," Jefferson explained. "That's where we're gonna go. There are all kinds of things there … stores, museums, theaters …"

He stopped, wondering how much of this would interest a four-year-old, or even a pair of seven-year-olds for that matter.

"Are there parks?" Matthew asked.

"Yes," Jefferson said. "There's actually a really big one near where I live. It's got a zoo and everything."

"Does it have swings?"

"Yes, I know it does."

This seemed to satisfy Matthew.

"It's amazing what'll make a kid happy," Cassandra commented under her breath. Jefferson chuckled.

They finished their meal in relative silence until Abigail and Taylor got into an argument about pickles. They were separated, Taylor walking with Cassandra while Abigail followed Jefferson and Matthew.

They reached the flight gate and figured they still had plenty of time before they would board. At Matthew's insistence, they found some seats by the large windows so he could watch the planes come and go outside. Soon enough, he was excitedly telling Jefferson about his plans to become a pilot when he grew up. He was no longer shy around his uncle.

Abigail had now become quiet and withdrawn again. She and Taylor watched as a flight at a neighboring gate let its passengers off and took on new ones.

When Matthew ran out of things to tell Jefferson about airplanes and the pilots who flew them, the latter decided to check his e-mail. He had left work rather suddenly, so he was sure that, despite the widespread knowledge about the cause for this sudden departure, there'd be things he'd have to deal with. He pulled his laptop out of his bag and turned it on. As he waited for the desktop to come up, he pulled a pair of earphones out of his jacket pocket and stuck one in his ear while sticking the plug into the computer's jack. When everything was set, he began typing. Using the hotkeys long-since engrained in his memory, he located a wireless connection in the airport and pulled up his e-mail account. Since the screen reader software didn't function with a mouse or touchpad, he used various keyboard commands to supplement this.

Sure enough, there were plenty of new messages in his inbox. Most were from colleagues and students offering their condolences. His boss wanted to know if there was anything Jefferson needed and when he would be back in New York. A few e-mails were from students who had questions about a reading assignment he'd left for them, at least two being quite apologetic for bringing this up now. One e-mail was from Eric, confirming the details for Jefferson's flight.

As Jefferson wrote replies to the most important messages, Abigail noticed his other earphone dangling by his elbow. Interested, she grabbed it and held it up to her ear, wondering what he was listening to. Jefferson felt her tugging at it and looked over at where he knew she was sitting.

"What are you doing?" he asked.

"What are you listening to?" Abigail queried, still holding on to the earphone. "What's that voice?"

"It's a program on my computer. It reads stuff on the screen to me because I can't see it."

Interested, Abigail leaned over the armrest between them to see the laptop's screen. However, her limited reading skills caught up with her and she became stumped by the e-mail's legal language. Nevertheless interested, she began punching keys on the keyboard, adding random letters to the reply Jefferson had been working on.

"Is it reading that?" she asked eagerly.

"Yeah," Jefferson replied while Cassandra chuckled. "It's reading the letters."

Satisfied, Abigail sat back in her own seat and watched as Jefferson finished his e-mail and sent it out. Deciding the department chair didn't need to see Abigail's amendment to his message, Jefferson quietly deleted this.

"Uncle Jeff?" Taylor asked. "Why are you blind?"

Jefferson paused, wondering how to explain this. The question had never really come up during his phone conversations with the kids.

"Well," he said, thinking carefully, "I was born blind. A part of my eyes didn't grow the right way, so I can't see."

"Was Daddy born blind?" Abigail asked, interested again.

"No, your daddy was lucky. He could see just fine."

The twins seemed satisfied with this explanation and the subject was dropped. Matthew, who hadn't heard a word, was still content with staring out at all the airplanes. He tried to count them but, between his early counting skills and the planes constantly moving around, he gave up after a few minutes.

* * *

Around 11:15, a voice over the PA system said, "Paging Jefferson Thomas. Jefferson Thomas ... please report to the nearest Delta Airlines counter."

Jefferson was sure he knew what this was about. Leaving the kids to stay with Cassandra, he made his way over to the gate agent's counter. Though she had heard the page, the woman working there had no clue what it was about. So, she called her supervisor, who in turn connected her to another supervisor, who then requested to speak to Jefferson.

"Mr. Thomas," the man said. "I just wanted to confirm that you are having two caskets transported on your flight, correct?"

"Yes," Jefferson said in a low voice so people around him couldn't hear. "they're the bodies of my brother and sister-in-law."

"They have arrived, and we will make sure they are loaded when your plane arrives. On behalf of Delta Airlines, I offer our condolences for your loss."

"Thank you."

The call ended there. Jefferson looked at the gate agent, who still seemed to be clueless as to what was going on. Lucky him.

"While I'm here, I'd like to get a pre-boarding pass for me and my family," he said.

"How many of you are there?" the agent asked.

"Four plus the dog," Jefferson told her.

"Sir, you can only take one person with you when you pre-board."

"The people with me are four and seven years old," Jefferson said, pointing back in the direction he'd come. "You really think it'd be a good idea for me to leave any of them behind?"

The man didn't argue further and instead handed over the necessary pre-boarding cards.

About half an hour after Jefferson rejoined the others, their plane arrived and passengers began coming out of the jet bridge. Cassandra decided now would be a good time to start saying "goodbye."

"You're gonna go with your uncle now," she told them. "You take care of yourselves."

She hugged each of them in turn.

"I'll stay just a few minutes more," she said. "But then you guys have to get on the plane."

She helped them gather up their things and they all walked over to where the pre-boarders were to wait. For this flight, Jefferson and the kids were the only ones in that group.

Matthew, who had originally not wanted to give up his spot where he could see the many, many planes, was now excited about getting to actually go on one. Taylor was silent and even Abigail seemed a little withdrawn as the impending trip came closer.

"We just have a few more passengers coming out," The gate agent said. "you can board after that. Would you like some assistance down the jet bridge?"

"No thanks," Jefferson replied. "Just show me to the door and we'll be fine."

"Okay. It'll be just a few more minutes."

"Then this is our cue for the last goodbye," Cassandra said.

She hugged each of the kids one more time, wishing them well.

"You listen to your uncle from here on out," she told them. "He's in charge now."

The three kids nodded. Cassandra took Jefferson aside

"You're in charge now," she said. "You ready?"

"I have no idea," Jefferson admitted.

"You have my number if you need any tips."

Jefferson nodded. He'd entered it in his phone before leaving New York.

"Good luck," Cassandra said, shaking his hand as her voice trembled a bit.

"Thank you," Jefferson replied. "For everything."

"Take care."

"Come on Uncle Jeff," Abigail called. "They said that we can get on."

"That's your cue," Cassandra said. Jefferson nodded and headed back towards the kids. He scooped up his overnight bag, which he'd tasked Matthew with watching, and herded them together.

"Boarding passes please," the gate agent said.

Jefferson handed them over. The agent put them through the scanner one at a time and handed him the stubs.

"You're all set," he said. "Have a good flight. The doors are straight ahead of you."

"Thank you," Jefferson said as he directed the kids and Presley through the doors into the jet bridge.

"Bye you guys!" Cassandra called after the group as she watched them walk down the tunnel. "Take care!"

"Bye!" the kids chorused back, turning to wave one last time. Jefferson, whose hands were full, was only able to look back and give her a nod. The group then disappeared around a bend in the tunnel.

"Good luck," Cassandra whispered.

Chapter 4

"Guten tag," the flight attendant said as Jefferson and the kids approached the plane's doors.

"Hello," Jefferson returned, hoping that, mixed with his lack of a German accent, would indicate his lack of any German speaking capabilities.

"Welcome aboard. Can I help you find your seats?"

"That would be great. We're in row twenty-eight, seats A through E."

"Where's the pilot?" Matthew chimed in, looking around as he followed Jefferson onto the plane.

The flight attendant laughed.

"The captain is in the cockpit," she explained, pointing at the nearby, vault-like door. "He's making sure everything is ready for us to leave on time."

Matthew stared at the door and Jefferson wondered if he was figuring out how to open it.

"I'll show you folks to your seats," the flight attendant said. She took two steps and stopped again.

"Oh," she said, noticing Presley for the first time. "You have a service animal as well. She is beautiful."

Jefferson could hear the swishing of Presley's wagging tail.

* * *

the group had the two seats by the window and three of the four seats across the right-side aisle. Thankfully, the airline had been able to block off one extra seat to give Presley room to curl up and lie down. This wasn't a courtesy Jefferson received often. Planes were usually full, and no seat could be blocked. Then again, he didn't fly much. When he did, it was for short, domestic trips and Presley usually just took the foot space in front of him.

"Here you are," the flight attendant said as they reached their row. "I can help put your bags in the overhead bin."

"We'll start with these," Jefferson said, indicating his briefcase and overnight bag.

"I can take those," the attendant said as she opened one of the overhead bins.

Jefferson paused to consider the best seating arrangement.

"Taylor, Abigail," he said, "you take those two seats."

He indicated the two seats by the window.

"Matthew," he continued, "you're with me and Presley on this side."

He would take the aisle seat with Matthew right next to him and the empty seat for Presley on the boy's other side. His legs were short enough that she could stretch into his foot space as well. Jefferson figured, with this arrangement, he'd be able to keep a sense of control over all three kids.

As the twins decided amongst themselves about who would get the aisle seat on their side, Jefferson and the flight attendant loaded everyone's bags into the overhead bins.

"We have some activity kits your children would enjoy," the flight attendant said. "I'll go get those."

She left, though Jefferson wasn't sure how she'd gotten around him and the kids, the group successfully blocking the narrow aisle. He was still processing what she'd said. "Your children." He supposed that was true, even if he still had to absorb it.

Abigail and Taylor seemed to have decided that Abigail could have the aisle seat while Taylor took the window seat so she would be left alone by anyone passing their row. Jefferson was surprised and relieved when their agreement was struck without apparent conflict. They settled into their respective seats and buckled up at his urging. Their compliance further helped him relax a little.

Meanwhile, Matthew decided he wanted a better view of what was going on outside the plane and stood up in his seat.

"Sit down," Jefferson encouraged, finding and tugging on his shirt.

It took a few tries, but Matthew finally complied.

"There's a very important airplane rule that you always need to remember," Jefferson told his nephew. "Always do what the flight attendants and pilot say. You need help buckling up?"

"They said to buckle up?" Matthew asked as Jefferson buckled his own seatbelt.

"They whispered it in my ear," Jefferson said, thinking quickly to cover himself. Matthew seemed to accept this as his uncle helped him buckle his seatbelt and the flight attendant returned.

"Here you go," she said, handing each of the kids a bag. "We've got some coloring books and crayons, stickers, and activity books … all kinds of fun things. You can do some of them with your Dad."

Jefferson froze, again absorbing her words. The kids might have missed what she'd said before, but they couldn't have missed it now.

"He's not our Dad," Abigail said. "He's our Uncle Jeff."

"Oh," the flight attendant said.

Jefferson sensed her pause. He didn't encounter it often, but he understood its meaning.

"Well, 'Uncle Jeff'," the attendant said. "My name's Lauren. Just hit the call button over your head if you need anything and I'll come right down. Have a nice flight."

She walked away and Jefferson was sure he was right. Seeming to draw the conclusion from his title "Uncle Jeff" and the lack of a ring on his finger, this woman was now interested. Had he been flying alone, he might have responded accordingly to the underlying flirtation in her final statement.

Jefferson's luck with the opposite gender varied. Some women couldn't get past his blindness while others seemed fine with it. Eric had once told him he looked like the actor Titus Welliver, which Jefferson figured was a good thing. Too bad it wasn't enough to keep Nancy around.

Thinking about the flight attendant again, Jefferson wondered what Eric would have to say about her. His friend usually described women around them, and flirtatious hints were usually a good cue to get him started. This woman, Lauren, did have a nice-sounding voice. But Jefferson knew that, even with the aid of Eric's descriptions, things were different now. The kids around him were the strongest evidence of that.

* * *

As other passengers filed through the aisle, Abigail greeted as many as she could while Taylor seemed to be trying to stay occupied by browsing through her new activity kit and then the SkyMall catalog she found in the magazine sleeve in front of her seat. While she had some reading capabilities, the catalog quickly had her stumped and she took to just looking at the pictures. Jefferson prayed she wouldn't stumble across anything inappropriate, though he wasn't too sure about what could define "inappropriate" in the SkyMall catalog.

"Hi," Abigail continued greeting the other passengers, a few of whom greeted her back.

"Settle down," Jefferson finally told her. "I think you've greeted enough people."

"Okay," Abigail said and also began going through the magazine sleeve in front of her seat, soon discovering the safety information card. She perused it, admiring the diagrams.

Jefferson texted his parents, as well as Eric and Amy. The messages were virtually identical. He and the kids were on the plane and it looked like they'd leave Berlin on time. Putting his phone away again, he felt thankful that all three kids were being quiet for now. But he was sure it would still be a long flight.

* * *

"Lunch time," Frank announced, entering the bookstore with several small plastic bags which bore the logo of the local Subway sandwich restaurant. Both Kathy and Monique looked up as he came over to them.

Since the store was kept open through the daily lunch hour, the routine was that one person would go and get lunch for everyone or they would order in. Either way, they'd be eating while they worked. No one had ever complained or cited New York's laws about lunch breaks.

Kathy reached beneath the counter by the register and emerged with a plastic tumbler identical to the one through which Monique had drank her coffee that morning. She secured it to the wheelchair and poured in the Coke Frank had brought back for his boss. Monique took her sandwich, and they all began eating.

"How's the hiring process coming along?" Frank asked after a while, taking a break from his meatball sub.

Kathy withdrew from taking another bite of her veggie sandwich and looked up with apparent interest.

"Slowly," Monique said. "I'm not sure if I've found anyone human enough who will accept what comes with the job."

She gestured at herself.

"I had one person ask if I even worked here," She continued. "That was the end of that interview."

"You'll find someone," Kathy assured her, setting her food aside as a man came towards the register with two books clutched in his hand. Monique only nodded as she watched the transaction being completed.

* * *

"Uncle Jeff," Taylor said from across the aisle, bringing Jefferson out of his dozing state, "can I go to the bathroom?"

"Sure," Jefferson replied, rubbing his eyes. "Just go to the ones right in front of us and come right back."

The lavatories were just two rows ahead of them. Taylor promised she would and got out of her seat. Matthew was asleep and Abigail, who had gotten her backpack from Jefferson, was busy coloring with her crayons. Jefferson couldn't help thinking that the flight was going pretty well so far. They only had about three hours left before they were due to arrive in New York. All three kids had eaten the meal provided earlier, though Abigail asked about a million questions regarding its contents before she began eating, and he'd be sure to have them take the snack that would be coming around before they landed. So far, everything was fine.

Then Jefferson realized it had been almost ten minutes since Taylor left. as far as he knew, she wasn't back. He didn't hear voices up ahead by the lavatories, so he didn't think there was a line where she was waiting.

"Abigail," he said, getting his other niece's attention, "do you see your sister?"

"No," Abigail replied, "but she went to the bathroom, remember?"

Great, Jefferson thought. How on Earth was he going to search the plane for this girl? What if she was locked in a lavatory? He knew that he couldn't just sit there and wait.

"Abigail," he said, "take my seat and watch your brother."

As Jefferson got up, Presley began to get up as well, believing he needed her

"Stay," Jefferson told her.

Presley was quick to settle down again, Matthew's feet dangling over her back.

"Hey," Abigail protested as Jefferson walked away. "I'm too young to baby-sit."

Jefferson didn't respond. He reached the lavatories and looked around.

"Taylor?" he asked. "Taylor? Are you around here?"

The only response he got was from a nearby flight attendant.

"Sir," the attendant asked, coming over, "is everything all right?"

It was possibly Lauren, the flight attendant from earlier. Jefferson couldn't be sure.

"My niece is missing," he explained. "She's seven years old, has red hair, and she's wearing a purple sweater and jeans."

Thankfully, he'd memorized what the kids had put on that morning.

"All right," the flight attendant assured him. "We'll go through the cabin. I'd like you to sit back down in your seat and we'll bring her back when we find her. She can't have gotten far."

Jefferson reluctantly followed her instructions. He left Abigail in his seat and took hers for the time being.

"What's going on, Uncle Jeff?" his niece queried from across the aisle. "Where's Taylor?"

He didn't respond to her inquiries.

"What's your brother doing?" he asked instead.

"He's sleeping," Abigail replied.

Jefferson figured a sleeping child couldn't cause him any grief at the moment.

Another flight attendant soon approached their row. This definitely wasn't Lauren.

"Sir," she reported, "we've found your niece."

Jefferson felt relief wash over him.

"Where is she?" he asked, tempted to just reach out for Taylor.

"Well, that's the problem," the attendant said. "She's curled up on the floor by one of the exit doors and she's refusing to leave that spot. She seems to be very upset."

bet I know what that's about, Jefferson thought as he rose and again left Abigail to watch her brother. The flight attendant led him up through another section in economy class. Most of the other passengers ignored the precession while a few looked up with mild interest. Jefferson could soon hear Taylor sniffling. They came up to where she was curled up on the floor with her head buried between her knees, which were pulled into her chest with her arms wrapped around them. Jefferson took the lead now.

"Hey," he said, crouching down in front of her. "What were you thinking, running off like that?"

"I don't want to go," Taylor said between sniffles. Her voice sounded muffled.

"You don't want to go where?" Jefferson asked, sure he knew the answer.

"I don't want to go to New York," Taylor said. "I want to go home. I want my mom and dad back."

Jefferson had hoped another episode like this would wait until they reached his house. But he did not have Cassandra Kingman's confidence or luck. He also wasn't sure if he had her bluffing capabilities. It wasn't like he could get far away from Taylor on this airplane, nor would he want to.

"You know that can't happen," he said.

"Why not?!" Taylor wailed. "I didn't do anything. It's not fair!"

Jefferson wondered if nearby passengers were now watching and listening. He didn't know or care if the flight attendant was still there.

"I know it's not fair," he said. "It stinks. It stinks for me too. I lost loved ones, just like you did. But we now have to make it work."

Taylor was quiet. Jefferson sat on the floor next to her.

"Listen to me," he continued. "When I first got the call and found out what happened, my first thought was what would happen to you guys. I knew your parents named me as your legal guardian, but that was a long time ago. You know what though? When I was told what happened, I said I would be in Germany as soon as possible."

Taylor stopped sniffling and looked up at him.

"It's not fair," she repeated in a softer voice.

"I know," Jefferson agreed, pulling her into his arms. "I know it's not fair. But we have to make it work. That's the only choice we've got."

He patted her head as she began to relax and uncurl herself.

"You ready to go back to your seat?" he asked after a few silent seconds.

Taylor nodded. He felt her head moving against his chest.

"Come on," he said.

He first took her to a nearby lavatory so she could wash her hands and face. With that done, they went to rejoin Abigail and Matthew, Jefferson using the seats they passed as his source of guidance.

"Can I have my seat back now?" Abigail asked impatiently as Taylor once again sat by the window.

"Wait another minute," Jefferson told her and sat down next to Taylor. Taylor looked at him, suspecting they weren't quite done talking yet.

"I need you to make me two promises," Jefferson said. "I need you to promise me that you understand that running off like that was wrong, and you have to promise me that you won't do it again."

"I'm sorry," Taylor said.

"Can you keep those two promises?"

"Yes. I promise."

"Good," Jefferson said and let Abigail have her seat back.

Soon, the flight attendants began handing out snacks, which once again prompted Abigail to begin her food-related interrogation. At that time, Matthew also woke up. He immediately asked how much longer the flight was going to be. It seemed the majesty of air travel was wearing off.

"Two more hours," Jefferson told the boy as well as himself.

Chapter 5

The plane landed at the John F. Kennedy International airport. Abigail, who had seemingly grown bored of flying in the last hour and a half, was now ready to move on to the next adventure.

"Let's go," she insisted.

"Calm down," Jefferson told her as people passed between them. "We'll wait just a couple more minutes and go when it isn't so crowded."

At his feet, Presley was fidgeting. She too wasn't content to wait. When Jefferson gave her the command, she bolted out of the row, ready to go.

Jefferson was expecting an airline employee to meet them at the end of the jet bridge. instead, they were met by a man who identified himself as Agent Keith Noble from the Transportation Security Administration.

"I've been instructed to make your reentry process a smooth one," the agent explained. "Since there is no notarized letter from the children's parents permitting them to accompany you as you enter the United States, we want to work to prevent any hiccups."

Jefferson wouldn't argue with this logic. Making sure the kids were with him, he took Agent Noble's elbow, Presley walking by his side.

They first went to the baggage claim to collect the kids' bags, which took a little while as the items had somehow been distributed throughout the plane's cargo hold. The last two bags were among the last few items to emerge onto the belt.

Agent Noble volunteered to push the luggage cart now baring the load of the six duffel bags. Noting the area sounded less congested, Jefferson instructed Presley to follow him.

"Stay close to me," he said over his shoulder more than once. None of the kids responded, but he got some comfort from hearing their small footfalls on the airport's linoleum floor.

"Welcome back to the United States," the customs official said when Jefferson's turn came. "Did you enjoy your trip abroad?"

"Not sure," Jefferson replied, unable to come up with a better answer as he presented his passport.

"Are you declaring any perishables? Any fruits, vegetables, or meats?"

"No," Jefferson replied, wondering when he would have had the time to get any of that stuff.

"Is your dog from the United States?

"Yes," Jefferson said, retrieving Presley's vaccination certificate from the side pocket of his overnight bag. "That's from my vet in Manhattan."

"And these are your children?" the official asked, seeming to notice the twins and Matthew for the first time.

"No," Jefferson said, retrieving an envelope from his overnight bag along with Maggie's passport. "Their passports are in here."

"What is your relationship to these children?" the official asked, taking Maggie's passport.

"I'm their uncle," Jefferson explained, "and now their guardian."

"Do you have any documentation to confirm this?"

the customs official sounded ready to summon the police. Jefferson presented the envelope, wanting to do anything to avoid outright saying Stanley and Margaret were dead.

"That's a letter from the U.S. Ambassador in Berlin, Germany," he explained. "It gives me permission to bring the kids here to New York with me."

Somewhat reluctantly, Cassandra Kingman had explained the State Department had no protocol in place for if one of its overseas employees and their spouse was killed, leaving their children in a foreign country without a legal guardian. Though she and Jefferson never met, Ambassador Kelly Ridder wrote the letter and affixed the seal of the United States next to her signature to affirm her government's support for the children's relocation.

The customs official read the letter and nodded slowly.

"Okay," he said in a more somber tone, stamping all the passports. "Welcome back to the United States."

* * *

the group emerged in the bustling public area of the airport's terminal building. Despite the onslaught of noise, Jefferson almost immediately heard his name being called through the crowd of waiting family members and limo drivers there to receive clients.

"Jefferson! Jefferson! Hey Jefferson!"

A man was finally able to make his way through the crowd to meet the group. He stopped to catch his breath before speaking.

"Hey man," he said. "How you doing?"

45

"I'm good," Jefferson replied, recognizing the speaker as his friend and colleague, Eric Nelson. "You sound like you've been having fun here."

"Oh yeah. Brutal crowds … old ladies too dumb to exist … screaming kids … expensive coffee … it's been a blast."

Eric's voice lost its sarcasm as He turned to Agent Noble.

"I'll take them from here," he said. "Thanks."

Agent Noble nodded, seemingly somewhat relieved to not have to push the cart anymore.

"You folks take care," he said and walked away.

"Guys," Jefferson said. "This is my friend, Eric Nelson. He was nice enough to come to drive us home."

All three kids greeted Eric. Abigail sounded cheerful, Taylor sounded indifferent, and Matthew sounded shy.

"Good to meet you guys," Eric said.

"Where'd you park the van anyway?" Jefferson asked.

"Amy's circling the building with it. I figured it'd be easier to bring her than try to park in this nightmare."

"How'd she feel about that?"

"She started calling the idea stupid in Latin, so everything's normal. Shall we?"

He moved behind the cart and began pushing.

"Jesus Christ!" he said almost immediately. "What did you pack in these bags? Bricks?"

Abigail giggled as she followed him. Given Eric was five feet, eight inches tall and weighed around a hundred and seventy pounds, Jefferson didn't find his complaints too unexpected.

They made their way out of the building, where Eric stopped the cart and called his wife.

"Trust me," he said, speaking loudly to be heard over the traffic, "we're hard to miss. Look for the Mount Everest of luggage."

Amy Nelson pulled up in their minivan a few minutes later and got out to meet the kids, ignoring the glares from a nearby police officer. Being two inches taller than her husband and a former track star, Amy was the most confident person Jefferson knew.

"I have heard so much about you guys," she said. "Welcome to New York. How was the flight?"

"I don't know how we're going to fit everything," Eric said, having pulled the luggage cart towards the back of the minivan and opening its rear door.

"Consilium capiemus," Amy insisted, pulling open the minivan's sliding door. "Jefferson, you get these kids in the car. Reach out straight ahead of you and you'll have the door. It's about five feet."

She moved to the back to help with the bags.

"Oh boy," she soon commented. "There is a lot in here. You travel with kids?"

"Told you," Eric said.

"I'm surprised they let them on the plane," Amy added, lifting the first bag into the back of the minivan.

"Abigail," Jefferson said, figuring out how to flip one of the middle row's seats forward, "you mind sitting in the back row with Presley?"

"Sure," Abigail agreed, scrambling past him into the minivan.

"Amy!" Jefferson called. "I'm going to see if Presley needs to go before the drive."

The dog hadn't had a chance to relieve herself since leaving Berlin. He moved towards the front of the minivan and extended Presley's leash a little, urging her to step off the curb.

"Get busy," he encouraged. "Busy. Busy. Busy. Get busy."

Not one to disobey a command, Presley peed. She didn't sniff around to select a spot to defecate and instead stepped back onto the curb, indicating this was all she needed to accomplish.

"Good girl," Jefferson praised. "Come on."

They stepped back to the open van door, where Amy met them with one of the duffel bags.

"Skootch over, Abby," she said. "I need to put this back there with you.

"I don't like that," Abigail replied.

"You don't like what?" Amy asked, confused and trying to hide the strain the heavy bag had on her.

"I don't like that name. My name is Abigail."

"Understood," Amy said with a patient smile. "Could you please move over so I can put this in?"

In the back, Eric shut the door as Amy heaved the last duffel back onto the seat next to Abigail. At Jefferson's urging, Presley climbed into the van.

"I need to tuck her tail in," Amy said. "I don't want it to get caught when I put the seat back down."

"Go ahead," Jefferson said. "Abigail, don't let her climb onto the seat."

Pushing Presley's tail away, Amy flipped the seat back down and turned to Matthew.

"See that booster seat?" she asked, pointing towards the far side inside the minivan. "That's yours. Hop in."

Matthew did so and she followed him, gathering the seat's straps in one hand.

"Both my sons sat in this," she explained as she buckled each strap. "Lucky we still had it in the garage. There … In Omnia Paratus."

"Huh?" Matthew asked.

"It means you're ready for anything."

"You're driving," Eric insisted, climbing into the front passenger seat. "The airport gave me a headache."

"Ain tu?" Amy replied as she slid out of the minivan again. "Don't get too comfortable. I need directions once we leave Queens."

"Whatever. Just stop with the Latin."

Amy smiled as she directed Jefferson into the van, followed by Taylor, and slid the door shut.

"I'll tell you where to go," Eric promised as she got in behind the wheel.

From the back, Abigail giggled as Presley licked her.

"Don't let her climb onto the seat," Jefferson reminded his niece.

* * *

The ride lasted about forty-five minutes, during most of which Abigail asked questions about almost everything she saw. Jefferson, Eric, and Amy answered everything as best they could.

"That's a butcher's shop," Eric said at one point after another query about a sign baring a cartoon pig. "Doubt you'll ever go to that one. It's a bit far from home for you guys."

Meanwhile, Taylor had fallen asleep, her head resting against Jefferson's torso. Glancing in her rearview mirror every so often, Amy smiled at the sight.

Much like his sister, Matthew was interested in their surroundings. He was still determined to find a park.

"I think there's one near where you live," Amy said, though she was far from certain.

By the time they pulled up in front of Jefferson's brownstone, Abigail was getting tired and had quieted down a bit. After executing a complicated maneuver to exit the van without waking Taylor, She and Matthew followed Jefferson up to the front door. He unlocked it and brought them inside. Showing them where they could leave their shoes and helping them hang up their jackets, he led Presley into his small backyard so she couldn't escape while the luggage was hauled in through the open front door. With two of the three kids settled on one of the den's couches, he went back outside to help Amy and Eric unload the cargo. They piled the bags up in one corner of the foyer with Jefferson making plans to sort it out later. For now, he just wanted the stuff out of the way so he wouldn't trip over it.

The last thing left in the van was Taylor, who never stirred despite the activity around her. Jefferson scooped her up and, with help from Eric and Amy, who made sure he didn't run into anything or trip along his way up the front steps, brought her into the house and set her down on the second couch. He and Amy pulled her shoes off and covered her with a blanket. Taylor still didn't flinch.

"That's everything," Eric said. "We'll see you tomorrow."

"Minime," Amy insisted. "We can't leave yet."

Jefferson and Eric stared at her.

"We have to go to a supermarket," Amy elaborated. "Jefferson probably never got a chance to go before he went to Germany. We need to get a few things for him and the kids."

"You don't have to ..." Jefferson began but Amy shook her head.

"You need to feed these kids properly," she admonished. "I'm willing to bet your milk's gone bad by now. You can't give them that."

"Don't fight it," Eric advised. "Trust me."

As he had done before, Jefferson marveled at the couple's union. Eric, a self-described "major nerd turned major legal nerd", and Amy, who never objected to her husband's description of her as "amazingly hot", getting together was almost a cliché from a cheesy teen comedy. Where Eric was thin, Amy was athletic, one hailing from the chess club and the other the track team. Eric's hair was blond while Amy's was auburn. He could be invisible in a crowd while she turned heads wherever she went. She stood about two inches over him and her skin was a darker, olive shade, so she looked like she always sported a light tan. Eric looked like he spent too much time indoors.

Still, the couple had their similarities. Both were smart and outgoing, having met in a library at Columbia University. They shared a passion for swimming, though Eric conceded his wife was better at it. And they were happy together.

Jefferson had just one problem with that ... Amy wasn't with him. She'd chosen Eric and he probably knew why.

Chapter 6

"I'll be back in ten or fifteen minutes," Amy promised as she and Eric left. "Stricta sit."

Nodding, Jefferson turned to Abigail and Matthew.

"You two wanna see your rooms?" he asked.

They seemed to be enthusiastic about this idea, so he took them upstairs, Presley bringing up the rear.

The brownstone's second floor had two empty rooms, a hall closet, and a bathroom. Jefferson explained how the three kids would share the bathroom and that he would figure out what they'd keep in the hall closet. He showed them the two bedrooms, describing how Abigail and Taylor would share the slightly larger room while Matthew would get the other one to himself. He also showed them the view both bedrooms had of the neighborhood, something they seemed to be impressed by.

The home's previous owners had carpeted the two rooms, which now saved Jefferson the trouble of having to do it. He had formerly used the rooms for storage, but the items once there had been moved to other parts of the house in great haste. Jefferson told himself he'd reorganize things more thoroughly once he had some time.

"Where's your room?" Abigail asked, realizing she'd seen the entire floor.

"I'm one floor above you guys," Jefferson told her, pointing at the ceiling. "My room and my office are on the third floor."

"How many floors do you have?" Matthew asked, looking up.

"There are four floors in this house. The fourth floor's the attic. Then there's also a basement below the first floor as well as the garage."

Both kids seemed awestruck by this.

"Hello?!" someone called from beneath them.

Jefferson realized Taylor was awake and probably confused about her strange surroundings.

"We're upstairs!" he called back.

Taylor soon joined them, and he showed her around her new living arrangements. Taylor surveyed the rooms with apparent interest.

"There's no beds," she finally commented. "Where are we gonna sleep?"

"I've got some air mattresses and sleeping bags that you guys can use for the time being," Jefferson said. "Once your furniture gets here, we can set up the rooms the way you want."

Though they rented most of the furniture they needed with every relocation, Stan and Maggie had purchased some items for the kids' rooms which would be moved with them. A moving company in Germany had packed up this furniture with the rest of the family's personal belongings and were shipping them across the Atlantic. Jefferson would probably sell a large majority of this stuff, but the kids' things would go in their rooms.

The doorbell rang and Jefferson went to answer it. Amy bustled in with two shopping bags, heading straight into the kitchen.

"Milk, a mixed pack of small cereal boxes to please all pallets, bread, eggs, orange juice, and bananas," she announced, setting the items out on the counter as Jefferson followed her. "Everything you'll need for breakfast for the time being until you have a chance to get reorganized and really go grocery shopping."

"Thank you," Jefferson said, taking out his wallet. "How much do I owe you?"

"You don't have to ..." Amy began, but Jefferson found her jacket pocket and stuffed two horizontally folded twenty-dollar bills into it. "Ut melius nosti."

Understanding it was futile, she decided not to argue.

"I'd better go," she said, exiting the kitchen. "I left Eric in the car."

"Hope you cracked a window," Jefferson remarked as he opened the front door for her.

"Nequicquam."

Amy stepped around him and moved to exit the kitchen. She then stopped and turned towards him again.

"I know Eric got a chance to say it before you left," she said, "but I didn't. And, I didn't want to say it in front of the kids. I'm really sorry for your loss."

"Thanks," Jefferson said, "and thanks for all your help today."

"Sure. Have a good night."

"Good night," Jefferson said, stabbed with one of those occasional pangs of jealousy. Shouldn't he be the one who had the house and the family in Queens with her? Or should they be in this house in Greenwich Village? Sure, he was happy for the couple, having stood up and spoken at their wedding, but those conflicts still lingered in his mind.

After Amy left, Jefferson put the food away in accordance with his system of organizing his kitchen. Abigail, Taylor, and Matthew soon came downstairs as well.

"We're hungry," Abigail announced, seeming to speak for the group.

"To be quite honest, me too," Jefferson admitted. "Pizza sound good for tonight?"

All three kids seemed to be okay with this idea. As Jefferson picked up his iPhone, they headed for the front door.

"Where are you going?" he asked.

"To get our shoes on," Taylor replied, confused. "I thought you said we were going to get pizza."

Jefferson understood the confusion. Germany, like every other country in Europe, wasn't known for restaurants that delivered. Sure, they existed, but not in the same volume as in New York.

"We don't have to go anywhere," he said and proceeded to explain the system of pizza delivery. This seemed to hold their interest for a little while.

"What do you guys want on your pizza?" Jefferson asked, holding up his iPhone. He soon regretted the question as they all shouted out different requests, with Abigail mainly listing what she didn't want.

"How about just cheese?" Jefferson asked, finally able to get their attention again. They seemed fine with this idea and asked to go and explore more parts of the house.

"Just be careful," Jefferson said as he located a pizzeria on Uber Eats.

They ran off while he placed the order and went to let Presley back in. The dog passed him and went to locate the kids. After placing their order, Jefferson headed into the den to sit on the couch. There was no real point in chasing after the kids. Before he left for Germany, he'd had enough sense to lock the doors to his bedroom, his office, the attic, and the basement/garage. Unless they goofed around in the kitchen, which he could easily prevent from his current position, there wasn't too much that could harm them for the time being.

After texting a few people, including his parents, to let them know he and the kids were now home, Jefferson got up again and headed back into the kitchen. He opened the refrigerator and took out his old half-gallon jug of milk. He took the cap off and sniffed it. Deciding Amy was right, he poured the remaining milk into the sink. When was the last time he'd bought milk? He only used it for his coffee and the occasional attempt at actual cooking.

His phone rang and he withdrew it from his pocket, not recognizing the number the voiceover software was reciting.

"Hello?" he asked.

The young-sounding caller identified herself as "Elizabeth" with Dodson & Dodson. It took Jefferson a moment due to the fatigue, but he soon recognized this was the funeral home he'd been in touch with.

"Mr. Thomas," Elizabeth said, sounding way too perky for this kind of work or this late in the evening. "We've received two sealed caskets with documentation from the funeral home in Berlin."

"Yes," Jefferson said, hoping the kids couldn't hear him. "Those are my brother and sister-in-law."

"We are very sorry for your loss. I want to assure you the caskets are still sealed and undamaged. All the paperwork is in order. Mr. Hurson will be in touch tomorrow to help you with the arrangements."

"Thank you," Jefferson said.

"How come there are locked doors?" someone asked as he ended the call.

Jefferson turned and realized the speaker had to be Abigail, though he couldn't be absolutely sure yet. The twins sounded almost as identical as they looked. He also couldn't be sure about how much of his phone conversation she'd heard. Her curiosity suggested little to none of it.

"Well," Jefferson said, "two of those doors go to my office and my bedroom, which, if I'm not in there, you guys are definitely not allowed in there. Then, the door that can let you up into the attic is locked for your own safety, just like the door that goes down to the basement."

Abigail seemed to accept this, though she also seemed disappointed to not be able to explore these parts of the house. She headed over to a window and looked out on to the street, probably wondering when the pizza would come.

"Hey," she said. "There's a ramp in front of your house."

She seemed to not have noticed it when they arrived earlier.

"Yep, there is," Jefferson confirmed.

"Where does it go?" Abigail asked.

"To the garage. It's underneath us."

"Do you have a car?"

"No, I just have the garage."

"Weird," Abigail commented.

The distraction of the ramp and the garage had apparently caused her to miss a car pulling up in front of the house. She didn't think anything was up until Jefferson's phone chimed and he headed to the front door.

"That's probably the pizza," Jefferson explained as he walked. "Go get your brother and sister. You guys gotta wash up for dinner."

Abigail ran back upstairs while he went to answer the door.

"Thanks," he said, taking the two pies.

He was setting them down on the kitchen table when the kids returned. After directing them to wash their hands in the kitchen sink, he set out plates on the table and distributed the slices of pizza. The kids were initially quiet as they ate.

"This is good," Matthew commented at one point.

"It's a good restaurant," Jefferson responded. "But anyone will tell you that New York has the best pizza ever … except maybe Chicago."

"What's Chicago?" Taylor asked.

"It's another city," Jefferson explained. "It's in another part of the country. It takes about two hours to get there by plane from here."

"Can we go there?" Abigail asked.

"Maybe someday."

* * *

"Okay," Jefferson announced, entering the den. "Bedtime."

While the kids watched TV, he'd spent the last hour setting up the air mattresses, sheets, and sleeping bags in their rooms. He couldn't recall why he had all this stuff in the attic. Maybe he and Nancy had intended to go camping at some point.

"But I took a nap," Taylor whined.

"Doesn't matter," Jefferson told her.

Taylor pouted as she continued to watch television with her siblings.

"Let's go, you guys," Jefferson insisted, locating the remote on one of the couches and switching off the TV. He received some whining and muttering, but no one seemed to have the strength for an outright protest. He too felt drained and could already picture his own bed upstairs.

Jefferson was thankful he didn't get any strong arguments. While Cassandra Kingman had given him a crash course in parenting at every chance she got while he was in Germany, he was not yet experienced enough to hold his own if one of the kids talked back repetitively.

Having already brought the kids' bags upstairs, he had them locate their pajamas, toiletries, and anything else they needed for bed. he would sort the rest out in the morning.

Everything was going fine until a fight ensued when they were trying to determine who would get the bathroom first.

"How about this?" Jefferson suggested. "I'm thinking of a number between one and ten. Whoever guesses closest gets to go first."

"Seven," Abigail offered.

"Four," Taylor guessed.

"Three," Matthew tried.

"It was four," Jefferson told them. "Taylor goes first, followed by Matthew, and then Abigail."

Abigail wasn't happy about being last and stood fuming in the hallway. The whole matter might have blown over then if Taylor hadn't blown a raspberry before disappearing into the bathroom.

"Settle down," Jefferson admonished.

* * *

"What will happen tomorrow?" Abigail asked, getting into her sleeping bag. It was meant for an adult and she took up about half of it.

Next to her in the other sleeping bag, Taylor seemed to have fallen asleep almost immediately, not caring about what was to come the next day. her earlier nap seemed to also have been forgotten.

"So?" Abigail asked again when Jefferson didn't respond. "What's gonna happen tomorrow?"

"We're gonna keep working on getting you guys settled in here," Jefferson replied. "We might go out and do some stuff, but we'll have to sleep first."

He wasn't sure if his answer satisfied her or if Abigail was too tired to question him further, but the next thing he heard was the little girl breathing as she slept. She was almost in rhythm with her sister.

Jefferson checked in on Matthew, who was also fast asleep, his air mattress made up like a bed with spare sheets and a blanket, and then headed up to his own bed, Presley following him. Despite the evening running smoothly after the bathroom squabble, even the dog was exhausted.

* * *

After locking up the store for the night, Frank and Kathy went home and Monique took her private elevator back up to her apartment. Joan arrived about fifteen minutes later and set to work on preparing dinner, which was potato salad. They talked about their respective days, with

Monique doing most of the talking since most of Joan's topics fell under nurse/patient confidentiality. When the salad was ready, Monique ate while Joan went to prepare her bed and pajamas.

After dinner, Monique went into her bedroom, where Joan got her into her other wheelchair, which she used to get into the bathroom. When she came out a few minutes later, Joan helped her change into her pajamas and get into bed.

"One of these days," the nurse said, "you're gonna tell me to scram as soon as possible so you can continue a date."

This was another frequent remark of hers.

"Don't count on it," Monique said.

Joan performed a quick check-up to make sure everything concerning Monique's health was in order. With that done, she made sure the water bottle Monique kept on her nightstand was full.

"Have a good night," she said. "Pleasant dreams."

Left alone, Monique didn't feel tired yet, so she began fumbling with the stationary remote control affixed to the side of her bed and watched the news for a while, though she found nothing good. When she finally began to feel tired, she turned off the television and went to sleep.

Chapter 7

Believing at first she was still dreaming, Monique woke up to a strange noise. Looking around her dark bedroom, she focused on her clock radio. The glowing red numerals told her it was 1:47 in the morning.

What the? she wondered.

The noises continued and she realized they were coming from below her bedroom. But the store should be … she thought when it hit her. Someone was in her store at a time when no one ought to be there. Someone was robbing her store.

Monique replayed the previous evening in her head. She'd used the keypad beneath the front counter to lock the front door at closing time. She, Frank, and Kathy went through their usual clean-up and inspection routine before they left via the back door. Frank had used his key to lock that door and Monique had double-checked it before returning to the front of the store and using the keypad to engage the alarm.

She looked over at a small screen mounted on the wall next to her bed's headboard. It showed her that, not only was the building's silent alarm engaged as she remembered, but that it had been tripped. The police would have received the alert by now, but Monique wasn't taking any chances. Managing to control her arm, she reached out and pushed a large red button below the screen. She hoped help got here soon.

Then, she heard the sound of a door below her being opened. She knew this led to a stairwell leading from the bookstore to her apartment and the storeroom above it. Since the doors to the store and the exterior door of the apartment were always locked, Monique had never bothered adding any type of lock to this interior door. Yeah, her office door had its own lock, but that was because she kept money and confidential personnel documents in there. Now, the burglar had discovered an access point to the rest of her building. Hearing another unsecured door open, Monique knew he was now in the main room of her apartment, twenty feet and one door from her bed.

Her heart racing, Monique lay in her bed. She wished now more than ever she could get out of bed on her own. Maybe then, she could hide or escape. But this wasn't an option.

She could hear the intruder walking around her apartment. She thought about calling 9-1-1 but decided against it. She had already manually triggered the alarm and the intruder was sure to hear a telephone conversation.

The handle of her bedroom door made a faint noise as it moved. Ready to have a heart attack, Monique shut her eyes and pretended to be sleeping. The room was dark, so he probably didn't see anything to suggest she knew he was there. Still, she feared the sound of her terrified breathing gave her away. The soft taps of his shoes on the floor rang in her ears, each step sounding like a clap of thunder.

The intruder stepped into the room. Opening her eyes just a bit, Monique could see a flashlight beam dancing across the wall. The intruder went to her closet and began looking through it but seemed to find nothing. He continued moving around the room, ignoring her. Shaking, Monique held her breath.

The intruder came up to the bed and shone his flashlight in her face. Monique involuntarily squeezed her eyes shut tight against the bright glare. She also couldn't withhold a gasp.

The intruder grabbed her shoulder and shook her. Too afraid to do anything else, Monique looked up at him but only saw shadows fall over his face.

"Don't scream," he told her in a soft, deep voice.

Monique nodded, terrified.

"Where do you keep your cash?" he demanded. "Tell me now."

"In the safe in the office downstairs," Monique told him truthfully. "I can give you the combination. And I've also got some money in my purse. It's in the hall closet outside in the main room."

"You're lying!"

the intruder was angry now. Monique was confused.

"I checked the hall closet," he snapped. "There's no purse in there,"

He grabbed her chin and squeezed it tight.

"Now," he said, "tell me the truth. Don't lie."

"Please," Monique whimpered. "I'm not lying. It's in there. I always keep it in there. Please don't hurt me."

The intruder let her go but he didn't move away from her bed.

"Please," Monique tried again, managing to prop herself up on her elbows. "I'll give you whatever you want."

Without a word, the intruder grabbed the edge of her blanket and pulled it back, shining his flashlight over her pajama-clad body. He reached out and stroked her leg.

Oh God, Monique thought.

Then, they could hear sirens outside. They were getting closer. The intruder froze, his hand still on Monique's leg. Monique was still as well, biting her lower lip to keep from crying.

All of the sudden, the intruder raised his flashlight and brought it down on the side of Monique's head in one sharp blow. The force of the impact caused her to pivot to one side, where gravity took over. She fell off the bed, her feet entangled in her blanket, crashing at the intruder's feet.

Leaving her there, the intruder fled the room. Managing to stay conscious, Monique could hear him unlock and open the door leading out of the apartment as the sirens got closer.

                    * * *

"What've we got?" New York City Police Detective Brian Casslebeck asked, arriving at the bookstore.

"Burglary," a patrol officer replied. "Some punk broke in through the back door down here and seemingly ransacked the place. We'll get someone to tell us if anything's missing, but it's definitely a mess."

Detective Casslebeck nodded and surveyed the store. It seemed as though every book had been pulled off the shelves. They lay strewn across the floor. The cash register had also been broken into and the cash drawer seemed to be missing. One coin roll had broken open and dull silver coins lay scattered across the counter and floor.

"Our intruder then went upstairs," the patrol officer continued.

"What's up there?" Detective Casslebeck asked.

"The owner lives up there. Her name's Monique Vasquez."

"Did she call 9-1-1?"

Detective Casslebeck hoped this was the case. that would mean she was still alive and maybe okay, physically speaking. The woman had to be terrified.

"No," the patrol officer explained, "the intruder tripped the alarm. We responded within five minutes of getting the call. The dispatcher said it was a priority because of her disability."

"Disability?" Detective Casslebeck asked. He knew the city had programs which allowed people to have such information entered in databases used by 9-1-1 operators and dispatchers so first responders would be able to act accordingly.

"Yeah," the officer said, "apparently she's paralyzed or something. Paramedics are upstairs looking her over."

Detective Casslebeck nodded and, making his way around two forensics technicians searching for fingerprints and fibers, went back outside and around to an external staircase he'd noticed earlier. He ascended it to find the door leading to the apartment above the bookstore. He entered and greeted another technician, hearing voices coming from a bedroom.

"I'm fine," a woman was saying. "Just put a bandage on it and let me get in my chair."

Stepping through the open doorway, Detective Casslebeck found two paramedics tending to a woman on a gurney. The woman seemed to be conscious and coherent as she was speaking with the paramedics, one of whom was bandaging a bloody wound on the side of her head.

"Ms. Vasquez, I assume," Detective Casslebeck said.

Monique turned and looked at him.

"That's me," she declared.

"I'm Detective Brian Casslebeck, NYPD. Are you all right?"

"The perp hit her across the head and knocked her off the bed," a paramedic explained. "She was conscious when we arrived. We're still checking for signs of a concussion."

"Hey," Monique protested. "I'm right here. I can speak for myself, thank you."

"As you can see, there doesn't seem to be any brain damage. We're gonna take her to the E.R. to make sure everything's okay though."

"Wo!" Monique said, ignoring the rude portion of his statement for the time being. "Wo! No way! I'm fine."

"Ms. Vasquez," the other paramedic said, "you were hit across the head with a flashlight and fell off the bed. You may feel fine, but there might be skin tears, broken bones, and other injuries none of us know about yet. Then there's still the possibility of a concussion."

Monique glared at both paramedics.

"Fine," she said, resigned.

"I'll be at the hospital in a little while to speak with you," Detective Casslebeck said as she was wheeled out of the bedroom. Listening to the ambulance drive away, he looked around the bedroom and then headed back downstairs to speak with the forensics technicians.

* * *

Despite Monique's continuing protests, the doctors at Beth Israel Medical Center's emergency room gave her a full check-up before being satisfied the bump on her head was her only serious injury and it wasn't a threat to her health. She had sustained some minor cuts and scrapes along her right side from the fall, which were easily treated and bandaged. She was lying in a hospital bed when, as promised, Detective Casslebeck came to speak to her.

"Can you tell me what happened?" the investigator requested.

As the sun's morning rays poked in through a nearby window, Monique recounted the previous night's events, adding how she was sure the intruder had planned to harm and possibly kill her.

"I just got the absolute chills when he touched me," she said. "The hairs on the back of my neck stood straight up. If you guys hadn't shown up when you did …"

Her voice trailed off with a shudder. Detective Casslebeck saw her being vulnerable for the first time that morning. He gently touched her shoulder.

"You survived," he assured her. "You're here and you're alive. That's what counts."

Monique nodded.

"Have you been released yet?" Detective Casslebeck asked.

Monique shook her head.

"I'm still waiting on the forms," she explained.

"I'll take you home when that's done," Detective Casslebeck said.

* * *

About an hour later, Detective Casslebeck's unmarked sedan pulled up in front of Monique's bookstore. The sun had fully risen by now and Kathy and Frank were anxiously waiting by the open front door. From the looks of it, the crime scene technicians and patrol officers were done and gone.

Kathy came forward to help Detective Casslebeck get Monique out of the car and into her wheelchair, which had been left in her apartment while she was in the hospital. She and Frank thanked the detective for all of his help. Detective Casslebeck wished them all well, promised to call with any news, and left.

Monique proceeded into the store, Kathy and Frank behind her.

"Are you sure you're okay?" Kathy asked almost immediately, eyeing the thick bandage on the side of her head.

"I'm fine," Monique insisted. "I took one blow to the head and they already released me. It can't be that bad. I also got some pain killers, just in case."

She pulled out a small vial of pills and shook it at them.

"Supposed to be the good stuff," she said. "Plus, there's definitely no concussion or anything like that."

"You will wanna lie down," Kathy insisted. "You've been up for most of the night."

"I'm fine. Come on. Let's get this place cleaned up so we can be open for at least part of the day."

The crime scene technicians had been kind enough to stack the books on the floor into piles, but there was absolutely no organization to this setup. Frank and Kathy set to work putting everything right again while Monique supervised and took a mental inventory. Some of the books looked damaged and might need to be discarded or donated. They'd do a full inventory once everything was cleaned up. Monique wondered if the intruder actually thought one of the books, or a bookshelf, concealed some sort of hidden treasure and that was why he'd tossed so many volumes onto the floor.

Joan soon arrived and Monique reluctantly allowed herself to be taken upstairs where the nurse checked her out. As she worked, Monique surveyed the apartment, not missing the fingerprint powder coating many pieces of furniture and spots on the walls and doors. The off-white splotches looked sickening.

Joan took an hour to clean the pale powder off Monique's bed and change her sheets. Despite her protests, Monique was put into bed and ordered to sleep for a few hours. She was given one of the prescribed pills with water.

"I'll come back later, and you can then go downstairs," Joan said before leaving, "if you sleep."

Stuck in bed, Monique had no choice but to comply. She released a long, shuddering breath.

* * *

Jefferson's alarm went off at 7:00 that morning. He sat up in bed, rubbing his eyes as he heard Presley getting up from her bed in the corner of the bedroom. The dog stretched and left, probably on a quest for breakfast. She'd be waiting by her bowl downstairs in a matter of seconds.

"Morning," a cheerful voice said.

Jefferson jumped in surprise before realizing it had to be Abigail.

"What are you doing in here?" he asked.

"You said we could be in here if you were in here," Abigail pointed out.

"Are the others in here as well?"

"No. Taylor went downstairs and Matthew's still in his room. We're hungry."

She seemed to have assumed the role of spokesperson for the group again.

"Okay," Jefferson said. "Give me a minute and I'll come down and make you guys something."

"Okay," Abigail said. "Remember. I don't like …"

"I think I remember. Get going."

"Okay," Abigail said and left.

Jefferson got out of bed and stretched. He headed downstairs, where he could now hear Taylor interrogating her sister about the status of breakfast.

"When's he coming?" she asked as he descended the stairs.

"I'll get started on it for you guys," Jefferson said as he entered the kitchen and put on coffee. "Go see if your brothers awake."

The girls scurried back up the stairs as Jefferson fed Presley and located his iPhone. Arranging the small cereal boxes Amy bought last night on the counter, he pulled up his Aira app and hit the "Call" button. After listening to a short segment of hold music, he was connected to a representative, or "agent", as this company called them.

"Connecting to Agent Jason," his phone's electronic voice recited.

Jason himself was then speaking.

"Thank you for calling Aira," he said. "What would you like to do today?"

Explaining his layout of the dozen small cereal boxes, Jefferson asked Jason to help identify them, holding up his iPhone so Jason could see the counter via its camera. In under a minute, they were identified and alphabetized.

"Is there anything else I can help you with?" Jason queried.

"No, thanks," Jefferson replied. "I'm good."

They disconnected and he pocketed the phone. As he took Presley out to relieve herself, he thought about how things like this didn't exist even ten years ago. Now, with the push of a button, someone in an office in another city could see what he was seeing and help accomplish minor tasks whose completion might otherwise be delayed due to his lack of sight. And, this was a professional company, complete with the promise of confidentiality.

When the girls returned with Matthew in tow, Jefferson had them wash up and presented their cereal options. Abigail quickly picked out Fruit Loops, something Jefferson found surprising when he considered the variety of ingredients supposedly in the cereal and how picky she normally was. But he decided not to dwell on the matter. She had made a choice and that was what counted. Most importantly, he'd been spared the recitation of her list, something he already found tiring.

Taylor was just as easy, if less surprising, picking out Smacks with little hesitation.

"Captain Crunch," Matthew said.

"I don't have that," Jefferson replied.

"Captain Crunch," Matthew repeated with a pout.

"He really likes Captain Crunch," Abigail offered from her seat, as though this information would somehow help.

Jefferson knew he'd need to buy Cap'n Crunch soon, but what could he give Matthew now? He racked his brain.

"How about Pops?" he asked. "They're kind of like Cap'n Crunch."

He held out the small box, not sure how valid his claim was.

"Okay," Matthew agreed after studying the box.

Jefferson sighed with relief as he set out cups of milk for the kids and added glasses containing their juice requests. Taylor wanted orange juice, which was readily available because Amy had bought it the night before, and Abigail and Matthew wanted apple juice. Since Jefferson could be considered a habitual drinker of the stuff, he had that readily available as well, though he himself was having coffee with milk that morning. Since none of the kids wanted eggs, he scrambled a few for himself and joined them at the table.

"What are we doing today?" Abigail asked between spoonful's of cereal.

"Let's see," Jefferson replied. "Amy and Eric are coming by later today and they're gonna help us settle you guys in more. Hopefully, the movers will get here today, and we can start getting your furniture set up in your rooms. I think that'll take most of the day."

"Are we going anywhere?" Abigail asked.

"I don't know," Jefferson replied. "Maybe we'll go out for dinner tonight."

They continued eating and soon all three kids were ready to leave the table.

"Did you guys drink the milk?" Jefferson asked.

Thankfully, he knew enough to see the importance of drinking milk for small children.

"You're not drinking milk," Taylor replied, giving away that she had not drank hers.

"Wrong," Jefferson corrected, testing the weight of her cup to confirm his suspicions. "There's milk in my coffee. I'm drinking it. So will you."

"Can we have some coffee?" Abigail asked.

Jefferson couldn't picture the idea of this already-energetic child on caffeine.

"No," he said, "but you are going to drink your milk. Otherwise, we're definitely not going anywhere today."

The twins gave in and returned to the table. Matthew, who had actually drunk his milk, ran off to play with a gleeful giggle.

When the twins were done and had run off as well, Jefferson cleared the table and deposited the dirty dishes in the sink. He called the kids together so they could go upstairs and get dressed. He let them pick out what they wanted to wear, provided they didn't make too much of a mess of the things in their bags. While the twins picked out pretty normal outfits, Matthew was a little more creative, picking an undershirt to wear with a set of swim trunks.

"Absolutely not," Jefferson said, heading for the stairs. "Taylor, come help me."

Using Taylor as his eyes, Jefferson proceeded to help him pick out something more appropriate. It took some pushing, but Matthew eventually agreed and changed.

* * *

Amy and Eric arrived at 10:30. While Amy went with the kids to mark their clothes with Braille tags to indicate their color for Jefferson's future benefit, Eric and Jefferson set to work on the box of legal documents Cassandra Kingman had packed up in Berlin. Jefferson had sent the box to Eric via expensive overnight shipping so the latter could start reviewing everything as soon as possible.

As a family court attorney, Eric had plenty of experience in legal matters surrounding adoptions, foster care, guardianship, and the like. Therefore, he was able to review the documents much more quickly than the embassy's legal counsel in Berlin. Jefferson sat with him at the kitchen table, his contribution to the process being to confirm what had already been faxed. He was pleasantly surprised to learn Cassandra Kingman had labeled everything with post-it notes as well.

The task took over two hours, in part due to Eric and Jefferson making half a dozen trips to Jefferson's third-floor office to scan and e-mail items as needed.

"Why didn't we just bring everything up here to begin with?" Eric queried during the fifth trip, eyeing the spare chair in the corner of the office.

"Let's not question our judgement now," Jefferson advised.

"Right."

Around the same time they finished, Amy and the kids emerged from the bedrooms to report their work was done. the clothes had been labeled with the aluminum Braille tags so Jefferson knew their colors and could match them up properly. Everything was now mostly put away in the closets.

"Mostly?" Jefferson asked.

"You need some more shelves in those closets," Amy told him. "What did you keep in there before?"

"Nothing, really. I never used those rooms much."

The rooms and their closets had come with the house. Jefferson wasn't going to decline the opportunity because of their existence and non-necessity at the time he bought the place.

Lunch consisted of sandwiches from a nearby deli. Then Eric and Jefferson left to file more papers with the courts. There'd be more to do once these documents came before a judge, but for now, everything was in order. Jefferson was the kids' official guardian pending a future hearing to decide if this arrangement ought to become permanent.

Chapter 8

Joan allowed Monique to go back down to the store around noon. By this time, it was established that Monique's purse had actually been on the kitchen counter next to the refrigerator instead of in its usual spot in the closet, explaining why the intruder hadn't found it. From what everyone could tell, he'd never entered the apartment's small kitchen.

Kathy and Frank had finished cleaning up and replaced the stolen cash drawer from the register with a spare kept in the storeroom on the building's third floor. Monique was impressed when they told her they were open again only an hour and a half later than usual. It seemed several people had stopped by throughout the morning to ask about the earlier police activity and were relieved to hear everyone was okay. Some even promised to stop by again soon to purchase something and help make up for the lost revenue. Monique had to smile. It was this exact loyalty which kept her store going despite the onslaught of chains and online venues.

The "lost revenue" amounted to just over two hundred dollars in small bills and change which had been in the stolen cash drawer. Another few thousand dollars was in the safe in Monique's office, which the intruder seemed to have tried to access without success, based on the pry marks in the office's doorframe. Frank had already summoned a locksmith to change all the locks as soon as the crime scene technicians were finished. The storeroom had been left untouched.

Monique was alarmed when she learned the locksmith had been in her apartment while she'd been sleeping. She glared at Frank, shaking a bit.

"I was there too," Frank added, making her feel a bit better. "Plus, I trust this guy. I went to college with his brother."

Monique relaxed as he handed her a large, padded envelope. Peeking inside, she noticed several rings of keys. She'd have to decide who got which keys and change out their old ones. She looked up at the bookshelves.

In addition to the stolen money, about a hundred books were deemed too damaged to be sold, some suffering at the intruder's hands while others were casualties of the police and forensics technicians' work.

Some were thrown out while the rest were bagged to be sent to a non-profit organization who could still use them.

"How are you feeling?" Kathy asked as Monique began maneuvering her chair down an aisle, holding onto the envelope of keys.

"I'm okay," Monique said. "I feel better. The store is secure again."

"Better than before," Frank said, but Kathy wouldn't let her boss deflect for long.

"I'm fine," Monique insisted and headed for the office in the back. There were insurance matters she needed to take care of.

"Get me the bill for the locksmith," she instructed. "I need to get that over to the insurance company along with everything else."

* * *

Around 3:00 that afternoon, the movers arrived and began lugging furniture into Jefferson's garage and house. Thankfully, someone had labeled absolutely everything, so there was little doubt about what went where. Jefferson was sure Cassandra Kingman had overseen this part of the saga as well. After all, the kids were taken to her house around midnight after the evening Stanly and Margaret were killed.

With Jefferson, Eric, and Amy pitching in to help, the process of hauling furniture took about four hours. When the movers were gone and everything was stored somewhere, Eric and Amy headed home as well.

"All right," Jefferson said to the three kids. "Now I'll take you out for dinner."

* * *

Gately's Diner didn't really lean towards a certain type of cuisine, nor did it really have any type of theme. But the food was good, and Jefferson knew their menu by heart. And it was close by.

So that was where he, Taylor, Abigail, and Matthew headed for dinner. Despite Abigail's constant reminders about what she would not eat, they all seemed excited about their first meal out in New York City.

"Mom and Dad told us there are lots of places to eat here," Taylor said.

"More than you could ever count," Jefferson confirmed.

The hostess knew Jefferson well and was delighted to meet his nieces and nephew, not lingering on why they were there with him for the first time ever. She seated them and informed him of the evening's specials.

"I recommend the macaroni and cheese," she added before stepping away.

"I think she likes you," Abigail said when the hostess had left.

"You do?" Jefferson asked, though he wasn't interested in women for the time being. His recent long-term relationship looked like it was pretty much over and he honestly wasn't looking to salvage it. He had more immediate concerns.

"All right guys," he said, changing the subject. "What do you wanna eat?"

He regretted the question seconds later as his ears were assaulted with responses.

* * *

Thanks to her long nap that morning, Monique was not tired yet and therefore lay in her bed that evening, watching television. She had made Joan check and recheck all the new locks in both the apartment and the store below it. Only when she felt sure everything was secure did she let the nurse go home.

"I can stay, you know," Joan offered. "I can just spend the night out on your couch."

"Then I'd just be worrying about the both of us," Monique argued.

Joan decided not to press the subject. Her patient had had a long day. Her home was secure, and she was fine. So, the nurse left after helping Monique take another dose of the prescribed pain medication.

So now Monique was awake, watching television, and listening for any unusual sounds. She knew it was going to be a long night. And the worst part was she needed to sleep. She had selected Samuel Bridges from her thin applicant pool and, since he was able to start immediately, the young man was coming the next morning. She needed to be coherent as she gave him the information he would need to successfully do his job.

* * *

Jefferson woke up the next morning, relieved to not find anyone waiting there at the side of his bed. He wasn't sure how any parent got used to that.

He found all three kids playing in their rooms among the boxes the movers had left the day before.

"When do we get our beds back?" Matthew asked.

"I'll get to work on those this afternoon," Jefferson promised. "But you might have to sleep on the stuff I gave you for maybe one more night. Come on. Let's get some breakfast."

As the three kids ate, Jefferson, keeping a bagel in one hand, took the cordless phone into the den and made some calls. Thankfully, the people he needed to speak to were awake and more than willing to help.

"Who were you talking to?" Abigail asked when he came back into the kitchen.

"Some people at your new school," Jefferson told her. "You're gonna go see them today. Hurry up and finish eating."

* * *

At 9:45 that morning, Jefferson entered PS 41 with the twins and Matthew in tow while their Uber drove away from the curb. The group was directed to the main office, where they waited in some chairs near the front desk. About five minutes later, a woman came out and stepped over to them.

"Mr. Thomas?" she asked.

Jefferson nodded and the woman introduced herself as the school's principal, Cynthia Langley.

"And this must be Abigail and Taylor," she said, turning to the twins.

"Hello," Abigail said, but Taylor remained quiet. She had become subdued again. Her new life was sinking in now more than ever.

"Give her time," Jefferson said in a low voice and Cynthia Langley nodded in understanding.

"I'd just like to talk to you in my office," she said. "There are a few forms that need to be filled out. We can have an aide show the girls around the school while we do that."

Jefferson agreed and set Matthew up in his seat with some crayons and a coloring book. After an aide arrived to take the twins, Jefferson followed Cynthia Langley into her office.

"They seem like sweet girls," the woman commented as she shut the door.

"They are," Jefferson said.

"How long have you had them?"

"This is my third day with them," Jefferson said and they both chuckled.

"You're on the right track already. Let's get started on the enrollment paperwork and talk about what we can do to help your family with this unusual situation."

Jefferson nodded as she produced the first form. He withdrew his plastic signature guide from his wallet, explaining it would help him sign on the lines she indicated.

"Just set it in place for me," he said, handing her the plastic square.

* * *

"So how did you guys like the school?" Jefferson asked as he and the kids waited by the curb for their Uber.

"It was cool," Abigail replied.

"It was okay," Taylor admitted.

"Well, you guys better like it," Jefferson told them. "You start there for real on Monday."

He and his brother both went through the public school system on Staten Island and later in Manhattan, so he had faith in it serving the girls well now.

His phone chimed, indicating the Uber was close by. One of the things he'd researched during his single, restless night in Berlin was taking cabs and rideshare services with young children. He'd learned that, while the twins no longer needed any type of car seat, Matthew was nowhere near the required age, height, or weight to be exempt as well. To his surprise, Jefferson had found that Uber offered an option to request a ride with a booster seat in the car, spending an hour figuring out how to incorporate this feature on his iPhone's app.

"Come on," he said as the car pulled up. "Let's get some lunch."

* * *

"Hey," Frank said, "new guy buys lunch."

Samuel looked over from the shelves he was restocking. His reddening cheeks told Monique that he didn't have enough money to cover lunch for the four of them.

"Don't listen to him," she said. "Go into my office. I keep some money in the top left drawer of my desk. Forty dollars should do the trick."

Once Samuel departed to fulfill the errand, Kathy and Frank immediately began gossiping about him.

"Guys," Monique admonished, "be nice."

They didn't listen and went right on with it. I guess practically hazing him wasn't enough, Monique figured.

"What do you think of him?" Kathy finally asked.

"He seems nice," Monique said. "But come on. He's been working here for half a day. Give him a chance."

She was thankful she'd managed to sleep enough to sound coherent as she orientated the young man to the store and its policies throughout the morning.

Frank and Kathy agreed but nevertheless continued their current conversation for a little while longer.

* * *

After lunch at a McDonald's, Jefferson and the kids took another Uber over to the Tate Sunshine Day Care Center. One of Jefferson's law school colleagues had a sister who brought her son here and spoke highly of the facility. Jefferson intended to check it out for Matthew, who was too young for even pre-school.

Leaving the twins in the lobby with some books to read, Jefferson, Presley, and Matthew were led into the facility by its Head Caretaker, Olivia Jordan.

After a tour, Matthew was allowed to go and play while Jefferson spoke with Olivia Jordan. Though he provided the twins' school records when he'd enrolled them that morning, the process still hadn't been simple. It was a little simpler this time.

"We'd evaluate Matthew during his first few days with us in order to determine how to best meet his needs," Olivia Jordan explained. "We will e-mail you the link for our standard online forms and the questionnaire that we require all parents to fill out."

Jefferson agreed and the meeting ended soon after that. He collected the three kids again and they left with the twins complaining the books they were given to read had been boring.

"Well, they're gone now," Jefferson told them. He decided they could walk around for a while before heading home.

* * *

"Hey," Taylor said after ten minutes and two blocks. "There's a bookstore up ahead. It looks neat. Can we go in?"

Since she'd been quiet and subdued earlier, Jefferson decided to encourage this sudden excitement. Abigail and Matthew also seemed to be interested in having a look, so he saw no harm in making the stop. After all, it wasn't a toy store.

* * *

Monique crumpled up her sandwich wrapper and managed to make a shot into the wastepaper basket, earning a comment from Frank about joining the WNBA.

"I'll consider it," she remarked, turning her wheelchair towards the register. She moved forward, occasionally taking a sip of her remaining iced tea through the straw.

The bell above the front door chimed but she paid it no mind. Customers were put off if she looked at them as soon as they came into the store, if they weren't put off by her chair first. For now, it was best to let them continue with their business, making it more likely for her to get their business in the end. No need to be a predator stalking her prey.

Monique rolled her chair down an empty aisle, absent-mindedly surveying the books on the shelves on either side of her. Everything seemed to be in order.

She turned into another aisle and saw a young girl up ahead who seemed to be looking at some children's books. She moved towards her.

"Hi," she said. "What's your name?"

Surprised, the girl turned around and seemed even more startled to see this woman in the odd-looking chair.

"Sorry," Monique said. "I didn't mean to scare you. What's your name?"

"Taylor," the girl replied. She seemed to have gotten over the fact Monique was in the wheelchair, reminding Monique about why she loved children so much.

"Hi Taylor," she said with a smile. "I'm Monique."

"Hi Monique," Taylor said. "Your chair looks cool."

Monique chuckled slightly. It always amused her when kids used words like that to describe her wheelchair. Most adults she knew wouldn't dare such a feat.

"Thank you," she said. "Tell me something. You're not here alone, are you?"

Taylor shook her head.

"No, my sister and my brother and my uncle are here too," she explained. "They're looking at other books."

"Okay," Monique said, nodding. "Is there a particular book I could help you find?"

Taylor shrugged her shoulders.

"let's look for something together," Monique suggested.

Taylor seemed okay with this idea. Monique turned her chair slightly to continue down the aisle, scanning the colorful book spines as she went.

"Anything particular that you're looking for?" she asked, earning another shrug from Taylor.

"What's that chair for?" the girl asked instead, pointing at Monique's wheelchair.

"It helps me get around because I can't walk. This little stick lets me control which way it goes."

Monique wiggled the chair's joystick very lightly with the tip of her finger.

"Okay," Taylor said, seeming to understand.

"Hey," Monique said, stopping, "pull out that book on the bottom shelf there. I think you might like it. All the way to the left."

Taylor found the one she was pointing at and pulled it out.

"Yeah, this should do the trick," Monique said. "It's about a girl who lives on a horse farm. Do you like horses?"

"I guess they're okay," Taylor said, sounding indifferent.

"Well, try this out and then come back and tell me how you liked it."

"Okay," Taylor said. "Thank you."

She walked away, presumably to reunite with her family. The store didn't have a problem with kids wandering out through the front door without paying. Plus, whoever was manning the register would prevent this, were it to ever become a problem.

Monique stayed in the aisle, continuing to check if everything was in order. Once satisfied, she headed back towards the register.

A man was standing by the counter, a guide dog, young boy, and a slightly older girl standing there with him. Monique recognized the girl immediately.

"Hello again," she said, maneuvering her wheelchair over to the group.

The girl turned but seemed confused.

"Hi," she said.

Monique noticed the book she was holding. It was a fictional story set in colonial times.

"What did you do with the book I gave you?" Monique asked. She was admittedly a bit pushy about keeping the inventory in order. God only knew where the other book had been stashed.

The girl looked confused. the man glanced back and forth between her and Monique.

"What's she talking about?" he asked. "What book?"

"I don't know," the girl replied. "She didn't give me any book."

Monique was about to respond when another little girl walked around the corner. This girl was definitely Taylor. And she was still holding the book Monique had given her.

"Oh," Monique said, realizing. "You guys are twins. I get it."

Everyone laughed and Monique wondered how she missed the fact the girls were wearing different clothes. Sure, they were a bit similar, with Taylor wearing a maroon top while her twin wore pink, but she ought to have paid attention. Also, the twin's jeans had flowers sewn on along the outer seams.

"That's my sister Abigail and my brother Matthew and my uncle Jeff," Taylor explained.

"Nice to meet you guys," Monique said. "I'm Monique and this is my store."

"It's cool," Abigail commented, though she was eyeing Monique's wheelchair.

"Thank you. Are you guys ready to pay?"

"I think we are," the man named Uncle Jeff said. "Are we?"

Both girls nodded and, seemingly remembering something, said they were ready. Monique was now sure this man was in fact blind and not training the dog in the guide dog harness.

"All right," she said to cover her silent pause. "the register's just over to the right. Give me a second and I can ring you guys up."

She maneuvered her chair around the counter and, willing her arms to stay steady, worked the register. Since he was paying, the man named Uncle Jeff was standing closest to the counter, waiting.

"So, are you guys visiting your uncle?" Monique asked as she held each book under the mounted scanner next to the register.

"No," Abigail replied. "We're living with him."

Thankfully, Monique noticed a slight wave of the man's hand and took the hint not to pursue the topic.

"That's $47.87," she said instead. The man held out his credit card, which she took it and ran it through the machine, taking a second to peek at the name on the card.

"Jeff" stands for Jefferson, she thought. She supposed it Suited him.

The credit card machine emitted its shrill beeps, confirming the transaction was successful. Monique always thought how misleading those beeps sounded. She, and many customers, first thought there was a problem when the equipment was updated to accommodate the new chipped cards. No, it was just someone's poor choice in sounds at the manufacturing level.

"Here you go," Monique said, raising her arm with the credit card in her hand. "Straight in front of you."

"Thanks," Jefferson said, finding the card and returning it to his wallet. Monique supposed he had a specific place for it in there.

"Hey," she said. "We're holding a book reading for kids here the Saturday after next. You guys should come. We've got one for the younger kids and then one for the older ones."

"Thanks," Jefferson said, taking his copy of the receipt. "We'll keep that in mind."

He left with the three kids in tow. Monique watched them go.

* * *

"That lady was nice," Taylor commented as they walked down the street.

"Really?" Jefferson asked, more interested in the fact Taylor seemed interested than anything else.

"Yeah, she helped me find a book. She moved down the aisle in her chair and found it for me."

"Her chair?"

"Yeah. She sits in a wheelchair. A big one."

Jefferson nodded. He'd actually believed that woman had just been really short … possibly a little person. Taylor's explanation cleared up the mystery of the motor he'd heard while in the store.

"Can we go back there sometime?" Taylor asked.

"We'll see," Jefferson told her as he took out his iPhone to call an Uber. "Come on now. We should get home."

* * *

Monique moved away from the register and found both Kathy and Frank staring at her. Samuel was somewhere else, probably restocking shelves, and Monique was glad for that. Both Frank and Kathy were wearing amused expressions on their faces.

"If you two wanna keep your jobs, tell me what's so funny," Monique demanded.

"You are," Frank said.

"What?"

"You are," Kathy echoed. "The way you were with that gentleman just now."

"How was I?"

Monique had no clue what the comment was supposed to mean.

"You were practically staring at him," Frank said, "and I'm pretty sure it wasn't because he was blind."

"What?" Monique asked. "You think I have something like a crush on him?"

"Like a schoolgirl," Kathy said.

"You told him about the readings," Frank pointed out. "Despite the big sign we have by the door, telling people all about it."

"He's blind," Monique defended. "He would have never noticed that sign, no matter how big it was. I did it to be nice."

"Yeah, that's it."

Monique shook her head.

"You two are crazy," she told them. "Go away."

Deciding to do as they were told, Frank and Kathy headed off to tend to other matters. Monique moved back behind the register to keep an eye on things.

She couldn't believe what those two were saying. It was insane. She had told that man about the readings because he would have never noticed the sign and kids weren't attentive to those sorts of details. She had done it to be nice. Or …

Monique had to admit he was cute. He reminded her of an actor, though she couldn't recall whom. Maybe she did want to see him again.

Chapter 9

"Hey Uncle Jeff," Abigail said as the group walked towards their house. "Who's that at the door?"

"I don't know," Jefferson said, confused. As they got closer to the house, he called out to whomever was there.

"Can I help you?" he queried.

"Yes," a woman replied when they reached her at the front door. "I'm looking for Mr. Jefferson Thomas. Do you know if he's home?"

"I'm Jefferson Thomas."

The woman's silence clearly meant she was taken aback by something, and he didn't think he'd have to work hard to determine what that was.

"Yes," the woman said, the rustling of papers suggesting she was checking something. "they mentioned something about your condition …"

Her voice trailed off as she kept rustling.

"I don't mean to be rude," Jefferson said, "but who are you?"

"Gloria Lawson," the woman said in a brisk, business-like tone. "Children's Protective Services."

"Oh, you're the social worker," Jefferson said, remembering Eric saying he could expect a surprise visit within a few days of filing the custody papers.

"Yes. are you going to invite me inside or should we stand out here all day?"

"Oh, right. I'm sorry. Just a second."

Jefferson dug out his keys and unlocked the front door.

"Come in," he invited as the kids already hurried inside the foyer. He immediately heard them tossing aside their shoes.

"Hey!" he called after them. "You guys know you're supposed to put those by the coat rack. I don't want to trip over them. And don't go anywhere just yet. I want you to meet this lady."

When their shoes were by the coat rack, Abigail, Taylor, and Matthew were introduced to Gloria Lawson, who greeted them warmly.

"I'm here to make sure you guys are safe and happy living with your uncle," she explained.

"We're happy," Abigail said. It was the first time Jefferson ever heard her sound suspicious.

"I'm sure you are," Gloria Lawson said. "But you children went through a lot these last few days. I just want to make sure you stay happy."

Abigail seemed stumped by this statement.

"How about you guys go and play while Miss Lawson and I talk," Jefferson suggested.

The kids seemed to like this idea and hurried off.

"As you can see," Jefferson said more seriously to Gloria Lawson, "they're pretty happy."

"I still have some questions," Gloria Lawson said.

"Then let's sit down," Jefferson said, leading her into the kitchen.

They sat at the table and Gloria Lawson took a moment to organize some papers.

"Have there been any serious incidents of any kind since you took custody of the children?" she asked, getting right to the point. "Anything at all come to mind?"

"One," Jefferson said and, without hesitation, recounted how Taylor disappeared on the flight from Germany. Gloria Lawson took notes the whole time he spoke, her pen scraping across her pad.

"Have the kids seen a professional child psychiatrist?" she asked.

"They're going to start with that next week," Jefferson told her. "I've set up appointments for each of the girls with the councilor at their new school and the day care center where I'll be taking Matthew also has a counselor who will meet with him regularly. I can take them to a child psychiatrist if it becomes necessary."

"So, you've enrolled the girls in school, and you've found a day care facility for Matthew," Gloria Lawson said, making more notes. "Might I ask where?"

Jefferson gave her the addresses of the school and day care. She seemed satisfied with his choice in regard to Matthew, but she frowned when she heard where Taylor and Abigail would be going to school that Monday.

"I'm surprised that, considering your financial standing, you didn't enroll them in one of this city's fine private schools," she remarked.

"Well," Jefferson defended. "I spoke to a number of my neighbors with children, and they all say good things about our local public school. Plus, my parents were well off and my brother and I went through public school all the way. We turned out just fine."

True, he was worth almost ten million, or maybe more once Stan and Maggie's will went through probate, but he didn't want to define himself by his money.

"You are a college professor, correct?" Gloria Lawson asked, sounding unimpressed.

"I'm a law professor," Jefferson corrected.

"How many classes do you teach?"

"Three this semester. I have off on Mondays, but I go into the office for a few hours in the morning and get some work done."

"That doesn't seem like a substantial income," Gloria Lawson remarked, definitely now sounding unimpressed.

"I make some extra from royalties on law books I've written," Jefferson said. "And I got a trust fund and stocks from my parents, which a friend of mine on Wall Street helps me invest."

"But something else could be."

Jefferson stared at her, waiting.

"The issue of your blindness," Gloria Lawson explained. "In all honesty, I'm concerned you will be able to always keep track of the children."

"I'll be interviewing candidates for a nanny's position to help me out," Jefferson told her. "I'll start with that after I get the girls to school."

"Do you think that would be sufficient?"

"Ma'am, if my blindness was an issue with those three kids, it would have probably revealed itself already, despite our short time together."

Gloria Lawson didn't argue, instead asking to see the house. Jefferson decided to oblige in the hopes she would leave soon.

The only real issue came up in the kids' rooms, where Jefferson was still in the process of putting together the furniture. Gloria Lawson was very unhappy with the potential danger the construction posed to the kids, despite assurances that everything was put away when not in use.

"See that it's finished soon," she said, making more notes.

Not long after that, Gloria Lawson bid Jefferson a stale-sounding "good day." Before she left, she reminded him this was the beginning of his year-long probation period as the children's guardian. A judge would still have to officially grant full custody after receiving a report from her.

"I look forward to it," Jefferson said. "Thank you."

"Why does she think we're not happy here?" Abigail asked, coming up behind Jefferson as he reentered the den after seeing the social worker out.

"It's a little more complicated than that," Jefferson told her. "Don't worry about it though. You guys are fine."

* * *

Every so often, Joan set Monique up in a standing frame in order to allow her to change positions instead of always being confined to her wheelchair. For this, she made an extra trip to see her patient, and that afternoon was such an occasion.

The standing frame was stationary, so when Monique was in it, she remained behind the counter and operated the cash register. True, she got a lot of looks from customers, but the regulars paid the frame no mind and Monique ignored the staring from the rest. Despite the fact she had no sensation from her mid-torso down, it felt good to stand up every so often.

An extra source of amusement came from watching Samuel trying not to stare at his new boss as she went about completing a customer's purchase while strapped to this odd device. But the young man was able to keep working, so Monique didn't call him out on anything. But she eventually decided to get him out of this phase where he averted looking at her.

"Hey," she called. "Do me a favor."

Samuel looked at her as best he could, waiting for instructions.

"There's a water bottle under the counter here," Monique said. "Could you get it and pour some water into my tumbler here?"

She nodded her head towards the cup strapped to the standing frame just above her shoulder.

Samuel hesitated but decided it was probably in his best occupational interest for him to do as he was asked. He came behind the counter, carefully stepping around the standing frame, and located the bottle. He came up with it and hesitated, looking at the tumbler, which looked like any plastic cup with a straw attached to it.

"Just pour the water in," Monique told him, remaining patient. "It's secure. There's no way you could knock it over."

Samuel seemed to be just under six feet tall, so he'd be able to see the inside of the tumbler as he filled it. He unscrewed the bottle cap and proceeded to pour the water into the tumbler. Monique pretended not to watch him but kept an eye on things anyway.

"That's good," she said when he screwed the bottle shut again and put it back beneath the counter. "See, I'm not fragile."

Samuel said nothing and returned to surveying the aisles for customers in need of assistance. Though she hadn't really been thirsty, Monique took a sip from the water anyway. It was good to see this kid start to feel a little more comfortable around her, but she knew she would still have to work on him. She rolled her eyes. Things like this were never easy.

* * *

There was one major step left in the machinery of dealing with Stanley and Margaret's deaths … their funeral. Though the Thomas family had largely left Staten Island decades earlier, the couple had intended to return and settle down their someday. Now, they were to be buried there.

On Friday morning, Eric arrived to help Jefferson go through some more paperwork from the funeral home and to provide an update on activity at the law school.

"Everyone misses you," he said. "Some students are actually asking when you'll be back. I wish they cared that much about me. By the way, you'll find some cards on your desk when you get back."

"Good," Jefferson said. "You'll be reading them to me."

"Looking forward to it. Where are the kids?"

"Upstairs. I talked to them about the funeral yesterday evening and they've all been quiet ever since."

Eric nodded as he removed his coat and sat down at the kitchen table.

"When do your parents get here?" he asked.

"In a couple hours," Jefferson said. "I'm setting them up on the sofa bed in my office."

"You're a good son," Eric said.

"At least my mom has to stop nagging me to turn those bedrooms into guest rooms."

"What about down here?"

The first floor had a small bedroom and bathroom which could be accessed from the den. Jefferson supposed the space was meant for a butler or something back when the house was first built in the 1930s, but he wasn't sure. History suggested the owners went bankrupt soon after completing the structure and never lived in it. Jefferson's parents never considered sleeping there.

"Something they might have to consider after a night on the sofa bed," Jefferson said, though he had another idea as well.

* * *

"They're here!" Matthew called excitedly, running in and out of the den and kitchen to ensure his message was received. "They're here."

"Girls!" Jefferson called up the stairs. "Come down."

He opened his front door as his parents emerged from their town car. Knowing his home well enough to not need Presley or a Kane, he came down the front steps.

"Hi, Mom," he said. "Hi, Dad."

Despite everything, William and Beth beamed as they hugged their son. Though they'd been in constant touch by phone and e-mail since Stan and Maggie died, this was their first face-to-face meeting since the accident.

"Can I take something for you?" Jefferson offered.

"About time," William said, thrusting a suitcase into his hand. He stayed behind to thank the driver while Jefferson and Beth entered the house.

The kids were waiting in the foyer, Matthew hurriedly describing his sighting the town car for his sisters.

"Come here!" Beth exclaimed, stretching her arms out wide. "My angels. You've all gotten so, so big."

While Jefferson's parents did use FaceTime to see the kids every so often, this in-person meeting was very different.

"Tell me," William said as he entered the house and shut the door. "Is your uncle spoiling you guys to no end?"

None of the kids knew how to answer this since Abigail and Taylor weren't sure what the word spoiling meant, and Matthew was completely clueless.

"Don't worry," William said with a smile. "Your grandmother and I will spoil you to no end, and trust me, that is a very good thing."

Jefferson withheld a groan.

* * *

New Yorkers their entire lives, William and Beth now lived in a small house in Charlottesville, Virginia, owning a second property near Nubanusit Lake in Hancock, New Hampshire. A twenty-year veteran of the New York City Police Department, William and four of his colleagues opened a security firm, IronDog Security, after their retirements. The firm quickly gained moderate success.

Though Jefferson's parents both decried the rash of mass shootings plaguing the country, no one could argue it helped the business grow. A number of private schools throughout the five boroughs sought IronDog's services and connections to major corporations were made through these institutions. In fifteen years, IronDog Security was now one of the top ten security firms in the United States, operating in all fifty states and often sending personnel overseas for special events. Rumors suggested they were a top contender to provide security at several upcoming Olympic Games.

While William and Beth lived in Virginia, he still sat on the company's Board of Directors. Jefferson and Stanly each received a two-percent stake in the business upon graduating from college and became millionaires themselves soon after, as happened to all of the founders' dozen children. Neither was interested in actually working for IronDog in any capacity, instead using the profits to fund their own paths. When his parents decided to move to Virginia, Jefferson bought the family's home for just under five million, a move Stan didn't argue with as he was in Tokyo at the time. Jefferson wondered if he would have bought a similar home on Staten Island once his work kept him stateside.

* * *

"How was the flight?" Jefferson asked.

He and his parents were sitting on his small patio, watching the kids chase Presley around the tiny yard.

"Short," William said. "The way I like them. We were able to get our driver's entire life history, thanks to your mother, while coming here from La Guardia."

"I take an interest in people," Beth admonished. "And he was a nice young man."

William's grunt suggested he agreed with her on this point. He just didn't appreciate the long Segway's it took to come to this conclusion.

"He came here from Iran when he was fifteen," Beth described. "He became a citizen three years ago and he owns the car he drives. He seems to have done well for himself."

"An entrepreneur," William said. While he didn't disapprove of his sons' career choices, the title "entrepreneur" always meant a little something more to him.

"How is everything going?" Beth asked with a glance towards the yard.

"We're doing fine Mom," Jefferson said. "Don't worry."

"Under the circumstances, allow us some wiggle room on worrying," William said.

Jefferson nodded. He could understand this.

"The kids look a little thin," Beth commented. "Are you feeding them enough?"

"They're fine Mom," Jefferson said. "I'm not even close to being able to count their ribs."

"Please allow me to worry anyway."

"Sure, Mom."

Jefferson found it somewhat amusing that his mother worried about how thin other people were when she herself was only a little thicker than a rail and had probably lost some weight recently.

"How are you guys doing?" he asked as William rose to join the kids.

"We're okay," Beth said. "It's been hard, but I am glad you guys are here now. It is a high price to pay for having my grandkids closer."

Jefferson didn't miss the catch in her voice.

* * *

The room was gloomy, illuminated only by the multitudes of candles which lined the walls. The bodies were laid out in the center. Jefferson, William, and Beth stood nearby, along with Maggie's sisters, Rachael and Olivia Easterling. Maggie's father had walked out on his family when she was three years old and, as Jefferson had heard her say so often, her stepfather wouldn't bother making the trip unless he had assurances of there being a fat inheritance and an open bar. Her mother had died of cancer two years earlier, so she and her sisters had been the only ones left. Neither Rachael nor Olivia objected the Thomas family's burial plans for their sister.

Taylor, Abigail, and Matthew weren't at the funeral home, instead staying home where one of Jefferson's cousins baby-sat them. It had been decided not to bring them to the wake, as the atmosphere would certainly only spook them. Adding to the creepiness was Mr. Garrett Hurson, the funeral home's director who, while being a friendly person, had the appearance of someone possibly overdue for lying in a coffin himself. For that and other reasons, the kids stayed away and would instead attend the funeral the next day.

As mourners came through the room to pay their respects and give their condolences to the family, Olivia took every opportunity to shoot

Jefferson a dirty look despite knowing he couldn't see them. Nevertheless, it seemed to satisfy her.

When Stan and Maggie named Jefferson as the guardian of their children, Olivia was livid. She felt she deserved the title, which was mainly what she wanted. She was a woman concerned with her appearance above all else. It was this self-centered behavior which caused Maggie to not consider her as a suitable guardian. Naturally, Olivia did not agree with this assessment.

Maggie's other sister, Rachael, lived in a small apartment in Chicago and traveled often for work. She had accepted that she would not make a good parent with that lifestyle and easily settled for the role of the doting aunt, making Jefferson promise to let her come and visit whenever she was in New York on business. So, with that agreement reached, they got along quite well. True, Olivia did still love her nieces and nephew, but her appearance still seemed to come first.

The wake took about two hours, after which Mr. Hurson approached the group, his footfalls always sounding heavier than his small frame would suggest.

"Do you have any final wishes before tomorrow?" he asked in his wheezy tone.

"No, thank you," William said, being unable to speak above a loud whisper as his voice shook.

"Okay. Have a nice evening."

Mr. Hurson shuffled away as William turned to Jefferson.

"No parent should bury a child," he said. "Take care of yourself, Son. Please."

* * *

Dinner that evening was late and a simple and subdued affair, consisting of potato salad and sausages. None of the kids said much except for answering their relatives' questions.

After dinner, the three kids got ready for bed and each asked to be tucked in. Jefferson obliged before heading back downstairs to spend some time with his parents.

"So how have they been since they got here?" Beth asked.

"They're okay," Jefferson said. "Sometimes they're quiet like now and other times they'll be happy without a care in the world."

"When do they start school?" William asked.

"Monday," Jefferson replied. "I'm going back to work on Tuesday."

"If you ever need anything, let us know," Beth encouraged. "We can be back here in no time."

"Thank you," Jefferson said.

"And remember what I said," William added.

Jefferson nodded, realizing how adamant his father sounded.

* * *

Jefferson stirred in his sleep. He quickly realized that, despite only having the kids for a short time, his hearing had already become much more acute to all sorts of sounds, and he was sure he now was hearing something out in the hallway. With Presley not stirring in her bed, he went to have a look.

When he opened the bedroom door, the sound became much more pronounced, and he now knew that it was someone crying. Feeling pretty sure he knew who it was, Jefferson moved slowly down the stairs, the sound getting louder. He soon felt something brush his leg. Reaching down, he found two heads, one of which was definitely crying.

"Let me in there," he insisted and one of the girls slid over. He sat on the steps, wrapping an arm around each girl. They both leaned their heads against him. Soon, one side of his t-shirt was soaked with tears.

Chapter 10

Around eleven that Saturday morning, the sun was out, and a light spring breeze blew through the cemetery. All in all, it wasn't the worst day to be outside.

With the funeral at the nearby Trinity Lutheran Church over, the mourners gathered at the gravesite for the final farewells. Along with Department of State personnel working stateside, the ceremony was being live-streamed to every U.S. Embassy and consulate around the world. College friends of Stan and Maggie also attended, as did a few of Jefferson's colleagues.

Not knowing many people, Abigail, Taylor, and Matthew stayed close to their uncle and grandparents, who were in the front of the crowd.

The minister prompted the relatives of Stanley and Margret, including their three children, to say one last goodbye before leading the group in a prayer. Cemetery workers then lowered the caskets into the ground.

"Pick up some dirt," Jefferson encouraged.

The kids all stared at him. Dressed in their best clothes, they long knew better than to get messy now. Taylor eyed the dark soil beneath their feet.

"Watch me," Jefferson said, scooping up a handful of dirt and, with William's guidance, sprinkling it over the caskets in the hole.

All three mimicked his action, followed by Beth, William, and a few other relatives. The workers then began burying the caskets.

"Are mom and dad gonna be okay down there?" Matthew asked.

"I thought Mom and Dad were in heaven," Abigail said.

"They are," Jefferson said. "Their souls went to heaven and their bodies stay here so you can always come visit them."

"Will they see us?" Matthew queried.

"Yeah."

Matthew stared at the hole, which was quickly filling with dirt.

Jefferson also looked towards the grave, picturing the couples' joint gravestone. His parents had commissioned it while he flew to Germany to retrieve the bodies and the kids. He spoke with them about it and knew the inscription by heart.

In Loving Memory

Margaret Bailer-Thomas
Stanley Allan Thomas

February 29, 1984 - February 2, 2019
May 19, 1981 - February 2, 2019

Parents, Children, Siblings, Friends

They've Kept Their Promises And Went The Miles
Now They Sleep

The last lines were a reference to Robert Frost. Maggie had minored in English Literature at Loyola University and devoured Frost's works. Stan's interest in the man grew as their relationship blossomed … Jefferson never wanted to consider the possible correlation.

"How about we head to lunch now?" Beth suggested, bending down to wipe Taylor's tear-streaked face with a tissue before proceeding to do the same for Abigail.

* * *

Lunch took place at a local up-scale but family-friendly American-style restaurant. Unfortunately, the ride over there was not short enough to prevent Abigail from reciting the list of foods she would not eat. She seemed unconvinced by everyone's promises to make sure these items didn't dare to come near her.

The group, which consisted of Jefferson, his parents, the three kids, and Maggie's two sisters, got the staff to push two tables together to accommodate them. Knowing Jefferson the best, Taylor and Matthew chose to sit with him. Abigail decided to be more adventurous and sat with her aunt Rachael, despite the fact they hadn't seen each other in the past one and a half years.

The meal went pretty well, with the adults mostly swapping fond memories of Stan and Maggie or asking the kids about how they were adjusting to their new lives in New York. Taylor mentioned Monique Vasquez and her bookstore, but the conversation didn't stay there long.

After lunch and dessert, the group drove back into Manhattan, where Rachael had to say "goodbye". she had to fly back to Chicago and prepare to leave for Hong Kong the following day. She promised to come visit soon. Olivia left soon after that, saying she had a long drive back to Columbus.

"What time is your flight tomorrow?" Jefferson asked when just he and his parents were in his den.

"1:29," William replied.

"Then let's do brunch tomorrow before you go. I think the kids will like that."

His parents agreed, smiling.

* * *

Monique moved down the aisles, dodging around customers examining the books. Saturday was probably the store's busiest day of the week, and she was thankful for that. She could always use the money.

She came back to the front of the store, where Kathy was working behind the register. Despite the store being busy, no one was actually making a purchase at the moment, so the two women spoke with one another.

"Did you try and track down that guy with those kids who were in here the other day?" Kathy asked.

Monique gave her a somewhat stern look before speaking.

"Okay," she said. "First off, that's called stalking. Second, no. And third, how is that any of your business?"

"I was just curious," Kathy said innocently. "You seemed interested in him, so I thought you might give it a shot."

Monique shook her head as a man approached the counter.

"Excuse me," he said. "I'm looking for the new book by that Sparks guy. My daughter is dying to get her hands on it. Do you carry it?"

"Sure," Monique said. "I'm sure we still have some copies. Hang on and I'll show you where …"

"That's all right. I'll find it. Thanks anyway,"

The man quickly moved away from the counter. Monique sat in her chair, fuming. That guy had seen her for what he believed she was, and he had declined her help. It was definitely not because he wanted to make her life easier. He wanted to make his life easier by not dealing with her.

"Let it go," Kathy advised in a whisper.

Easier said than done, Monique thought. But she knew Kathy was right. Idiots like this would always be around, and she'd just have to deal with them, whether she liked it or not. Plus, if he found and bought the book, it was still a win for her.

* * *

William and Beth had gone to bed early after packing their luggage. With the kids also asleep, Jefferson sat by himself in his den, reliving the day's events and considering what came next.

There was one step left in this grim process before the kids would be set. Stan and Maggie's will was still migrating through the legal channels. It was highly doubtful anyone would contest its contents and stipulations, but that didn't mean there wasn't a waiting period.

Jefferson already knew what it said, Stan and Maggie having gone over the terms with him when he'd agreed to be named the kids' guardian in the event anything happened to them. Stan's holdings in IronDog Security, plus his and Maggie's savings, was to be placed in a trust fund for the twins and Matthew, helping with things like college expenses. Jefferson, as their guardian, would be named as the trustee to oversee the fund until each of the kids turned twenty-five, at which point they'd receive equal thirds of the remaining money.

Jefferson planned to just put the money in the bank, not touch it, and let the interest rates take care of the rest. If his calculations were correct, each child would receive two to three million after they'd all finished college and, he hoped, graduate school.

He himself would not be getting any money and he was fine with that. He didn't need it. True, Stan and Maggie would probably leave him some random items of personal value, but their kids were the priority, even after their deaths. He was fine with that. He just wanted to get the will settled and move on.

True, there was also the matter of Jefferson needing to officially be granted full custody of the kids, instead of the probationary guardianship status he was on now. But he wasn't worried about that. Eric had assured him that he had seen a lot of kids go to homes worse than his and the judges considered those suitable. And, seeing he worked in family court all the time and now taught the subject matter on the side, Eric would know what he was talking about. So, there was no need to worry.

* * *

Monique met Joan in her apartment as usual and had some pasta with alfredo sauce and cucumber salad for dinner. Joan then got her ready for bed and made a joke out of tucking her in.

"Very funny," Monique commented.

"You'll miss that when I'm gone," Joan reminded her.

Monique nodded slightly. Joan would be going away to visit family members and she was leaving late on the following Wednesday evening, shortly after their regular session. Another nurse would be filling in for her during the five days she was gone.

"Maybe we can find out if I'll actually miss you while you're gone," Monique commented.

"Very funny," Joan shot back, smirking.

* * *

The next day was Sunday, the last day before the girls would be going to their new school. Though all three kids' beds were now assembled and being used, some of their other furniture wasn't. So, Jefferson's morning consisted of finally getting that done with William's help.

The brunch turned out to be a more subdued affair than Jefferson had anticipated. He figured the kids were still affected by the funeral and were probably bummed that their grandparents were leaving in a few hours. True, New York and Virginia were a lot closer than Germany and the United States, but Matthew and the twins were too young to put that difference into perspective.

* * *

Thankfully, because they moved around a lot, Stan and Maggie had never acquired a lot of personal property. Everything fit in Jefferson's one-car garage with a few extra boxes currently in the main house. Even with the progress he'd made with help from Eric, Amy, and his parents, there was still plenty to sort through.

Jefferson set to work and almost immediately found some papers and envelopes in a desk. These documents had apparently been missed when Cassandra Kingman and other Embassy staff went through everything in search of the will and other necessary legal materials, someone later taping the drawers shut for transport. Jefferson made a pile on top of the desk, intending to take everything up to his office later. He had a scanner up there which was equipped with software that could read him the documents, provided they were typewritten. Handwriting was still an issue with the technology. He figured most of the papers would end up in the garbage or his shredder, but he knew he needed to check first.

"Knock-knock," someone said.

Startled, Jefferson jumped back, knocking a pile of boxes against the wall. He hoped there wasn't anything fragile in those. Hearing the woman stifle a laugh, he realized who his visitor probably was.

"Sorry," she said. "It's Amy. The door was open."

Having noticed how hot the garage seemed to get as he'd worked, Jefferson had opened the door to get some ventilation. True, it was March, but the cool air was helping. Hearing Amy remark about it now, his heart skipped a beat, as it often did whenever she arrived.

"What brings you here?" he queried, straightening the pile of boxes again.

"We didn't get a chance to talk at the funeral," Amy said. "How are you doing?"

"I'm okay."

The funeral had been a whirlwind for Jefferson. Being co-organizer with his mother left little time to take in the gravity of the event.

"Par angusta ad augusta," Amy said.

"Huh?" Jefferson asked. Amy liked to use her Latin-speaking skills in conversation at random moments.

"Through trial to triumph," Amy explained. "It'll get better."

Jefferson nodded.

"I just hope you're taking time for yourself as well," Amy added. "You need to."

She stepped forward and then wrinkled her nose.

"Oh deus meus," she commented. "Seems like you've been working in here for a while."

"Lots to sort through," Jefferson said. "I gotta figure out what to keep, what to get rid of, what to put in storage for a later time … maybe there's stuff the kids can use someday."

Amy nodded.

"Are the girls ready for school tomorrow?" she asked.

"Almost," Jefferson replied. "I'm going to get the remaining supplies with them later this afternoon."

"Nullo modo. Not smelling like that you aren't."

Amy surveyed the garage, wrinkling her nose again.

"You've got a lot to do here," she said. "Give me some money, at arm's length, and I'll take them. You keep working and then take a long shower … a very long shower."

* * *

With money and a printed list, Amy and the twins were gone within half an hour. Occasionally pausing to check on Matthew, Jefferson kept going through boxes, sometimes pulling up the AIRA app on his phone for sighted assistance to identify items.

While most of the contents would require pickups for donation or disposal, he was able to fill half a dozen garbage bags. Deciding to quit for the day, he grabbed the pile of papers he'd collected on the desk. Carrying them up to his office, he left them on his own desk, next to his keyboard. Then, he hopped in the shower.

* * *

"Uncle Jeff!"

He was drying himself off when he heard it. Abigail could actually be heard from two stories down, having seemingly just returned with Taylor and Amy. Jefferson briefly wondered if he'd get a noise complaint from his neighbors. The brownstones here were set close together.

He got dressed and went downstairs to find the twins laying their new school supplies out on the kitchen table.

"They want to show you what they got," Amy reported. "Nice to smell you've showered, by the way."

* * *

The tour through the two piles of school supplies took half an hour. With Amy's help, Abigail and Taylor described each item for Jefferson's benefit before putting it in their backpacks. Abigail had gotten a variety of designs and pictures on her notebooks, folders, etc., while Taylor's were more muted, occasionally containing stripes or large spots.

"Very nice," Jefferson said. "Thank Mrs. Nelson for her help and then put those in your bags. I'll get started on dinner."

"I should get going," Amy said, rising from her seat after the girls went upstairs.

"Thanks for all your help," Jefferson told her. "Have a good evening."

"It'll be a quiet one. Eric's watching a baseball game at a sports bar with some friends of his and Sam and Keith are both at friends' houses for the evening."

"On a school night?" Jefferson asked with a raised eyebrow.

"What, are you SuperDad already?" Amy asked with a chuckle. "They've got a curfew and Eric's picking Keith up on his way home."

"So, you're by yourself for dinner?"

"Sic EGO coniecto."

Jefferson supposed that was some Latin form of "yes".

"You wanna eat with us?" he offered. "Consider it a sign of gratitude from me."

"Depends," Amy said. "What are you having?"

"Not a clue."

* * *

With Amy's help, Jefferson prepared a meatloaf, mashed potatoes, gravy, and carrots.

"Who knew I could put this together with all the random things I've got around this place?" Jefferson remarked, semi-amazed.

"Ire figure," Amy agreed.

Upon hearing what they were having for dinner, Abigail began listing everything she wouldn't eat, assuming Amy needed to hear this. Amy was patient and assured the girl everything would be safe, which Abigail seemed to believe. Nevertheless, when she was given her portion, she poked her meatloaf slice with her fork as though this would reveal some hidden ingredient. Amy couldn't help being amused by this.

"I've got two sons at home," she commented. "I tell you, if either of them were a picky eater, I'd probably have to take them to the doctor. They'll eat anything."

"How old are your sons?" Abigail asked, momentarily ignoring her food.

"Sam is fourteen. Keith is ten, but he'll be eleven in July."

"Where do you live?" Taylor asked, taking an interest as well.

"I live in Queens with my husband and kids. Actually, I live pretty close to that airport where you guys landed. We're in Kew Gardens Hills."

"Where do you work?" Abigail asked.

"Guys," Jefferson admonished, "you can't go snooping around Mrs. Nelson's private life."

"It's okay," Amy assured him. "I don't mind."

"See," Abigail said, satisfied. "She doesn't mind."

Seeing defeat, Jefferson kept quiet as Amy explained she was a librarian. Listening to her talk, he supposed she didn't feel burdened by the kids' inquiries.

* * *

Jefferson came back down after getting the kids to bed. Amy was in the kitchen, finishing her drink. She'd stayed a while longer after dinner to chat with the kids before their bedtime.

"Tell me something," she probed. "What do you do if any of them demand a bedtime story? I can't imagine too many of those come in Braille."

"According to my research, some do," Jefferson said. "Takes forever to ship them here though. So far, except for the occasional story about their parents, the twins aren't very demanding. As for Matthew, I memorize stuff I find on the internet and put a bit of my own spin on it whenever I don't remember something … you know, improv."

Amy chuckled and downed the last of her wine.

"I'd better get going," she said. "Thanks for dinner. It was fun."

"I'm glad you had a good time," Jefferson said. "Thanks for all your help."

Amy set her glass down on the kitchen table and grabbed her coat from the back of her chair. She headed for the front door.

"Oh," she said, stopping. "I almost forgot. I got these in the mail, and I thought you might like them."

"What are they?" Jefferson asked.

"They're brochures for a youth soccer program the city runs every fall," Amy explained, coming back and handing them to him. "They're already getting sent out now. I think Matthew might still be too young, but if the girls are interested …"

Her voice trailed off.

"We'll look into it," Jefferson said, reaching out for the pamphlets. "Thank you."

"Sure."

His fingers brushed the back of her hand before he found the pamphlets. Amy flinched, though she wasn't sure why.

"I can scan these," Jefferson commented, taking the pamphlets.

"Yeah," Amy said, wondering if she ought to have just provided the program's website address instead. They both had e-mail.

They stood there, staring at one another.

Chapter 11

"Uncle Jeff!"

Jefferson woke to the sound of his name being called from somewhere in the house. He checked the time.

"10:08 p.m.," the clock's electronic voice recited.

Realizing it had to be one of the kids, Jefferson got up and found his pajamas. He threw them on and went to investigate.

Out in the hallway, he found Matthew coming up the steps. The boy stopped when he saw his uncle.

"What's up Champ?" Jefferson asked, trying to sound casual while his heart began racing. He had to redirect the boy.

"I'm thirsty," Matthew announced. "Can I have some water?"

Relief washed over Jefferson. This problem required a simple solution which could be found far from his bedroom.

"Sure," he said. "Come on."

He took Matthew down to the kitchen and handed him the requested water in a plastic cup. After Matthew drank it, Jefferson took him back up to his bedroom and tucked him back in. Matthew was asleep in less than a minute.

Jefferson returned to his bedroom to hear the sound of ruffling clothing. Amy was getting dressed. He did not know what to say.

"I really should go," Amy said from across the bed. "I … I need to …"

She too seemed to be at a loss for words, English or Latin.

"I'm sorry," Jefferson said, standing still. "I never wanted to do this to you … you or Eric."

The silence told him the mention of his friend and Amy's husband was not welcome at this moment.

"I really need to go," Amy said. She sounded different now, like she was bending down and the bed blocked her voice's otherwise clear path to Jefferson's ear. Jefferson figured she was putting on her shoes.

"I don't know what to say," he tried.

"We can't talk about this now," Amy said, sounding like she was standing up straight again. "I need to think about this. It needs to sink in. And I really need to get home."

Jefferson couldn't begin to come up with a possible explanation she could give Eric about where she'd been or what she'd been doing, so he didn't try. He just nodded as she pulled on her jacket.

Their descent down the stairs was silent, Amy leading the way. Presley, who had been sleeping until now, brought up the rear.

Amy grabbed the handle of the front door and paused. Then, she opened the door and walked out without a word, pulling the door shut behind her.

Jefferson sighed, locked the door, and headed back upstairs, Presley still following. The dog would probably be relieved to return to her bed. The last couple hours weren't life-changing for her.

* * *

On Monday morning, Jefferson got out of bed and went downstairs to find the twins already there and ready for school. He made them breakfast just as Matthew was coming down.

"What about me?" he asked, eyeing the twins. "What do I do today?"

"You and I are gonna hang out today," Jefferson told him.

Matthew seemed awestruck by this idea. The twins were too busy talking about their plans for their first day of school to notice … well, Abigail was doing most of the talking while Taylor seemed to be listening and agreeing.

After getting himself and Matthew into more decent clothes, Jefferson, Presley, and the three kids left the house, Abigail still chatting excitedly about what was to come. The twins had claimed to be old enough to walk to school alone, but Jefferson knew enough about children not to believe that theory.

"Let me make sure you get there safely," he said. "You've never seen a city like this before."

He then heard a car pull up to the curb.

"Morning," Eric said, emerging from the vehicle.

"Morning," Jefferson returned. it took pretty much all of his energy to greet his friend as though nothing was the matter. Thankfully, Abigail was kind enough to step in.

"What are you doing here?" she queried.

"I'm here to walk you guys to school," Eric explained. "Your uncle doesn't know exactly which way it is so I'm gonna help him learn it and then he can take you all by himself in the future."

He looked at Jefferson.

"Isn't that right?" he asked, mockingly patting Jefferson's shoulder.

"Let's go," Jefferson said, not sure how to react at that very moment.

"All right then. Off we go."

As they walked, Eric pointed out various landmarks to Jefferson that were unlikely to change, such as signs, sewer grates, benches, and more. He explained to the kids that Jefferson would memorize all this and that would be how he would then be able to take them to school himself.

"Like this crack in the sidewalk," he said, pointing it out. "I'll bet the city never gets around to fixing it. It's big enough to give Presley there pause and your uncle will then know he's on the right track."

Presley indeed paused at this crack, only continuing when prompted.

Along the way, Jefferson found himself thinking about Amy and what happened between them. He wondered how it had happened to begin with. It seemed like one minute she was giving him some brochures for a youth soccer program, and the next minute, they were in his bed together. How on Earth did that happen?

He was also wondering what, if anything, Eric knew or suspected. He hoped he wasn't acting too weird.

Jefferson knew this wasn't as simple as him having slept with his best friend's wife. These things were never that simple. He'd had a crush on Amy ever since he and Eric, then second-year law students, met Amy, a junior undergrad, in the law library, where she was working. While becoming friends with both of them, she'd chosen Eric.

Jefferson didn't fault either of them for this outcome, but he did wish things had happened differently.

* * *

The walk to school wasn't a long one, so Jefferson wasn't able to dwell on his thoughts for very long. He needed to listen as Eric was describing the route to him. He snapped back to attention as they approached an intersection. Based on the traffic sounds crisscrossing ahead of him, he could tell the light was red. Eric, who knew his friend could easily figure these things out, didn't say anything as they waited to cross.

Soon, the light changed, and the sounds of the traffic started up alongside the group instead of crossing in front of them. They could now cross the final intersection before they'd reach the school.

"would you like me to hold your hand while we cross?" Eric asked with a smirk. Jefferson thought about possible comebacks, but he

100

decided to let it go. The girls giggled as they began walking while Matthew seemed to have missed the comment altogether.

"here we are," Eric announced once they were across.

The group found themselves among the other parents and kids arriving at PS 41 that morning.

"All right you guys," Jefferson said to the twins. "This is where I leave you. Good luck. I'll see you here this afternoon."

"Bye Uncle Jeff," the twins chorused and hurried towards the school building's front doors.

"Nice," Eric commented. "I'm what exactly?"

"Merely a guide," Jefferson said. "Like with Presley, they shouldn't interact with you when you're working."

Eric rolled his eyes as they turned to head back the way they came.

"You're new in the neighborhood, aren't you?" someone commented.

Jefferson stopped and turned to learn it was a mother who had just dropped off her son and daughter. He could hear her sending them off, her attention briefly diverted. Eric waited, interested in seeing where this would lead.

"Your family's new here, right?" the woman asked once her kids were heading into the building. "I haven't seen you around here before."

Jefferson couldn't be sure if this woman was flirting with him or not, but at the moment, he had too much on his mind to care. He was sure Eric wasn't going to get him out of this. If there was even a hint of flirtation, His friend was probably enjoying the show.

"No," Jefferson explained. "I've lived here for several years. Those are my nieces. They're new."

He had never interacted much with the families who lived in the neighborhood, so it wasn't too surprising that he was an unfamiliar face now.

"Oh," the woman said. "You two aren't ..."

It took a moment for the implication to sink in.

"No," Jefferson said, wondering if his denial would somehow sound offensive. These days, one never knew.

"We're not together," Jefferson clarified. "My friend Eric is just helping me learn the route."

He could imagine the gigantic grin Eric was trying to conceal. His friend would have a joyous laugh about this later.

"Well," the woman said, "new or not, it's nice to meet you. Your nieces are very pretty."

"Thank you," Jefferson said. "You have a nice day."

He walked away with Matthew and Eric.

"Well," Eric said when they were a block away. "That made my year."

He began laughing. Jefferson let him be, figuring the secret he was holding on to would obliterate the man's current joy.

"Who was that?" Matthew asked eagerly.

"Just another parent," Jefferson told him, glad for the diversion. "Don't worry about it. Come on."

"She was cute though," Eric said, recovering.

Jefferson ignored him.

* * *

Abigail and Taylor walked down the hallway together, surrounded by the swarm of their new fellow students. Both were somewhat apprehensive, but Abigail was clearly the more excited of the pair.

"Here's my room," she said, pointing out the number for Taylor. "See you later."

She disappeared before Taylor could say anything.

Now alone, Taylor kept moving down the hallway, checking the room numbers against what she had been told hers was. Unfortunately, she felt more alone now than ever before. She didn't even have her uncle to turn to.

Then, to her relief, she found room 11. Her nerves still strong enough, Taylor entered the classroom.

Some students were already there but didn't seem to notice her. She saw the teacher, a young-looking man, sitting behind his desk. He seemed to be checking something on his computer. She made her way over to him.

"Excuse me," she said in a timid voice.

The teacher turned and smiled down at her.

"Can I help you?" he queried.

"I ... I'm Taylor," she said, still nervous. "I'm new here and ..."

Without looking, the teacher snatched a piece of paper off his desk. He pulled a pair of glasses from his shirt pocket and put them on. Taylor waited as he studied his note.

"Taylor Thomas?" he asked.

She nodded.

"Our world traveler," the teacher said, beaming. "Don't worry, you're in the right place. Welcome. I'm Mr. Wallace, but you can call me Mr. W if you want. Just take that seat over there for now and I'll introduce you to the class when I make my morning announcements, all right?"

Taylor nodded and quietly sat down at the desk he pointed out for her. She felt a bit better knowing she was in the right room and that the teacher was nice.

* * *

Having left Matthew downstairs with a coloring book and some crayons, Jefferson sat in his office, deep in thought. So many things were running through his head, not least of all being his worries about how the girls were doing at school. Though she tried to hide it, he'd noticed that morning how Taylor was apprehensive about the whole thing. Then there was the fact that she was known to suddenly break down in grief over her parents' deaths.

All that worried him. Thankfully, Abigail was a bit easier, not that he didn't worry about her as well. He was just glad he didn't have two emotionally unstable kids to deal with.

He was also still thinking about his one-night-stand with Amy. One thing was absolutely certain. Intended or not, he'd done something he'd hoped to do for years. She'd lived up to his fantasy, at least until the guilt sank in for both of them soon after the deed.

He replayed the previous evening's events in his head. Amy had eaten dinner with them. Afterwards, he, she, and the kids talked before Matthew and the twins went to bed. Alone, the two of them talked a bit more, standing in the foyer as she gave him the information about the soccer program. They'd stepped closer and closer to one another. Jefferson supposed he was motivated by the wine they'd been drinking. Neither was drunk, but they were definitely buzzed. With three inches left between them and a four-inch height difference, he'd leaned down and kissed her.

Though initially shocked, Amy soon kissed him back, their lips mashed and tongues dueling. When they broke apart, they stared at each other, breathing heavily as their hearts raced. That ought to have been a good opportunity for sense and decency to sink in again. It didn't.

"Upstairs?" Jefferson had asked.

"Okay," Amy had replied.

With that, Jefferson fulfilled his dream of bedding Amy Bovio, now Amy Nelson. Was his guilt worth it? He knew he'd kept Matthew away from his bedroom for more than just wanting to prevent a four-year-old from walking in on two naked adults in post-carnal dozes.

Jefferson sighed. He finally gave up on getting any work done and went downstairs to spend time with his nephew. Very soon, he'd be interviewing candidates for the nanny position.

* * *

"Okay class," the teacher, Ms. Turner, said. "We're now gonna find a partner and you will work on these math problems together."

Not knowing anyone didn't stop Abigail from getting out of her seat and going around the room. Most of the kids were quickly pairing up with friends of theirs, but she had little trouble finding a girl who did not yet have a partner.

"Hi," she said. "I'm Abigail."

"Hi," the girl replied. "I'm Mallory."

"You wanna work on these math problems with me?"

"Okay."

As the two girls pushed their desks together, Ms. Turner watched from afar. The new student seemed to be fitting in just fine and she was glad for it.

* * *

The phone rang. Monique, who happened to be in the office, hit the speakerphone button to answer the call. Since she was in the room alone and the door was closed, she could do it this way no matter who it was, a method she preferred over using a headset or trying to handle the receiver.

"Hello?" she asked.

"Miss Vasquez?" a male voice asked.

"Speaking," Monique said, not recognizing the caller's voice, though it sounded vaguely familiar.

"This is Detective Brian Casslebeck," the caller said.

"Oh hi," Monique said, remembering the detective. "What can I do for you?"

"I just wanted to give you an update," Detective Casslebeck said. "Unfortunately, there isn't much to report. Since only a small amount of money was taken, we really have no way of tracing it. I'm sorry I don't have any better news for you."

"That's all right," Monique said, though she couldn't help feeling disappointed.

"I assume you've spoken to your insurance company about the damage done?"

"Yes, and I've had all my locks changed."

"Well, that's the best you can do in these situations. The truth is that the longer a case like this lingers, the less likely it is that we'll ever be able to catch the guy who did it. In all honesty, I think it was some punk who just got lucky. I doubt he'll come back."

"Hmmm."

"We'll keep looking," Detective Casslebeck assured her. "I'll let you know if we find anything. Feel free to get in touch if you have any questions."

"Thank you," Monique said, though she didn't feel very thankful.

When the call was over, she pressed her head back into the headrest of her wheelchair. She felt numb all over, different from how she usually felt.

True, the thief hadn't gotten much out of his heist. Just the little money that was left in the cash drawer. He hadn't gotten the safe open and he hadn't found Monique's purse. He also hadn't stolen any books. The insurance covered the small loss, as well as the repairs and modifications to the security system. So, all in all, no real harm was done.

But plenty of harm had been done. Monique could still remember how the intruder had come into her room and threatened her. She remembered how he had touched her. Had the police not shown up when they did ... Monique didn't even want to think about what could have happened. After all, he'd stayed long enough to hit her with his flashlight.

Though she was making no big deal of this in front of other people, it was a very different situation when she was alone. Before heading up to her apartment for the night, Monique was making it a point to double and sometimes triple check to make sure everything was securely locked up. Nevertheless, she was always worried that the thief would return, and she'd had more than one nightmare about the matter. She considered the idea of seeing a psychiatrist but was always putting it off. She was still functioning, and the store was okay, so she saw no need to rush. But, when she admitted it to herself privately, Monique knew she was scared.

* * *

Jefferson heard the doorbell ring. He got up from the kitchen table, leaving his laptop behind. He was sure this was another woman sent by the agency he was using to find a nanny. She would be his fourth interview that day. He hadn't seen much wrong with the first three, but at the same time, he hadn't seen anything really outstanding about them either. And true, two were somewhat put off by his blindness.

Briefly stopping to check on Matthew, who was playing with blocks in the den, Jefferson answered the door to a woman who, according to the information the agency provided, was in her late twenties. She introduced herself as Anya Motkova. There was no doubt she had an accent and that it was Eastern European, but it wasn't so thick that she couldn't be understood. Her English was clear, and she sounded intelligent.

"Come on in," Jefferson said.

Presley was waiting in the foyer, armed with a toy to show the newcomer. Anya Motkova smiled.

"She is beautiful," she said. "She looks well taken care of."

"Thank you," Jefferson said. Though he did pride himself on doing whatever he could to keep Presley, and her two predecessors, as healthy as possible, he did pause to wonder if the woman's compliment was a line to try and win his favor.

"May I pet her?" Anya Motkova queried as Presley danced around her feet.

"Go ahead," Jefferson said. They were at home and Presley wasn't wearing her guide dog harness. It was perfectly okay for her to be a dog.

After a couple pets, Jefferson and Anya Motkova sat at the kitchen table.

"They told me that you are blind," Anya said, taking a flash drive out of her purse. "I brought a copy of my resume on this flash drive."

She gave it to him, and he inserted it into his laptop. After a quick, automatic virus scan turned up no threats, he was impressed. He opened the document and skimmed it to refresh his memory.

"You're an immigrant?" he asked, quickly scrolling through the resume while his screen-reading software read the text to him via an earphone.

"Yes," Anya said. "I am from Saint Petersburg. I came to America seven years ago to study at the City University of New York ... the Lehman College specifically. I was given a scholarship to study psychology and I took cooking classes for fun."

"Psychology," Jefferson said, slightly confused. "How'd you wind up becoming a nanny?"

"I understood the subject and liked it," Anya explained. "I especially liked the children. But I found that being a professional in the field was not for me. I liked cooking and I still liked the children I worked with during my studies, so I thought to combine the two ... I began working as a nanny and found I liked that."

Jefferson was skeptical, but her resume backed up her statements, so he decided to believe her. Plus, she had already scored points with the flash drive.

"The agency told me you've been doing this for almost three years," he said. "Tell me about your experiences."

* * *

Not needing Eric to show him the route this time, Jefferson arrived at the school shortly before dismissal with Matthew in tow. He did his best to blend in with the parents who were there to pick up their own kids and found himself running into the woman he had spoken to that morning.

"I never did introduce myself," she said almost immediately. "I'm Linda. Linda Carrows."

"Jefferson Thomas," he said, shaking her hand.

"Our third president flipped around," Linda commented with a chuckle.

"So I've been told."

Jefferson had heard the observation many times before and was indifferent to it. He wondered if she had sought him out and orchestrated this second meeting.

"Well Jefferson," Linda said. "I have a question. How is it that you've suddenly enrolled your two nieces here and are walking them to and from school with, I presume, your nephew, coming along?"

"It's a long story," Jefferson told her.

"I hope I can get a chance to hear it someday," Linda said with a smile as the first students began trickling out of the building.

Jefferson said nothing to this, sure she wouldn't be so curious if she had a clue about that story's context. Plus, having made three serious mistakes with the opposite gender in the past five years, he'd made the decision to slow down in that area for a while.

Chapter 12

"Hey Uncle Jeff," Taylor said, looking up from the game of Go Fish she was engaged in with Abigail. "That lady at the bookstore told you there was something going on there, right?"

"Yeah," Jefferson said, vaguely remembering what the woman had said. "I think it was some sort of reading this Saturday."

"Can we go?"

Abigail and Matthew, the latter of whom had been playing with his Lego Duplo blocks on the floor, also seemed mildly interested.

It was Thursday afternoon, and the newly formed family were all sitting in Jefferson's den, each engaged in their own activity. So far, the girls had gone through four days of school, and while they were still adjusting, they seemed to be doing fine. They had each met up with the school's psychiatrist once so far to set the groundwork for future sessions, and though Jefferson hadn't heard anything, he decided not to interfere too much in a subject matter he knew little about.

Matthew had now spent three days at the Tate Sunshine Day Care Center, and he seemed to like it. The family's morning routine had become somewhat solid, with Jefferson dropping the girls off at school before taking Matthew to the day care center and then heading over to New York University, where he would be either teaching or working in his office until it came time to pick up the girls. He would pick up Matthew along the way, and he'd be back in charge that afternoon. True, this routine would have to be changed once a new semester rolled in and his teaching schedule changed, but it was working for now, and that was all Jefferson cared about.

More recently, Jefferson had earned the attention of teenaged girls who lived in the neighborhood and made their money baby-sitting. One of them had come by the previous Tuesday afternoon to tell him all about their qualifications and the like. So far, Jefferson had promised to consider calling them if he needed to and he was quietly asking parents at the school about them. Most of the parents had positive things to say about the pair, with the rest not knowing them.

Jefferson was still working on finding a nanny. He'd finished interviewing people for the time being and was now working to narrow down the field of candidates. Never in his life had he imagined this decision being so hard. He was finding flaws in every aspirant. But he had to keep going. He needed a nanny.

With this new life slowly falling into place, Jefferson was back at work. Eric had been right about the cards which were waiting in his office, along with some flowers and one box of chocolates. Jefferson had packed everything away and took it home to go through at a later time. He had also received many condolences from colleagues and students about his loss. Though he hadn't mentioned it before leaving for Germany, word spread about his taking in his nieces and nephew. Many people having previously believed he was simply traveling to Germany to settle his brother's affairs. Of course, they all now wanted to hear how everyone was adjusting and to see photos of the kids, a request he only granted to a few.

"Uncle Jeff?" Taylor asked.

"I'm sorry," Jefferson said, having been lost in his thoughts. "What's up?"

"Can we go to the bookstore on Saturday?"

"Maybe. I'll look into it."

Taylor seemed satisfied with his answer and turned her attention back to her game with Abigail.

"Ten more minutes," Jefferson told them. "Then you guys have homework to do."

He was somewhat surprised not to hear any pushback or protests. Maybe his negative memories of the concept were more associated with his high school days.

* * * *

"Okay," Jefferson said. "despite an order from the President of the United States, telling states like Texas who had Mexican nationals on Death Row to reconsider the individuals' sentences because they were not granted their right to seek assistance from the Mexican consulate upon their arrests, Texas went ahead and executed José Medellín as scheduled in 2008. Can anyone tell me why no laws were broken by this action?"

He faced his class of NYU law students, none of whom made a move to respond. It was Friday morning, and he was sure they were all already planning their evening of binge-drinking before hitting the books again around noon on Saturday. They weren't first-years anymore. They'd earned this one night of freedom per week.

"Come on people," Jefferson said, making his voice boom through the lecture hall. "Can anyone come up with an answer. It's still Friday, for God's sake. It is not the weekend yet."

"Texas isn't bound by the President's order because of states sovereignty," a voice answered. "Only an act passed by Congress would have required Texas to comply with the President's order. Otherwise, he has no influence on their individual criminal justice systems."

Despite his better judgment, Jefferson couldn't hide a smile. He recognized the speaker as Paula Franks, a young divorcee who came to law school after her husband ran out on her with his secretary. She had taken his class last year and he was sure why she was here now. But he wasn't going to bring that up in front of everyone else.

"Care to share your thoughts about the international laws that were broken?" he instead prompted.

"Simply put," Paula Franks continued, "the United States violated the International Court's ruling which prompted the President's order for Texas to comply. But the court can't punish the U.S. for this because the order does not apply to the individual states, just the country as a whole. We, particularly Texas, just have a bit of a negative image in the eyes of some other nations."

"Correct. There is also the fact that American citizens arrested abroad may face similar treatment from the host nations."

He checked the time and saw that class was over.

"That's all for today," he said. "I expect you all to be ready to discuss Grutter v. Bollinger on Tuesday. And, some more enthusiasm would be appreciated."

The class rose and began to leave. As people filed out of the room, Paula Franks moved towards the front, where Jefferson was busy packing up his briefcase. She noticed his jacket was hanging over the back of the instructor's chair, indicating he hadn't stopped by his office that morning.

Jefferson seemed to sense her lingering there. He looked up but said nothing. Paula Franks was silent as well, waiting for him to initiate the conversation. Presley remained lying by the desk, sleeping, waiting to be needed.

"As I recall, you passed my class last year," Jefferson finally remarked.

"I know," Paula Franks said in an innocent tone. "I just wanted to check on you. How are you doing?"

"I'm fine. If you'll excuse me, I've got a lot to do today."

"I heard your nieces and nephews are living with you," Paula Franks said, undeterred.

"They are, which is why you'll understand why I won't have lunch, dinner, coffee, or anything else with you later today."

Especially given recent events, Paula Franks was not a mistake Jefferson would make. He was due for some common sense.

"It must be so hard," Paula Franks went on as though she hadn't heard anything he'd said. "If you ever need anything, you'll let me know."

She turned around and left. Hearing the door of the lecture hall slam shut, Jefferson let out a groan. Paula Franks was definitely a bright woman, but she was also doggedly determined in all of her pursuits, including him. He was now sure he knew who had sent him the box of chocolates as a form of condolences.

* * *

Monique was working in her back office, preparing for the readings taking place the next day as well as catching up on various other things. She had gone to her bi-weekly physical therapy session that morning and though her condition wasn't expected to improve, she was deemed to be in good physical health. Since that was always good news, Monique took it gratefully. It'd take a scientific breakthrough to alter the status quo in that regard, so she always proceeded under the current circumstances with no expectations of change. It was simpler than scouring the medical journals for signs of hope.

When she returned to the store around noon, Kathy gleefully informed her that Jefferson Thomas had stopped by earlier that morning to inquire about the exact times of the readings the next day. Monique excused herself and headed to the back office to get away from the comments Kathy and Frank were formulating in their heads. She figured if she hid out behind her desk long enough, they'd lose their steam and forget about Jefferson Thomas's visit. At least she hoped so.

* * *

Having stopped at the bookstore belonging to that woman Monique to check what time the readings were on that coming Saturday, Jefferson had been running late that morning and hadn't been to his office at all. But a custodian had unlocked his door as usual, so he was able to just greet the department secretary and walk right in after his first class. He tossed his coat over the back of his chair, sat down, and turned on his computer.

As he waited for the computer to get to his desktop, he leaned back in his chair and thought about what sort of things he had around his office. His diplomas from Columbia University and its law school hung on the wall and he had a few knick-knacks on his desk, including a Newton's cradle and a ceramic sculpture of the Dogs Playing Poker painting. Otherwise, his office was pretty bare.

He knew many of his colleagues had photos of loved ones, especially children, displayed in their offices. People had always encouraged him to put up more stuff in his own office for others to see, even if he couldn't see it himself.

Now that he had Abigail, Matthew, and Taylor in his life, Jefferson was considering this advice with a new prospective. He figured that he ought to at least hang pictures of them somewhere in his office. After all, they were his family. He then recalled that he had a nice photo of Stan and Maggie, a few years younger, stashed away somewhere at home and thought he might put that up as well. He paused, thinking about this. The photo was around the time of their last visit. It'd been taken a day before his brother was called away to an emergency in Washington, a time he preferred to forget, so far without success.

His thoughts were interrupted when the speaking software on his computer came to life and he set to work on checking his e-mail. But it wasn't even a minute later when the secretary poked her head into his office.

"There's a woman here to see you," she told him. "She says she needs to urgently speak with you."

"Send her in," Jefferson said, figuring if it was Paula Franks again, he could very easily show her the door.

Someone walked into his office and shut the door. They didn't speak and, after a few silent seconds, Jefferson decided to get the ball rolling.

"Can I help you?" he queried.

"Hello Jefferson," Amy said.

Jefferson almost fell out of his chair.

"A... Amy?" he asked, trying to keep some composure. He hadn't seen her since last Sunday night, when she walked out of his bedroom, regretting what happened between them.

"Hey," she now said. "Can we talk?"

"Sure," Jefferson replied, waving his hand towards an empty chair. "Have a seat."

Amy sat down. It didn't sound like she removed her jacket or set down her purse. Jefferson came around his desk and took the other empty chair. Somehow, putting the desk between them didn't seem like the best idea right then. What Amy wanted to talk about surely had no business components to it whatsoever.

"I want to talk about what happened between us," Amy said, cementing that notion.

Jefferson nodded.

"It was a mistake," Amy said. "It was a stupid mistake, and I can't understand how it happened."

"That makes two of us," Jefferson replied.

"I know things haven't always been … easy between us, but I thought we were in a good place."

Jefferson sometimes wondered how much Amy knew about his feelings for her. He'd dropped hints at Columbia but worked hard to tamp them down after she and Eric became serious and then got engaged. He knew she wasn't stupid, but it still wasn't clear how much she ever knew.

"I have a family," Amy said. "I love them. I love my husband. I know I can't take back what I did, but I don't want to ruin what I have."

"I wouldn't want you to," Jefferson said.

"Can we just bury this forever? Go back to the way things were? I don't want to hurt Eric."

"Me neither," Jefferson said, no stranger to the idea of burying. "I'm willing to do whatever it takes to somehow make things work here. If that involves burying what happened, I'll do it."

For the first time, Amy managed a smile.

"I can't believe I took so long to bring this up," she said, sounding relieved. "I thought this was going to be so much harder because …"

Her voice trailed off and Jefferson could sense her embarrassment.

"That night was fun," he admitted, "but that was all it was … fun."

He would not admit it'd been more than "fun" for him. Not now.

Amy nodded, making a noise of agreement.

"It's not worth ruining our lives for," she said. "Gratias tibi ago."

"I'm just happy we're okay," Jefferson said.

"Yeah. I'd better get going before people get suspicious. I had a hard enough time explaining to Eric why I was home so late that night. I don't want him to hear about this on top of it."

Jefferson nodded as he got up and reached out to open the door for her. He wouldn't ask what she'd told Eric that night.

"Hey," Amy said. "You really don't know how it happened?"

Jefferson shrugged. They hadn't been inebriated, but the course of events still didn't make sense.

"Best I can piece together, we hung out and had some drinks after the kids went to bed," he recounted. "Things just sort of … happened after that."

"I guess we'll have to settle for that," Amy said. "Bye Jefferson."

She left and Jefferson sat down behind his desk again, feeling drained.

Eric entered the restaurant and located Jefferson, already seated in a booth with Presley asleep on his feet. He greeted his friend as he slid in across from him just as the waitress came by.

"Will you be joining him?" she asked.

"Yes," Eric said, looking past the waitress at the specials board, "and I'll have a Coke and the shrimp pasta."

Jefferson knew the shrimp pasta came along for about a week every couple months and Eric never missed the opportunity. And Eric called him a creature of habit?

The waitress took a moment to write down Eric's order after giving Jefferson his water. When she was gone, Eric looked across the table.

"I worry that if they ever shut this place down, you'll go hungry," he remarked. "You are aware that Manhattan has other places where you can go for lunch, right?"

"I am," Jefferson said, "but how would you find me?"

"I'd probably take the easier route and find new friends," Eric said as the waitress brought his Coke.

"Always nice to know I'm so easily replaceable."

"Well, that's life," Eric said, raising his glass. "To this year being over sooner rather than later."

Jefferson chuckled and raised his glass as well. They never actually toasted, just raised their glasses for whatever reason which struck them at that moment.

"Thank God for it," Jefferson commented after having taken a long sip. "The sooner Paula Franks graduates, the happier I'll be."

"She's still pursuing you?" Eric asked.

"Like never before. I tell you … I think I'd rather stick my head into a pool of hungry piranhas."

"Hey, let's not get crazy here. I mean, she isn't bad looking."

"Aren't you married?" Jefferson asked, a sudden reminder of his fling with Amy flying through his head. He was able to keep a straight face, but so much for "burying". Maybe that plan had been easier the last time thanks to geographic distance.

"No harm in looking," Eric said innocently. "But I know what you mean. Paula Franks is very smart, but she's also a perfectionist to the extreme. I remember when I gave her a low grade on a midterm paper. She spent three months trying to get it changed."

Jefferson emitted a slight chuckle.

"So how is your love life?" Eric asked, somewhat changing the subject. "Any prospective candidates?"

"Not right now," Jefferson said. "I figure I'll put the brakes on that for a while. I'm having better luck finding a good nanny."

He had narrowed the field of candidates a little more, but it was still difficult to choose.

"You hear from Nancy at all?" Eric asked.

"Nope," Jefferson said without a hint of regret.

"So, it's over? You're just gonna throw five years away like that?"

"Yeah. She was pretty adamant. I had to make a choice, which I did."

Nancy had been a mistake long before Stan and Maggie died.

Eric nodded.

"Then you did the right thing," he commended. "Besides, you're a handsome guy. The women will throw themselves at you soon enough."

"Thank you for adding that last part," Jefferson remarked. "Being called 'handsome' by my best friend is something I want to be striving for."

"Glad to help."

* * *

Monique sat in her living room, still strapped into her chair. She waited patiently as she watched the weather channel, checking on tomorrow's forecast. It looked like it was going to be a beautiful spring Saturday, perfect for enticing people to leave their homes and perhaps come down to her bookstore for the readings. She wished there was a park or a courtyard or something nearby where they could hold the event outdoors. But alas, nothing was close enough. So she'd have to settle for people simply being driven out of their homes by the nice weather.

She froze, hearing the door to her apartment being unlocked. She looked over and relaxed when she saw Joan's temporary replacement, a young nurse named Erika Stoult, entering. The woman was now well into her second day of working with Monique and things were going okay so far. True, Monique preferred Joan, but this woman wasn't so bad.

"Same routine as last night?" Erika Stoult asked, and Monique nodded. "What do you want for dinner?"

"Is there any chicken in the fridge?" Monique asked.

Erika Stoult checked and found some. She set to work on making chicken tenders with mashed potatoes, peas, and gravy. As she worked, she began asking Monique about her day, which required some background information about Monique and the bookstore in order for everything to make sense. At least the longer-than-usual conversation helped pass the time.

"There we go," Erika Stoult soon said. "The chicken is in the oven and everything else's on the stove. I'm just gonna go make sure your bed and pjs are ready for you."

She left the main room and Monique turned her attention to watching the evening news. She was watching a story about a possible cutback in the city's funding of public schools when Erika Stoult came back out and joined her.

Dinner was ready about fifteen minutes later. Monique ate while Erika Stoult went about loading the pots and pans into the dishwasher and occasionally making small talk with her temporary patient. After Monique was finished eating, they headed into her bedroom and the nurse began helping her get ready for bed.

"Would you like me to come by sometime tomorrow to put you in the standing frame?" Erika Stoult asked at one point.

"No, I'm fine," Monique said, seriously doubting that this little person had the strength for that task. Joan always required help when doing it and she could probably take this woman with one hand behind her back and a debilitating disease crippling her. In fact, Monique herself could probably shock-put this woman out to Long Island if necessary.

Despite her small stature, Erika Stoult was able to help Monique get into bed. She checked to make sure her water bottle on the nightstand was full, asked if Monique needed anything else, and, when everything was set, wished her patient a good night and left.

Now alone, Monique couldn't help thinking that, despite this woman not being so bad, she still missed Joan. If nothing else, it was because the usual routine was disrupted.

* * *

Jefferson allowed himself to sleep in that Saturday morning and therefore didn't get up until around eight. Nevertheless, he found the

117

kids awake and playing in their bedrooms, which finally actually looked like kids' bedrooms, with the exception of the bare walls. He hadn't even thought about getting them painted.

During breakfast, Taylor pestered him about the bookstore's readings. He explained he had looked into the matter and found out the first reading would take place at eleven for the younger kids. the older kids would have their turn at noon. Since all three kids seemed interested in going, they would be sticking around for the full two hours. None of the kids had a problem with that, finding the bookstore pretty interesting. I'd hate to see what they think of a toy store, Jefferson mused as he cleaned up after breakfast.

* * *

At 10:30, the group left the house. It was a sunny morning with a spring breeze blowing through the neighborhood, so they decided to walk the few blocks to the bookstore. Jefferson was sure he had the route memorized, but kept his phone's GPS on, just in case.

* * *

With Monique supervising, Kathy, Frank, and Samuel began setting things up for the readings around 10:00. The store's children's section wasn't big, but the store itself wasn't that big. Still, size wouldn't be a problem. They'd always managed with the available space and received positive feedback for it.

They arranged large colorful cushions in a semicircle for the audience to sit on. All makeshift seats faced a stand equipped with a small frame and page turner for Monique to use in order to show the kids the pictures in the books she read. The books themselves were stacked up in one corner.

"I just hope my arms will stay in check so I can hold them," Monique commented with a half smirk.

"You'll be fine," Kathy told her.

"If you're worried," Frank chimed in, moving a table out of the way and dragging another large cushion into place, "you can test yourself by actually lending us a hand with this stuff."

"I would," Monique retorted, "but I need my hands to sign your paycheck."

Frank didn't say anything else as he kept working.

* * *

Families began trickling in around a quarter to eleven and browsed the shelves while they waited for the first reading to begin. Leaving Frank and Kathy to finish setting up, Monique sent Samuel into the shelves to be available if anyone needed anything while she went up front to watch the register.

It was while she was there that she saw the man named Jefferson Thomas come in with his guide dog, his two nieces, and his nephew. One of the girls noticed her almost immediately. Which twin was she again?

"Hi Monique," she said, waving.

"Hello," Monique said back with a smile.

Jefferson was then momentarily distracted by a small boy coming over and asking if he could pet Presley.

"No, she's working," he replied, being polite about it. "She can't be pet when she's wearing this harness."

The boy wandered back towards his mother, who was reading the back cover of a novel, and Abigail's attention was captured by this topic.

"Why can't people pet Presley when she is wearing the harness?" she queried, watching the dog with curiosity.

"Petting distracts her," Jefferson explained. "She needs to pay attention to do her job. People can't distract her by petting her. I could get hurt otherwise."

"Oh," Abigail said, these potential consequences seeming to not concern her. "Okay."

Monique watched all of this, finding it interesting. She had always played around with the idea of getting a service dog to help her out, but she had never seriously pursued it. It was interesting to see one in action, even if it was for someone with a different disability.

* * *

Eleven o'clock soon rolled around and Frank took charge of the register while Monique headed back to the children's section. Kathy had already set the first book into the frame and handed Monique an identical copy to read from along with the remote for the page turner. Monique maneuvered her chair around so she faced her young but captive audience. She was sure that it was her chair which held their attention.

"Hello," she said. "I'm Monique and I'd like to welcome you to my store."

Her greeting received some responses from the kids and the parents who were sticking around rather than browsing through the shelves.

"I'm going to tell you right now that I love books," Monique continued. "I love them because they allow each of us to have adventures and to see and hear things, we never would have thought possible. Now, we're going to go on some adventures together. Are you ready to get started?"

* * *

Jefferson, Presley, and the twins browsed the bookshelves in the unoccupied area of the children's section, hearing Monique reading but not really keeping up with what she was saying. Jefferson was sure Matthew was having a good time though. The boy hadn't come looking for him yet.

* * *

Matthew watched and listened with fascination as Monique read a story about knights and dragons while using a remote to turn the pages so everyone could see the book's pictures. He sat on a big bright red cushion, currently not caring where his uncle and sisters had gone off to.

* * *

Monique finished around 11:50, leaving a ten-minute break before the reading for the older kids was to begin. The younger kids began rising from the cushions, some coming up to thank her while others went to find their parents. Some parents who knew Monique also came over to make small talk, generally about upcoming releases due to appear on her shelves.

Around noon, the older kids, ranging from seven to ten, began sitting down on the cushions as Kathy set up a new stack of books. This stack was a bit shorter than the earlier one, but since the books were a bit longer, it evened out in the end.

This selection of books didn't contain pictures, so Kathy folded up the page turner and set it aside. Monique again introduced herself to the group. She then began to read.

When it was over around 12:50, the kids got up from their cushions and began rejoining their parents. Abigail and Taylor quickly found Jefferson and Matthew, who had been sitting in the back and listening in.

"Do we have to go already?" Taylor asked.

"I'll give you guys ten more minutes," Jefferson said. "Then we're definitely leaving."

Taking advantage of the opportunity, the three kids headed off to look around some more.

* * *

With the readings over, Monique was once again moving through the aisles and mingling with customers. A brief change in her routine came about when she had to help convince a little boy that "The Silence of the Lambs" was not a book about a farm. It seemed he hadn't yet learned the meaning of the word "silence", but "Lambs" had grabbed his attention.

As she was moving towards the front of the store, Monique ran into Taylor. The little girl had a book in her hands and explained she was going up to the register to meet up with her uncle.

"Come on," Monique offered. "I'll go with you."

Taylor's uncle and siblings weren't at the front of the store yet, so Monique suggested they wait, figuring the others would be along shortly.

"You live with your uncle?" Monique queried.

"Uh-huh," Taylor replied, nodding her head.

"Where are your parents?"

Taylor's eyes very suddenly and very quickly went to her feet.

"They're dead," she said in a small voice. "Uncle Jeff came and got us to live with him when they died."

Monique was stunned. Never in the world could she have seen this answer coming. Sure, asking about parents was sometimes a touchy issue, what with the divorce rates out there. But this was something different.

"I'm so sorry," Monique said.

Taylor said nothing as her uncle came up behind her with the other two kids in tow. Only now remembering his subtle hand gesture from last time when the subject almost came up, Monique knew he had heard everything. he didn't look thrilled.

"Go wait by the register," he told the kids, steering Taylor off in that direction with one hand. The other two obeyed without question. Maybe they hadn't overheard.

Monique looked at Jefferson and saw no anger in his face, but rather stress and some anguish.

"I'm sorry," she said. "I didn't know ..."

"Forget about it," Jefferson said. "Just forget about it."

He went to the register, where Samuel was currently working, and paid for the books the kids had picked out. Monique silently watched them go, feeling terrible. She noticed Taylor was on the verge of tears.

* * *

"Hey," Jefferson said, stopping about half a block from the bookstore and crouching down to be somewhat at eye-level with Taylor. Even he could tell she was ready to cry. Abigail and Matthew, who'd missed what happened earlier, waited but were rather impatient about it.

"Hang on a second," Jefferson told them and turned back to Taylor. "You okay?"

Taylor sniffled.

"She didn't mean anything by it," Jefferson assured her. "She didn't know."

Taylor continued to sniffle, and Jefferson hugged her tightly.

* * *

Though she never started crying, Taylor remained subdued for the next few hours, only coming around by 4:00. She was relatively cheerful again by dinner and joined the others in a game of Trouble.

* * *

"Everything okay?" Erika Stoult asked as Monique ate her dinner. "You're usually more upbeat than this. Did your reading not go well?"

"No, it went fine," Monique replied. "It was afterwards where I really screwed up."

"What happened?"

"I made a little girl relive the fact her parents are dead. That really doesn't fall into the 'Highlights of My Life' category."

"And that's all there is," Jefferson said. "The story's over."

"They got to keep the dog?" Matthew asked.

"Yep," Jefferson told him as he stood up. "Now go to sleep."

He quietly left the room, feeling thankful to have found a digital version of the story online. His mother had read him all the books from the series when he'd been that young. he was right in thinking Matthew might like them now.

Checking in on the girls and hearing nothing, Jefferson went back downstairs and sat down on the couch. he switched on the TV, figuring he'd listen to the news for a while.

* * *

"Anything else you need before I say good night?" Erika Stoult asked as she set Monique's full water bottle down on the nightstand and adjusted the straw slightly for her patient to have easy access.

"Yeah," Monique said. "my iPhone is on my desk back in the main room. Could I have it please?"

* * *

The phone rang and Jefferson got up to answer it, leaving the TV on for the time being. He hoped it was a wrong number.

"Hello?" he queried, hoping he sounded weary enough.

"Hi," a voice he didn't recognize said. "Can I speak to Jefferson Thomas?"

"This is him."

"Oh hi," the voice said, sounding a little surprised. "Sorry, I didn't recognize your voice. It's Monique, the horrible woman from the bookstore."

Jefferson realized who it was. He figured she found him in the White Pages. And he was sure what subject was on her mind.

"I'm sorry for intruding like this," Monique continued. "I just wanted to apologize again for upsetting your niece today. I didn't know."

"It's all right," Jefferson assured her. "Like you said, you didn't know."

"Is she okay?"

"She's fine. She bounces back."

"Good. I'm glad to hear it. And I hope you guys will come back to the store sometime soon."

Jefferson had no idea when that might happen.

"Sure," he said. "Thanks for calling."

He was sure she sounded genuine. that this wasn't just to try to get some good PR.

"Um," Monique said. "Could I ask you a question ... something personal?"

"Sure," Jefferson said, nonetheless cautious.

"I got the feeling the kids lost their parents recently. Is that the case?"

Jefferson took a deep breath.

"Yeah," he confirmed.

"I'm sorry," Monique said. "If you ever need anything ..."

Her voice trailed off as she wondered if she really should be saying that to someone she barely knew.

"I don't think I ever really introduced myself," she said to cover her silent pause. "I'm Monique Vasquez."

"Jefferson Thomas," Jefferson said. "But you already knew that."

"Sort of. Nevertheless, it's nice to meet you."

"Same here. Thanks for calling."

Monique disconnected the call, having used the speakerphone function on her iPhone instead of trying to keep it pressed against her ear. After all, she was alone for this call.

She set the phone on her nightstand, still thinking about those kids. She knew it was wrong to pry, but her curiosity got the better of her. Now she couldn't get them out of her head. And she couldn't help wondering what happened to their parents. Then, she thought of her own parents.

Adjusting her body as best she could on the bed, Monique drifted into an uneasy sleep, her mind still locked on those kids and her hope that she would see them, and their uncle, again.

Chapter 14

With the outside world looking like the air had been replaced by rainwater, Jefferson worked on preparing breakfast and lunches for the kids while summoning an Uber on his iPhone. He figured it was best to avoid the risk of anyone drowning on the walk to school. Problem was, all of Greenwich Village seemed to have the same idea. It had been ten minutes and no driver had accepted his fare yet. Granted, needing the booster seat for Matthew limited his options, but Jefferson thought a place like New York City had the resources to make this work.

"Come on," he muttered, checking his phone again. "Somebody. It's a short trip."

He put the phone back in his pocket just as the twins and Matthew came down the stairs. the house was beginning to show the effects of its newest occupants, who had been living there for almost five weeks now. More coats and shoes had been unpacked and now stood alongside his in the foyer, looking like the attire of dwarves next to the items which accommodated his six-foot, two-inch frame. Likewise, small, colorful plastic plates and cups stood alongside his dishware in the kitchen cabinets. Two crates of toys occupied corners of the den and it wasn't unusual for him to find a stray toy which hadn't been put away again. The kids' rooms were now painted, the walls being blue in Matthew's room and a light purple in the twins' room. Only the third floor and the attic remained as they were before Jefferson received the news about Stan and Maggie.

Jefferson had eventually settled on a nanny and hired Anya Motkova. Their agreement included her living in the small bedroom adjacent to the den with its own bathroom, which he'd furnished and affixed with a lock similar to the one on his front door. She'd moved in two weeks ago, abandoning the basement apartment she'd previously occupied in Chelsea. With Jefferson still running the house, her job was to help him as necessary, particularly when his blindness became an impediment, and keep an eye on the kids. Previously, Jefferson had hired a house-cleaning service to help him keep the place neat, but that was no longer needed with Anya around.

Anya proved to be easy-going, her only requested addition in her new home being a bookshelf as she liked to read when not working.

She was easily twice as competent and industrious as she was easy-going. She awoke at 5:00 every morning and went out for a thirty-minute jog, showered, and met Jefferson at 6:00 as he was getting his first cup of coffee of the morning. She cleaned and ran errands while others were out and took a nap in the early afternoon. By the time Jefferson and the kids returned from work and school, she was prepared to hear about everyone's day. She also proved to be adept at math, a subject Taylor struggled with, and actually took notes when Abigail recited the foods she did not like. Jefferson wondered who'd been foolish enough to give her up.

"Do we have to walk in the rain?" Taylor asked, eyeing the horrendous weather outside as Anya followed them downstairs.

"I'm getting a ride for us," Jefferson assured her, though his fare had yet to be accepted. This had to be a record.

He glanced out the window again, hearing the rain battering the glass. Even Presley wasn't keen to go out there, rushing to relieve herself in the backyard earlier. She lay in one corner of the kitchen, which now smelled like a wet dog.

Having skipped her morning jog for fear of slipping on the wet sidewalk, Anya had helped prepare breakfast before going to assist the kids with getting ready for school. She corralled them towards the kitchen table. Jefferson kept checking his phone, resisting the urge to curse out … he wasn't quite sure whom to target.

He was surprised when the doorbell rang. He went to answer it and found the visitor was Linda Carrows.

"Hey," she said, stepping into the foyer. "I thought you guys could use a ride. I've got my minivan, so there's room."

"A minivan in Manhattan?" Jefferson asked with a raised eyebrow.

"I don't actually use it much. Just for days like this or when I'm traveling outside of the city. Besides, I'm not planning to do any parking. So, you want the ride? Because I've got the room. It's just me and my two munchkins right now."

"Sure," Jefferson said, deciding not to rely on Uber anymore. "That'd be great."

Among the parents of PS 41's student body, Linda was the closest to what he could call a friend. They chatted regularly outside the school and she'd advised him on how to handle several school functions due to occur before the summer break.

Jefferson was canceling the Uber request when Anya came into the foyer. He didn't miss Linda falling silent upon her appearance. She hadn't met the nanny before, though she knew he'd recently hired one.

126

"Linda," Jefferson said, "this is Anya, my new nanny. Anya, this is Linda. Her kids go to the same school as the twins and she's being kind enough to give us a ride during this downpour."

In the back of his mind, he wondered if that was still the case. Neither he nor Anya were naive. In part thanks to Eric, they both knew she was smart, professional, blonde, slender, and stood on legs as long as her hair. Rumors had begun circulating in the neighborhood after she moved into Jefferson's home, mainly because she greeted early-morning commuters during her jog. She wasn't flirtatious, just friendly, and her jogging attire wasn't that flattering to the eye. But the rumors spread. Eric had clarified the situation to Jefferson after meeting her for the first time, later claiming to have almost suffered a stroke.

"She's every heterosexual guy's and homosexual gal's wet dream," he'd said. "Heck, I'm sure she can turn the heads of some gay guys and straight women as well. Think Jennifer Lawrence in that Russian spy movie. The woman could probably make garbage look appealing, and she is living in your house. People are going to wonder if you two have a side arrangement going on."

"We don't," Jefferson replied firmly, "and we won't."

Between Anya's professionalism and his disastrous love life, he refused to compromise the arrangement they had made ... the only arrangement they had made. Plus, the kids loved her, and Jefferson did not want to get in the way of that.

Eric had accepted this, though Jefferson suspected he too might have previously wondered if there was something going on between him and Anya. Linda's silence now suggested she too was suspecting the possibility.

"I will go clean up in the kitchen," Anya said, her melodic accent not helping the situation. "It is nice to meet you. Stay safe in this weather."

"Nice to meet you, too," Linda returned.

Anya disappeared and Linda looked at Jefferson again.

"My kids are finishing breakfast back at the house," she said. "Want me to circle back in about fifteen minutes?"

* * *

Though her own words indicated she didn't drive often, Linda proved to be a typical New York driver, mainly in that she wouldn't let another motorist get the better of her. Jefferson was thankful she didn't crash or curse as they maneuvered through the dense morning traffic, further hampered by the still-dark sky and the continuing rain.

Not that surprisingly, many cars had replaced the usual crowd of parents who walked their kids to school, most of them probably Ubers and Lifts. So, letting out the twins and Linda's two kids became almost like an act normally performed by circus acrobats. There were aides outside to help coordinate the traffic, but their apparent lack of experience with such madness made them kind of useless. Nevertheless, Jefferson and Linda got their kids to the front doors of the school, where they parted ways with them and hurried to drive away to keep from annoying too many people by holding up traffic. For both, it was the shortest drop-off ever ... no chit-chatting with anyone.

"Where to next?" Linda asked as she drove away from the front of the school, her wipers on their highest settings.

"You don't have to," Jefferson told her. "Matthew and I can catch a cab or something from here."

He'd learned about a subway station near the Tate Sunshine Day Care Center and figured he could further avoid the rain by catching a train over to the law school's neighborhood. That'd be easier than trying to get a cab or Uber for that leg of the trip.

"In this weather?" Linda asked. "Yeah right. Come on, tell me where to go next. It's no problem."

* * *

After dropping Matthew off at the day care center, Linda continued by insisting she could drop Jefferson off at the law school instead of letting him take the subway as he intended. He again politely tried to decline her offer, but she again wouldn't hear of it, so he again gave in.

The ride to the New York University Law School buildings was longer than the previous trips, so the pair spoke as she drove. They'd exchanged brief snippets while dropping off or picking up their kids at school over the past few weeks, but this was their first real conversation.

Linda was a divorced mother of two who defined her relationship with her ex as "good love ... better friendship." Her husband worked for a multi-national engineering firm, so the alimony checks took care of the expenses. Nevertheless, she worked part-time at the Metropolitan Museum of Art as an assistant curator.

"I need to work," she explained. "I'd go crazy if I didn't have a place like that to go on a regular basis."

This made perfect sense to Jefferson, who didn't need his NYU professorship, even with the kids now in his life.

Linda went on to explain how her husband traveled a lot for work, so their custody agreement was based around when he was home. She was thankful he at least made an effort to be a part of their lives, even if he wasn't as involved as much as she would like.

"I have friends who have it a lot worse," she said.

Jefferson couldn't even picture having to share Abigail, Matthew, and Taylor with anyone.

"So," Linda then asked, "what's the deal with you and the Russian nanny? She seems very nice."

Jefferson had both accepted and dreaded this probe. But he'd deal with it.

"Nothing," he said, hoping his tone indicated this was true and it was nobody's business.

"Okay. She a hard worker?"

Jefferson was surprised. Apart from Eric, anyone who dared to mention Anya to him never made such an inquiry.

"Absolutely," he said.

"The kids like her?" Linda asked as they stopped at a red light.

"Yes. I can't imagine what would happen if I got rid of her."

"Then forget about the rest."

Linda and Jefferson exchanged a smile as the light turned green.

* * *

"All right," Linda said, driving through a huge puddle and leaving Jefferson wondering if the van was about to be flooded. "Here we are … New York University School of Law."

"Thanks very much," Jefferson said, opening his door. "I owe you one."

He grabbed his briefcase and moved to exit the van.

"It's no problem," Linda said again.

Jefferson paused.

"Then how about I take you out for dinner?" he suggested.

"Why Jefferson Thomas," Linda asked with a sly smile. "Are you asking me out?"

"In a manner of speaking," Jefferson admitted.

Sure, he remembered his personal pact from last month, the one where he'd decided not to date or enter into a relationship for a while. But Linda wasn't the same as his mistakes. She was nice, unattached,

129

seemed interested in him, definitely loved kids, struck him as intelligent and motivated, and, according to Eric's description, was "Not bad looking."

"She could maybe challenge Amy in the looks department," Eric had once said over lunch. "And I'm not even including your new nanny in that calculation. Please never tell Amy I said any of that."

While his short affair with Amy still stung, Jefferson was now able to filter that out and see Eric's point.

"So, there's really nothing going on between you and your nanny?" Linda asked.

"No," Jefferson said, taken aback. He considered withdrawing his invitation for dinner.

"All right then," Linda said. "Dinner sounds nice. I'll call you and we'll work something out. Your number is on the class list, right?"

Jefferson paused, still considering.

"Sure," he said. "Looking forward to it. And thanks again for the ride."

* * *

"Hey Samuel," Monique said. "Go fetch another box for the science fiction section from the back room. The shelves are starting to look a little under stocked."

"On it," Samuel said and headed for the storeroom.

The storeroom was actually the space on the building's third floor, consisting of one large room turned into a labyrinth made of boxes and supplies. It was the only part of her own property which Monique did not have access to, her ambulatory employees taking the stairs and unlocking the door. Her private elevator, installed upon her return from college at Syracuse, only went to her apartment on the second floor. A small lift had been installed to move newly-delivered books into storage or retrieve inventory to replenish shelves. But Monique never saw enough value to get a loan to rip out her current elevator, expand its shaft, and reinstall it. The only occasion for a prolonged stay up there was to do inventory. And how was she supposed to operate her chair while Balancing a large box of the latest Game of Thrones volumes on her lap? It wasn't worth it.

As she watched Samuel disappear between the shelves, Monique thought how the kid had become easier to work with over the past few weeks. He began seeing her less as a disabled person and more like his boss, which made his quick responses to her instructions and requests a little amusing. At least he wasn't treating her like a china doll anymore, though he still had some work to do.

Monique was behind the cash register that morning, where Joan had once again set her up in her standing frame. The nurse would be back shortly after lunch, when she would get Monique down and then drive her over to her physical therapy clinic. Normally, Monique's appointments were in the morning, but one appointment needed to be rescheduled for that afternoon, warranting this change in her routine.

* * *

Jefferson sat in his office, listening to the rain outside and trying to decide what to do for lunch. He was not particularly keen on the idea of going out there to get something to eat. But he was hungry, and he had another class to teach before he could pick up the kids and go home. Since he wasn't going to rely on Linda giving them a ride back, he had already scheduled an Uber. A driver had accepted the three-stop fare ten minutes ago.

With that done, Jefferson focused on figuring out where and when to take Linda to dinner. True, her last question had stung, but he was getting over it. He did owe her for the ride and he genuinely wanted to pursue this and see what possibilities might come. His designs did not include the idea of marriage, but it'd be nice to have some regular female companionship. His personal pact to halt his dating was officially abolished.

Jefferson's thoughts were interrupted by a knock on the door and Eric entering without waiting for a response. The smell indicated he was carrying cartons of Chinese food. Eric set the cartons down on Jefferson's desk and pulled up a chair.

"Thought you might not want to go out," he said. "I also wanted to remind you that there are other cuisines besides Italian. Sweet and sour chicken?"

"Thank you," Jefferson said, taking the carton being offered.

"So," Eric queried in a muffled voice, his mouth full of lo mein, "any developments in your love life?"

"Nothing yet. It's kind of hard when you're not married but have kids waiting for you to come home."

"What about the places where you take the kids? Like their school? There's bound to be a few good-looking single moms around."

Jefferson sometimes seriously believed his friend was psychic

"I did ask out this one woman," he confessed. "She's got two kids in the girls' school."

"There you go!" Eric exclaimed. "That's something. That's a start. Heck, it's a 'development'. I know her?"

"Linda."

"The one who thought we were gay?"

Eric shook his head and smiled.

"Not bad," he said. "I mean, she ain't bad-looking, though your nanny is an Olympic gold medalist compared to everyone else on Earth. This one's got black hair, always wears some kind of blouse and slacks, light-pink fingernails … do I have that right?"

"Sounds like how you've described her before," Jefferson said.

"Where are you taking her?"

"I have no idea," Jefferson replied with a shake of his head.

"You'll figure it out," Eric assured him. "Just, whatever you do, don't fixate on Italian food."

* * *

By the late afternoon, the rain finally let up, so Monique decided to wait outside for the cab that would pick her up from her physical therapy session. She sat near the clinic's front doors, attracting the occasional stares from passing pedestrians as she watched the traffic.

Her session, though rescheduled, had gone well. In her case, no news was always good news. The only real problem she was having was that she wanted to spend more time in one of the clinic's pools. The facility had two, a heated therapeutic pool and a regular lap pool. Monique was willing to settle for the therapeutic pool just as long as she got to spend more time just moving around in the water. To her, the lack of gravity offered some sense of freedom from her chair, even if she was then confined to the water. She had frequently asked her physical therapist to give her more time and he was promising that it would happen soon, so she now settled for pestering him about the matter every chance she got.

"Excuse me," a voice said, pulling Monique out of her thoughts. "Do you need help?"

It was probably the tenth time she'd been asked this.

"No, thanks," Monique said, pulling up one of her usual responses. "I'm just waiting for my ride home"

She'd been asked this question thousands of times in her lifetime and she always had a response prepared so she would be left alone.

"Oh, sorry," the voice said. "It's just that I walk by this place every day and I've never seen you before, so I wasn't sure if …"

Monique looked up to see the speaker was a handsome man about her age who was dressed in a dark-gray suit. He seemed friendly enough and Monique decided he shouldn't just be blown off.

"I'm normally here in the mid-morning," she explained. "My appointment was rescheduled."

"That's too bad," the man said. "I was kind of hoping you were a new face here and this would be your regular time."

"Oh, really?" Monique asked, surprised and slightly cautious. "Why's that?"

"So I could get to know you a little bit before I asked you out for dinner or coffee or something," the man explained. "But now you've forced me to accelerate my plans. I'm Brad Myers, by the way."

He didn't move to extend his hand to shake, seeming unsure if Monique could reciprocate.

"Monique Vasquez," she said, extending her own hand as best she could.

Seeming more confident, Brad Myers now shook her hand, though a little too gently for Monique's taste.

"So," he said, "you come here in the mid-morning, right? Meaning you would get out around lunchtime?"

"Yeah," Monique replied, suddenly feeling very hopeful. Could he really be interested in her?

"Then how about lunch?" Brad suggested. "There's a great diner just around the corner."

"Sure," Monique agreed. "That sounds great."

They exchanged phone numbers before Brad insisted he had to run. Monique's cab arrived and she said she had to likewise get going, giving him one more smile before he kept walking.

Chapter 15

The bookstore was as busy as it always was on a Saturday. Monique was near the register, mingling with customers, mainly children. She looked and smiled as Jefferson came in with Presley, Abigail, Taylor, and Matthew. The group was accompanied by a blonde woman Monique didn't recognize. She was young and very pretty. Samuel, who was behind the register, definitely looked and Monique feared he'd need a long bathroom break later.

"Hey, you guys," she said, focusing on the kids.

"Hi Monique," Taylor said, beaming. She then looked up at her uncle.

"Can we go look around?" she asked.

"Sure," Jefferson permitted. "Just don't make a mess. And we're not buying anything today."

The kids hurried off and Jefferson looked at Monique.

"They look good," Monique commented.

"Thanks," Jefferson said. "Tell me something … this is our fifth time coming here since those three came to live with me a few weeks ago. From day one, Taylor, who is normally reserved around people she doesn't know, even family members, is bright and sunny with you. Can you explain that?"

Monique shrugged her shoulders as best she could.

"I just have that effect, I guess," she said. "Reach kids who don't want to be reached. I really can't explain it. It just sort of happens."

"Well," Jefferson said, "whatever it is, thanks. It's doing wonders for her."

"No problem. Now let's go find them before you all rob me blind."

She, Jefferson, and the unidentified woman headed off in the direction the kids had run off in.

"Can you show me your secret?" the woman requested as they moved down one aisle. "With the children, I mean. I am still learning."

She spoke with an accent, suggesting she was from Eastern Europe.

"Em, sure," Monique said, uncertain of who this woman even was.

Her answer seemed to trigger something within Jefferson.

"Monique," he said, "this is my new nanny, Anya Motkova. Anya, this is Monique Vasquez, the store's owner and manager."

Having watched Monique operating her wheelchair, Anya extended her hand, which Monique promptly shook. The attractive blonde was observant and intelligent.

"Jefferson has told me a lot about this store," Anya said. "I was wondering if you have any works by Andrey Dementyev?"

Monique had never heard the name. She promised to help Anya look to see if, on the off chance, he was in her inventory.

"Thank you," Anya said as they found Matthew.

* * *

Monique was actually shocked when they came across Andrey Dementyev's work in the store's miniscule poetry section. She supposed she'd purchased the volume as part of some package deal with one of the publishers or distributers she regularly dealt with.

As she plucked the book off the shelf, Anya explained the author was a well-known poet in her native Russia who'd died a couple years ago.

"He was a patriot," she explained, "but he stood against what Russia has become today in the world's eyes. You will find great compassion within his words. He enjoyed the simple things and could be very funny."

Monique had to agree on some level. She got her amusement watching Anya pay for the book while Samuel seemed to be trying not to faint as he completed the transaction. Thank you, Mr. Dementyev. Monique glanced at Jefferson, wondering how he had found this woman.

* * *

Jefferson's quandary about what tie to wear was interrupted by the doorbell. He went downstairs and let in Ellen O'Bryan, the kids' babysitter for the evening. He and Anya had agreed her workday ended at 5:30. That evening, she had zipped out the door around 6:00.

It wasn't the first night she'd gone out. She usually left shortly after quitting time about three or four evenings a week. She never said where she went, and he frankly didn't care. She was reliable and if anything did require her assistance, her number was in his phone.

"Hey," he said to the babysitter. "The kids are playing in their rooms. Go on up and introduce yourself. I'll be back in a second."

He hurried back upstairs to his own room. It didn't take him much longer to decide to abandon the idea of a tie altogether. He instead grabbed his jacket and went to find Ellen in the girls' room, where she was introducing herself to the three kids. Abigail was being her usual friendly self while Taylor and Matthew were reacting more shyly towards this newcomer.

"You guys gonna be okay?" Jefferson asked.

"We'll be fine, Mr. Thomas," Ellen said. "Have a good time."

Jefferson gave her the last-minute instructions, including where to find the emergency numbers and dinner for herself and the kids. He promised to be back by eleven and left, successfully avoiding Abigail's recitation of all the foods she would not eat.

* * *

Jefferson and Linda had agreed to meet at Wildair, a French/American Restaurant in the East Village. In texts sent back and forth, they called it their "safe choice".

Jefferson was seated at the restaurant's bar when Linda arrived. The host told them it would be about another ten minutes before their table was ready, so she perched herself on the stool next to him and ordered a Vodka Tonic.

"You clean up pretty good," she commented, surveying Jefferson for at least half a minute.

"Thank you," Jefferson returned. "That's a nice perfume you're wearing."

"Thanks. You haven't done this in a while, have you?"

"What?"

"Dating someone new. This conversation gives away the fact that it's been a lot longer than when your nieces and nephew moved in."

Jefferson managed a chuckle.

"Am I that transparent?" he queried. "Yeah, I actually just got out of a five-year relationship."

"You weren't married, were you?" Linda asked.

"No, nothing like that. It was just something I thought I was committed to. Recent events have shown me otherwise."

Linda nodded, seeming to understand.

"I've pretty much lacked any type of social life since my divorce," she said. "Everything revolved around my kids, even when I didn't have them with me. I've had a few coffee and lunch dates, but this is my first dinner date in a while."

"How's it going?" Jefferson asked.

"So far, so good. I'm not sure if the fact we're drinking already is the best thing, but who am I to talk."

They chuckled as the host came over to let them know their table was ready. They finished off their drinks and followed him into the restaurant, Jefferson leaving a twenty on the bar.

"You want me to read you the items in the menu?" Linda asked once they were seated, noticing no one gave Jefferson a Braille menu.

"Would you?" Jefferson asked as Presley made herself comfortable underneath his chair.

"Sure, no problem," Linda said and began to read.

They soon received fresh drinks and gave the waiter their orders. Jefferson picked up his drink and looked at Linda.

"So, what do we talk about now?" he asked.

"We can definitely skip that awkward moment where we have to confess we have kids waiting for us back home," Linda replied.

Jefferson smiled.

* * *

"Hey Taylor," Ellen said, coming into the bedroom. "Abigail and I are gonna play Old Maid. You wanna join us?"

Taylor, who had been busy drawing with crayons at her desk, glanced up. This lasted for a second or two before she resumed what she was doing. She didn't seem interested.

"Come on," Ellen encouraged, stepping closer. "Everyone else is downstairs. You really wanna be alone up here all night?"

Taylor didn't answer.

"Your uncle's coming back," Ellen promised. "He just went out for a few hours. You've got no reason to worry."

Taylor still didn't say anything, instead continuing to draw.

"All right," Ellen conceded. "I'll make you a deal. One game. If you have no fun with us, you can come right back up here and I'll leave you alone until your uncle comes back."

Taylor seemed to consider the offer. She finally set down her crayons and headed out the door. Ellen followed her with a smile. This game would be fun.

* * *

"Wait," Linda said, laughing as she tried to maintain a normal tone. "You mean to tell me that when your brother and his family came to visit you, you stuffed everyone into this tiny apartment you were living in at the time?"

"Yeah," Jefferson said, also laughing. "They shared my old sofa bed while I stayed in my bedroom, which was about the size of a shoebox. The twins slept in this portable crib thing they had back then, and I guess I should be thankful that Matthew wasn't around yet."

The visit happened almost five years ago. Jefferson wasn't sure why he was sharing it now. It'd been the last time he saw Stan and Maggie alive and in person. Video calls weren't the same.

"And they spent the entire long weekend there?" Linda asked, still laughing. Jefferson nodded, finding this story very amusing to tell … at least, this part of it.

"Stan had to go back down to Washington D.C. for business for one night," he clarified. "Some emergency … I don't remember the details. But otherwise, they were all there with me. All in all, we had fun."

He paused, hoping he wouldn't be prompted to continue. Now, he wasn't sure why he'd told this story to begin with.

"And that was the last time you saw them?" Linda asked, getting serious again.

"Yeah," Jefferson said. "Stan got sent out to his new post in Tokyo just a week later. They lived in Japan for a few years and he then got sent to Germany."

That was now the second reason he didn't like to tell this story. Who wanted to share the moment they last saw a now-deceased loved one?

"Okay," Jefferson said, changing the subject. "Your turn. Tell me about Detroit."

* * *

Ellen sat cross-legged on the couch, watching TV. The kids were all asleep, their requests for water, stories, and everything else satisfied. Now it was just a matter of waiting for their uncle to come home.

Ellen was thankful she managed to convince Taylor to come and play Old Maid. Despite losing to her sister quite frequently, she stuck around until bedtime, though Ellen had noticed her constantly looking towards the front door. In her unprofessional opinion, that girl had some serious attachment issues. But, unless she was asked to give such an opinion, she'd keep it to herself. She did wonder how these kids had wound up suddenly living with their uncle, but that again would stay in her head. Jefferson Thomas was giving her and her friends his business, and she wanted to keep it.

* * *

Jefferson and Linda walked out of the restaurant, having shared one final drink before paying the check, splitting it at Linda's insistence.

"Having the man pay is so old-fashioned," she chided. "We're living in the 21st Century."

"Well," Jefferson said. "I'm paying next time."

Linda smirked at him.

"You're that sure that there will be a second date?" she asked.

"Who said anything about a second date?" Jefferson asked. "I'm talking about right now. It's only 10:30. We could stop at a bar for a nightcap."

"I really think I've had enough. I'd like to be somewhat sober when I slip in and kiss my kids good night. Can't have them showing up to school, hung over because I breathed on them after consuming liberal amounts of alcohol."

Jefferson nodded, supposing she was right.

"Fair enough," he conceded. "So, about that second date?"

"We'll talk," Linda promised. "For now, live with the fact that this went pretty well."

"I can definitely live with that," Jefferson said, though he wasn't quite sure.

They each pulled out their phones to summon Ubers. They weren't planning to let their respective kids in on their possible relationship yet, so they figured it was best to part ways at the restaurant. Linda's ride arrived first

"Good night Jefferson," Linda said and climbed into the back of the Toyota.

* * *

Jefferson and Presley arrived home around 10:50. He paid Ellen and had her take his Uber to get home rather than walk this late at night, no matter how safe their neighborhood was. The driver had dozens of four and five-star reviews, so he figured that was the better options.

He poked his head into the kids' rooms and heard nothing, so he let them sleep and headed up to bed himself, hearing Anya coming home around 11:30.

* * *

The phone rang and Samuel answered it. Frank, Monique, and Kathy figured the call was just business. Samuel would summon one of them when he needed them, so they paid him no mind. Their attention was peaked when he called for Monique to come over.

"It's someone named Brad Myers," Samuel reported. "He's looking for you."

Monique was surprised as she had Samuel plug in her headset and put it on.

"Hello?" she asked, speaking into the mouthpiece.

"Hi," the voice said. "It's Brad, the guy from outside the rehab clinic."

"Hello."

Monique was surprised to hear from him. Sure, he'd been friendly, but she hadn't counted on him following through.

"Sorry for calling you at this number," Brad said. "I looked it up and thought it'd be easier to reach you here."

"That's okay," Monique assured him. "What's up?"

Out of the corner of her eye, she noticed Frank and Kathy moving closer.

"I was wondering if you wanted to set a time for that lunch," Brad explained. "At the Sweet Life Cafe?"

"Sure," Monique replied. "I have a physical therapy session on Tuesday. I get out at 11:30. We could meet up at the diner right after that."

She'd seen the Sweet Life Cafe several times when riding away from her physical therapy clinic in the West Village, but she'd never been there. It sounded better than what Brad's initial mention of the word "diner" had suggested.

"Great," Brad said. "I'll see you then."

Monique ended the call and turned to see Frank, Kathy, and Samuel watching her.

"What?" she asked.

"That sounded like a personal call," Frank said. "You never let us use that phone for personal calls."

"Well, that's the benefit of paying the phone bill and signing your paycheck. I get to do whatever I want. You don't."

"So?" Kathy asked. "who was that?"

"Just someone I'm having lunch with."

"Hey Samuel," Frank said, turning to the young man. "Did that sound like a male voice to you?"

"Yeah," Samuel said nervously.

Monique recalled the young man had said Brad's name earlier, so the issue of the caller's gender ought to be obvious without requiring verification. Frank was having fun.

"Sounds like more than just 'someone'," Frank said. "You're abandoning us for lunch with him."

Monique rolled her eyes.

"Be nice and I might tell you someday," she said.

* * *

"When's Ellen coming back?" Matthew asked as he, Jefferson, Presley, Abigail, and Taylor headed towards the girls' school.

"Not sure yet," Jefferson said.

"She was nice."

Matthew's statement was a simplification of the kids' feelings. All three of them admitted to having fun with their baby-sitter.

"Glad to hear it," Jefferson said as they immersed themselves in the crowd of students and parents by the front doors. He bid the twins farewell and headed off to the day care center with Matthew.

* * *

"Hey Monique?" Frank asked as he restocked some books. "Isn't your big date today?"

"No, it's tomorrow," Monique replied. "And it ..."

"I know, I know. It's not a date. You're just having lunch with this guy who seems to be interested in you."

"And don't you forget it."

* * *

"Show me a rough draft by Thursday," Jefferson instructed. "Then we'll see where to go from there."

"Thank you, Professor," the student said. She rose and left his office.

Jefferson leaned back in his chair and sighed as he pinched the bridge of his nose. He was glad Eric hadn't been around to witness this meeting. He would have been roaring with laughter if he had heard how this student was trying to flirt with him. True, she wasn't as insistent as Paula Franks, but it was nonetheless annoying.

Jefferson knew the student well and did not believe for a minute that she was having trouble with one of his assignments. No, he had seen her act so often before. Ever since he had started teaching at the university three years ago, the female students had been making any excuse to come see him during his office hours. They had then tried every method of seduction in the book, quickly abandoning the appearance angle after they came to understand more about his blindness. Undeterred, verbal flirting and the occasional so-called casual touching became the most popular venues. So far, Jefferson had turned them all down cold, but every year brought a new set of ambitious women willing to give it a shot. He was thankful he now had his responsibilities for Abigail, Taylor, and Matthew to use as an excuse, though this only drew sympathy from some students.

Thankful to be alone, Jefferson went on his computer and pulled up an outline for a new book he was starting. The project had first been brainstormed with a few of his colleagues shortly before Stan and Maggie's deaths. He had made some progress on his part ever since returning to the United States, but now it was time to really get to work on it once again.

Fate apparently had other plans as Jefferson's cell phone rang. He answered it while trying to keep some focus on the outline.

"Hey," Linda said. "Am I bothering you?"

"Not really," Jefferson said, the outline now forgotten. "What's up?"

"I was just wondering why you never called me. We had such a good time last Saturday, but I haven't heard from you since then. You didn't even stop to chat this morning."

"Sorry. I was in a hurry. And in regard to the calling, I've never been good at figuring out when to do that after a first date."

"Well, that's reasonable, I guess. I had a good time that night."

Jefferson smiled.

"Me too," he agreed.

"You wanna talk about that second date yet?" Linda asked mischievously.

"I don't know," Jefferson said. "Easter is around the corner. What are you doing then?"

Chapter 16

"Okay," Monique said in an annoyed tone, "this is getting ridiculous."

Actually, she thought the point of ridiculousness had passed a while back ... maybe an hour ago.

She was in her bedroom, seated in her less elaborate wheelchair and clad only in a bra and matching panties. Joan was busy going through her closet, trying to find just the right thing for her to wear for her lunch with Brad.

"It's not a date," Monique protested more than once when the nurse used that word. "And, I'm getting cold. Can we hurry up?"

Despite the fact the only other person in the room had seen her in much more compromising positions, she couldn't help feeling self-conscious. Context really did make a difference.

"You still have to look nice," Joan insisted. "You never know."

"Right now, I don't even know if I'll make it on time," Monique protested. "I'll wear anything ... anything! I'll settle for sweats at this point. Please just give me something."

Joan finally chose a light blue blouse. Since Monique absolutely refused to wear a skirt, they settled for khaki pants with a pair of sandals to complete the ensemble.

"You're making too big a fuss out of this," Monique said as Joan gave her some cereal and toast for breakfast.

"Well," Joan pointed out. "I can't come by later today to help get you ready, so I have to do it now."

"Hooray."

* * *

"Ow!" Abigail exclaimed, whining and tugging her head away. "You're hurting me."

"Do you want this done or not?" Jefferson asked, ready to abandon the project if she gave a hint she'd let it go. "Stop squirming."

They were standing in the den. Abigail had recently come across a box of her mother's hair accessories and wanted to wear some of them to school. Jefferson agreed to let her wear some of the cheaper-looking hair clips and he was now helping her get them right. Unfortunately, it wasn't going well and Jefferson was prepared to blame this on the fact he was both blind and male. Taylor, who was watching from the sidelines, was having the time of her life. Thankfully, she had opted out of having her hair accessorized by her uncle. Matthew was still upstairs, picking out what to wear that day with Anya's help.

"There," Jefferson said, adjusting the last clip. "That's as good as we're gonna get it."

Abigail didn't seem entirely happy about the hairdo.

"Go get your book bag," Jefferson instructed. "We don't wanna be late."

* * *

Mainly to avoid their comments, Monique volunteered to go out and fetch coffee for Frank, Kathy, and Samuel. The kid behind the counter of the local Starbucks didn't know her and immediately offered to help carry the cups, which were already in a cardboard carrier, but Monique politely waved him away and headed out of the store on her own. She doubted he'd be so eager once he realized it was a two-block trip.

When she was about half a block from the coffee shop, Monique was greeted by Jefferson, Presley, Abigail, Taylor, and Matthew.

"This is a nice surprise," she said. "Where are you off to?"

"School," Taylor replied.

"Some of us, at least," Jefferson added.

"Abigail?" Monique asked, noticing the hair clips she was wearing. "Who on Earth did those for you?"

Abigail, who still wasn't thrilled about the outcome of Jefferson's work, pointed directly up at her uncle. Monique laughed.

"Oh, that makes sense," she said. "You got a man's touch. That won't do. Here, let me help you out with that."

She had Jefferson take the cups of coffee and motioned for Abigail to step closer to her wheelchair. Moving her arms as carefully as she could, she proceeded to properly arrange the hair clips.

"My nurse usually does this for me when I want to wear something in my hair," she said as she worked. "I've watched her do it for so many years that I think I have a grip on the process ... okay, I think that's it ... there, now your head doesn't look like a construction site."

"Thanks Monique," Abigail said, now happier about how her hair looked.

"You're welcome. Happy to help."

Monique was all too aware about the fact she could probably never get her arms to cooperate in a way so she could do that for herself, but at least she was able to help someone else.

"Come on you guys," Jefferson said. "We need to get going. Besides, I think we've spent enough time going over the fact that I have no hair-styling skills."

"Aw, come on," Monique said. "You're a guy. It's natural for you to have no such skills."

The twins giggled.

"Thank you," Jefferson said with a smirk. "If we're done profiling me, can we get going?"

"Well, I've got to run as well," Monique said, taking the coffees back from Jefferson.

"Big day?"

"Maybe. It could be. I don't really know yet."

"Good luck."

Monique smiled, considering the possibilities today might hold.

"Thanks," she said. "Let me know if you ever need help with the girls' hair again. It's too precious to ruin."

She cast an admiring glance at the twins' long, red strands.

"I'll keep that in mind," Jefferson said as he continued on down the sidewalk, following the kids.

* * *

"Okay class," Mr. Wallace said. "As you probably remember, we won't be seeing each other again until Wednesday of next week because of the Easter holiday. I hope all of you have lots of stories for me about what you did while you were at home with your families. Maybe you went on a trip … maybe someone came to visit … maybe you just played a game you like … whatever it is, I'd like to hear about it the following week."

A low murmur rippled through the class, but Mr. Wallace called for silence again as he retrieved a stack of papers from his desk.

"I have something very neat which I want each of you to give to your parents when you get home today," he explained. "In two weeks, we will have Career Day here in our class and your parents are all invited to come in and tell us what they do when they go to work. Here, I'm gonna hand these out and then we'll get started with our reading assignments."

As he passed out the fliers, the class began talking again. Most of the students seemed interested in Career Day. Others didn't seem as interested.

Taylor sat in her seat, staring at her desk. She wordlessly took the flier from Mr. Wallace and pretended everything was fine.

* * *

When Brad Myers arrived at the Sweet Life Cafe, Monique had already secured a table for them. The staff had taken away a chair and she'd moved her wheelchair right up to the table, looking almost like any of the other patrons.

"You got in here okay?" Brad asked as he sat across from her.

"Yeah," Monique replied. "No sweat."

She hadn't dared to be fashionably late for fear that some unforeseen obstacle might arise to interfere.

They surveyed their menus, with Brad offering to hold Monique's for her.

"No, thanks," she said and began reading the long, laminated sheet of paper.

When the waitress came to take their order, Monique instructed her to bring some water and pour it into the plastic tumbler attached to her wheelchair. It took the woman a little time, but she eventually understood.

"You probably run into that a lot," Brad commented as the waitress walked away.

"Sometimes," Monique admitted. "I just handle it and let it go."

"You're so patient about it though. I don't think I could do that."

Monique managed a shrug and sought to steer the conversation away from her chair.

"What do you do when not having lunch at diners?" she asked.

"I'm an accountant," Brad explained.

"And you're out of your office during tax season? I'm not sure mine has ever left his office, period."

"I try to give myself some social time, even now. Otherwise, I'd go crazy. Plus, my father's friends with one of my firm's partners."

Monique nodded and smiled.

"So, what about you?" Brad asked. "You have a job?"

"I run a bookstore," Monique said. "I took it over after my mom retired and moved to Pennsylvania."

"That's cool. It's set up for you to get around without problems?"

"Yeah," Monique said, starting to feel off about all this, "and the other people who work there help me out when I need it, but I do pretty well on my own."

"That's cool," Brad said as their food arrived. "It's really incredible."

Monique felt a lot of adjectives were not being applied in the right way in this conversation.

* * *

"Hey Uncle Jeff," Abigail said on the walk home from school, "my teacher gave me this."

She handed Jefferson a sheet of paper.

"What's this?" Jefferson asked, taking the paper despite not seeing its text.

"It's for Career Day," Abigail explained excitedly. "Parents come to our class and tell us what they do at work."

Jefferson nodded.

"Hey Taylor?" he asked. "Did you get one of these fliers as well?"

"Uh-huh," Taylor said, keeping her eyes fixed on the sidewalk ahead of her. "It's in my backpack."

"Can you come?" Abigail asked eagerly.

"I'll have a look at this when we get home," Jefferson said. "We'll see."

* * *

"What's on the menu tonight?" Jefferson asked, coming into the kitchen where Anya was working. She usually prepared dinner before quitting at 5:30, often joining Jefferson and the kids to eat.

"Solyanka," Anya replied, her Russian accent prominent as she pronounced the dish's name.

"Sol-what now?" Jefferson asked.

"It is a thick piquant soup with beef, cabbage, smetana, pickle water, cucumbers, olives, capers, tomatoes, lemons, lemon juice, kvass, and finally, salted and pickled mushrooms."

Jefferson gaped at her, stunned.

"If you get Abigail to go near that, I'll double your pay," he said. "Heck, if you get me to go near that, I'll double your pay."

Anya gave him a mischievous grin.

"I am kidding," she confessed with a giggle. "I am making pasta with cheese sauce. I'm also baking a loaf of garlic bread to go with it. Abigail should be okay with that, if we just say it is plain bread."

She had already been subjected multiple times to Abigail's long list of foods she wouldn't touch.

Relieved, Jefferson chuckled as well. Anya had proven early on she had a sense of humor, which he had no problem with. She never overdid it, and her jokes were clean for the kids' benefit.

"You need help with anything?" Jefferson asked.

Anya shook her head. A few seconds passed in silence.

"Anya?" Jefferson queried.

"Oh, I am sorry," Anya said. "I have not remembered yet. No, I do not need any help. I am almost finished."

Jefferson nodded. There were still some minor hiccups in their system.

* * *

Taylor sat on her bed, staring at the wall. Abigail was nearby, playing with a puzzle on the floor. They both looked at Jefferson when he knocked on their open bedroom door.

"Dinner's in ten," he told them. "Abigail, we're getting those clips out of your hair before that. Come on."

Abigail did not look thrilled as she got up and walked towards her uncle.

"Hey Taylor," Jefferson said. "Is everything okay? You've been pretty quiet all afternoon."

"I'm fine," Taylor said half-heartedly.

"All right. You'll come talk to me if anything's wrong, right?"

"Uh-huh."

Jefferson decided to leave her alone and took Abigail to the bathroom to get the hair clips out.

When they were gone, Taylor got off her bed and retrieved the Career Day flier from the top of her dresser. She briefly looked at it before crumpling it up and throwing it against the wall. Then, with tears in her eyes, she hurried downstairs to where her shoes lay.

* * *

"I like them," Abigail said as she and Jefferson came out of the bathroom, her red hair now clipless. "I look pretty."

"Well, when you get older, you're not gonna be looking so pretty," Jefferson told her. "I think your dad will want me to make sure of that."

"Why?"

"I'll explain when you're older," Jefferson said, thankful the removal of the hair clips had been a lot easier than getting them in there.

They entered the girls' room, where everything was quiet. Jefferson figured Taylor was still unhappy about something and he planned to talk to her after dinner. Hopefully, he could get her to share what was bothering her.

"Come on Taylor," he prompted. "Time to wash up for dinner."

There was no response.

"Come on," Jefferson said, clapping his hands. "Let's go,"

He still got no response.

"She's not in here," Abigail reported.

"I guess she already went downstairs," Jefferson concluded. He knew she couldn't be in the bathroom because they just came from there and they hadn't passed her in the hallway.

Jefferson and Abigail went downstairs, summoning Matthew for dinner along the way.

"Where's Taylor?" Abigail asked, looking around.

"What are you talking about?" Jefferson asked, his heart rate increasing.

"She's not down here," Abigail reported as Anya poked her head out of the kitchen.

"She is not in here with me," the nanny added. "I thought she was upstairs."

"She was …" Jefferson said. "Abigail, take a look out in the backyard.

He hurried back up the stairs to check the third floor. But the doors to his bathroom, bedroom, the attic, and his office were all closed, the attic door also still being locked. A quick sweep of the other rooms proved they were empty.

Coming back downstairs, Jefferson found the basement door was locked as well. Taylor couldn't have gotten into any of those places.

"Any luck?" he asked as he came back into the den.

"She is not in my room and definitely not in the kitchen," Anya said. "I have checked again and again."

"She's not in the backyard," Abigail reported. "Her shoes aren't here either."

"What?!" Jefferson asked, alarmed. His heart rate sped up even more.

"Her shoes are gone," Abigail said. "She didn't take a jacket."

Jefferson and Anya hurried into the foyer.

"Her sneakers are gone," Anya said with a gasp.

Jefferson bolted to the front door and found it was unlocked, which was definitely not the way he had left it. He yanked the door open and hurried outside.

"TAYLOR!" he called frantically. "TAYLOR!"

Standing on his front steps, he whipped his head left and right. Where had she gone?

Chapter 17

A Police cruiser from the NYPD's 6th Precinct soon arrived at Jefferson's house. Two patrol officers began filling out a Missing Person's report, questioning Jefferson about Taylor's description and where she might have gone. Anya quickly provided a description of what Taylor was wearing before going out to check the neighborhood.

"I have no idea where she would go," Jefferson said desperately. "She doesn't really know anyone here yet."

"Have there been any problems at home?" one of the officers asked. "Sometimes it might be something minor and she is blowing it way out of proportion."

"Well, I mean, she's had some problems adjusting to the move here."

Jefferson explained the circumstances in more detail. Both officers nodded as they took notes, their pens scratching across their pads.

"It's more likely than not that she hasn't gotten far," one of them said. "We'll get word out to all patrol units in the precinct to be on the lookout. We'll just need a current photo of the girl to pass around."

Linda soon arrived to help with finding a photo that had been taken of Taylor shortly before the move. The officers took it and promised to call as soon as they knew something. They then left and Linda stayed with Jefferson. Anya came back a few minutes later, having run around the block twice in the hopes of catching up with Taylor.

"I did not find her," she said, sounding defeated. She took a deep breath and looked around.

"Where are Abigail and Matthew?" she asked.

"Upstairs," Jefferson said. "I figure they can't escape from the second floor."

Sighing in relief, Anya went upstairs to check on them anyway.

"And you can't think of any place Taylor might go?" Linda asked, sitting on the couch with Jefferson. "School maybe ... the local ice cream shop ... someone's house?"

"The school's closed," Jefferson said. "She wouldn't stay there if she found no one. Same with the ice cream shop. As for anyone she might try to visit, she doesn't know where they live. Oh God. Where did she go?"

He buried his face in his hands as Linda placed a comforting arm around his shoulders.

* * *

Monique was still in her office, giving her tax paperwork one final review before she'd file it, when Joan arrived. It took some doing but the nurse finally convinced her patient to abandon her work for the day and come upstairs for dinner.

"The others left you here?" she asked as Monique shut down her computer.

"Yeah," Monique replied. "Frank left about five minutes ago. He locked the back door on his way out, so we just have to turn off the lights and set the alarm."

The two women headed towards the front of the store. Following Monique's instructions, Joan began flipping the switches on the wall behind the cash register, turning off the lights one by one.

They both stopped when they heard a noise. It sounded like something had been knocked over.

"What was that?" Joan asked.

Monique didn't answer, considering the possibility of another intruder. But this made no sense. She'd been in her office for the past four hours with the door open. She'd have heard any unauthorized entries. Frank, Kathy, and Samuel hadn't reported any problems. Still, someone was in the store.

Monique headed down one of the aisles to investigate. If someone was here and intended to harm them, they'd have done so already. Seeing no other choice, Joan flipped a few lights back on and followed her.

Great, Monique thought, A quadriplegic and her nurse investigating a strange noise at night. That's really safe. Memories of the recent robbery were slivering into her head and she tried hard to push them back. Sure, this probably wasn't the same, but the comparisons presented themselves anyway.

The two women quietly inspected each of the aisles but found nothing. Then Monique headed into the store's children's section, where several large pillows and bean bag chairs were piled in one corner. Normally, they were laid out for the kids to sit on and read among the bookshelves. There were also some small tables and chairs meant to serve the same purpose.

Moving further, Monique saw the noise she had heard was a chair which had been knocked over. What she didn't expect to find was a little girl standing next to the fallen piece of furniture.

"Taylor?" Monique asked, recognizing the small redhead immediately.

"Hi," Taylor said in a small voice, knowing she was caught.

"Did you come here by yourself?"

Taylor gave a small nod.

"You crossed multiple streets to get here?" Monique asked, shocked. "In the dark? Do you have any idea how dangerous that is?"

Taylor looked at her feet.

"I'm sorry," she said in that same small voice.

Monique took a deep breath. This interrogation was getting her nowhere.

"It's okay," she said, nudging her chair closer. "I'm not mad at you."

Taylor looked at her, waiting to see what would happen next.

"All clear, Joan!" Monique called over her shoulder, turning her head as best she could. "Just an unexpected visitor."

Joan came over and was just as surprised to see Taylor.

"Who's this?" she asked.

"Her name's Taylor," Monique explained. "She lives near here."

Surveying the area as she spoke, she now saw the pillows and bean bag chairs which were piled into one corner so Kathy could vacuum after closing earlier. The pile had been disturbed. She guessed Taylor had snuck in shortly before Frank left and hid in the pile until she thought everyone was gone. The child's ultimate goal still remained a mystery.

"I have her uncle's number on my phone," Monique said. "It's in my office next to my computer. Go get it. He's gotta be worried sick."

Looking back at Taylor, she noticed the little girl seemed to be getting upset about something.

"Joan," she said, "hang on a second and get me out of this thing."

She slapped her palm against her chair's armrest for good measure. Joan undid the wheelchair's straps and helped Monique sit down on the floor with her back against the pile of pillows and bean bag chairs, which gave her some support. Monique then pulled Taylor over to her while the nurse went to find the number.

"Hey," she said, seeing tears welling up in Taylor's eyes, "what's wrong?"

"Uncle Jeff's gonna be mad at me," Taylor replied.

"Well, that's probably true. But I'm sure he's really worried and wondering where you are. Taylor, why did you run off from home and come here like this?"

"I don't know," Taylor whined.

"Come on. It's gotta be something. You can tell me."

Taylor began to cry.

"I want my mom and dad!" she wailed.

Oh boy, Monique thought. She vaguely knew about what was going on with this issue, but the full story was still a mystery to her. Nevertheless, Taylor was now upset and letting her see her parents was obviously not an option. As best as she could, Monique pulled Taylor close to her, speaking softly to her as she cried into her blouse.

"It's okay," she said. "It's okay. Don't be upset."

She thought of her father, but then pushed the thought aside. She needed to focus.

"Taylor," Monique said when the girl had calmed down a bit. "it's okay to miss your mom and dad, but it is not okay to run away from home because of that. I'm sure your parents wouldn't want you to do that."

"I didn't run away because of that," Taylor said.

"Then why did you?" Monique asked, wondering what else could be mixed into this mess.

Taylor hesitated before speaking.

"At school today," she explained, "the teacher told us about Career Day. That's when the parents come in and tell us what they do at work."

Monique nodded, encouraging her to continue.

"He gave us a piece of paper about it to give to our parents to invite them to come to our class," Taylor continued. "Abigail got one too for her class."

"And you're upset about this?" Monique asked. "Why?"

"Uncle Jeff is not my parents," Taylor said.

The situation was becoming clearer in Monique's head.

"You don't want him to come to Career Day because he's not your mom or dad," she concluded.

"I don't know," Taylor whined.

"Did you tell your uncle this?"

Joan returned with some tissues and the conversation was halted so both women could focus on cleaning Taylor's face.

"Your phone was ringing when I got to the office," Joan reported. "I answered it and it was this Jefferson guy. He wanted to talk to you about his niece, so I told him she was here. He's on his way."

"Okay," Monique said when they were done. "Taylor, did you tell your uncle what you just told me?"

Taylor shook her head.

"Why not?" Monique asked. The answer hit her almost immediately.

"You didn't want to hurt his feelings, right?" she asked.

Taylor nodded.

"Taylor," Monique said. "I think your uncle's feelings will be even more hurt if you don't tell him. If you're honest with him, I'm sure he would understand."

Taylor said nothing.

"I want you to tell him the truth," Monique insisted. "Can you do that for me?"

Taylor was about to answer when the group heard knocking on the front door. Figuring it had to be Jefferson, Joan went to answer it. She soon came back with Jefferson and Presley right behind her. Accompanying them was Anya, Jefferson's nanny.

"Hey," Monique said. "She's okay. She's right here next to me."

"Taylor," Jefferson said, sounding relieved.

He came over and hugged her tightly. After that, he grabbed her shoulders and held her at arm's length.

"Don't you ever do that again," he said, sounding very angry now. "Do you have any idea how much you scared me?"

Taylor was beginning to whimper. Anya seemed stunned by her boss's behavior.

"I think you need to calm down," Monique advised, but Jefferson appeared not to hear her.

"I think she is right," Anya said, taking a step forward.

But Jefferson ignored her as well.

"Do you understand how dangerous this stupid idea was?" he asked Taylor. "You could have been killed!"

"I'm sorry," Taylor said, beginning to cry again.

"You really need to calm down," Monique said. "You're upsetting her ..."

"You promised you were never going to do this again," Jefferson said, still focusing on Taylor. "Do you remember that? You promised,"

He shook her slightly.

"I'm sorry," Taylor wailed.

"That's enough!" Monique said and, with all her might, reached out and grabbed Jefferson's arm.

"Joan," she said, "take Taylor up to the front of the store and clean up her face again please. Her uncle and I are going to have a little chat."

Jefferson tried to free his arm, but Monique held on with a vice-like grip. Seeing she wasn't giving in, he let go of Taylor's shoulders and let her be led away by Joan. Recognizing the two of them were better off left alone, Anya followed Taylor and Joan.

"Okay," Monique snarled. "I don't know what sort of stress you're under, and right now, I don't care. What I care about is the fact that girl is seven years old. She understands that what she did was wrong and that you're upset with her because of it. Yelling at her isn't going to help anything."

"She's done this before," Jefferson shot back. "She's done this before, and she promised not to do it again."

"She's a kid," Monique said. "She's going to break promises and you're gonna have to forgive her for it. It doesn't matter what she's said before. Look, I'm sure that she isn't doing this specifically because of you. There's something else going on here, and you need to try to figure out what it is. And again, yelling at her isn't going to help the matter."

Jefferson mumbled something as he finally wrenched his arm free from her grip.

"Excuse me?" Monique asked.

"Stop trying to push your way into my business," Jefferson told her.

"Excuse me?!"

Monique was shocked and angry.

"You heard me," Jefferson said. "Ever since I met you, you've been trying to push your way in with the girls and Matthew. You did it just this morning."

"What?" Monique asked. "The hair clips?"

She couldn't believe this was actually an issue.

"I was just trying to help," she protested.

"Well, don't," Jefferson said. "I have enough to deal with."

"Fine. Suit yourself. But open up your thick skull long enough to let this sink in. Your niece may want to talk to you about something important in the very near future, if you haven't completely scared her out of it. When she does, listen."

Jefferson turned around and had Presley guide him away. He headed back to the front of the store, where Taylor was waiting, still whimpering slightly.

"Come on," Monique heard him say. "Let's go home."

"I'm sorry," Taylor said in that timid tone.

"I know," Jefferson replied in a flat tone. "Come on."

They left the store with Anya right behind them. Joan locked up and then went to get Monique, who was now in a very bad mood.

* * *

"Uncle Jeff?" Taylor asked as they walked down the sidewalk. "Am I still in trouble?"

They were a few blocks from the bookstore and maybe three minutes from home. It was the first time any of them spoke since leaving, with the exception of Jefferson giving Presley instructions.

"Oh yeah," Jefferson said. "You are so grounded."

"What's grounded?" Taylor asked.

"You'll learn."

Anya walked behind the pair, unsure of what to say.

* * *

"Hey," Linda said, sounding relieved as Taylor, Jefferson, Presley, and Anya came home. "Glad to have you back. Are you okay?"

Taylor responded with a single nod.

"Go up to bed," Jefferson said. "We'll talk more tomorrow."

Taylor silently disappeared up the stairs. Linda looked at Jefferson.

"Everything okay?" she asked, glancing at Anya's blank face.

"No," Jefferson admitted. "Things didn't go so smoothly at the bookstore. Right now, I just wanna get a few hours of sleep and then figure out my next move."

Linda nodded.

"Call me if you need anything," she said. "Good night."

She gave him a quick kiss on the cheek and left. After he locked the front door, Jefferson went to the couch and sat down, burying his face in his hands.

"I will go to bed as well," Anya said in a cautious tone.

Jefferson looked up at her, seeming to just realize she had been there all this time.

"Sure," he said. "I'd like to talk to you tomorrow."

"Okay," Anya replied. "Good night."

"Good night."

* * *

"Everything okay?" Joan asked.

157

Lying in her bed, Monique didn't reply as the nurse pulled the blanket over her torso.

"Don't worry about what that guy said," Joan advised. "You're not pushy. You just care. It's one of your many flaws."

"Way to make me feel better," Monique remarked.

Joan gave her a quick hug before leaving. When she was gone, Monique released a very long sigh.

* * *

Jefferson didn't get much sleep that night. He wound up being awake around five the next morning and decided to start his day early. He was in the kitchen, making coffee, when Anya came in from her morning jog.

"Good morning," she said, not sounding as cautious as the night before.

"Morning," Jefferson returned and offered her some coffee. Anya took the mug and sat down at the table. Jefferson sat down as well.

"Couldn't sleep?" he asked.

"I did sleep for some time," Anya replied.

"Lots to think about?"

Anya admitted she did think about the previous evening's events.

"Not my brightest moment," Jefferson said. "I'm sorry about how I acted. That's not me. I just got mad, and I handled it completely the wrong way."

Anya looked at him for a long time.

"It is all right," she finally said. "I have seen angry men when I lived in Russia. You are quite tame compared to them."

Jefferson did not know what to think of that.

"I understand that what happened last night was not your normal behavior," Anya continued. "It is okay."

Jefferson managed a slight smile.

"Thanks," he said. "Now I just have to talk civilly with Taylor."

"You will be fine," Anya assured him.

* * *

Taylor soon learned being grounded meant that, with the exception of meals and going to the bathroom, she was confined to her room. She argued at first but was quickly reminded of what she had done to end up being disciplined like this, after which she was quiet.

To make matters more unfortunate, Gloria Lawson, who had made a few surprise visits to the house since her initial meeting with Jefferson a month and a half ago, showed up three days before Easter. She of course learned all about Taylor's flight and subsequently interrogated Jefferson about what actions he had taken, how everything worked out, and what punishments were imposed. Throughout all this, she was always sweet to Taylor, who told her Jefferson had been mad when he had picked her up from the bookstore but that things were better now. Deciding to be honest, Jefferson admitted he had raised his voice with Taylor that night, upsetting her, and he gave her Monique's information for if she wanted to verify anything. Gloria Lawson wrote so fast that it was a wonder her notepad didn't catch fire. But since Taylor showed no signs of abuse and understood why Jefferson had been angry with her, Jefferson thought it was doubtful if this would actually hurt him. He was also sure Gloria Lawson would still try. The woman had developed a straight-forward dislike for him. But she left without taking the kids, so that was a good sign. Maybe the fact he now had Anya around played in his favor, even if the social worker had made remarks about the woman's youth and appearance.

* * *

On the afternoon after Gloria Lawson's visit, Taylor left her bedroom and went downstairs to find Jefferson cleaning up in the den. He didn't notice her until she spoke up.

"Uncle Jeff?" she asked.

"I told you to stay up in your room," he said, frustrated.

"I know, but ..."

Taylor clenched and unclenched her fists.

"But what?" Jefferson asked. "You know you're grounded."

"But ..." Taylor said, "I need to talk to you. It's important."

Jefferson was about to say something else when he stopped. Monique's last bit of advice was ringing in his head. He took a deep breath and looked at his niece.

"Come on over," he said, sitting down on the couch. "Tell me what's up."

Chapter 18

Taylor was grounded until Easter morning. Upon her release, she was instructed to get ready. They were all going out to the New York University Law School dean's home in Bay Ridge for an Easter brunch. It was an annual event where the law school's faculty and their families gathered at the dean's home for an outdoor brunch and casual socializing.

Anya was also invited, but she stated she had other plans. Jefferson had to admit he was curious who she always had plans with when she had time off, but he didn't pry. After all, it was her business and he couldn't afford to lose her.

Jefferson had invited Linda and her two kids, Jessica and David, who accepted. The group was all loaded into Linda's minivan. With Jefferson navigating, she negotiated the Manhattan and Brooklyn traffic and they soon arrived.

Sending their kids off to play with some other children, Jefferson and Linda joined the adults at the gathering, where Jefferson introduced his colleagues to his new friend.

"What?" one person asked. "You're not calling her your girlfriend?"

"We're not quite there yet," Linda said, stepping in to defend Jefferson.

The conversation soon turned to the upcoming exams, which was when Linda just held her glass and nodded politely. After all, she had been a studio art major in college and worked as a museum curator. The law had never really interested her.

But thankfully, the subject soon switched to everyone's upcoming summer plans. She was able to contribute to this conversation.

The party broke up around noon with people going home to continue with other Easter festivities. Linda drove Jefferson and the kids back to his house.

"That was fun," she said when she and Jefferson were alone in front of his door. Abigail, Matthew, and Taylor had gone inside. David and Jessica were waiting in the minivan.

"I'm glad," Jefferson said. "They seemed to like you."

"What can I say?" Linda replied. "I'm a hot single mom."

Jefferson smiled.

"You'll hear no argument from me," he said.

"So," Linda queried, "you think I can work my way up to being called your 'girlfriend'?"

"Maybe," Jefferson teased. "You still want the title?"

"I don't have to put out, do I?" Linda asked and they both laughed.

"I'll call you."

"That works."

Linda thought about kissing him, but she was sure her kids were watching from the minivan, so she decided against it.

"I'd better get going," she said instead. "Thanks again for inviting us."

She headed back to her car and Jefferson entered his house.

* * *

It seemed the New York City School District hadn't used all of its allotted snow days, and the remaining time was being added to school breaks throughout spring. Since Jefferson's Easter break was therefore one day shorter than the kids', Anya was in charge for the time he had to go to the university.

He was not entirely surprised to find some chocolate eggs waiting for him when he arrived at his office. Feeling confident they were from Paula Franks, he tossed the whole basket into the trash. He was more surprised and less thrilled to receive a visit from Gloria Lawson just a few minutes later.

"The kids aren't here," he pointed out.

"Uh-huh," Gloria Lawson said. "Where are they?"

"At home. My nanny's watching them."

He did not move to rise from behind his desk.

"Does anyone besides your nanny ever stay with the kids?" Gloria Lawson queried.

"I've hired a couple of baby-sitters on occasion," Jefferson replied. He prayed she wouldn't want to interrogate those poor teenagers.

"Are they trustworthy?"

"They're well-liked by all the families in the neighborhood, and I haven't had a problem with them."

"Do you expect a problem in the future?" Gloria Lawson asked, pouncing on his choice of words.

"No. Now, do you want to tell me why you are here, Ms. Lawson? As I've said before, the kids aren't here."

"I just want to see what sort of work you do. See how it carries over into your home life."

Gloria Lawson seemed to be more surprised that he actually had a job than anything else. Jefferson had seen this before.

"I'm a law professor," he said. "I think that's mentioned in my file. I'm sure I've told you that before."

"It is," Gloria Lawson said. "Now tell me ... have you ever had any sort of inappropriate relationship with any of your students, especially the female ones?"

"I wouldn't have this job if I did."

Jefferson hoped Paula Franks was as far from the university as possible right then. Then again, maybe these two crazy ladies ought to meet sometime, preferably with him far away during such a meeting.

"Do you date?" Gloria Lawson asked. Her tone suggested the answer ought to be "no."

"Yes, I go out when I can," Jefferson said.

"Are you seeing anyone in particular right now?" Gloria Lawson queried.

"Yes, a woman who has two kids who go to the same school as Abigail and Taylor."

Gloria Lawson narrowed her eyes suspiciously.

"She's divorced," Jefferson added, sensing her suspicion. He wondered when he could report her for this behavior.

"Would you enter into a relationship with a married woman?" Gloria Lawson asked.

"No," Jefferson said, though he thought of Amy. But that definitely did not count as a relationship.

"Would you ever become involved with the woman you hired as a nanny?" Gloria Lawson asked.

"No," Jefferson said, actually surprised she would suggest that. "Never."

"The reason I ask all this is to make sure all aspects of the children's new lives are stable. For example, a man who frequently dates one woman after another for short periods wouldn't be so suitable."

Jefferson nodded, though he was sure she was really just fishing for a reason to discredit him. He again wondered at what point he could report her and what repercussions that might bring.

"What about this woman from this bookstore that the kids seem to be so fond of?" Gloria Lawson asked. "Would you consider her?"

"I've honestly never thought about it," Jefferson said, though he was sure Gloria Lawson would not be asking about Monique if she knew

Monique was in a wheelchair. What was this woman doing anyway? Playing matchmaker? If so, for whom?

"Do the children know about your current relationship?" Gloria Lawson asked.

"No," Jefferson said. "I thought I'd wait a while to make sure it lasts before subjecting them to that."

Gloria Lawson said nothing to this.

"I have a faculty meeting to get to," Jefferson said. "Is there anything else?"

"Not at this time," Gloria Lawson said. "But expect to see me quite often until your custody hearing."

She left without another word. Jefferson packed up his briefcase and left his office as well. He was sure Gloria Lawson would try to find more ways to discredit him and take away custody of the kids, but he wasn't worried. Eric, the self-proclaimed expert on the matter of child custody cases, had told him repetitively that his lifestyle didn't offer many problems for including kids. Jefferson was certain that not even Taylor's little field trip would be enough to warrant anyone taking custody of her or the other two. No, Gloria Lawson had nothing on him, and it definitely angered her.

Nevertheless, Jefferson released a sigh as he walked. Despite not having to worry about Gloria Lawson, he had something else on his mind. He needed to take care of it, but he just didn't have the time right now to do it.

* * *

Monique was in her office, dozing in her wheelchair, when someone knocked on the door. She stirred and came to life as Kathy entered.

"What's up?" she asked.

"There's a gentleman here to see you," Kathy reported. "He says he wants to talk business."

"You can tell him I'm not interested."

Monique knew all too well the meaning of "business". But, like some people before him, this man wasn't yet ready to quit. He barged right into the small office.

"Now wait just a minute," he said in a thick southern drawl. "Don't go judging until you've heard what I've got to say."

"Kathy," Monique said, "you can go back up front. I'll take care of this."

163

Happy to leave, Kathy stepped out of the office. Monique looked at this man, who looked like he could be from Texas or Louisiana or any of those southern states. He wore a brown suit with a string tie and cowboy boots.

"So?" Monique asked, "what shouldn't I be judging before I hear it, Mr. ..."

"Teller," the man said, thrusting out a hand. "Evan Jay Teller, of Teller's Books. We're an expanding chain from McAlester, Oklahoma."

Monique accepted his hand but found the handshake to be all business, lacking any personal touch.

"And what can I do for you?" she asked.

"Your parents retired young," Evan Teller said, stating it as a simple fact.

"My father didn't. What does that have to do with anything?"

The fact her visitor claimed to have done his research and didn't seem to know this irked her.

"I'd simply like to offer you the same opportunity that your mom had," Evan Teller said.

"By buying my store and turning it into a part of your franchise," Monique concluded.

She knew all about Teller's Books. They were mainly a southern chain, but the owners were trying to expand. Their stores were actually quite similar to Monique's, but she saw them as "cookie-cutter" locations, each the same as the next while trying to put on a homey façade.

She'd gotten offers from Teller's Books before to sell her store, but she never expected the company's head to come waltzing in himself. She wondered who he might be visiting in New York as no amount of desperation would warrant such a trip just to meet with her.

"We're prepared to make you a generous offer," Evan Teller said, placing a packet of papers on Monique's desk, "and we'll of course be willing to carry over any of your employees who want to stay. Otherwise, we can make their transition to another occupation as easy as possible. You'd be able to retire anywhere with what we're offering you just for the store itself."

He slid the proposal closer to Monique, who didn't move to pick it up.

"I'm quite happy where I am," she said.

"With this offer, you'd also be able to improve your standard of living quite nicely," Evan Teller said. "I'm sure that's important to you, given your disability."

Monique narrowed her eyes.

"And who made you the expert on my disability?" she asked. "Mr. Teller, you might have done enough research on me to know it would be okay to shake my hand, but you know nothing about me. I'm happy here, as are those people you saw on your way in. I have received so many offers like yours before, and I've turned them all down. My store is doing well. People in this neighborhood like us and are therefore loyal customers. I have no intention of selling to you or anyone else. Now, if you'll excuse me, I have to manage my store. You can show yourself out."

"If you could at least look over my proposal, I'd greatly appreciate it," Evan Teller said, clearly determined not to walk away yet. "My numbers are on the cover sheet. Thank you for your time."

He left without another word. Monique waited a few minutes in silence. She then picked up the proposal packet and pushed it through her shredder.

Chapter 19

As Monique ate breakfast, the phone in the kitchen rang. Joan answered it. After briefly speaking with the caller, she looked over at Monique.

"It's for you," she reported. "A Mr. Brad Myers."

Monique nodded and Joan held the phone to her ear so she could speak.

"Hey," Brad said. "How are you doing?"

"I'm good," Monique replied.

"That's good. Listen, I was just wondering if you'd maybe like to get some dinner this Thursday night. There's this great seafood restaurant that's completely wheelchair accessible. Osteria 57 … it's on West 57th. Would you be interested?"

"Sure," Monique said, deciding to give him another chance despite the fact he seemed to be a little too focused on her disability. After all, he called her, which put him far ahead of many men she'd encountered.

They took a minute to finalize the arrangements before Monique signaled for Joan to hang up.

"Anything I should know?" the nurse asked.

"Yeah," Monique said. "I need you to come see me twice this Thursday evening."

* * *

Jefferson entered his office and found a message from Paula Franks on his voice mail. Hearing it made him be thankful that, unlike some of his colleagues, he did not give his cell phone number to his students. With such information, Paula Franks would probably never leave him alone.

Paula Franks's message was straight-forward. Since he only had office hours that morning and no classes, she wanted to have a long lunch with him. Jefferson deleted the message and leaned back in his chair.

Jefferson did not think of himself as the poster boy for scruples, but he liked to think he had some. So, apart from the fact he'd definitely be fired if he were caught, he did not date his students, past or present, seeing such an action as inappropriate. Paula Franks was unwilling to accept that, so it had come to the point where she continued to persist and he continued to blow off her advances. True, she was an intelligent and attractive woman, assuming Eric's description of her was accurate. And, if she weren't a student and he didn't know how absolutely persnickety she was, he would definitely consider dating her. Jefferson chuckled at this thought. It was like needing to prove all of a law's elements in order to apply it in a case.

Jefferson was sure the woman would stop by later to see if he got her message. Thankfully, he actually had other plans for later that day, so he could easily play that card if his usual refusals didn't work. If he was really lucky, he wouldn't be there when she came around.

* * *

"Hey orphans!" a boy called.

Abigail and Taylor, both having heard this line before, ignored it and continued with their game. A few of the girls they were playing with looked up, but seeing no reaction from the twins, didn't do any more. The boy, seeing his best attempt wasn't working, gave up and walked away as recess continued.

* * *

Monique was on her computer, reviewing an order she was making with a publisher. She double-checked the store's inventory records and then finalized the purchase.

As she was reading the publisher's confirmation e-mail, someone knocked on her door. She called for the person to enter, thinking it was either Kathy, Frank, or Samuel. She was not expecting to see Jefferson Thomas walking in with Presley by his side.

"Can I help you?" she asked suspiciously. "The books are out there."

"Can we talk?" Jefferson asked.

"About what?"

"Please."

He seemed genuine, so Monique gave in.

"Pull up a chair," she instructed. "It's right in front of you. And shut the door."

Jefferson did so.

"What's up?" Monique queried, not in the mood for a drawn-out conversation.

"I want to apologize," Jefferson said. "The other night … I was out of line. I shouldn't have been so rough with Taylor … and I shouldn't have rejected your attempts to help. I'm sorry."

Monique had definitely not seen this coming. For a few moments, she was speechless.

"Okay," she finally said. "I guess I have to apologize as well."

"For what?" Jefferson queried.

"I just wanted to help. I don't know … when I first met you and then learned your story, I thought you were doing so well … and I didn't want to see it fall apart. I butted in too much. I'm sorry."

"That's okay."

"How's Taylor doing?"

"She's good. She understands what she did was wrong and she's sorry. Grounding her for a few days did help."

Monique said nothing, waiting to see if there was more.

"She told me about Career Day," Jefferson added. "She said she wasn't sure if she wanted me to come. So, you were right about me needing to listen."

"What are you gonna do?" Monique asked.

"I figure I'll wait to see if she makes up her mind. I'll sign myself up with her teacher, and I can simply take myself off if she doesn't want me there. I'm going to Abigail's class that day anyway, so I'll be in the neighborhood regardless."

"That's good. Are you okay?"

"I guess," Jefferson said, taking a deep breath. "I guess I'm still getting used to playing the parent role as much as they're getting used to having me in it."

"The other two seem to be okay."

"I figure they just adjust faster."

Monique nodded.

"I hope you guys all come back soon," she said.

"Thanks," Jefferson said. "I'd better get going."

Monique nodded as he got up and headed to the door. He stopped with his hand on the handle and looked back at her.

"Hey," he said, "you would say we're friends, would you?

"I suppose," Monique admitted. They'd chatted often enough when he and the kids came to the bookstore and the topics were sometimes about more than just books.

"Then how come we've never hung out outside of this place or our random meetings on the street?" Jefferson asked.

"I don't know," Monique replied with the best shrug she could manage. "I guess we should though."

"Yeah. How about we do lunch sometime?"

"Sure. We could work something out."

Jefferson nodded, bid her a good day, and left. He left the door open and Monique stared through the doorway long after he'd disappeared.

* * *

That Thursday evening, after making sure the front door was locked, Monique bid Joan farewell and moved her wheelchair up into the ramp in too the accessible taxi. The driver secured the chair and then rejoined the traffic, executing smooth maneuvers despite the usual mayhem around them.

The drive over to Osteria 57 took about fifteen minutes. Brad Myers was waiting by the front doors, which he immediately held open for Monique when she arrived.

"You look nice," he said as they waited for their table.

"Thank you," Monique said with a smile. It was nice to hear a complement from him that didn't involve her disability.

A waitress came by in just a couple of minutes to let them know their table was ready. Brad offered to push her wheelchair, an offer Monique politely declined. She also ignored the people staring at her as they were escorted through the dining area. Rather than try to hand Monique the menu, the waitress simply put it down on the table in front of her.

"You want me to read you this?" Brad asked, picking up his own menu.

"No," Monique said. "I've got it."

Managing to keep control of her arms, she began scanning the menu. She knew it would not play in her favor if her arms suddenly now decided to spasm and go off on their own accord. Brad was already seeing her like a fragile china doll. He didn't seem to remember her successfully reading the menu and ordering her own lunch at the Sweet Life Cafe.

"That's pretty cool," Brad commented, watching her read the menu.

Monique ignored him as she tried to decide between the tilapia and the swordfish.

The waitress returned to take their drink orders, at which point Monique had her take the plastic tumbler off her wheelchair to fill with the wine she ordered. Thankfully, this woman took only a few seconds to get it and headed back to the kitchen again, tumbler in hand.

"You said you were a quadriplegic, right?" Brad asked.

"I am," Monique said, not bothered by talking about it but nonetheless wondering how it had suddenly come up.

"But you can move your arms. I thought that wasn't possible."

"Quadriplegia is defined by the location on the spine that's effected, not by what you can still move," Monique clarified, seeing this misconception quite often. "I'm what's called a C6 quadriplegic, and I'm blessed I still have the use of my arms."

"Then what's the difference between you and a paraplegic?"

"The location on my spine where the injury effected it. If it was just a few vertebrae further down, I'd be considered a paraplegic,"

Brad nodded. Monique was sure he had done a little research to learn the very basics, but he had only done the basic research. But she wouldn't hold that against him. After all, it was more than some of the other guys she had gone out with. She supposed that, maybe, this was actually a second date.

Their drinks soon arrived with the waitress reattaching the tumbler and inserting the straw as Monique instructed. They then gave her their dinner orders and she disappeared again.

"I'm guessing a toast is out of the question," Monique said, nodding to the tumbler now situated over her shoulder, secured to the wheelchair and immovable.

Brad hesitated and then laughed slightly, realizing she was joking.

* * *

The phone rang and Jefferson got up to answer it. The caller turned out to be Linda, who wanted to chat since all the kids were asleep.

"About what?" Jefferson queried.

"About where you wanna go for dinner this Saturday night," Linda said. "And if you want dessert at my house afterwards."

They had planned to go out again that coming Saturday night, so the first half of that statement came as no surprise to Jefferson. The second half surprised him, and he dared to consider the possibilities.

"There's a good Thai place not far away," he said. "GAllanga. As for dessert, I'd still have to be home by eleven to relieve the baby-sitter."

He figured he would not interfere with Anya's evenings yet. He still had no clue where she went so often every week.

"That sounds good," Linda said. "Though I must say I don't think I've ever gotten the baby-sitter excuse from a man when I've offered sex."

"Oh, was that what you were offering?" Jefferson retorted, relieved to hear his assumptions being affirmed. "Well, it's the truth."

"I know. But hear this ... one day soon, I'm going to fulfill that craving I know you have."

"I look forward to that."

* * *

Joan was already waiting in the apartment when Monique came out of the elevator. Since she had eaten, they proceeded straight to her bedroom, where Joan helped her get undressed.

"So how was it?" the nurse asked.

"All right," Monique said. "He is still having trouble looking past the fact I'm in this chair. He didn't even try to kiss me good-night ... he didn't try anything for that matter."

"Maybe he's a gentleman."

"No, there are gentlemen, and then there's guys like him. He practically wants to keep me sterile."

"Give it time."

Monique sighed.

"I guess so," she agreed. "I mean, he's stuck around this long. That's saying something."

But the reality was that she wanted someone who did more than just stick around. While she wasn't looking for the childish passion she had in college, she wanted some sort of intimacy. She was a woman after all. She wasn't sterile.

Chapter 20

Monique entered the Starbucks on 6th Avenue and was recognized and greeted by a barista while she was still more than ten feet from the counter.

"The usual? Ms. Vasquez?" the young woman queried, her fingers already hovering over the register's keyboard.

"No," Monique replied. "Thank you."

She spotted Jefferson, who'd secured a small table with Presley lying underneath it. She moved towards them.

"So, no coffee yet?" she queried after they'd exchanged greetings.

"I'm blind, remember?" Jefferson asked with a smirk. "How am I supposed to order anything if I don't know what's on the menu?"

"Well, you do realize we're in a Starbucks coffee shop, right?" Monique asked. "I hear they generally serve coffee."

She proceeded to read from the nearby menu board.

"You're going up there and getting the coffee," she insisted when she'd finished. "I'm in a wheelchair, remember? I'll have a small cappuccino in my tumbler and one of those lemon cake slices."

"What tumbler?" Jefferson asked.

Monique told him where it was and how to get it off her wheelchair before sending him on his way. Unfortunately, her day turned out to be busier than she had anticipated. Therefore, they weren't able to meet up for lunch as planned. They settled for coffee instead. Thankfully, the fact Jefferson only had to go into work on Monday mornings made his schedule considerably more flexible than hers, so they still found a time which worked for them both.

"There you are," Jefferson said when he came back, reattaching the tumbler as Monique instructed and setting the lemon cake down in front of her. "So, how was your weekend?"

"Is that what this friendship will amount to?" Monique asked. "A talk-about-the-weather question like that? I thought you were deeper."

"Okay? "what should I ask?"

"Why I switched out our lunch for coffee would be a nice start."

Jefferson raised an eyebrow.

"You said you had to work," he countered.

"Yeah, but I might want to elaborate," Monique pointed out. "Don't assume, Jefferson Thomas."

"All right. Why did you have to change our lunch to coffee?"

"I have a lot of work I need to get done."

Jefferson looked dumbfounded.

"I never said I would elaborate," Monique pointed out. "I thought you were a lawyer."

"Very funny," Jefferson said. "So, how's your life outside the store? How's Mr. Wonderful?"

He'd heard about Brad Myers through their recent telephone conversations.

"I wouldn't brand him that just yet," Monique admitted. "He's still got some work to do."

"You don't think there's a future there?" Jefferson queried.

"I don't know. I would like to think there could be. I mean, I'm not planning the wedding or anything, but I don't want to pass a Dead-End sign on day one."

Jefferson nodded.

"In all honesty, I believe in true love," Monique said. "I think it's possible. What I don't believe in is love at first sight. I think that concept is ridiculous. I mean, if you love someone when you first meet them, what is there to work up to?"

"I guess that makes sense," Jefferson said. "Given your premise, you think this guy you're seeing now could maybe be someone you could fall in love with?"

"I don't know. I think he first has to work past the fact I'm strapped into this chair."

"Ah. I had that in college and law school. Supposedly people grow up, but I haven't always seen proof of that."

"how many were there in college?" Monique said, pouncing on the opportunity with a mischievous grin.

"Three," Jefferson replied. "Then there were two more in law school and two after that before I met my then-girlfriend Nancy."

"Really? Are you still seeing her?"

"We broke up last March," Jefferson said.

Monique was surprised.

"Oh," she said. "That's … recent. After what … five years? Are you okay?"

"Yeah, I'm fine," Jefferson replied.

"But five years … you invested so much in it …"

173

"I did, but then I saw her for what she really was. I broke away clean."

"It took you five years?"

Now, Monique was astonished.

"I was blind for a long time," Jefferson said.

Monique decided to ignore his choice of words for the time being.

"For a while, I thought she was perfect because I had unwittingly molded myself to be perfect for her," Jefferson clarified.

"And now you're the real you again?" Monique asked.

"I think so."

"Well, I don't think I'd wanna meet that other you. You're fine."

"Thanks."

"Are you seeing anyone now?" Monique asked, expecting him to say "no."

"This woman I know through the girls' school. We've gone out a couple times."

"That's getting back on the horse pretty quickly."

"Well, my only regret about being with Nancy so long is not getting out sooner," Jefferson said, working to push the memory of Amy out of his head. "Otherwise, I've got nothing about it holding me back."

"Five years though," Monique contemplated. "That's not bad. The longest I had was three years with a guy in college. He was pretty much my only one in college."

"What happened there?"

"He went off to graduate school in Houston."

"Houston, Texas?"

"Yeah. What else would I mean?"

"There's a Houston, Idaho."

"That's Huston, Idaho, not Houston."

"Oh."

Jefferson was momentarily sheepish. Monique waved it off.

"He kind of expected me to follow him," she explained, "but I had my heart set on coming back here and eventually taking over the family business. Last I heard, he's married with a little boy."

Jefferson nodded.

"See," Monique said. "This is a real conversation. None of this how-was-your-weekend junk."

* * *

Jefferson left the coffee shop about thirty minutes later and headed home. As he walked, his cell phone rang.

"Hello?" he asked.

"Hey," Linda said. "Listen, I've got a bit of a situation here at my house."

"What's that?" Jefferson asked, concerned.

"Well," Linda said, her tone of voice suddenly changing to a more mischievous nature, "there is a naked woman in my bed and she's lonely."

Jefferson smiled.

"And what can I do about that?" he asked, playing along to see what else she might say. The implication seemed pretty obvious, but he'd made so many mistakes with the opposite gender, he wanted it to be more than obvious.

"You know where I keep my spare key and you've got a few hours before you have to pick up your kids from school and day care," Linda replied. "I'm sure you can figure something out."

Jefferson supposed he could.

* * *

"How was your date?" Frank asked as Monique came into the store. A customer who had been paying for some books looked over with interest.

"It was coffee," Monique said. "It wasn't a date."

Frank waited for the customer to pay and leave before pouncing on Monique again.

"Well, the crumb on your lower lip suggests it was more than coffee," he said with a smirk.

Monique found and picked the crumb off her lip. She flicked it in his direction, but her aim wound up being wildly off.

"I had some lemon cake," she said. "I didn't make out with the guy."

"Right," Frank said, still smirking. He really enjoyed tormenting her like this.

"I've got work to do," Monique said. "If there are any more stupid comments anyone would like to submit, here's your last chance."

Frank couldn't think of anything else. Nor could Kathy or Samuel, though the latter had never made a snarky remark to Monique since being hired.

With no one saying anything else, Monique headed back to her office.

"You are an interesting man," Linda commented, turning her head to look at Jefferson, who was lying next to her on the bed. "It takes me until our third date to get you to kiss me and, just two days later, you're more than willing to accept my booty call."

"I like to work in mysterious ways," Jefferson told her.

Linda smiled.

"Well, they bring excellent results," she commented.

Jefferson leaned forward and kissed her.

"We've got about an hour and a half before school lets out," Linda said, pulling the covers up over her nude body. "I'm going to take a nap. You're more than welcome to stay. Otherwise, lock up on the way out."

* * *

Jefferson did stay and also took a nap in Linda's bed. They then showered, got dressed, and took an Uber over to the Tate Sunshine Day Care Center together. Linda waited outside while Jefferson picked up Matthew. when questioned, they explained to the boy they had met up and decided to walk together. Both were thankful he was too young to make other, more accurate conclusions.

* * *

As Monique worked in her office, Brad Myers called. He explained that a client of his firm had given them a bundle of tickets to a gala at the Natural History Museum that was set for the coming Friday. He'd snagged two and wanted to know if she would like to go.

"Sure," Monique agreed. "that sounds like fun. I've always liked that museum."

"Great," Brad said. "I'll see you at eight."

Monique ended the call and leaned her head back against her chair. I'm giving him a chance, she thought. Maybe it would work out.

* * *

"And that's what a veterinarian does," the father at the front of the class said, finishing his speech.

At Ms. Turner's prompting, the class gave him a round of applause.

"Now, we have one more guest who's going to speak to us before we go to lunch," Ms. Turner said. "Abigail's uncle, Mr. Jefferson Thomas, is here to tell us what he does. Let's all give him a big hand."

Everyone clapped and Jefferson, despite being blind, was sure Abigail was absolutely giddy about this whole thing. She had never had a problem with Career Day, which probably could have come along much sooner in her mind. But it was scheduled for the second Wednesday after Easter, and now that it was here, so was he.

"Hi everyone," he said. "I'm Abigail's uncle and I am a law professor. Basically, it's my job to teach people how to tell the difference between right and wrong. If you think about it, I'm a bit like your teacher, except my students are all a lot older than you guys and they have to work while they go to school."

"Why?" one boy asked.

"Well, many of them don't live at home anymore," Jefferson said. "They have to take care of themselves when they're that old."

The students all seemed dumbstruck by this possibility, certain it would never happen to them.

"Any other questions?" Jefferson asked.

"You're Abigail's uncle, right?" the same boy asked.

"I am," Jefferson said, not sure if he liked where this was going.

"Where's her mom and dad?"

Jefferson saw this coming, and he had no clue what to say without causing some form of a disturbance. How was it harder to deal with kids than opposing litigators?

Luckily, Ms. Turner stepped in right then.

"Class," she admonished. "Mr. Thomas is here to talk about his job. So, if there are any questions about that, feel free to ask them. Otherwise, keep it to yourself."

Jefferson answered a few more questions before the class aide, Ms. Harris, came to take the students to lunch. As the class lined up, a few students went to greet their parents and Abigail came over to Jefferson.

"Hey," Jefferson said. "you liked that?"

"Yeah," Abigail said. "Thanks for coming, Uncle Jeff."

"No problem. Enjoy your lunch."

As Abigail left the classroom, Jefferson approached Ms. Turner.

"I'm sorry that almost got ugly," the teacher said.

"Don't worry about it," Jefferson assured her. "Thanks for the backup."

"Not at all. It's part of my job description."

"Which is why I'll stick to teaching at a university. How's Abigail doing?"

"She's adjusting well. A lot of the students like her, and she always has some exciting stories to share

."I guess it pays to be the daughter of someone who works for the State Department."

"I guess so."

* * *

Monique was about ready to kill herself. She had spent the last four days reviewing the store's inventory and placing orders based on her findings and it's financial standing. She had sometimes had to go through the store until her wheelchair battery threatened to die on her in order to check the shelves. Meanwhile, the others were moving through the storeroom upstairs. She hated this part of her job, but she had to get it done a few times every year, even if she wished to shoot herself every time.

Deciding to take a break, Monique reached for the headset by the phone and put it on, always preferring it over handling the receiver. She adjusted the microphone and voice-dialed a number.

* * *

Having brought along Anya's egg salad wrap for lunch, Jefferson sat on a bench not far from the girls' school, eating it while Presley looked on with jealousy. Even the dog recognized Anya's culinary skills, and she only had the scents as a basis to form her opinion.

Jefferson interrupted his meal when his phone rang.

"Hello?" he asked.

"Hey," Monique said. "how's Career Day going?"

"So far, so good. One down."

"And what about the other?"

"I don't think it's going to happen. I don't think Taylor wants it."

"Don't worry about it. Give her time. Maybe next year."

"Yeah. I just worry about when Matthew's in elementary school as well. Then I'll have to juggle all three of them."

"You'll manage. You've done good so far."

"Yeah, but I'm pretty sure all three of them would prefer my brother and sister-in-law."

Monique sighed over the phone.

178

"That's probably true," she admitted, "but this isn't a perfect world. You just remember that you stepped up when they needed someone. That's what'll count in the long run."

"Thanks," Jefferson said.

"And let me know if you ever need advice or help with something. Believe me, I am stripped naked and put in the shower by someone else every morning. I'm the last person who would look down on you for asking for help."

"Thanks," Jefferson repeated.

"Just putting it out there."

"I appreciate it. I've gotta see about this Career Day thing with Taylor. Consider it the 11th hour."

"Good luck."

Jefferson hung up, wrapped up the remainder of his food, and packed everything away again.

* * *

"Hello?" Jefferson asked. "Mr. Wallace?"

Mr. Wallace looked up from his computer and immediately came over.

"Taylor's uncle I presume," he said. "The dog gave it away. I've heard plenty of stories about you two."

"Glad to know I have a fan," Jefferson said. "Listen, I'm here about Career Day ... I don't think it's going to happen ... Taylor just doesn't seem comfortable with the idea just yet."

Mr. Wallace nodded.

"I understand," he said.

"How's she doing in here otherwise?" Jefferson queried.

"She is a bright girl ... no argument about that. She will only answer questions every so often, but her assignments are all very well done."

"I can take no credit for that. How's she doing socially?"

"Well, except for me and two or three other students, she doesn't really talk to anyone. I try to get her to interact with others through group projects, but she will only participate as much as she has to."

The teacher thought for a moment.

"She does stick to her sister and her friends during recess," he added. "One of the aides mentioned it to me once. Maybe she has some friends there. There is one boy I've heard about who's been calling her an 'orphan', but as far as the aides have seen, both girls are ignoring him. One of them has spoken to him about it and it hasn't happened that often yet. The thing is … Taylor hasn't said anything to me about it. I don't want to push her and make her feel uncomfortable."

"She hasn't said anything to me either," Jefferson echoed.

"Then I think the best thing we can do is monitor the situation and step in if it persists or escalates."

Jefferson nodded.

"Thank you," he said. "I'd better get going."

"Sure," Mr. Wallace agreed. "I'm sorry it didn't work out today."

"Don't worry about it," Jefferson told him and left.

* * *

Not far from the classroom, Jefferson heard a group of students approaching. He stopped and stepped up against the wall to let them pass, trying to figure out how this changed his perspective of the directions he'd been given earlier and was now tracing back to the school's front door.

"Uncle Jeff?" someone asked.

He was surprised to hear Taylor addressing him but then figured this had to be her class. They were heading in the direction of her classroom.

"What are you doing here?" Taylor asked, coming over to him.

"I just went to speak to your teacher," Jefferson explained. "Listen. I'm not going to stick around for Career Day today. Is that cool with you?"

"Uh-huh," Taylor replied, and he was sure he heard relief in her voice. "Is it okay with you?"

"Oh yeah. I'm fine. I'll pick you up this afternoon as usual."

"Okay."

She really did sound okay with this arrangement.

"All right," Jefferson said. "Go catch up with your class. Maybe I'll come speak to them next year."

"Uh-huh," Taylor said and kept walking.

Jefferson kept walking the other way and soon ran into Linda. She had been speaking to her daughter Jessica's class about working as a museum curator.

"You're not sticking around for the second class?" she asked.

"Not this year," Jefferson replied. "Taylor's not up for that. I just spoke with her."

"Oh," Linda said, understanding. "Maybe next year."

Jefferson nodded.

"So," Linda said, her voice taking on a mischievous tone, "we've got the afternoon off. What should we do?"

Chapter 21

"Uncle Jeff!"

Jefferson, who had been getting ready for work in his bedroom, stopped when he heard the blood-curdling scream from below. With his shirt half-buttoned and only one sock on, he hurried to investigate.

He ran into Abigail on the second floor. She was running up to her bedroom as fast as she could, Anya not far behind.

"What's wrong?" Jefferson asked, managing to stop the little girl.

"There's a monster outside!" Abigail wailed, trying to keep running.

"A monster?"

"I have been in the kitchen, making lunches," Anya reported. "I do not know what she means. There is someone in the yard. The one you told me would come, I believe."

"No," Abigail insisted. "It's a monster. In the backyard."

"All right," Jefferson told her. "I'll go take a look."

He let her hurry off to her bedroom and continued on downstairs, fixing his shirt along the way. He crossed through the den to the rear sliding door.

"Hello?!" he called, opening it and stepping onto the patio.

"Oh hey, Mr. Thomas," someone responded. "It's Craig from Poop-and-Scoop. I came early today because we're trying to beat a bad storm that's supposed to come later."

"Oh okay," Jefferson said, now understanding. "My niece saw you and panicked."

He'd gotten a text from the company early that morning and had updated Anya. He hadn't thought to update the kids.

"Sorry about that," Craig said. "I forgot you once mentioned you now had some kids living with you."

"No problem," Jefferson said, heading back inside. "You have a good day."

He first explained the situation to Anya, who had met Craig on previous occasions as he normally came when the kids were in school. She relaxed, finding the circumstances somewhat amusing.

"I suppose a child might find that uniform scary," she concluded, looking out at the man as he worked. "I have never thought about it."

Jefferson nodded in agreement. He knew the Poop-and-Scoop employees wore thick, dark-colored overalls, matching gloves and caps, and facemasks. How there wasn't a rash of heat strokes among them during the summer was a mystery.

Jefferson went back upstairs and found Abigail hiding in her closet. Once he convinced her to come out, he was able to explain what was going on. Craig was from Poop-and-Scoop, a service which came to the house once a week to clean up Presley's business in the small backyard. To do this, they wore thick coveralls and had a vacuum-like device strapped on to their back, giving them an unusual appearance, possibly making a child think they were seeing a monster.

"But there's no monster," Jefferson said. "I swear."

Abigail seemed to accept this explanation and calmed down.

"Come on," Jefferson told her. "We've gotta finish getting ready or we'll be late."

He hoped that, in his haste to respond to her earlier cries, he hadn't knocked his other sock off his bed. That would only delay him further.

* * *

"Hello," Joan said, entering the bookstore. "I thought you might want to do some standing up for a while."

"Okay, sure," Monique agreed.

"Where are Frank and Kathy?" Joan asked as she moved the standing frame into place behind the cash register. She would be needing help from at least one of them to get Monique up into it.

"Frank has an appointment to get new glasses," Monique explained. "And Kathy's daughter is visiting from Ohio. Given this gathering of random luck, I'm a bit short-staffed today."

"Is anyone else here?" Joan asked. She almost immediately noticed the twinkle in Monique's eye.

"Samuel!" Monique called.

The young man emerged from between the shelves.

"Hey Samuel," Monique said. "Joan wants to get me up into my standing frame. She needs a second set of hands though. You wanna help her out?"

"Em ... sure," Samuel said, hesitating. "What would I have to do?"

"Come on around here," Joan said as she started to undo the straps holding Monique in her wheelchair. "Grab her shoulder and keep her sitting up while I get the straps on her legs."

Samuel did so and was not prepared for when Monique's upper body fell forward, no longer supported by the straps. He quickly pulled her back up and tightened his grip.

"Didn't see that coming, did you?" Joan asked with a grin.

Samuel said nothing as she undid the last ankle strap.

"Okay," Joan instructed, "put your hands under her arm there. Get a good grip on her. On my mark, we're gonna lift her into a standing position and get her over into the frame. Get her shoulder into the molded foam and hold her there until I can get her strapped in. Got it?"

"Yeah, I think so," Samuel said.

"All right. Lift her up ... now."

They lifted Monique out of the chair and maneuvered her around to the frame. As he lifted her a little higher in order to get her shoulder into the mold, Samuel let out an involuntary grunt.

"Heavy, isn't she?" Joan asked as she began strapping Monique in.

Samuel didn't reply, probably out of fear for losing his job.

"Relax," Monique told him with a nod in Joan's direction. "I'm more likely to fire her first."

Samuel still said nothing as Joan came over to his side and continued securing the straps over Monique's torso and legs.

"You can let go now," the nurse said about a minute later, tightening the last strap over Monique's shoulder. "She's all set."

"Yes," Monique added. "I'm one step from becoming Hannibal Lecter."

Samuel let go of Monique's shoulder and stepped back. At Joan's instruction, he moved Monique's wheelchair aside so no one fell over it if they wanted to get to the register. He then headed back into the shelves.

"Hey," Monique said. "Thanks."

Samuel glanced back and nodded before he disappeared.

"He's still nervous around you," Joan remarked in a whisper.

"He's learning," Monique said. "This was a nice lesson for him."

Joan nodded in agreement.

* * *

"There you are," Joan said. "Professional and sexy all rolled into one."

Monique, who still refused the idea of wearing one of the few skirts she owned, looked at herself in her bedroom's full-length mirror and felt she had to agree. True, the straps across her slack-covered legs looked a bit off, but she would have to live with that. And besides, Joan had done a good job with making sure everything looked right. And, there was always the hope the blouse and jacket Monique was wearing would distract anyone from noticing her legs too much. The white blouse wasn't that revealing, but its shimmering threads did draw attention upwards.

"You're gonna knock his socks off tonight," Joan told her.

Monique hoped so.

* * *

The taxi pulled up to the Natural History Museum's main entrance and Monique was unloaded and, at her insistence, left to fend for herself. She headed inside, finding Brad waiting for her in the lobby. The way he looked at her gave her hope that he maybe saw her as more than just a person in a wheelchair. There was definitely a hint of lust in his eyes as he surveyed her.

"Hey," he said.

"Hello," Monique replied.

"You look nice."

Monique couldn't help beaming.

They headed over to where a museum employee was checking tickets for the gala, which was immediately followed by a security checkpoint.

"Ma'am," one of the security guards said. "we'll need to check your chair. Can you walk at all?"

"No, she can't," Brad said just as Monique was opening her mouth.

"All right," the guard said, speaking directly to Brad now. "I'll need to wand her and the chair."

Brad nodded and the guard set to work while Monique sat quietly, absorbing the scene and fuming.

Eventually, neither Monique nor her chair were considered a threat and they were allowed to move on into the gala itself. With Brad leading the way, they mixed into the crowd standing around and talking or looking at exhibits set out for the event.

Brad soon located some of his colleagues and introduced them to Monique, assuring a few of them she could shake hands.

"I can speak for myself," she told him as quietly as possible while still being sure he could hear her, but he didn't seem to be listening.

"So, Monique," one of his colleagues said, "do you work?"

"Yes," Monique replied, keeping her emotions in check. "I run a bookstore."

She hated it when people assumed she didn't work due to being disabled. The attire she was wearing cost almost a thousand dollars. That ought to be an indicator.

"She does it well too," Brad said. "She's got it all set up so she can get around by herself."

How would you know? Monique thought with some bitterness. he'd never been to her store.

But she held her tongue.

A waiter came by, offering champagne. Taking over again, Brad quickly told him to pour the contents of one glass into the plastic tumbler on Monique's wheelchair. As he did this, the waiter nudged the straw askew. As Monique raised her hand to readjust it, Brad reached over and pushed it back.

"Thanks," she said somewhat coldly. She told herself to relax and have the drink. After all, Brad was clearly no longer worried about offending her. He had moved on to believing she was incapable of doing anything. Wonderful, she thought, sipping her champagne. For one brief moment upon her arrival, she'd considered the possibility of them going to bed together. That seemed so long ago now.

Brad and his friends began talking about work, and though Monique had taken a few accounting and finance classes in college, she was quickly uninterested and turned her attention to one of the nearby glass cases. It contained a stuffed monkey. Despite never having been much of a history or science buff, Monique was nevertheless interested and moved in for a closer look. Reading the plaque below the case, she learned that the monkey was in fact a howler monkey. The brief blurb went on to explain a bit about the species, but Monique quickly grew bored and looked at the monkey itself, sure she had seen photos of the animal before. Another waiter came by and offered her a bruschetta, which she took and ate while admiring the exhibit. A few minutes later, Brad came over.

"We're moving over to the other room," he told her. "You wanna come?"

"Sure," Monique said, deciding to take a chance. "Listen. Don't always speak for me. I can express myself, all right?"

Brad almost looked offended by her request.

"I'm just trying to help," he said.

"I know," Monique said, "but I'm a big girl. I've been living like this for over thirty years. I know what I'm doing."

"Sure. Okay."

Monique smiled.

"Thanks," she said. "Let's go."

Feeling better, she followed him into another room, which had more visitors and more exhibits. She got a refill on her champagne while she examined a few more items in glass cases and continued to mingle. Brad was busy talking to colleagues or clients and thankfully not treating Monique like an incapable moving statue. She was beginning to enjoy his company again.

Soon, everyone's attention was directed towards a nearby podium, where a gray-haired, bespectacled gentleman wearing a tuxedo was preparing to address the crowd.

"Some hotshot from the museum," Brad explained in a low voice. "It's time to thank all the big donors."

Monique nodded, half-listening to the man's speech. It was pretty boring, and she hadn't contributed anything to the museum.

After the speech and promises of more speakers to come during the night, the guests all began talking with one another again and Brad found a friend of his who worked at the museum. He introduced him to Monique, calling her his guest.

"So, you're his special lady," Brad's friend, Wade Swane, remarked. "He's said good things about you."

"Did he now?" Monique asked with a smile.

"I bet he helps you out with all sorts of things, right? I mean, strapped in that chair all day, it's gotta be a nightmare to get a thing done. Good thing you've got my boy Brad now."

To her horror, Monique noticed Brad chuckle along with his friend as he received a pat on his shoulder.

"I manage just fine," she said, keeping herself in check.

But they weren't listening, instead talking about a recent baseball game. In a split-second decision, Monique turned her chair around and headed for the exit, pushing her joystick forward a little harder than necessary. Thankfully, while people did notice her as she made her way through the crowd, no one really paid her any mind except to step out of her way.

She made it outside and managed to pull her cell phone out of her jacket pocket. Why had she allowed it to be put there to begin with?

Not wanting to risk waiting for a wheelchair-accessible Uber she summoned at the last minute, she dialed the number of a cab company and waited. A part of her wondered if Brad had noticed her absence yet and hoping he wouldn't until she was gone.

When an operator finally answered, Monique gave him her location and stated that she was in a wheelchair. After giving a few more bits of information, including her cell phone number, Monique hung up and waited anxiously, wanting to go home. She noticed there was some champagne left in her tumbler. She began drinking it, watching the traffic go by and noting the many yellow cabs among the organized madness. It was relatively easy to get a wheelchair-accessible cab in New York City, but it sometimes wasn't easy enough.

* * *

Since Linda's ex-husband had taken their kids for the weekend, she came to visit Jefferson a little while after Matthew, Taylor, and Abigail had gone to bed. They immediately retreated up to his bedroom and locked the door, a bottle of wine and two glasses in hand.

* * *

"Monique!" Brad called, coming out of the museum, a somewhat bewildered guard watching him. "Monique!"

Monique cast a brief glance back before continuing to watch the traffic, willing her cab to appear.

"Hey," Brad said, coming up next to her. "I've been looking everywhere for you."

"Really?" Monique asked sarcastically. "Was your search perimeter wide enough. I mean, I couldn't have gotten that far on my own."

"What are you talking about? Wait. Is this about what Wade said?"

Monique was angry now.

"No," she snapped, "it's about the fact you basically agreed with him. No ... actually, it's everything. You went from constantly worrying about offending me to trying to do everything for me to letting people believe I'm incapable of doing anything without you. I told you before that I am perfectly capable of living my own life. You didn't listen, so now it doesn't include you."

"So, you're breaking up with me?" Brad asked.

Monique wondered if this accountant was really that dense.

"Yes," she said, "because you're clearly too stupid to realize what you're doing wrong. So do one intelligent thing and go away and never call me again ... burn my number and believe that I will burn yours."

A large van with the cab company logo then pulled up to the curb. The driver stuck his head out the window and looked at Monique.

"You call for taxi?" he asked in broken English.

At that moment, Monique couldn't tell where he was from, and she didn't care.

"Yes," she confirmed.

"Where you go?"

"Right now," Monique replied, coming over to the side of the van, "just get me away from here."

Brad stood there while the driver lowered a ramp. Monique rolled her chair up into it and he strapped her chair down to prevent it from moving during the ride. Once the doors were closed and the driver was back behind the wheel and Brad couldn't hear, Monique recited her address.

"Okay," the driver said and then yelled in a foreign language at a sedan which attempted to prevent him from rejoining the traffic flow.

Monique kept her eyes locked straight ahead in order to avoid seeing Brad through the van's windows as she left.

"Rough night?" the driver asked.

"You could say that," Monique replied. For her, it was the understatement of the year.

* * *

Sipping some more wine, Linda leaned against the headboard of Jefferson's bed, shutting her eyes and relaxing. She didn't protest when Jefferson reached over and gently pinched one of her nipples.

"You wanna go again?" he asked.

Linda smiled.

"When?" she queried, surveying him.

* * *

Joan arrived at Monique's apartment to find that her patient was already home and had successfully managed to overturn a bowl of fruit in her fit of rage. Rather than ask, she simply cleaned up the spilled produce and took Monique into her bedroom. She changed her into her pajamas and got her into bed. Deciding to still not try to press the matter, she wished her a good night and left.

* * *

Jefferson lay in bed, Linda lying next to him. Their empty glasses stood on the nightstand next to the partially empty wine bottle. Both were sleeping peacefully, enjoying their time together before they'd have to wake up early so Linda could slip out without the kids knowing she was ever there.

* * *

Monique lay awake in her bed, alone. The room was dark, and her blinds were shut, so she couldn't even see the moon. Her blankets were tucked all around her, keeping her warm and effectively trapped. Her water bottle stood on the nightstand, the plastic straw protruding from it.

"Little paralyzed girl," Monique murmured, "safely tucked into bed,"

At that thought, she began to cry.

Chapter 22

"He really laughed at that?" Jefferson asked incredulously.

"He did," Monique confirmed.

"And you left?"

"I did."

"Unbelievable. How can anyone be that stupid?"

"I honestly have no idea."

They were having lunch in a Subway restaurant on 8th Avenue, not far from Monique's bookstore. Throughout the meal, Monique recounted the details of her miserable date at the museum, leaving out what had happened in her apartment afterwards.

"And that makes you single again?" Jefferson asked, a smirk playing across his lips.

"Yeah," Monique said, chuckling slightly. "Why? Are you interested?"

"Me? No, I'm taken. I was just going to pass your name around to some guys over at the university."

"I don't think I'm that desperate yet," Monique said, picking at her sandwich.

"To date law professors?" Jefferson asked, taking a big bite of his own sandwich.

"No, to have my name passed around on a piece of paper with the phrase 'For good time, call'."

"Oh, come on. I wouldn't portray you like that … I would put 'For pleasant encounter, cell number:'. It's classier."

"Ha-ha," Monique said while he laughed. "Maybe I should just give up with guys altogether. I mean, I haven't had any luck with them. Maybe lesbianism is the answer … I mean, Joan's kind of cute and she's seen me naked, so that hurdle is overcome …"

"She'd be lucky to have you," Jefferson remarked, taking another bite of his sandwich. "Any woman would be."

"Are you even listening to me?"

Jefferson swallowed before responding.

"I am listening," he said. "You wanna get it on with your nurse … sounds like a great plot for a porno flick."

He began laughing again.

"Hey," Monique said. "I'm being serious here. If we didn't know each other so well, I would have a good mind to just leave right now."

Jefferson took a moment to stop laughing.

"I'm sorry," he said. "You'll find someone. Don't worry about it. You're a great catch."

"I think I found your earlier comments more comforting," Monique remarked.

"You will find someone. Granted, I'm not the best person to be talking to you about this. I mean, I spent five years with the wrong one, but the right one is out there … for the both of us. Trust me … I believe that there's someone out there for everyone."

Monique studied him, turning his words over in her mind.

"You think Linda might be the one for you?" she queried.

"I don't know yet," Jefferson replied. "I'd like it if she was. It'd be nice to stop looking."

"Well, when you're married and happy, just promise to invite me over for Thanksgiving."

"Sure, but you'll be too busy with your own family. I'm willing to bet on that."

Monique groaned.

"I'm gonna die an old maid," she lamented.

* * *

The phone rang. Still mostly asleep, Jefferson reached over to the nightstand to check what time it was.

"5:30," the electronic voice of his apple-shaped clock recited.

5:30, Jefferson wondered with a groan, Who on Earth calls at 5:30 in the morning?

He picked up the receiver and almost immediately heard a voice recording that regarded the twins' school. The recording stated that, due to some vague maintenance reason, the school would be closed for the day.

"Okay," Jefferson said to himself when the recording had finished and was repeating itself. "what do I do now?"

He couldn't take off from work anymore. His vacation days were gone for the semester. Matthew would still go to the day care center, but he'd have to find someone who could watch the girls.

But first, he needed coffee. Hanging up the phone, he decided to start his day a little earlier.

* * *

Abigail, Taylor, and Matthew came downstairs for breakfast to find Jefferson on the phone, learning the high school was open and running a normal school day, so Ellen O'Bryan and all her fellow baby-sitters were not available. Linda had to work for part of the day, so she was sending her kids over to her parents for the morning. Anya had a doctor's appointment in a few hours, followed by a mysterious lunch plan, so she couldn't watch the twins. Since Jefferson's parents lived in Virginia, that was not a possibility either. There was quickly only one option left.

"Okay," Jefferson told the girls over breakfast. "You two are gonna come to work with me, all right?"

Taylor and Abigail seemed interested in this idea.

"Go get some stuff to keep yourselves busy," Jefferson instructed. "We're leaving at the same time as always."

* * *

Thankfully, Matthew had no problem with still going to the day care center, so Jefferson only had the responsibility of keeping track of two kids in a university setting.

"You guys are gonna be law students for the day," he told the girls as they waited for the Uber that would take them from the day care center to the law school.

* * *

With Abigail trying to greet every person they passed, Jefferson, Presley, and the twins made their way into one of the law school's buildings. As they headed up to his office, Taylor remarked it looked a lot like the buildings where her parents had worked.

"I guess they're not too different," Jefferson commented, having no idea about the validity of this statement.

They reached his office and both girls were eager to explore the room. However, they quickly sounded disappointed.

"What's wrong?" Jefferson asked.

"This isn't a classroom," Taylor observed.

"It's not."

"You said you're a teacher."

Jefferson nodded, understanding.

"I am," he said. "It works a little differently here. Every teacher has their own office, and they borrow the classrooms when they want to teach."

"Don't you teach all day?" Abigail asked.

"I do, but here, you teach a class for a little while and then you take a break."

"Okay," Abigail said, seemingly accepting this explanation. "Who do the classrooms belong to?"

"The school owns the classrooms," Jefferson said, going around his desk and sitting down at his computer. "Hang out for a minute. I just have to check something and then we're going over to one of the classrooms."

As he waited for his computer to boot up, he felt one of the girls brush against his leg as she came around the desk and seemed to be trying to look at something on it. She was having trouble due to her height and was trying to stand on tiptoes to accomplish the task.

"Is there something I can help you with?" Jefferson queried.

"There's no pictures," Abigail observed, no longer trying to look at the top of the desk. "Our parents had pictures in their offices. Ms. Turner has pictures on her desk at school. Why don't you have any pictures?"

"He can't see them," Taylor pointed out.

"That is true," Jefferson said. "But that doesn't mean I can't have some pictures in here to show other people. I've always wanted to do that, but I keep forgetting to get some."

His computer was ready to go, and he set to work. With his attention on that, the twins amused themselves by looking out the window behind him. Having heard his screen reading software so often before, it no longer interested them.

After entering grades for papers he'd reviewed at home, Jefferson announced they would now go to a classroom.

* * *

"Sorry to hear it didn't go so well with your accountant guy," Frank said as he swept up dirt someone had tracked into the store. "If you'd like, I know some single guys."

"I'm okay," Monique said. "Thanks though. I'm just gonna tough it out on my own for a while before I try dating again."

She was sure she probably would pursue a sexual relationship with Joan before she ever took Frank's dating advice.

"Well," Frank said, "we're all here for you."

"Thanks," Monique said.

* * *

"Okay," Jefferson said, pulling two spare chairs over to the small table he'd gotten a custodian to set up on one side of the lecture hall, "you two can have these seats. Play with what you have, but do it quietly while I teach, all right?"

Both girls seemed okay with this arrangement.

"You need anything else before class starts?" Jefferson asked. "Water? Bathroom break? Anything?"

"No," the twins chorused, slightly out of sync with one another.

"Good," Jefferson said, pointing out the nearby lectern. "I'll be right over there."

He allowed himself to believe this might actually go well.

Students soon began trickling into the classroom. One downside of the twins' location was that some students had to walk right past them to get to their own seats, prompting Abigail to begin greeting them. A few returned the greeting, some actually stopping to greet her back. Taylor also said "hello," but at a much less frequent pace.

"Okay," Jefferson said. "Let's sit down now. Remember, I'm not above the idea of flunking any of you for the semester right now."

The students took their seats and pulled out their laptops and notebooks, somewhat ready for his lecture.

"Good morning," Jefferson said at 10:00. "As you have noticed, my nieces are visiting us today. Their elementary school officials finally realized that some old pipes need to be replaced ... after they broke and caused some considerable water damage in the building. Better late than never."

Some students snickered.

"We'll be running class pretty much as usual," Jefferson continued. "Just keep your comments G-rated please ... Mr. Willis."

There was considerably more laughter to this comment as several people looked over at the student named Claude Willis, who wore a proud grin on his face.

"We left off last time with New York Times Co. v. United States ..." Jefferson began.

* * *

The door chimed, signaling the arrival or departure of a customer. Monique ignored it as usual as she continued working behind the register, once again strapped into her standing frame. As it turned out, a woman had come in with a little boy and girl in tow. They came directly to the counter.

"Excuse me," the woman said. "Do you carry the new Sergio Ruzzier book?"

"Yeah," Monique said, "it's in our children's section that way."

She pointed towards a nearby aisle.

"If it's not there, let me know," She continued. "There are definitely more copies in our storeroom. It's been quite popular."

"Thank you," the woman said and headed off with her children still in tow.

They seemed to have found what they were looking for and were back about ten minutes later with "Good Boy" by children's author Sergio Ruzzier, along with a copy of "The Silent Patient" by Alex Michaelides, a work definitely too advanced for the kids. Monique didn't comment as she rang up the purchases.

"No school today?" she instead queried.

"School's closed," the boy said. "The pipes broke."

"Did they now? That's $28.11."

The woman pulled a credit card out of her wallet and hesitated, clearly unsure if she ought to just hand it to Monique. Monique solved the problem by holding her hand out for it. As she ran the card through the card reader, she noticed the card holder's name was "Linda Carrows". She recognized it immediately. This was Jefferson's girlfriend.

Linda Carrows had meanwhile taken the opportunity to glance around the store with apparent interest. Monique got her attention again by sliding over the card and the accompanying receipt.

"This is a nice place," Linda commented as she took the card and the slip of paper. "I've lived in New York for many years and I've never been in here."

"We've been around for a few decades," Monique said. "We mainly serve the immediate neighborhood and the occasional passerby."

Linda nodded.

"A friend of mine told me about this place," she commented. "He said it was a good place for kids. I finally got the opportunity to see for myself."

"Come back on a weekend," Monique encouraged as she put the books and Linda's receipt into a bag. "It's more exciting around here."

"I might just do that," Linda said, taking the bag. "Thank you."

She corralled her children, and they took their leave. Monique remained where she was, amused by the fact Jefferson was this woman's source of information about her store.

"Word of mouth," she muttered, chuckling. "You gotta love it."

* * *

Eric entered the restaurant and quickly located Jefferson. He came over to the table and was surprised to find Abigail and Taylor already sitting there.

"law students are getting younger every day," he remarked.

Abigail giggled.

"Shouldn't you two be in school?" Eric queried.

"School's closed," Abigail reported, and Jefferson explained the situation more fully.

"Wish I'd had that kind of luck back in the day. You guys mind if I join you for lunch?"

No one objected and he slid into the booth next to Taylor.

"Has your uncle been reading you the menu?" he asked.

"He's blind," Abigail said, giggling again. "He can't read it."

Eric looked at Jefferson.

"They've lost track of their Braille copy of the menu," Jefferson explained, answering the unasked question.

Eric snickered.

"Really?" he asked. "I would think that you're here so often that they wouldn't have a chance to lose it."

He cracked open the menu and began reading the options. Since the restaurant mainly served a college crowd, there were no specific entrees for children. Eric and Jefferson instead resolved to have the twins share a cheese pizza, thus also satisfying Abigail's list of foods she would not touch.

The waitress, who looked no older than nineteen, soon came over to take their orders and was very surprised to see the twins, again a sign that the restaurant was not used to serving children. It took a little while for Jefferson to get through to her that she should please bring out two plates with the pizza so the twins could share it. She finally got it and wrote everything down before leaving.

"Clearly a freshman," Eric muttered, and Jefferson smirked. "how's it going on your first day of law school?"

The girls began telling him about how they were allowed to go to Jefferson's class. Jefferson added the anecdote about how, at one point during his lecture, they had started squabbling about something regarding the drawings they were working on and he had to stop teaching to settle the matter, subsequently jokingly referring to the interruption as an example of an early version of family court.

As the waitress brought them their drinks, Eric's cell phone rang. He had to control his laughter before he could answer it in order to sound halfway sane.

"Hello ..." he said, still chuckling. "Oh hey ... you are? ... I'm at Mindy's, having lunch with Jefferson. Come on over ... No, it's fine. He'd be more insulted if you didn't ... yes, you know Mindy's ... it's the pizza and pasta place where I always seem to wind up for lunch. ... Yes, that place ... come on over ... all right, a Coke and ... Got it ... not too much cheese ... I promise. ... See you soon."

He hung up.

"Amy's on her way," he reported. "She decided to try to meet me for lunch."

He got the waitress's attention and ordered a Coke and a plate of spaghetti with marinara sauce, explaining that a fifth person would be coming for lunch. He then took a chair from a nearby table and placed it at the end of their own since there was no room for his wife in the booth itself.

Thankfully, he didn't seem to notice Jefferson looking slightly less comfortable. This was the first time Jefferson would be seeing both Eric and Amy together since his one-night-stand with the latter. He had no idea how this would go, despite Eric's apparent continuing obliviousness to the incident.

Amy arrived a few minutes later and was as surprised as her husband had been to see the twins there. Jefferson once again explained the situation as she sat down in the chair, putting her right between him and Eric. Her tone of voice told him she wasn't entirely comfortable with this arrangement either, something else Eric thankfully seemed to miss. Amy kept her head movements very controlled, looking mainly at her husband and the twins.

"What was so funny earlier when I called?" she asked as the waitress brought her Coke along with a placemat and silverware.

Eric forced Jefferson to repeat the story about the twins' squabbling. Amy laughed, finding this very funny while also being glad to have something to make her feel less awkward.

"So," she asked after calming down. "which do you like better … elementary school or law school?"

"We get to draw more here," Abigail said. "That's fun."

"I think there are people who would disagree with you," Eric remarked as their food arrived.

Since Jefferson and Eric were in a better position to assist, they began separating the pizza slices from one another to move them onto the girls' plates. Unfortunately, they hadn't been cut well and the men were having trouble with it. Amy watched them with amusement. They finally managed to give each girl one slice to start with and Eric cut the rest completely through with his own knife.

"Hey," he said as he started on his own food. "Don't you have the Stevenson twins in class this afternoon?"

Jefferson thought for a moment and chuckled.

"Who are the Stevenson twins?" Amy queried.

"They're identical twins in their second year here," Eric explained. "They'll be in Jefferson's class this afternoon."

"And I assume they're female," Amy concluded, now chuckling as well, the irony sinking in.

Eric nodded.

"People are gonna have a field day with this," he remarked.

"Looking forward to it," Jefferson muttered.

They ate in silence for a while, the only exception being when one or both of the girls asked for more pizza or when Amy apologized when hers and Jefferson's hands accidentally brushed against one another due to the confines of the table. Jefferson apologized as well. This exchange didn't go over Eric's head.

"If I didn't know any better, I'd say he just shocked you," he remarked. "I don't think I've ever seen you pull your hand back that quickly. Everything okay?"

"Yeah," Amy said. "It was static electricity, I guess."

"Yeah," Jefferson agreed, thankful for her quick response.

"All right," Eric said, deciding to leave it at that despite them both acting odd.

Jefferson and Amy were relieved he didn't pursue it further.

"How's Linda?" Eric asked instead.

"Who's Linda?" Amy queried.

"Jefferson's new lady friend. She's a divorcee whose kids go to the same school as … umph."

Having taken a moment to orient himself, Jefferson successfully kicked his friend's leg beneath the table, but the twins' attention was already captured.

"Linda's your friend?" Taylor asked.

"Yeah," Jefferson said, thinking quickly. "She comes by every so often and helps me with stuff when I need it."

"Kind of like I did," Amy added, scowling at Eric.

"Yeah," Jefferson said, pouncing on this, "but Linda lives closer, so it's easier to ask her for help."

Thankfully, the twins seemed to accept this explanation.

* * *

Monique soon learned more about the local school closing as more parents and their children stopped by her store. Anya also came in with a friend of hers, though neither stopped to chat. Joan eventually let Monique out of the standing frame and back into the wheelchair, so she was then able to move around the store again. Unfortunately, this came along just in time for her to meet a little boy who desired nothing more than to play with her chair, being brazen enough to try and grab the joystick. With his mother not reacting, Monique swiped his hand away and turned the chair around to leave the aisle.

She occasionally ran into children like that but didn't worry about it. After all, kids were kids, and some were just more interested in her chair than anything else. What bothered her was the parents' inactions to resolve the situation, people's excuses ranging from not caring to wanting to allow their children to be curious and explore. All such "reasons" were idiotic.

Chapter 23

After lunch, Amy took the twins into the restaurant's restroom to clean them up while Eric and Jefferson paid the bill.

"Hey," Eric said. "I'm sorry for running my mouth about Linda. I forgot that you weren't telling the kids anything yet."

"It's all right," Jefferson assured him. In reality, he had been glad to have the issue come up as a distraction, drawing attention away from how he and Amy were behaving around one another.

"It's gotta be difficult dating these days," Eric remarked.

"It's all right," Jefferson said. "Linda's got kids, so she understands. That does help."

"How do you two actually find the time to pursue this relationship? I mean, Amy and I are married with just two kids, and we sometimes have problems with getting time for just us. It's gotta be a nightmare for you two."

"We manage," Jefferson said, calculating the tip he owed the waitress.

"How?"

"Creativity, compromise, and knowing someone who you can call on to watch the kids."

Eric nodded.

"Hey," he said. "aren't you supposed to talk about that prostitution case today? The one that tried to spin Lawrence v. Texas in the 9th Circuit?"

Jefferson groaned.

"I gotta figure out what to do," he said. "I can't talk about prostitutes with Abigail and Taylor there."

"What's a prostitute?" someone asked.

Both men realized Amy had returned with the twins.

"What's a prostitute?" Abigail repeated.

Neither Jefferson nor Eric knew how to answer her.

"It's something grownup women do for work," Amy said. "But it's not something people talk about, so forget it, all right?"

"Can I be a prostitute when I grow up?" Abigail asked.

"No," Amy, Eric, and Jefferson all said at once.

* * *

Jefferson's afternoon class went pretty well, except for when Abigail accidentally sent one of her crayons flying halfway across the front of the room and had to run after it. Of course, having the Stevenson twins in the class didn't pass anyone by either and some students found jokes in that. But all in all, it went well, including Jefferson's last-minute substituting ESPLERP v. Gascón with Korematsu v. U.S. Many students did not miss the unmentioned cause for the change, glancing towards the twins every so often.

* * *

Unfortunately, Gloria Lawson showed up for one of her surprise visits a few minutes after Jefferson and the kids got home. The girls told her about going to work with Jefferson that day and she seemed to approve after learning no other means of supervision had been available. But things quickly went sour when Abigail let something slip about having heard the word "prostitute."

"Where did she learn that word?" Gloria Lawson demanded after the kids went outside to play with Presley.

"She overheard it," Jefferson admitted. "I was talking to a friend of mine about having to change the discussion topic for a class of mine and she came back from the bathroom before I realized it."

"Well," Gloria Lawson said, writing furiously in her notepad, "I strongly suggest that you make sure she learns another, more appropriate word and forgets this one."

Jefferson promised he would, and she left soon after that. When she was gone, he headed for the phone.

"Hey," he said, calling Monique. "You wanna do lunch tomorrow?"

"Sure," Monique agreed. "Subway again?"

"Sure," Jefferson agreed. "I'll see you at 12:30."

He hung up and dialed another number.

"Hey there," he said. "Listen, I'm just gonna be blunt about this … I need sex. Can you come over tonight?"

"Rough day?" Linda asked.

"Yeah."

"You can tell me all about it. I have to see about tonight though. If not, definitely tomorrow night."

"Okay," Jefferson said, rubbing his temples.

What a day, he thought as he hung up.

* * *

"Oh God," Monique said, laughing. "Tell me she's learned a different word by now."

They were back at the Starbucks, which was becoming one of their regular lunchtime haunts. Jefferson was recounting the twins' day in law school.

"Yeah," he said, taking a bite of his cookie. "I think she's forgotten about it. I'm just praying I don't get a call from school about her suddenly remembering it."

"Consider it a lesson," Monique remarked. "Always watch what you say. Always."

She took a long sip from the water in her tumbler.

"Thanks for the tip," Jefferson said.

"What I'm here for," Monique replied, grinning.

* * *

Against her better judgment, Amy pressed the bell by Jefferson's front door, an overnight bag tucked under her arm. She waited anxiously for him to answer. His approaching footsteps on the other side of the door told her there were seconds left.

When Jefferson opened the door, Amy managed a smile.

"Hey," she said.

"Hey," Jefferson returned, stepping aside to let her in. "Thanks for doing this."

"No problem," Amy said, relieved he wouldn't be there. She set her overnight bag on the kitchen table as Jefferson began feeding her information, such as where the emergency phone numbers were kept.

"Eric's okay with this?" he asked after this fact was relayed.

"Yeah, he'll be fine without me for two nights," Amy said. "Besides, he has no reason to worry because he doesn't know."

Jefferson nodded and called for the kids to come downstairs.

"Thanks again so much for doing this," he said, turning back to face her.

"Id est bonum," Amy assured him. "You need a weekend for yourself. Have a good time ... but, before you do, could you tell me where I can grab a spare pillow and blanket for the couch?"

"The third-floor hall closet by my bedroom," Jefferson told her. "But you can just take my bed for the weekend ..."

"Nihil," Amy interjected. "I really don't think that's a good idea. I'll be fine on the couch."

Jefferson nodded, understanding. Just then, the twins and Matthew came down and the subject was dropped.

"Okay you guys," Jefferson said. "You be good and listen to Mrs. Nelson while I'm gone. I'll be back on Sunday afternoon. Sound good?"

They nodded as Anya emerged from her room, a large backpack hanging off one shoulder.

"I am leaving now," she told Jefferson. "Have a good trip."

She turned to the three kids.

"I will see you soon," she said, hugging them each. "Proshchay."

She'd begun teaching the kids to say simple words and phrases in Russian. They mimicked this parting phrase with apparent accuracy and she left.

"What does she have planned?" Amy asked.

"I have no idea," Jefferson admitted. "All I need to know is she'll be back. I've gotta get going too though. You all set?"

"We'll be fine. Non forsit."

Somewhat satisfied, Jefferson went upstairs and got his bag, along with a pillow and blanket from the hall closet. He headed out the front door with a final wave, Presley leading the way.

When he was gone, Amy turned to the kids.

"Okay," she said. "We've got a few hours until dinner. What do you guys wanna do?"

* * *

Of course, late Friday afternoons in New York City were nightmarish times to try to obtain any form of public transportation, so Jefferson had thought ahead and reserved an Uber the day before. Therefore, he was right on time when he reached Grand Central Station.

Linda arrived about five minutes later in her own Uber, clearly sounding haggard, momentarily muttering incoherent phrases.

"You all right?" Jefferson inquired.

"Yeah," Linda replied. "It was just one of those Fridays where everything happened at once. You know, the kind before a weekend that won't allow for any time to catch up. Murphy's Law at its finest. Nevertheless, I made it out."

She embraced Jefferson and kissed him.

Next to them, Presley wagged her tail, hoping from one paw to another. But, to her disappointment, Linda knew better than to give her any attention while she wore her harness.

"It's not often that I get to do that when I first see you," she instead remarked with a smile.

Jefferson kissed her again, running his hands over her body. After all, this was New York City. Despite the heavy foot traffic surrounding them, no one took notice of them.

"What's that your wearing?" he asked, catching a whiff of her neck.

"It's called 'Celebration'," Linda described. "You like?"

"Very much. And the outfit's nice too."

"Thanks. I fixed myself up at work for you. Now come on. We've got a train to catch."

* * *

"All right," Amy said, reviewing the board on the den's coffee table. "It's Taylor's turn."

She and the twins were playing Junior Monopoly while Matthew sat nearby, playing with some toy cars. Taylor took the dice and rolled them half-heartedly, getting a six.

"Everything okay?" Amy asked as Taylor bought the bumper cars she landed on.

The little girl nodded.

"Hey," Amy said, not buying this response. "He'll be back before you know it."

She wondered what might have happened the last time this girl saw her parents to cause such attachment issues. It had to be more than them dying so suddenly.

* * *

The train ride up to Albany took about three hours. Once there, Jefferson and Linda rented a car and drove another two hours to reach Proctorsville, a small town in southern Vermont, where the Golden Stage Inn Bed and Breakfast was located.

They checked in with an older woman who ran the place and proceeded up to their room on the second floor, having eaten sandwiches during the drive. Jefferson got Presley settled with food and water and then pounced on Linda, who was already lying on the bed after having taken off her shoes.

"You're not wasting any time, are you?" she remarked as he began unbuttoning her blouse.

"I wanna get going before I get too tired," Jefferson replied.

Linda laughed and began undoing his belt buckle.

* * *

The alarm on Amy's phone crowed and she stirred, sending her blanket to the floor. She sat up on the couch, rubbing her eyes and taking a moment to remember where she was. Then, she took another moment to remind herself she had not slept with Jefferson again. Having taken stock of her surroundings, she snatched her phone off the coffee table before its alarm could wake the kids.

I'm losing my mind, she thought as she got up and headed towards the kitchen for some coffee. Despite the agreement she and Jefferson had made to put their one-night-stand behind them and stay friends, the practical application wasn't going so well.

Amy remembered her work study program in the Columbia University Law School's library almost fifteen years earlier. She could visualize the two second-year students who approached her between the shelves, where the nosy and bossy law librarian couldn't see them. God forbid anyone engaged in a casual conversation within a hundred feet of that woman.

Like ninety-nine percent of the Earth's population, Amy's eyes immediately fell on the guide dog accompanying one of the men. He was a large yellow Labrador Retriever/Golden Retriever cross. Using the dog as their opening, the men introduced themselves as Jefferson and Eric. The dog's name was Emerald.

Then a junior at Columbia, Amy was able to make five minutes' worth of conversation with the pair before she heard the librarian looking for her. The three of them scattered before the woman had the opportunity to discover their "unauthorized chatter".

It'd been three weeks before she saw either of them again. Taking a lunch break at a pizzeria just off campus, she spotted Jefferson sitting in one of the booths and engaged him in conversation. She was surprised he remembered her. Their chat turned into a lunch and that ended with an invitation to a party Jefferson and a bunch of his friends were hosting.

Amy wasn't sure exactly when it happened, but she was Eric's girlfriend within a few months of that second meeting. Jefferson was supportive of their relationship and served as Eric's best man at the wedding after they'd all graduated. But Amy supposed she always knew, on some level, there was another side to his feelings. He'd been very happy to see her again at the pizzeria, even remembering her voice and her name.

The three sometimes joked about what might have happened if Amy had ended up with Jefferson. Those jokes hadn't come up in a while and Amy now wondered if they'd ever felt like jokes to Jefferson. She also wondered how exactly she ended up with Eric. After all, she'd seen Jefferson again first and they'd had a nice lunch.

Though he wasn't lonely, Jefferson sometimes lamented the fact many women were intimidated by his blindness, fearing they might either offend him or seeing it as a potential burden on them. Amy feared she might have subconsciously considered this as well. She could admit she was now more mature than that undergraduate so long ago, but would she have been that shallow back then?

The coffeemaker finished just as Amy heard noises above her. Time to get started, she thought as she added milk and sugar to her cup.

* * *

"Morning," Linda said softly as Jefferson opened his eyes, running one hand through his hair.

"Morning," Jefferson returned, kissing her. "I gotta say … it's nice having you stick around in the mornings instead of watching you get out of bed and hurry off."

"Is it now?"

* * *

As best she could, Monique spent her morning helping Frank and Samuel restock some shelves to make space in the storeroom. They were expecting a delivery on Monday and they would need the space. So, the laws of physics required that every available gap in the shelves be filled.

Monique couldn't help thinking about Jefferson and the fact he was taking his girlfriend up to Vermont for the weekend. He'd mentioned this plan to her a few days back and she was envious in the sense that she didn't have anyone who would do that for her. The last time she had been on such a trip was in her senior year of college when she and her boyfriend had spent a weekend at a vineyard in upstate New York. They had had fun, despite her having some difficulty with the wine-tasting due to her being unable to properly hold the glasses. Now, with the exception of complicated trips to western Pennsylvania to see her mother, she hadn't been on a vacation in years.

* * *

After breakfast, Linda persuaded Jefferson to go to a local antique fair she'd read about. In exchange, she agreed to drive ninety minutes north to the Ben & Jerry's factory with him that afternoon. On their way back, she put forth the suggestion that they go on a hayride that evening, adding that dinner would consist of a cookout which was included.

"Can I sneak you off into the woods to do the wild thing?" Jefferson asked mischievously.

"I think we might scare the horses," Linda replied, nevertheless pleased about the fact such spontaneity was an option with their kids back in Manhattan.

* * *

While the twins watched a cartoon, Amy sat on the floor, helping Matthew build a fort with his blocks. By now, the kids, especially Taylor, had warmed up to her more and seemed to believe her when she said Jefferson and Anya would both be back the next day. And she had been able to shed some of her misgivings about staying in Jefferson's house. All in all, it wasn't going that badly, even if the memories persisted.

* * *

As the wagon bumped along the wide dirt road, Linda looked up at the night sky, describing what she saw for Jefferson's benefit. There were ten people on the hayride plus Presley, who was fascinated by the horses pulling the wagon through the woods. The view of their backsides and hearing the occasional snort or neigh was enough to hold the dog's interest and the ride came with its own theme music, consisting of a steady thumping as tail met wagon floor.

"We'll be at our cookout site in about ten minutes," the driver announced at one point, keeping a firm grip on the reins.

A few people acknowledged his announcement while others didn't speak, instead admiring the scenery around them.

"This remind you of that time we took that carriage ride around Central Park?" Linda asked.

"This is quieter," Jefferson remarked, wrapping his arm around her waist and pulling her close.

Linda smiled and leaned her head against his shoulder.

True to the driver's word, they reached a large clearing about ten minutes later where several people were already busy preparing food or putting the finishing touches on a large campfire. The menu consisted of burgers and sausages, which the hayride's passengers consumed with drinks as they sat around the fire.

"My God," Linda commented, looking back up at the night sky. "You can see so many more stars here than in the city. It's beautiful."

Jefferson nodded.

* * *

Amy sat on the couch in her pajamas, watching television. The kids were asleep, and she couldn't find any program which held her interest. She couldn't sleep either.

She finally switched off the television and dug a book out of her overnight bag. "Remembering Virginia, the first installment in the "2nd Time Around" series by Christian Becker. Having secured this advanced copy from a friend, she curled up on the couch and picked up at the spot where she'd left off.

But this too failed to stimulate her this time. Amy set the book down on the coffee table and looked around the room, feeling uneasy. Here she was, staying in the house of the man she had stupidly had sex with while her husband was at home, thinking everything between them was fine.

Of course everything between them was fine. What she had done with Jefferson was nothing more than an extremely dumb mistake. Eric had nothing to do with what happened.

Now, alone in Jefferson's den while in her pajamas, Amy was reliving the stupidity. Maybe this wasn't getting easier.

Thankfully, her day had been busy keeping track of the twins and Matthew, but now that they were asleep, there was nothing to keep these thoughts at bay. How could it have happened?

Amy remembered she'd had a few drinks after dinner that night, just like Jefferson. But she didn't think of herself as being drunk. Her thoughts and speech had still been clear and lucid and the same seemed to apply to him. She recalled how she was about to leave when she remembered the pamphlets she wanted to give Jefferson. They were for that soccer program. Their fingers had innocently touched, and they subsequently joked about it. Then, after some more time and tension, they were suddenly kissing and going upstairs to his bedroom, pausing only long enough to come to a verbal two-word consensus on the idea.

"Upstairs?" Jefferson had asked.

"Okay," Amy had replied.

The rest had been a flurry of undressing and the subsequent act itself. It had all been stupid … just stupid sex.

And Amy was still kicking herself for it. She was sure Jefferson felt guilty about it as well, even if he didn't always show it. She was also sure she felt so much worse. After all, after she left that night, he had been able to just go back to sleep. She had to endure the taxi and subway ride home. She had to walk into her house. She took a shower and climbed into bed next to her husband, making up an excuse about where she had been for so long. Amy couldn't even remember what she had said and was thankful Eric never brought it up again.

Feeling overwhelmed, she had quietly cried that night. And now, it was happening again. Amy curled up on the couch, burying her face in her hands.

* * *

Linda kissed Jefferson passionately as they stood in the middle of their room in the Golden Stage Inn. Presley was off in a corner, chewing on one of her toys and they didn't worry about her right then.

"How about you make yourself comfortable?" Linda suggested softly, leaning close to Jefferson's ear. "I'm just gonna go change and freshen up in the bathroom."

"I think I can do that," Jefferson told her.

Linda smiled as she headed into the small bathroom.

Jefferson kicked off his shoes and sat down on the bed, staring up at the ceiling as he waited. He was sure he had some idea of what Linda had in store for him, but the woman nevertheless had a way of surprising him.

Linda came back out a few minutes later and he could smell the fresh dose of perfume she'd put on. She'd explained she worked at a high-end makeup boutique during her graduate studies and knew tricks which could make Hollywood look amateurish. So far, Jefferson believed her.

He could hear the click-clacks made by the high heels she was now wearing as she crossed the wood floor to the bed. For one brief moment, Jefferson found himself wondering what she'd done with the boots she'd worn during the hayride. The thought evaporated as fast as it had formed.

"Hey handsome," Linda said in a sultry voice as she took one of Jefferson's hands in both of hers. "You wanna know what I put on for you?"

Jefferson nodded and she took his hand and guided it up to her torso, letting him feel the silk material of her nightie.

"You like that?" she asked.

"Oh, definitely," Jefferson said.

"That's good," Linda said, climbing on to the bed and straddling him. "Now, I want you to go ahead and explore. Find out exactly what I'm wearing. Enjoy. Just don't take any peaks at what isn't showing yet. No sneak previews."

Chapter 24

Jefferson entered his house to find Amy ready to leave, her overnight bag packed and by her feet. He could hear the kids playing upstairs.

"How was your trip?" Amy asked.

"It was good," Jefferson told her. "How were things here?"

"A little rocky at first, but we fell into a rhythm. We got along pretty well."

"That's good. Thanks again for doing this."

"It's no problem. I left the blanket and pillow folded up on the couch. I'll just say 'bye' to the kids and ..."

Amy's voice trailed off and Jefferson could tell she really wanted to leave.

"Hey guys!" he called up the stairs. "Guess who's back!"

The sounds of playing stopped and all three kids charged downstairs to greet their long-lost uncle. Presley, out of her harness, squeezed in to lick whoever's faces and appendages she could reach.

"Okay you guys," Jefferson said, interrupting their cheerful, incomprehensible chatter. "Say thanks to Mrs. Nelson first. She has to get going."

All three kids immediately thanked Amy and added a message of farewell at Jefferson's urging.

"Bye you guys," Amy said. "I had fun."

Jefferson sent the three kids away again and turned to Amy.

"Everything okay?" he asked. He could tell something was up.

"Yeah," Amy lied. "Everything's fine."

"Are we okay?" Jefferson asked, not buying her act.

Amy hesitated.

"I don't know," she admitted.

"I never meant for it to happen," Jefferson told her.

"I know."

"Can we just put it behind us? Forget about it? Like we planned?"

"I don't know," Amy said and hurried out.

Jefferson was about to shut the door when he heard a car pull up. He then heard Anya talking to someone, but construction on the next block successfully muffled her voice. He only understood her calling out an

English farewell to someone as they drove away. She walked towards the house and was surprised to see Jefferson.

"You are back already?" she asked. She then checked her watch, realizing she was late.

"I am sorry," she added quickly. "I lost track of the time."

"No problem," Jefferson assured her. "I just got back myself. Who's your friend?"

"She is just a friend," Anya said but she was noticeably defensive when she said this.

Jefferson thought about her pronoun slip, but he decided against it.

Anya came into the house and greeted the three kids, giving them each a small knick-knack she bought while apparently traveling to Philadelphia.

"It is a fascinating city," she told them. "A lot of interesting history, just like here in New York."

The kids thanked her and ran back upstairs to play. Anya turned back to Jefferson.

"The lady left already?" she asked.

"Oh, Amy?" Jefferson replied. "Yeah, you just missed her. She was leaving when your friend dropped you off."

He thought he could actually hear Anya stiffen. She was obviously not going to talk about this friend.

"I will go put my things in my room," she said instead and turned to head towards the den.

As he locked the front door, Jefferson let out a long sigh.

"Women," he muttered.

* * *

"Okay," Mr. Wallace said. "Now we're going to have Show-and-Tell. Today, Andrew, Vince, Leslie, and Taylor are going to share what they brought to show us."

Rather than just encourage the kids to bring something to show the class, he long ago decided to make it an assignment, picking a few kids for each occasion, in order to encourage those who normally wouldn't do such a thing as speak to others in the class to do so. Taylor was a prime example for why this system was needed. She was way too quiet all day.

Vince was up first, showing the class his prized eraser collection. Mr. Wallace let him talk for about five minutes, during which he described how he had acquired all these different erasers from the same

Staples store near his apartment building, before telling him to wrap it up and let someone else have a turn.

Leslie was up next. She had brought a photo of herself with her family's two terriers, both of whom were licking her face. The photo was passed around as she proudly described how she had gone with her mom the year before to pick the dogs up from a breeder out on Long Island.

"Taylor," Mr. Wallace prompted when Leslie was done.

To his surprise, Taylor did not look too nervous as she walked to the front of the room, carrying a cloth bundle.

"What did you bring to show us?" the teacher queried, genuinely curious.

"I brought a flag," Taylor explained as she unfolded the bundle.

Mr. Wallace came over to help and it was revealed to be an American flag.

"This is very nice," Mr. Wallace commented. "Where did you get it?"

"It used to hang in my dad's office," Taylor said. "He worked for the government. He took it with him every time we moved to another country."

"Very interesting," Mr. Wallace commented, happy to have her talking.

"It normally hangs on the wall in my sister's and my room. But my uncle let me bring it into school today. My nanny helped me fold it so I could carry it in my backpack."

"Very patriotic."

* * *

"She took the flag to school today?" Monique asked.

"Yeah," Jefferson replied. "She took it for show-and-tell."

"Good for her."

They were having lunch at La Bonbonniere, a diner on 8th Avenue. Monique was on the verge of peppering Jefferson with questions about his weekend, something he had managed to avoid for the past few days.

"So, is this going somewhere serious?" Monique asked with a sly grin. "With Linda, I mean."

"Yeah," Jefferson admitted. "I think it is."

"I'm glad. How good was the sex?"

"There's no way you're getting that out of me."

Despite his firm tone, Jefferson's smile gave him away.

"Then I guess I'll just have to sleep with you sometime to know how good you are," Monique remarked.

Surprised, Jefferson raised an eyebrow.

"I'm not that curious," Monique added.

* * *

Linda was loading plates into the dishwasher as she hummed along to the radio. She knew she would have to pick up the kids from school soon. It would her a chance to see Jefferson, even if she couldn't act on her desires right then. She hoped they could share their secret with all their kids soon so they wouldn't have to keep on sneaking around.

The doorbell rang. Linda put the last plate in the dishwasher and started up the machine before going to answer it. She was somewhat surprised to see Grant Hawkins standing on her front steps. She thought he was in St. Louis this week.

"Hey Grant," she said, giving him a smile. "What's up?"

She noticed he looked distressed about something.

"Is everything okay?" she asked.

"Yes ... no ..." Grant said. "Can we talk?"

His eyes were pleading. Linda could tell this was serious.

"Sure," she said, stepping aside. "Come on in."

* * *

Jefferson was in his office, updating some grades, when Paula Franks came in without knocking.

"I heard your nieces were here not too long ago," the woman remarked.

"They were," Jefferson admitted.

"I'm sorry I didn't get a chance to meet them. I've been so busy lately with preparing for my last final exams."

"Good for you," Jefferson said. In truth, he was relieved when Abigail's and Taylor's visit to the law school had ended without them running into Paula Franks.

"Let me know if they're ever here again," Paula Franks said. "I would love to meet them."

She was already on her way out again.

"Will do," Jefferson muttered under his breath, happy to hear her leave.

* * *

The phone rang and Jefferson wearily opened his eyes to answer it. He had no clue about what time it was.

"Hello?" he asked in a groggy voice.

"Jefferson," Linda said. "Can we talk?"

"It's two in the morning," Jefferson said, finally checking the clock on his nightstand. "Is everything all right?"

Linda didn't say anything.

"This better not be some booty call," Jefferson said, half-joking.

Linda didn't laugh.

"I'm downstairs at your door," she said. "Could you let me in please."

Jefferson realized she did not sound tired.

"Sure," he said. "I'll be right down."

He hung up and went downstairs to find Linda was indeed standing at his front door, her cell phone still pressed to her ear.

"Sorry," she said. "I thought about ringing the doorbell, but I didn't want to wake your nanny or the kids ..."

Her voice trailed off as she finally put the phone away.

"And me?" Jefferson asked, half-joking again. But he could tell Linda was not in the mood. He led her over to the couch and encouraged her to sit down. She did so, looking at him with tear-filled eyes.

"Please sit down," she said. "If it can be, it might be easier for me."

At this point, Jefferson hoped Anya was still asleep and wouldn't hear. She had never said anything about noise during the night before, but then again, Linda was never in his den this late at night before.

"Sure," he said, deciding to risk it, and sat next to her on the couch. "What's up?"

Shifting away from him, Linda hesitated and swallowed.

"Grant came by today," she said.

"Your ex?" Jefferson asked.

"Yeah. He came over while the kids were still in school. He wanted to talk. He was very distraught."

"And what did he want to talk about?" Jefferson asked, not sure if he wanted to know.

"He just began blubbering. He was saying that ending our marriage had been a mistake, how he still loved me, how he missed us all being a family, and how he wanted us to move out to Saint Louis with him."

"Saint Louis?"

Jefferson hadn't been sure what part of her narrative to process first. Somehow, St. Louis won.

"Yes," Linda continued. "He's being transferred there by his firm. He was practically crying. I comforted him and we just began talking about what went wrong between us. It got to the point where I had to stop and call a neighbor to ask them to go and pick up Jessica and David from school and watch them for the afternoon. Grant and I just kept talking. He promised to cut back on his work and be there for us more. All these old feelings we had for each other began spilling out again and we wound up making love in my bedroom."

Jefferson definitely did not want to hear about this.

"Does Grant know about me?" he asked.

Linda nodded as she began to cry.

"I ... told him ... all ... about us," she said.

"And?" Jefferson queried. "What are you going to do?"

Linda took a deep, shuddering breath.

"Jefferson," she said, "these past six weeks have been great. Honestly, I believed you and I had something. But I'm gonna go back to Grant. I wanna give our marriage another try. I'm sorry."

Jefferson was stunned. He had most certainly not wanted to hear this.

"So that's it?" he asked. "You're just throwing us away?"

"I'm sorry," Linda said. "I still love Grant."

"You left him," Jefferson said incredulously. "What's to stop history from repeating itself?"

"I don't know. But it might just work this time. I have to try."

"Linda, I'm not going to hang around and wait to see if it does or doesn't."

Linda nodded, making a noise which suggested understanding.

"You have to choose ..." Jefferson insisted. "Him or me?"

Linda hung her head.

"I'm sorry," she said. "I believed that we had something but ... he's my husband. I'll be calling a realter tomorrow to get the house on the market."

* * *

"Morning," Eric said happily, though his mood faltered when he saw how haggard Jefferson looked as he made his way down the hallway to his office, Presley taking cautious steps as her handler's body swayed left and right.

217

"What happened to you?" Eric asked, concerned. Jefferson looked both upset and hung over.

"Linda came over last night," Jefferson explained.

"And ..." Eric inquired, but he was unable to come up with a sarcastic remark.

"She left me. She's going back to her ex-husband. They're moving to St. Louis ... all of them."

"Oh man," Eric said, all attempts at humor gone now. "I'm sorry. You okay?"

"I'll be all right," Jefferson said, having trouble convincing even himself.

"You seem more upset about this break-up than the one with Nancy."

Jefferson would not disagree with this observation.

"I probably loved Linda more than I ever loved Nancy," he admitted.

"That's saying something," Eric said. "You gonna be okay to teach today?"

"That's the least of my worries."

Eric's eyes widened.

"What else could be on your mind?" he asked, bewildered.

"Gloria Lawson came by early this morning," Jefferson explained. "She wanted to observe how I got the kids ready for school and day care."

Eric groaned.

"And with you being drunk, hung over, and completely exhausted, that could not have gone well," he remarked.

"Let's just say we all survived," Jefferson said with a tone of relief. "I think she was glad to see me get rid of them. I managed to get rid of her near the day care center. Thank God Anya was there."

"Tell me the kids are wearing clothes."

"They are. Like I said ... we survived ... and we had Anya."

As it turned out, Anya had heard nothing the night before and was as surprised to find Jefferson in a similar state as Eric's discovery. She heard him out and was sympathetic, helping him get the kids ready for school and even offering to take them herself. Jefferson declined that part, saying he needed to get out of the house anyway. Plus, Gloria Lawson arrived before they could settle the matter.

"What are you going to do now?" Eric asked.

"I'm gonna go catch a few minutes' sleep in my office," Jefferson said. "Then I'll grab some coffee, teach, and wait for today to end."

"That's as good a plan as any," Eric said. "Take a few more minutes for that nap and I'll have the coffee waiting outside your door."

"Thanks."

Jefferson continued down the hallway towards his office.

"And don't worry about Linda," Eric said as he walked with his friend. "I figure she's not the one for you. You'll find someone else. You've bounced back before."

"Yeah," Jefferson said.

"There's always your nanny. I mean, you know how people think of her. 'Bombshell' is an understatement. You could have a beautiful Russian lady on your arm."

Jefferson managed a slight smile, but only to humor his friend.

"And I could loan you Amy if you ever need pity sex," Eric added.

Jefferson's smile faltered.

Chapter 25

Jefferson was in his home office, putting together a lesson plan. He got up and went to the bathroom, only to come back and find someone rifling through his desk drawers.

"What are you doing?" he asked as the rustling and muttering stopped.

"Looking for paper," Abigail replied. "Taylor and I need some more."

"What did I say about not coming in here when I'm not in here?"

"But the door was open," Abigail protested. "I thought you were in here."

Jefferson stopped, seeing her point.

"You're gonna make a great lawyer someday," he remarked as he pulled a few sheets of paper out of his printer tray and handed them to her.

But Abigail's attention had been caught by whatever was in the drawer she'd been looking through when Jefferson caught her in the act. She pulled out a DVD case and examined it.

"I think that's my name," she remarked, trying to read what was scrawled across the cover. "Uncle Jeff, what is this?"

"I think that's one of the home movies your mom and dad made," Jefferson said, taking the case from her and putting it back.

"All of these?" Abigail asked, looking at the dozen or so DVD cases.

"Yeah," Jefferson said, shutting the drawer.

Stan had been a videographer by hobby. He'd filmed and downloaded hours of footage, much of which he burned onto DVDs.

"Can we watch them?" Abigail queried, interested.

"Maybe another time," Jefferson replied. "I've got some work I've gotta get done."

"Okay," Abigail said, finally taking the paper she'd come for and hurrying out of the office.

Jefferson sank back into his desk chair, but he couldn't concentrate like before. The home movies were now on his mind, and consequently, so were Stan and Maggie.

He'd found the DVDs in some piece of furniture or box of stuff that was shipped over from Berlin. He'd stored them in his desk, and they'd been there ever since. He hadn't watched any of them and he hadn't told any of the kids about them until now. He wasn't sure why, but he just hadn't. Abigail was sure to tell her siblings all about her discovery, and they too would be asking him about them soon enough. But for now, he had to push the home movies out of his mind and get some work done.

* * *

Jefferson entered his office at the university to find Paula Franks waiting for him. He couldn't help silently calculating how many days she had left until her graduation.

"Is there something I can help you with? He queried, sure she'd come in shortly after the custodian completed his morning run through the building, during which he unlocked all the office doors.

"I came by to see how you were doing," Paula Franks said in her sweet and innocent tone. "I heard you broke up with your girlfriend."

"It's hit the papers already, huh?" Jefferson remarked, wondering how she had heard this.

"I'm always here when you need me."

Until you graduate, Jefferson thought, thankful when she was gone.

* * *

Jefferson was in his kitchen, thinking deeply with his face in his hands. An unfolded letter lay on the table in front of him, his iPhone lying next to it, the KNFB Reader app still open.

Matthew came downstairs to find his uncle in this position. In the background, Anya could be heard cleaning up the den, singing to herself in Russian.

"What's wrong, Uncle Jeff?" Matthew inquired.

"Nothing," Jefferson said to his nephew. "I'm fine. What do you want?"

"Juice,"

Jefferson retrieved a juice box from the refrigerator's top shelf.

"Thanks," his nephew said.

With Matthew's needs having been met and the twins seemingly not needing anything, Jefferson grabbed the letter and headed upstairs to his office. He locked the door behind him. He wanted to keep the kids out at all costs for the time being. Grabbing the phone receiver on his desk, he dialed a number he knew by heart.

"Hello?" Monique answered after a few rings.

"Hey," Jefferson said. "It's me."

"Oh, hey. What's up?"

"I need a favor."

"Does it require construction? I'm not good with hammers and nails and all those things."

"No construction, I promise," Jefferson assured her, not quite getting the joke. "It's this awards dinner that gets held for the graduating students at NYU every year. It's basically a rubber chicken dinner which I'm obligated to attend every year. I just don't wanna be the single guy there."

"And you were wondering if I could be your date for the evening."

"If you wanna be considered that. I really just want someone there to keep me from being the lone guy at the bar."

He'd originally planned to take Linda, but he'd never even had a chance to ask her.

"Is that bar an open bar?" Monique asked.

"Yeah," Jefferson replied.

"It might not be that bad. I guess I'm in. What's the dress code and how rubbery is that chicken?"

* * *

Two days later, Jefferson discovered a pipe underneath the sink in his kitchen was leaking. Having zero expertise about these things, he immediately called a plumber, who told him it wasn't an emergency. Someone would be there the next day and he should catch the dripping water in a bucket for the time being.

So, knowing he'd have to wait around at home for the plumber to show up, Jefferson was thankful he didn't have any final exams to Procter the next day. He simply took the girls to school and Matthew to the day care center, figuring it was easier to keep everyone out of the way. After all, he had originally planned to go to the law school for a few hours to post some final grades. With any luck he might still be able to do that.

By 2:00, the plumber had not shown up and Jefferson was getting nervous. It looked like going to the law school was out of the question by now, but he had to pick up the twins and Matthew. The problem was that if he left now and the plumber showed up while he was gone, the latter would simply leave. They could start this whole process over again. Anya was out grocery shopping, he wasn't sure when she'd be back, and she'd forgotten her phone. Jefferson needed someone's help.

However, he soon discovered everyone he called seemed to be either busy or unavailable. He wouldn't dare call Linda, the two having broken off all communication despite her not having left for St. Louis yet. So, resigned to taking a more complicated route, Jefferson called Monique.

"Hey," he said. "I need another big favor."

"It's not a massage with a happy ending, is it?" Monique asked.

Jefferson wondered where and why she came up with these responses.

"No," he said, focusing. "Unfortunately, it's a bit more complicated than that. Are you free right now?"

"I run a bookstore and make up the staff timetables," Monique replied.

                    * * *

The large, wheelchair-accessible taxi van pulled up to the curb and the driver helped Monique get out. She gave him twenty dollars so he'd wait before she headed into the day care center.

She explained the situation to the receptionist at the front desk, producing a letter Jefferson had e-mailed her, saying he was giving the day care center permission to let her pick up Matthew. The letter was inspected and reviewed, as was Monique's ID, and Matthew was eventually released into her care after Jefferson's signature at the bottom was compared and verified with their records.

Thankfully, the taxi was still there when Matthew and Monique came back out, with the latter explaining why she was picking him up. They headed over to the girls' school. Once there, the driver said he wouldn't wait this time.

"Do you know how chaotic the end of a school day gets?" he asked as he undid the straps securing Monique's wheelchair.

"That's okay," Monique conceded. "We'll walk from here. Thanks."

It was a nice day, and the walk wouldn't be far. The driver helped her get out and sped back into the Manhattan traffic, earning some disgruntled honks along the way.

Getting plenty of stares from the parents and nannies waiting outside the school, Monique made her way over to an aide who was already stationed near the front doors in anticipation for the upcoming dismissal time. She showed the woman Jefferson's letter giving her permission to pick up Abigail and Taylor. Rather than having Monique come into the school, the aide went inside by herself to fetch the principal, Cynthia Langley. It seemed to only take mentioning the Thomas twins to get the principal to come outside. She looked at Jefferson's letter and then at Monique and her chair. She glanced at Matthew before returning her attention to the letter.

"Okay," she declared. "Just move away from the doors a bit. It'll be like a dam bursting in a few minutes."

Pleased that everything was going smoothly, Monique moved back with Matthew in tow.

"See," she commented, "I'm just as fun as your uncle."

Matthew shrugged, unsure of what to say.

Students soon began pouring out of the building to meet up with their parents, many of them slowing down to stare at Monique before moving on and questioning their parents about her. The aide, now back at her post, decided to help Monique out by calling for the twins and pointing them her way. I could have done fine on my own, Monique thought as the twins spotted her and came over.

"Hey girls," she said, abandoning her thoughts.

"Hi Monique," Taylor said. "What are you doing here?"

"Your uncle and your nanny are busy at home, so he asked me to pick you guys up from school. Come on. I'm gonna walk you home."

The twins paused, probably to develop a proper retort for Monique's comment about "walking", but they abandoned the idea and followed her.

* * *

The trip to Jefferson's house took about ten minutes longer than usual because of Monique's chair, but no one complained too much. Matthew eventually got tired of walking, so he was allowed to ride in the chair by sitting on Monique's lap. However, he kept moving around, making it somewhat difficult for her to see where she was going.

"Sit still," Monique instructed more than once. "You're going to fall."

They finally reached Jefferson's house and the twins and Matthew hurried up the three front steps, leaving Monique behind.

As it turned out, the plumber had shown up while Jefferson would have been gone, so he had made the right call. He also made the right call when assuming that when the kids had burst in through the front door, they'd left Monique behind. He headed outside to speak to her. As he came out, Anya also returned home, carrying several tote bags. She greeted them and apologized for forgetting her cell phone.

"It's okay," Jefferson assured her. "I've done that plenty of times as well."

"Thank you," Anya said and headed inside to store the groceries away.

"How's the pipe?" Monique asked.

"It's getting looked at," Jefferson told her. "Thanks for your help."

"No problem. I got quite the workout today."

"You want me to call a cab for you?"

"That's okay. It's not far and the weather is nice. I'll be fine."

Jefferson nodded.

"Thanks again," he said.

"See you on Saturday," Monique replied and headed off.

Jefferson listened to her depart before going back inside in time to find Abigail interrogating the plumber. He sent her outside to play in the backyard with Taylor and Presley just as the doorbell rang.

"Close the screen door," he called to the kids as he went to answer it.

Momentarily believing it was Monique, he quickly reminded himself she could not get up the front steps. It turned out to be Gloria Lawson.

"Hello," she said. "I figured you would have the girls home from school by now and I thought I'd check up on things."

"Come on in," Jefferson said, figuring there was nothing she could call him out on today.

But Gloria Lawson quickly came across the plumber, who was finishing up, and used this to dig into Jefferson.

"How long has he been here?" she demanded.

"An hour," Jefferson replied. "Maybe a little less."

"You left him here alone while you picked up the kids?"

"No," the plumber said, coming out from underneath the sink. "He was here the whole time."

Jefferson wished he wouldn't help.

"You let them walk home alone?!" Gloria Lawson asked, furious by now.

"No," Jefferson said as the plumber packed up his tools. "A friend of mine picked them up. I sent e-mails that gave her permission to do so."

He was sure Gloria Lawson passed Monique during her drive to the house but had paid her no mind. Going by her general attitude, Monique was probably invisible to her.

"Fine then," Gloria Lawson said. "That's all for now. Everything seems to be in order. I'll be back."

She left without another word.

"Tough lady," the plumber remarked.

You have no idea, Jefferson thought.

The plumber also soon left but not before stopping to stare at Anya, who was reviewing the receipt from the grocery store. She was either unaware of his leering or just chose to ignore it.

"I will go do some laundry," Anya told Jefferson, heading towards the basement door after he left.

Jefferson sat down on the couch, listening to the kids playing out back. A few minutes later, the doorbell rang again.

It's like Grand Central Station today, he thought as he got up to answer it.

This time, a young-sounding woman who introduced herself as Virginia Miller was standing on his front steps. She didn't seem to be surprised by the fact Jefferson was blind, suggesting she knew who he was. Jefferson couldn't recall her at all.

"Can I help you?" he asked. He wondered if this was a student who had somehow obtained his home address.

"I'm looking for Anya," Virginia explained. "I wanted to drop something off for her."

"Come on in."

As Virginia entered the house, Jefferson went to the open basement door.

"Anya!" he called.

The nanny came up in under a minute. She was surprised to see Virginia.

"What are you here for?" she asked.

"You left your jacket at my apartment," Virginia explained, handing it to her.

"Oh," Anya said, taking the coat. "Thank you. I am sorry but I have work to do."

"Oh, yeah. Right."

Anya turned to Jefferson.

"It's no problem," he assured them.

Anya then seemed to remember something.

"Virginia," she said. "This is my boss, Mr. Jefferson Thomas. This is my friend, Virginia."

She was acting particularly nervous as she spoke.

"Are you okay?" Jefferson asked, noticing her tone. He wondered if Virginia was a drug dealer or something.

"I am all right," Anya told him.

"No, you're not," Virginia said. "Sweetie, what's wrong?"

The gasp escaping from Anya's mouth told Jefferson everything he needed to know. The expression on his face told Virginia everything she needed to know.

"I'm just gonna give you two a few minutes," Jefferson said and went outside to join the kids, closing the sliding glass door behind him.

Chapter 26

Virginia left a few minutes later. Anya then began completing every little task she could find, often repeating things, in order to avoid speaking with Jefferson. She was silent at dinner and Jefferson wouldn't try to get some answers out of her while the kids were around.

Nevertheless, he wanted to talk to her. Some questions were answered, but more emerged. They needed to talk. He wasn't interested in her sexual orientation. He was interested in why she treated the issue like she was carrying some deadly virus and didn't want to get too close to anyone for fear of infecting them. He was absolutely certain about few things, but him not being homophobic was an absolute certainty. He knew he never gave indications to the contrary.

Jefferson finally managed to stop her early the next morning, just after she'd loaded the breakfast dishes into the dishwasher, practically forcing her to sit down at the kitchen table. She looked up at him, saying nothing.

"Virginia seems nice," Jefferson opened, sitting down as well.

Anya still said nothing.

"How long have the two of you been going out?" Jefferson queried as casually as he could.

"Ten months," Anya said, seemingly waiting for something.

Jefferson noticed she answered his question the way a witness in the courtroom would, short and straight to the point, giving no unnecessary information to satisfy the inquiry.

"She seems pretty open about your relationship," he said.

Anya slammed a hand onto the table. Jefferson jumped, surprised.

"If you want to fire me, just do it," Anya demanded. "I do not want to just talk first."

"You think I wanna fire you?" Jefferson asked. He strongly suspected this was why she had avoided talking to him as much as possible since Virginia's visit.

Anya hung her head.

"Some of My past employers were not happy if they found out," she explained. "It was even more difficult when I was living in Russia. Virginia does not like that we hide who we are, but she understands. I love my job and I love working for you, but if you want me to leave, I will understand."

She fell silent again, waiting.

"Anya," Jefferson said, "you've been reliable, trustworthy, and just plain great to have around, and that's probably an understatement."

A brief smile flickered across the nanny's face.

"Who you date means nothing to me," Jefferson continued. "It's obviously not affecting your performance here. If I judged you on something like that, I'd be the biggest hypocrite you've ever met."

"What do you mean?" Anya queried.

"If you judged me on my blindness and held that against me, I'd resent you for it. In my book, it's the same concept."

Anya now felt somewhat hopeful.

"Here's the problem," Jefferson said and that hope faltered. "I don't care that you didn't tell me, but the fact you acted so defensive about it, as though I would have burned you at the stake, does eat at me. Anya, we need to trust each other if we can continue to make this work. It's none of my business about what you do with your private life, but just don't automatically believe I'd hold anything like this against you."

"I am sorry," Anya said.

"So, can we trust each other? I can trust you."

"I trust you, too."

"Good, because this is your one and only warning. Break that trust and you're out the door."

"I understand."

Anya rose to do some work. But Jefferson stopped her.

"I said before that your private life is none of my business," he said. "If you want to have company during your off hours, that's fine with me. Just don't let the kids walk in on anything I wouldn't let them walk in on."

Anya nodded, understanding.

"Thank you," she said.

* * *

Jefferson adjusted his tie and put on his jacket before heading downstairs to give the kids their dinner. Ellen O'Bryan showed up a few minutes later and he then left with Presley, his Uber having also shown up. Anya was also gone, most likely on a date with Virginia. She seemed much happier when she left earlier.

Monique was already waiting for him outside of Slattery's, where the law school had rented the Empire Room for the occasion. She had put on a blouse with a matching jacket and pants, looking rather professional. She also wore clips in her hair to keep it out of her face.

"You look good," Jefferson remarked after she'd described the ensemble.

"How would you know?" Monique asked.

"Can't I just pay you a compliment? You know I would mean it if I could see."

"All right. I'll take it … for now."

"Thank you. I apologize for how boring this evening will be."

"It won't be so bad if there's alcohol," Monique remarked, having been to her fair share of such events, mainly within the book business.

Jefferson led the way inside. As usual, Monique was stared at, but not as many people were guilty of it this time. She figured it had to be because of their interactions with Jefferson, noticing how only the hotel staff was staring at him and Presley.

They entered the corridor just outside of the banquet hall, where cocktail hour was already underway. They got drinks and began mingling, with Jefferson introducing Monique to his colleagues.

"What?" one of them asked. "You've replaced Linda already?"

"Not really," Jefferson said.

"We're sort of in limbo about that," Monique added, trying to help him out.

"Well, at least you always bring smart ones to these things," the colleague remarked. "Remember that woman Jonson brought last year?"

Both men burst out laughing at the memory. Monique patiently waited for them to collect themselves before speaking.

"Do I really want to know?" she queried.

Jefferson shook his head and she decided not to press the matter.

They continued to mingle, Monique soon finding herself face-to-face with the school's dean. He at first believed she was a new professor before she and Jefferson set him straight. He apologized and made small talk before moving on.

"It's nice to know I can pass for a lawyer," Monique commented when he was gone.

"He might have already had a few drinks," Jefferson remarked.

It was soon time to go into the banquet room itself. Since the seating arrangements were made long before Monique's presence was known, no one had informed the staff that she needed a free space at a table.

The place assigned to her still had a chair in it. A waiter was summoned to move it away and she was then able to pull right up to the table, meeting Eric and Amy for the first time. She couldn't help noticing a strange look on Amy's face as Jefferson introduced the two of them. It didn't disappear as she shook Monique's hand. She decided to let it go for the time being as everyone sat down.

With the wait staff moving through the room, taking drink orders, the dean stepped up to a lectern in the front. Having seemingly gotten past any effects from his earlier alcohol consumption, he welcomed the students and faculty to the awards' night, adding how the professors and other staff have worked tirelessly to ensure the students' hard work was recognized during the night's presentations.

After the dean said his bit, the class president stepped up and basically said the same thing but used different words. By this time, people were only half-listening and instead quietly spoke with one another. Monique and Amy were among them, neither really understanding much about the law but finding common ground in their work with books. Monique was quickly warming up to this woman as the fact she was strapped into an elaborate-looking wheelchair didn't seem to matter.

After the class president was finished, there was a break where drinks were served and dinner orders were taken, with the choices being chicken or vegetarian. As a waiter poured Monique's drink into the plastic tumbler on her wheelchair, he asked if she wanted the kitchen to cut her chicken for her, but Monique politely insisted she could do it herself. Amy was about to comment on this exchange when Eric spoke up.

"Don't look now," he said. "Here comes Jefferson's stalker."

Sure enough, Paula Franks soon made her presence known at the table. Judging from Jefferson's unspoken but clear desire to disappear told Monique exactly who this was.

"Hello Jefferson," Paula Franks said. "How are you this evening?"

"I'm fine," Jefferson said, clearly preferring the idea of sticking a fork into his throat over talking to her. "How are you?"

"Who's your friend?" Paula Franks asked, her eyes surveying Monique. She wasn't even trying to hide the fact she was silently sizing up the woman.

"This is Monique," Jefferson said rather reluctantly. "Monique, this is Paula Franks, a former student of mine."

"Very nice to meet you," Monique said, reaching out to shake Paula Franks's hand. She didn't expect to complete such a transaction, but she might get a surprised reaction by revealing her capability to do so.

Predictably, Paula Franks didn't move to reciprocate, leaving Monique's arm hanging in mid-air. She pulled it back and smiled before any spasms could begin.

"I've gotta run," Paula Franks said. "My date's waiting."

She pointed out a man about her age who was sitting a few tables away. As if on cue, he looked up and gave the group a wave.

"Nice seeing you, Jefferson," Paula Franks said and walked the way she'd come.

Jefferson released a sigh while Monique took a long drag from her drink.

"Lovely girl," she commented.

"Well, that's what happens when you forget your cyanide pills at home," Eric remarked.

"How does she expect you to know she's got a date waiting at another table?" Amy asked. "I mean, you couldn't see the guy waving or anything."

"I'd have to care before I could look into that," Jefferson replied.

"I think she hired the guy," Eric remarked. "I'm willing to bet that if we look up male escorts on the internet, we'll find him. I mean, you can't see it, but he basically looks the part. Wonder where he got the shoes or the teeth."

Jefferson chuckled, trying to picture teeth Eric could see from his current vantage point.

* * *

"Okay," Ellen said, setting up the DVD and selecting "Play Movie" on the menu. "You're all set."

The twins thanked her and then turned their attention to the movie while she went to help Matthew build some kind of fort out of his blocks, trying to find the best memory in her brain to help block out Frozen 2, a film she'd seen her entire babysitting career.

* * *

After Paula Franks's visit, the evening moved along more smoothly. Both Jefferson and Eric had to present awards, the latter not hesitating to complain throughout the process, but neither of them received anything, which they were both fine with.

"Maybe it's for the best," Monique commented. "Had you gotten something, I would have had to give you a congratulatory kiss."

"Which would have been so painful for you?" Jefferson asked.

"Maybe."

The awards' portion of the evening ended shortly before dessert was served. People ate the cheesecake and talked with one another a while longer. It wasn't long after dessert that they began to depart.

Eric and Amy soon made their exit, saying good-night and telling Monique it was very nice to meet her. Once several people had left and the area wasn't so congested anymore, Jefferson and Monique headed out as well.

"So, was this a date?" Monique asked as they crossed the lobby.

"I don't know," Jefferson admitted. "Do you want it to be?"

"Do you normally use the first date to take a woman to a law school awards dinner?"

"No, not normally. But I couldn't get tickets to the Oscars."

Monique chuckled.

"What do you normally do at the end of a first date?" she inquired.

"To know that, you'd have to consider this a date," Jefferson pointed out. "Do you?"

Monique made a noise which seemed to indicate she wasn't sure.

"How about we don't consider this a date?" she suggested. "You asked me to come as a friend, which I did. That sound good?"

"Okay," Jefferson agreed, wondering where she was going with this.

"And then we go on what we'd both consider a real date," Monique finished.

Jefferson stopped walking and stared at her.

"You wanna do that?" he asked.

"Sure," Monique replied. "Why not?"

"You do realize that we're risking our friendship, right? We might cross a line and not be able to turn back."

"Or something really great could happen. You're one of the few people I know who doesn't just see a girl in a wheelchair. You see a person, just like I see you. I think we've got something there. And frankly, I'd like to see what we can do with that."

Jefferson said nothing to this.

"Come on," Monique insisted. "One date. If it doesn't work out, we'll go back to being friends. We won't have sex or anything like that. Come on. Take a chance."

Jefferson thought this over for a long moment.

"All right then," he agreed. "Let's give it a shot."

Chapter 27

"Uncle Jeff!" Taylor called. "Abigail tied my shoes together!"

Jefferson sighed and went to see what was going on. He didn't doubt Abigail had tied Taylor's shoes together, but he wondered why. He was sure it had something to do with the fact she recently started learning how to tie shoes and seemed to like practicing. Taylor was learning this skill as well, but she wasn't as obsessed with it.

Jefferson found the girls in their room, where Taylor was already trying to undo the knot Abigail had created. After making Abigail sit in a corner of the room for a while as punishment, he set to work on helping undo the mess.

As he untangled the shoelaces, Jefferson soon had to put Taylor in another corner after the girls began squabbling in a mixture of English and what he guessed to be very sloppy Russian. He was finally able to separate the shoes but kept the girls in their corners for another few minutes. He eventually released them and then headed back up to his office.

"Sure hope Matthew doesn't pick up this stuff," he said to himself, his even bigger fear being what the twins could be like as teenagers. They were definitely very comfortable around him by now. And what if they got better at speaking Russian. He'd have to get lessons from Anya to keep up.

* * *

"No," Monique said in the firmest tone she could muster. "No little black dress. There's a very good reason why I don't own one."

If she had to wear a dress, she preferred something that went far past her knees as that presented less of a chance of giving someone a show.

"Come on," Joan said. "You wanna look good. You really seem to like this guy."

"That doesn't mean I wanna wear something that suggests I'm ready to hop in the sack tonight," Monique defended.

"All right then. How about a dress you actually own?"

* * *

Jefferson bid the kids a good night, leaving them in Anya's care, and headed out to meet his Uber. Sure, it cost him more, but Anya was happy to work overtime, adding that Virginia was also working late.

They'd chosen Amélie, a French restaurant in SOHO. When Jefferson arrived, the hostess reported his table was ready and that the woman he was there to meet had already been seated.

Sure enough, Monique was there, wearing a navy-blue dress, the matching jacket and purse draped over the back of her wheelchair.

Jefferson wasn't that surprised none of the staff had commented on Monique's appearance. She was in a wheelchair and, rather than risk getting themselves in trouble by saying something offensive, they simply didn't make any comment about her at all. Wait staff had mentioned a few positive things about Linda when Jefferson went to meet her at restaurants. But Linda wasn't disabled, so they saw no risks with her.

All this quickly left Jefferson's mind as he sat down and greeted Monique while settling Presley underneath his chair. Since the restaurant couldn't find their Braille menu, it fell on Monique to read the entrees out loud. Given she spoke some French, she was fine with this. They soon gave their orders to a waitress and handed back the menus.

"So," Monique said, "what happens next on a date with you?"

* * *

"All right children," Anya said. "Time for bed."

"Already?" Abigail whined. She had been trying to sing along to some songs on a CD of Jefferson's she'd found. Anya had barely gotten a chance to study the case to make sure the music was age appropriate. She deemed the list of Phil Collins songs to be okay and endured the subsequent karaoke night.

"Yes, it is already time," Anya told her, stopping the music. "The Same time as always. Come on now."

The kids grudgingly obeyed and headed upstairs to wash up and put on their pajamas. Anya straightened up a few things in the den before following them.

Neither of the twins were interested in a story, but Matthew was. Anya studied the books on the shelf in his room and selected a Curious George volume. When all three kids were asleep, she went back downstairs, where "Rebel" by Beverly Jenkins waited for her.

* * *

After dinner, Jefferson took Monique to the Spot Dessert Bar back in Greenwich Village. They bought ice cream and sat kitty-corner at a small outdoor table where Presley could curl up by Jefferson's feet, as she liked to do.

"I cannot believe I've lived in this city my entire life and never heard of this place," Monique commented, using a small plastic spoon to eat her strawberry shortcake ice cream. "How'd you find it?"

"A law school buddy of mine lived in this neighborhood," Jefferson replied. "He let me in on the secret."

"So now you bring all your dates to it?"

"Sometimes."

Monique gave her ice cream a thoughtful stare.

"I had a good time tonight," she said.

"Me too," Jefferson agreed. "And it doesn't look like any lines were crossed."

"I guess not."

Jefferson reached over, found and brushed her cheek with his fingers, and then leaned over and kissed her. Though startled at first, Monique soon found herself reciprocating.

"How about now?" Jefferson asked when he pulled away again.

"I'm not sure," Monique teased. "I might have to try one more time."

She leaned towards him as best she could, her ice cream now forgotten.

* * *

"this is my stop," Monique said as they approached the bookstore's front entrance.

"That's too bad," Jefferson said. "We'll have to pick this up another time."

"Yeah," Monique agreed with a smile.

Jefferson leaned down and kissed her for the third time that night. In the back of her mind, Monique was wondering if Joan was watching from an upstairs window. She couldn't remember the last time someone walked her home.

"Good night, Jefferson," she said when he pulled away.

"I'll call you," He promised. "Good night."

he walked away with Presley as Monique entered the bookstore and locked the door, her key serving as a back-up for the keypad beneath the front counter.

Not surprisingly, she found Joan waiting for her up in her apartment. The nurse was giving her an amused look.

"How was your date?" she asked.

"Fine," Monique said, shrugging as best she could.

"Your smeared lipstick and ruffled hair suggest it was more than fine."

Joan's amused expression grew.

"Believe what you want," Monique retorted.

* * *

"You went through with it?" Eric asked, trying to make the water cooler work. "You went out with Monique?"

He and Jefferson were standing in the corridor of the law school.

"Yeah," Jefferson said as Eric pounded on the cooler's plastic jug. "Is that so weird?"

"No way," Eric said, now kicking the base of the cooler. "I'm happy for you. She seems like a great catch. Why is it not coming out? I mean, I can see the water in the jug. It's definitely there."

He released a groan of frustration and smacked the jug.

Deciding to leave his friend to his quest, Jefferson headed down the corridor to his office. With final exams over, he had to finish preparing for the summer class he would be teaching, which would begin less than a week after the graduation ceremony. Thankfully, it was now only a matter of days before Paula Franks would be out of his life.

His phone was ringing when he got into his office and he reached out to answer it. The caller turned out to be his mother, Beth Thomas.

"How is everyone?" she inquired.

"We're fine, Mom," Jefferson insisted. "The kids are all still in one piece."

"I'm sure they are. Nevertheless, your father and I want to come up to visit you and our grandchildren."

"Well, could you wait another couple of weeks? I've gotta get my summer class up and running. Then I'd have the time to see you guys."

Knowing full well his mother would now demand a date, he pulled Outlook up on his computer.

"When can you make time in your busy schedule to see your parents?" Beth asked, being as predictable as always.

"How about you guys come down on the week of June 11th," Jefferson suggested. "Things should be running smoothly by then."

He secretly hoped he could recruit them as baby-sitters so he could go out with Monique.

"All right," Beth said, giving in, "but you've got to stick to that. Your father and I can't go changing our plans at the last minute just because something came up for you."

"I won't, I promise," Jefferson said. He never did such a thing anyway, but his mother still insisted on reminding him of these kinds of manners.

* * *

"Your parents are coming down to visit, huh?" Monique commented. "Great. Maybe I could get to meet them."

"I am not sure if I'm ready to drop that bomb on myself or you," Jefferson replied.

Though they were admittedly involved in a relationship, which now consisted of three dates, they didn't give up meeting up for lunch whenever they got the chance. It was simply another excuse to see each other.

"My mother will interrogate you to no end, and my father was the police detective in the family," Jefferson continued. "He will just go on and on about his days on the force to any adult who hasn't heard them a hundred times before. And he will then go on and on about IronDog. I guarantee you that your ears will bleed."

"All right," Monique said, giving in. "I'll wait. When you're ready to let me meet them, that'll be it."

"Maybe I'll first do something about those steps in front of my house."

"One thing at a time then," Monique agreed, dipping a cracker into her soup.

* * *

The kids were more enthusiastic about having grandma and grandpa come to visit, though it was still three weeks away. Jefferson was sure they knew all about what it meant to be spoiled by now and expected nothing less from his parents.

Anya was somewhat interested but stated it was none of her business. Jefferson told her his parents could help out with the kids while they were there so she could take some extra time off. She said she would consider the offer and thanked him.

* * *

Amy took a deep breath and rang the doorbell. She waited as Jefferson came to answer it.

"Hey," she said. "Eric mentioned you had some movies you wanted to put Braille labels on. I was in the neighborhood and I've got some time, so I thought I'd come by and offer to help."

"Oh, yeah, sure," Jefferson said, having not expected her. "Come on in."

He'd been working on the syllabus for his summer class, but he could afford to take a break.

"The kids have been asking about them for a few weeks," he explained. "I just wanna know what I'd be getting myself into."

He left out the fact he wasn't entirely comfortable about asking Anya for help with this matter. Though she knew the basics, the subject of his deceased family members didn't come up with the nanny.

"I understand," Amy said.

"I keep them upstairs in my office," Jefferson told her, leading the way up the steps.

Amy hesitated before following, passing Anya, who was carrying an overflowing laundry basket.

They reached the third floor and Amy stopped dead in her tracks.

"Everything okay?" Jefferson asked.

"Oh … Oh, yeah," Amy said, surveying the floor's three doors. "Just a second."

She took a deep breath and quickly walked past the first door on the right, the one to Jefferson's bedroom. She walked through the door at the end and into his office.

Jefferson pulled the dozen or so DVD cases out of the drawer and piled them onto his desk. Amy sat in the chair while he went to retrieve his Braille label maker. He pulled over the spare chair for himself and they set to work.

"'Kids' First Steps'," Amy read, studying the cases. "'1st Birthdays'. Looks like they filmed the events for each of the kids and put them together on one disc."

"Guess so," Jefferson agreed as he began making a label for the first DVD. "My brother was always good at those things."

"Looks like he labeled the discs as well," Amy said, opening the case. "Everything matches so far."

They discovered the same thing had been done for vacations and holidays.

"Who films Thanksgiving?" Amy queried, studying another case.

"Only Stan," Jefferson remarked, making another label.

"Hey," Amy said, waiting. "How can you be sure none of this is porn in disguise?"

Jefferson looked at her.

"I'm kidding," Amy admonished. "Relaxat."

"Stan wouldn't do that anyway," Jefferson said. "Besides, there's no need to do that with the Internet being so handy."

The task was completed in twenty minutes.

"You miss them, don't you," Amy observed as Jefferson put the DVDs back into the desk drawer.

Jefferson looked at her for a long moment.

"Yeah," he admitted. "Yeah, I do."

"Look," Amy said. "the only experience I've got with this is when my grandfather passed away a couple years ago. It'll get easier with time. That's all I can really tell you."

"Thanks."

"Par angusta ad augusta."

"What's that mean again?"

"Through trial to triumph," Amy reminded him, tapping the closed drawer with her foot. "And watch some of these home movies. It might help."

Jefferson nodded and they both rose from their seats.

"Hey?" he asked. "Are we okay?"

Amy seemed startled by this question and stayed silent for a moment.

"I'm not sure," she admitted. "What we did ... I'm ... it's complicated ..."

"Do you want to tell Eric?" Jefferson asked.

"I don't know. I mean, he's my husband. We have a family. But this would kill him ... I mean, this would literally kill him. I just don't know."

Jefferson nodded, trying to recount how many times they'd had this conversation.

"He's my friend," he said. "My best friend. I feel like I've stabbed him in the back."

"I have to go," Amy said. "I've got some things I need to get done."

She darted out of the office before Jefferson could say anything else.

"Thanks for your help," he said anyway, listening to her bounding down the stairs as fast as she could.

Chapter 28

"Hey orphan!" a boy called.

Taylor, who had been quietly sitting on a bench in the school's playground, turned her head. She didn't know this boy's name. Why was he talking to her to begin with?

"Yeah Orphan!" the boy continued. "I'm talking to you! What are you doing?!"

"Sitting here," Taylor said, though she had now decided to get up and walk away. He'd tried this before.

"We saw the movie 'Annie' in our class yesterday," the boy said, coming over. "She didn't have a mom and dad neither, and no one wanted her. You've got red hair just like her."

Taylor could feel angry tears filling her eyes. She'd always been proud of her red hair, especially when people said she looked like her mother because of it.

"Maybe we should call you Annie!" the boy said loudly. "Orphan Annie! Orphan Annie!"

Taylor clenched her fists as the tears began rolling down her cheeks.

* * *

"Hey," Monique asked, "everything okay?"

"What?" Jefferson asked, distracted.

"Are you okay? You've barely touched your food. What's on your mind?"

"Nothing," Jefferson said, starting to actually eat his lunch. "I'm fine. I've just got a lot on my mind."

They were having lunch at Subway, intending to make it quick as both were busy.

"I hope you would tell me if something's bothering you. Otherwise, I don't know how it's gonna work between us."

Jefferson nodded as his cell phone rang. He answered it and spoke briefly to the caller, his face quickly becoming anxious. He hung up and looked at Monique.

"I've gotta run," he said. "Something's happened at the girls' school."

* * *

Taylor was sitting on a bench in the school's main office, not speaking to anyone. Her head was down and she clasped her hands together in her lap. That was exactly how Jefferson found her when he arrived with Presley at his side. She looked up at him but didn't say a word, though he could hear her shuddering breaths.

"Fighting?" Jefferson asked. "Really? I thought I'd be waiting a few more years when I had to come to the police station for your first DUI."

Taylor didn't seem to understand the joke, so he dropped it.

"You wanna tell me what happened?" he asked instead, sitting down next to her. "The school said you hit a kid during recess. Is that true?"

"He called me an orphan," Taylor said in a low voice. "He called me 'Orphan Annie' and that made me really mad."

"And you hit him?" Jefferson asked. On the one hand, he was happy she so readily disclosed what happened to him. On the other, she'd hit another kid.

"Uh-huh," Taylor said. "I was really mad, and I hit him."

Jefferson let out a long breath and draped an arm across her tiny shoulders.

"And do you think that was the right thing to do?" he asked.

Taylor shrugged.

"I was mad," she said. "Really mad."

"That's no excuse," Jefferson said. "You can't go around hitting people when they make you mad … even really mad."

Taylor said nothing as the principal, Cynthia Langley, emerged from her office.

"Mr. Thomas," she said, "Can I speak with you?"

"Stay here," Jefferson told Taylor. "I'm gonna go find out how much trouble you're in."

He got up and followed Cynthia Langley into her office. The principal closed the door behind them.

"How's the kid she hit?" he asked as they both sat down at her desk.

"The nurse gave him some ice for his cheek," Cynthia Langley replied. "He'll be fine. I think Taylor was aiming for his nose and he moved at the last second, so he was lucky. An aide broke it up immediately."

"And what about Taylor?"

"We don't doubt that she was provoked. The boy was telling the nurse all about how 'the orphan' had hit him."

Jefferson nodded, though he was sure Taylor wasn't off the hook.

"Mr. Thomas," Cynthia Langley said, "this incident does raise some concerns. Taylor is very quiet in class. She does the work and does it well, but she doesn't participate unless she's pushed to. Also, the school psychiatrist says that she doesn't open up about her feelings concerning her parents' deaths. As we've seen today, bottling up those feelings does not do her any favors."

Jefferson nodded.

"Abigail's made a much easier transition," Cynthia Langley continued. "She is very talkative and readily participates in just about anything. She does express some distress to our psychiatrist, but it's nothing we wouldn't expect. The bottom line is that we're not worried about Abigail like we are about Taylor."

"Okay," Jefferson said. "What happens now?"

"We are going to send Taylor home for the rest of the day. Apart from a note in her record, she won't see any other disciplinary actions about this on our part. We would like to add an extra weekly session for her with the school's psychiatrist and then have both girls continue with an outside child psychiatrist over the summer. We want to crack the shell that Taylor has built up around herself and we want to make sure Abigail doesn't regress."

Jefferson nodded, thinking how Taylor hadn't been as open with him until more recently. And he was family.

"Okay then," he said. "We'll do that."

＊ ＊ ＊

Monique, who had accompanied Jefferson to the school, was waiting outside, watching the traffic go by. Taylor was surprised to see her when she, Jefferson, and Presley emerged from the school building.

"What are you doing here?" she inquired.

"I was having lunch with your uncle when the school called him," Monique explained. "I came to make sure you were okay."

Taylor nodded.

Jefferson and Monique had agreed not to disclose their relationship to the kids yet, despite how comfortable they were around her.

"Come on," Jefferson said. "Let's go home."

"I'll call you later," Monique said, deciding it was best to part company with them here. She needed to get back to the bookstore anyway.

Jefferson nodded and headed off with Taylor.

* * *

Jefferson forbade Taylor from watching television when they got home, so she retrieved some paper and colored pencils to draw pictures at the kitchen table. Anya watched her while Jefferson returned to the school and the day care center to pick up Abigail and Matthew. Abigail, having heard about the fight but having not witnessed anything, pestered him for information about what happened, but he told her to drop it.

"I saw the aide take Taylor away," she recounted. "That's all I saw. I was by the swings."

"That's all you need to see," Jefferson told her. "Everything's fine."

* * *

Not surprisingly, Gloria Lawson showed up the next day, having heard all about the fight from the school, who were required to inform her. Jefferson explained what happened and she fired off about a thousand questions. Had he seen this coming? What was he doing about it? She also questioned Taylor, though she was considerably friendlier towards the girl. As always, Jefferson was happy to finally show her the door.

"Hang on just a second," Gloria Lawson insisted. "I've been hearing things."

"What sort of things?" Jefferson asked, having no idea what she knew about now. Whom was she hearing things from?

"You've been frequently seen in the company of a woman in a wheelchair," Gloria Lawson said. "The school's seen her a couple of times."

"That's Monique," Jefferson said. "I know her. The kids know her and she's great with them."

"What is your relationship with this woman?" Gloria Lawson asked, scribbling something in her notepad.

"We were friends," Jefferson said, knowing the kids were upstairs and couldn't hear him. "Now we're dating."

"Uh-huh," Gloria Lawson said, still making notes. "And do you think it is wise to expose the kids to that sort of thing?"

"They don't know that our relationship has evolved. To them, she's just a friend of the family."

Jefferson was becoming seriously bothered by how much this woman dug into his personal life. He began weighing the idea of reporting her conduct against how doing so could jeopardize his chances of keeping the kids. He'd need to consult Eric about this and possible repercussions.

"I mean, do you think they understand her condition," Gloria Lawson clarified.

"They understand she can't walk just like they understand I can't see," Jefferson replied. "She's just a person to them."

Gloria Lawson wrote down something else before leaving.

* * *

Jefferson's yard was a thousand square feet, a little bigger than a two-car garage, with one-third of this being the patio. The wooden fence was seven feet tall and blocked any views except that of the sky.

There was a side gate which opened onto the small patio which could be accessed from the street via a narrow path between Jefferson's home and the neighboring brownstone. For years, the only people using this gate were the Poop-and-Scoop employees who cleaned the small yard every two weeks. Now, a second regular visitor would make use of the gate.

Monique could move through the space between Jefferson's home and his neighbor to reach the gate, which he'd be there to unlock for her. She could then enter his home through the rear sliding door, which provided a seven-foot-wide entryway.

"Nice place," Monique commented as she moved around the first floor, studying everything. "The bachelor pad is still trying to hang in there despite the kids' best efforts."

"It is relentless," Jefferson replied, putting the finishing touches on their lunch. "Maybe you could deliver the finishing blow."

Monique smiled as she came to the table.

"Might that not be moving a little fast?" she queried.

"It's not like I'm asking you to come upstairs and stay the night," Jefferson remarked. "It's just so you can do something like come by and survive my cooking."

Monique eyed the stairs, knowing his bedroom was on the third floor.

"What if it doesn't work out between us?" she asked.

"I'll change the lock to the gate," Jefferson remarked, and they laughed.

"Your parents are coming next week, right?" Monique asked as they sat down to eat.

"Yeah."

"You ready?"

"Yeah. I've got the couch ready for them."

"What, down here?"

Jefferson shook his head.

"It's actually a sofa bed up in my office," he clarified. "I've offered my room, but they always insist on that. I'm still surprised they never nagged me to use the empty rooms as guest rooms. I don't think they'll nag now that the kids took those."

Monique nodded, studying the stairs again. She then studied Jefferson.

* * *

"Why can't we go down to the platform?" Abigail queried as Jefferson again reminded her to stay close to the bench he was sitting on.

"Because I'm not risking any of you going off over the edge on to some train tracks," Jefferson said. "We can wait right here. Grandma and Grandpa know where to find us."

"Are you sure?"

"I am," Jefferson said, checking his watch. His parents were due in any minute.

Suddenly, a voice called his name. Next thing he knew, all three kids were running off to meet their grandparents, whom they had seen from afar. He and Presley went to join the group at a much steadier pace.

"Hi Mom," Jefferson said. "Hi Dad."

After hugging and kissing their grandchildren, Beth and William Thomas each embraced their son.

"How was the train ride?" Jefferson asked.

"It was fine," Beth said. "It might have been better if your father didn't keep reminding the conductor to make sure no cars were stuck in the train crossings."

"Do you know how often that happens?" William asked. "I can't even count the number of times I've responded to such a call while on the force. I didn't want us to get delayed."

"I'm sure they appreciated the help, Dad," Jefferson said. "Shall we?"

At his mother's insistence, he took one of the big suitcases so she could walk with her grandchildren.

* * *

Taking two cabs, the group got back to Jefferson's house. After the kids received the presents their grandparents brought, Jefferson was tasked with lugging the two large suitcases up to his office. He then introduced his parents to Anya, who immediately hit it off with Beth while William turned his attention to the twins.

"So," he asked, "when are you girls done with school?"

"Next week," Taylor replied.

"And then you'll have the whole summer for fun. You will have to come visit us down in Charlottesville. I can tell you all about the days when I was a policeman."

Both girls were interested in hearing such stories now, but Jefferson managed to deter this for the time being, saying the kids needed to have some lunch.

"I'll help Anya with lunch," Beth insisted, following the nanny into the kitchen. "Later, you can tell me all about this new woman you're seeing."

* * *

"You're cute," Monique said, leaning up against Jefferson. "Do you know that you're cute?"

"I've been told that on occasion," Jefferson remarked.

Monique chuckled and kissed him.

They were sitting on the couch in the living room of Monique's apartment, the wheelchair and Presley not far away. Monique had invited Jefferson over for a movie and Chinese food.

"how's it going with your parents?" she queried.

"It's going fine," Jefferson said. "I'm surviving. My mom really likes Anya."

"And the kids? Are they 'surviving'?"

"They're thrilled to have their grandparents there. I think they barely noticed that I left tonight."

"Don't worry. You'll have them all to yourself again next week."

Jefferson nodded and kissed her.

"Let's not talk about my kids," he insisted.

"Then what do you want?" Monique asked.

"You."

"Is that right?"

Jefferson began kissing her more insistently.

"You do know what you want," Monique remarked and kissed him back.

A sudden sound from outside caused her to quickly pull away.

"That's Joan coming up the outside stairs," she said.

Sure enough, the nurse then entered the apartment, looking at the two of them.

"Am I interrupting something?" she asked with a smile.

Monique was sure she hadn't seen anything, but the nurse was perceptive.

"Nothing that's any business of yours," she retorted. "It's not putting my health in danger."

"Okay," Joan said. "So, who's this helping you not put your health in danger?"

Monique knew she couldn't avoid this. There was no point in even trying.

"Jefferson, this is Joan, my nurse," she said. "Joan, this is my boyfriend, Jefferson Thomas."

The two shook hands. Joan then turned back towards Monique.

"If you two aren't planning anything else, I'll get you ready for bed," she insisted.

She helped Monique off the couch and back into her wheelchair. They went into the bedroom. Now alone, Jefferson packed up the remaining Chinese food.

"He's cute," Joan commented after shutting the bedroom door. "And he seems to really like you."

"That would be my business," Monique said. "I don't dig through your love life."

"Feel free to try. You'll make some interesting discoveries."

Monique decided not to pursue this topic. She let the nurse check her for any of the usual injuries and get her ready for bed.

"Anything else you need?" Joan asked as she made sure Monique's water bottle was full.

"Yeah," Monique said. "If you manage not to scare him off, let Jefferson come in here."

"All right," Joan said with a sly smile. "I'll just say 'good night' now then."

She left the room and found Jefferson still in the living room.

"She wants you," the nurse reported. "I'll just put this food away and let myself out. Should I expect you here tomorrow morning?"

Jefferson didn't answer and she left as he headed for Monique's bedroom.

"Hey," he said, coming in. "Lovely nurse. Really involved."

Monique laughed.

"Sorry about that," she said. "She's just worried about me."

"It shows," Jefferson said. "What's up?"

"I didn't want that to be the end of the night for us," Monique explained, adjusting the head end of her bed so she was somewhat sitting up. She patted a spot on the mattress next to her.

"Sit," she insisted. "Five steps forward and you'll hit the bed."

Jefferson did so and they began kissing again.

"We're really picking up right where we left off," Monique remarked.

Jefferson nodded and smiled.

"I love you," Monique said.

Jefferson stopped kissing her and stared.

"I mean it," Monique said, feeling bold, "I do love you."

"Now who's moving fast," Jefferson teased.

"I can't help the way I feel about you."

Jefferson kissed her again.

"Honestly," he said. "It's been a while since I've heard that."

"Says the man who's rarely been alone," Monique remarked.

"Nancy didn't say it much anymore during our last year together, and Linda and I hadn't gotten there yet when we broke up."

"I haven't had anything like this since college."

Monique looked at Jefferson.

"So, you know why Greg and I broke up," she said. "Why did you and Nancy split? I know you said you realized she wasn't for you, but what triggered that."

Jefferson took a deep breath.

"One day, I got a phone call," he described. "That was when I learned my brother and my sister-in-law were killed in a car accident. As I was still absorbing this information, the caller reminded me that I had long ago volunteered to be the kids' guardian if anything ever happened. They wanted to know if I was ready to now take up that responsibility."

Monique nodded, listening.

"I immediately said I would," Jefferson continued. "But Nancy flipped out. See, she never wanted to have kids."

251

"But she had to know you were named as the kids' guardian," Monique pointed out.

"She did. She even encouraged it when Stan and Maggie first asked me. But I guess she wasn't ready for it to be real. She gave me an ultimatum … her or the kids. I sent her to the curb the same day and left for the airport twenty-four hours later."

Jefferson became quiet. Monique reached out and pulled him up against her.

"You made the right choice," she told him. "They needed you. And besides, we might have never met."

Jefferson chuckled.

"It all worked out for the best then," he remarked. "Except for the fact I miss my brother and his wife."

"I know," Monique said. "I know it's hard. You can miss them. It's okay."

"I haven't seen any of them in five years. I mean, I never met Matthew in person until I became his guardian. How messed up is that?"

Monique shook her head.

"It's not messed up," she insisted. "They were abroad, and you had your own life to worry about here."

"I always thought about visiting them," Jefferson said. "We talked about it and made vague plans. I just never did it. Maybe I thought it was for the best."

Monique stared at him.

"Why would you think that?" she asked.

Jefferson fell silent.

"Jefferson," Monique said, still holding him close. "Please tell me. I won't judge, I promise."

Jefferson took a deep breath.

"I had a one-night-stand," he said. "I had a one-night-stand with Margret. I had a one-night-stand with my sister-in-law. I had a one-night-stand with my brother's wife."

Monique looked at him for a long time. She didn't say anything. She had not expected this.

"I'd better go," Jefferson finally said, moving to stand up.

"No," Monique insisted. "Stay. What happened?"

Jefferson took another deep breath.

"Before my parents moved to Virginia, I lived in this little apartment," he recounted. "It had a tiny main room, an even smaller bedroom, and a miniscule bathroom. I didn't need more space, even though I could afford it. One weekend, Stan, Maggie, and the twins come to stay with me. The twins were two at the time and Matthew hadn't been born yet. Maggie wasn't even pregnant yet. Anyway, they all came to visit before Stan got sent overseas. They brought this portable crib that the twins slept in while they took this sofa bed I had in my main room at the time."

Monique nodded, listening.

"On Saturday afternoon, Stan got a call," Jefferson continued. "Apparently, there was a paperwork problem or something down in Washington which they needed him for. So, he takes off, leaving Maggie and the girls with me and promises to be back the next morning to salvage what's left of the visit."

"It was just you and Margret then," Monique said, slowly putting the pieces together.

"Yeah," Jefferson confirmed. "We were hanging out. I helped her feed the girls as best I could. We drank some margaritas and talked. I never really knew her that well except for the fact Stan loved her, and I've always trusted his judgment. So, she was cool with me. Anyway, we're knocking back these margaritas and we're starting to feel a little buzzed. All of a sudden, we started kissing and one thing led to another. We're in my bedroom … you know. We wake up together the next morning with terrible hangovers and deep regrets. We shower and straighten up before Stan gets back and we agree never to tell him. It was a stupid mistake and that was it. They moved less than a week later, and I never saw her again. I always thought this distance between us was a good thing. It allowed me to pursue a relationship with Nancy, though that later turned out to be a brilliant idea … call it mistake number two."

He looked uncomfortable.

"I never saw Stan and Maggie again after that," he said. "And the next time I saw any of the kids, I was picking them up in Germany."

"Were you dating Nancy at the time?" Monique asked urgently. She needed to know.

"No," Jefferson said. "I met Nancy about a month later in a local coffee shop where she worked at the time," Jefferson said and, sensing what Monique had been thinking. "I've made some really stupid mistakes, but I would never cheat on anyone like that. I would never do that to you."

Monique decided she could trust him. But then something hit her.

"What other mistakes have you made?" she asked, narrowing her eyes.

Jefferson didn't say anything.

"Wait a second," Monique said. "The librarian ... the wife of your buddy at work ... Amy ... I saw the way she looked at you when I met them at that law school dinner ... she looked really uncomfortable ... you slept with her, didn't you?"

Jefferson nodded. He wouldn't even try to hide it, even if Monique appeared to be super-perceptive.

"My God," Monique said. "What happened?"

"Pretty much the same story," Jefferson said. "She came over to help with some things for the kids. We were drinking wine and talking. One thing led to another ... it was a mistake."

He looked at her, half-expecting to be kicked out right then.

"I've made my own sort of mistakes," Monique said, deciding to open up herself.

"Like what?" Jefferson asked.

"My store was robbed a couple of months back. The guy came up here, looking for more money. He found me and, when he heard the police coming, he hit me across the head with his flashlight and ran. I was so sure he would have done worse if he'd had the time."

"That's not your fault. It isn't the same."

Monique shook her head.

"But keeping my feelings about it bottled up is my fault," she insisted. "The truth is that I am so afraid that he'll come back. They never found him. I'm just so scared that he'll come back one day and kill me. I'm always double and triple-checking the locks and the alarm."

She began to cry. Jefferson put his arms around her as the tears flowed.

"Tonight ..." Monique said. "tonight was the first night I've felt safe. It's because of you. I know it is. And I know I love you. I love you."

Chapter 29

The house was silent when Jefferson and Presley entered through the front door. Since it was shortly before midnight, it was not surprising that everyone was fast asleep. Jefferson let Presley out of her harness and quietly headed upstairs to his bedroom.

* * *

Beth was already making breakfast when Jefferson came downstairs and poured himself some coffee.

"You were out late last night," she commented.

"Did I break curfew?" Jefferson asked.

"Were you with that girl? Monique?"

"I was."

Beth studied him.

"Does she know you have three kids living here with you?" she inquired.

"She's met them," Jefferson said.

"How does she feel about that?"

"She's supportive. She definitely likes kids. There's no problem."

Beth nodded once.

"I've already lost a son and a woman I considered a daughter. Be careful. I don't want to see you get hurt."

"Uncle Jeff!" Taylor called from upstairs. "Grandpa's making strange sounds! We can hear him!"

The moment between mother and son was broken.

"He's probably trying to sing in the shower," Beth remarked.

* * *

Monique was rolling up and down the aisles of her store. It was a slow day, and nobody seemed to need her help. Frank was up by the register, reading a magazine. Kathy was out that day, meeting a friend visiting from Oregon, and Samuel was up in the storeroom, cleaning up.

"What's with you?" Frank asked, noticing Monique's glazed-over eyes.

"I'm thinking," Monique said absent-mindedly.

"About your boy toy? What did you two do last night?"

"Nothing you need to be concerned about."

Monique wouldn't tell him anything. But she did need to talk to Jefferson. She turned around and headed to her office.

Once inside and set up behind her desk, Monique dialed Jefferson's home number. An older woman answered the phone and she guessed it was Jefferson's mother.

"Hi," she said. "I'm looking for Jefferson Thomas. Is he there?"

"I'm sorry, but he's not," the woman said. "He's teaching. He should be home soon though. Could I take a message?"

"No, that's all right. Thank you and have a nice day."

She did not want this to be an unofficial introduction between herself and her boyfriend's mother. She instead tried Jefferson's cell number. This time, Jefferson answered.

"Hey," Monique said. "Can you talk?"

"I just finished up my class," Jefferson said. "What's up?"

"I just wanted to talk. We kind of unloaded a lot on each other last night."

"Yeah. You okay?"

"I'm fine. I just wanted you to know that I'm okay with your mistakes. I wasn't in your life then. The past is the past."

"Okay. Thanks."

Monique waited a moment.

"But I also need you to know that if you ever do that to me, it's over between us," she said. "It happens and we're done. I won't stand for that."

"Sure," Jefferson said. "Thanks for your honesty."

"And I meant what I said last night. I love you."

* * *

Jefferson finished the call and pocketed his cell phone. He considered his conversation with Monique and what he meant.

He thought back on his affairs with Maggie and Amy. One was a mutually defined drunken mistake which now had little chance of ever being revealed. The other had yet to be defined, though it bothered him a bit less now and had almost no chance of being revealed. The leap of faith he and Monique took to get to this place carried no regrets.

Smiling, Jefferson checked the time and continued down the corridor.

* * *

"I'm looking for Monique Vasquez," Jefferson said.

"She's working in her office in the back," the man behind the register told him. "What's this regarding?"

"I'm a friend of hers. I need to speak to her."

He could tell from the man's snicker that he knew exactly what "friend" meant. For the first time since requesting an Uber from the law school to the bookstore, he began to wonder if this was the right way to do this.

"Turn left and go straight back," the man told him. "You'll walk right into her door."

Jefferson did as he was told and located the door. He knocked loudly.

"Come in," Monique said.

Jefferson entered. Monique was definitely surprised to see him.

"What's up?" she queried.

"I just wanted to tell you ..." Jefferson said, his voice faltering. "I have to tell you ... oh for God's sake! I love you ... I love you, too."

Monique emitted a slight gasp. Jefferson came around the desk and kissed her.

"Guess we have that settled," Monique remarked, and they shared a laugh.

"I wish I could stay," Jefferson said. "But I've gotta get home."

Monique understood.

"I love you too," she said. "I'll call you later."

Jefferson left and Monique could see Frank and Samuel standing by the open office door. Frank was wearing an enormous grin on his face and Samuel was unsure of how to act. Monique was sure Kathy would hear all about this very soon.

"Someone better be watching the cash register," she warned. "I find any money missing, I'm taking double that amount out of all your paychecks,"

Frank and Samuel quickly disappeared from view.

* * *

Jefferson's parents left a few days later, promising to visit again soon. Not long after that, the girls were out of school for the summer and, with Anya around and quite comfortable in the house, Jefferson decided to also keep Matthew home from day care. The kids stayed with Anya every day that he had to go and teach. He did the rest of his work at home and only stayed late if a student wanted to talk to him.

* * *

Monique was eating dinner when the phone in the kitchen rang. Joan went to answer it. After a few seconds, she handed the receiver over to Monique while wearing a big grin.

"Hello?" Monique asked, sure she knew who it was. As she worked to handle the receiver with one hand, she waved Joan away with the other.

"Hey," Jefferson said. "You busy?"

"No," Monique said, making sure Joan had retreated into the bedroom. "I'm just eating dinner. What's up?"

"I've got an offer for you. The 4th of July's just around the corner."

"It is. Just a few weeks away."

"I've got dinner reservations at this great place that's practically on the river. You ever hear of High Street on Hudson?"

Monique smiled.

"Yeah, sure," she confirmed. "In the West Village, right?"

"That's it," Jefferson confirmed. "You in?"

"How could I say 'no'?"

"Okay then. There is one more thing. The girls' school is doing this indoor camping trip thing next week. They're calling it a summer kickoff. Anyway, I've got Anya, who could potentially watch Matthew for that same night."

Monique's smile widened.

"What could you be getting at now?" she queried mischievously.

* * *

"Hey," Eric said, coming down the corridor in the law school, ducking around two students along the way. "How are you?"

"How is it that you're not teaching a summer class and you still come here?" Jefferson wondered aloud.

"Better coffee, and maybe I wanted to say 'hi' to you."

"Thanks."

They stepped out of the way of an approaching custodian pushing a cart.

"No problem," Eric said. "How are things? I hardly get to see you anymore."

"Teach a class during the summer," Jefferson suggested. "It'll give you an excuse to get out of Queens every so often."

"Amy's still working. Someone's gotta stay home and keep the boys and the house intact."

"You're here now."

"The boys are in summer camp. The house will stand on its own for a few hours."

Jefferson nodded.

"You should consider getting your Rugrats into a summer camp," Eric added. "It does wonders for the rest of your life."

"Maybe next year," Jefferson said. "I've had the kids for three months. I'd like to get to know them a bit more before I send them away."

* * *

Monique looked at herself in the full-length mirror attached to the inside of one of her closet doors. She normally didn't like to use this mirror as it brought her wheelchair into full view, making her see herself the same way others saw her. She did not like to see herself that way. She wasn't just some woman strapped into a wheelchair.

But tonight was different, or at least it would be. Tonight, a man was on his way over and he wanted her sexually. That hadn't happened in a long time and Monique couldn't help feeling excited. Seeing her wheelchair in the mirror didn't matter.

Not surprisingly, Joan had deduced Monique's exact plans. While she wouldn't be around when Jefferson arrived, she did come by a little earlier to make sure Monique was okay. She also helped spruce her up a bit, though Monique absolutely refused her suggestion to dress up in some sort of sexy outfit. After all, she and Jefferson would be having dinner first.

There was a knock on the door. Monique came out of her bedroom and went to let Jefferson in. He'd brought along a bouquet of flowers, which he handed to her.

"Already?" Monique asked. "I'd have thought you'd wait until after tonight to see how things went first."

"What can I say," Jefferson replied, coming inside. "I'm an optimist."

Monique shut and locked the door behind him. Jefferson let Presley off her harness and the dog immediately began exploring the apartment. Monique took the opportunity to pet the affectionate animal. She then had Jefferson retrieve a vase and a bowl from her kitchen.

"The sink is to your right," she directed as she followed. "Fill both up with water."

The bowl went on the floor for Presley while the flowers went into the vase and were set on the kitchen counter.

With Jefferson's help, Monique then freed herself from the confines of her wheelchair and they sat down on the couch to begin digging into their dinner. This evening's cuisine consisted of Indian takeout.

"Do you ever eat American food?" Jefferson asked.

"I'm a bit more exotic than that," Monique said. "Life's more fun that way. Here, help me with this thing."

Jefferson helped her set up her TV tray, as her coffee table was way too low for her to eat off of and she didn't trust her hands to be able to hold any food dish for very long. The tray's height worked much more in her favor, so she could eat while the firm couch cushions allowed her to remain seated relatively upright.

"You don't like handling glasses or dishes, huh?" Jefferson asked.

"I don't have the strength in my hands to keep a good grip on them for very long," Monique explained, carefully nudging her plastic cup a bit closer so she could drink from the straw. "I've dropped my fair share of plates and glasses and stuff."

"Uh-huh."

They ate in silence for a while, each consumed with anticipation about what was to come. Presley was nearby, amusing herself with a toy Jefferson had brought for her.

"Not much of a romantic setting," Jefferson commented at one point.

"Well," Monique remarked. "It's not like either of us is a virgin. I think what'll happen later is when it'll really count."

"I like your confidence."

After they finished eating, Jefferson cleared away the empty plastic dishes and threw them out. He then returned to the couch and began kissing Monique.

"I love you," he told her.

"I love you too," Monique said.

Thankfully, Presley was ignoring this make-out session.

"Okay," Monique finally said, pulling slightly away from Jefferson. "We can continue this one of two ways ... either you help me back into my chair or you carry me into my bedroom."

"I think I like that second one," Jefferson said, scooping her up.

"Just don't decapitate me on the door frame," Monique warned and began directing him on where to go.

They entered her bedroom and Jefferson put her down on her bed. Monique quickly pulled him on to it with her. They resumed kissing as they ran their hands over each other.

"Keep your hands further up," Monique advised at one point. "By my shoulders ... I can feel them there.

"How far down do you feel them?" Jefferson asked.

"Just past my nipple line."

Jefferson began fondling her breasts through her blouse.

"I guess I should have kept that a secret," Monique remarked as she ran her hands up his chest. She found the first button on his shirt and began to try to undo it, but she lacked the fine motor skills necessary to accomplish this.

"Having some trouble?" Jefferson teased.

"Maybe a little," Monique admitted in a smile and a pouty tone. "Buttons are hard."

Jefferson unbuttoned his shirt while she slid her hands down. She was able to unbuckle his belt, but she needed help with the button and zipper of his pants.

"Hey," Jefferson said as he pulled his pants off. "How come I'm the only one getting undressed here?"

Before Monique could respond, he pulled her blouse up over her head and tossed it aside. Her slacks soon followed.

Now clad only in their underwear, they began another furious make out session.

"Hey," Monique said. "This is probably a really bad time to bring this up, but you brought a condom, right?"

"Yeah," Jefferson said. "I've got one."

Monique kept on kissing him. At this point, he wasn't teasing her by touching her breasts. No, the way his hands explored them and the rest of her body made it inescapably clear he wanted her. He wanted all of her. That was no problem, as she wanted him just as badly, if not more.

She felt his hands on her upper back and a moment later, she felt her bra loosen around her chest. Jefferson pulled the garment away as she let one of her hands graze the front of his boxer shorts. Taking the opportunity to remove one of his articles of clothing on her own, she pushed them down his legs as far as she could reach. Gravity helped and they landed on the floor, followed shortly by her panties.

Jefferson stopped to seemingly survey her now nude body and Monique momentarily felt as though he could actually see her. She, being able to see, wasted no time in doing some surveying of her own.

As though he realized he couldn't see her, Jefferson once again let his hands roam across her skin, both where she could feel them and where she couldn't. His lips meanwhile moved across her collarbone and shoulder.

Monique was loving every minute of his attention. Maybe it was because she hadn't been in this situation with a man in years or because she truly loved the man she was now in this situation with, but she just wanted more and more from him.

"Get the condom," she finally said, breathless. "Now. Go get it."

Jefferson obligingly got off the bed and found his pants hanging by a belt loop off one of Monique's bedposts. He needed to check three pockets before finding the condom.

Monique managed to prop herself up on her elbows and watched him work, her body tingling with anticipation. She had long ago learned that, while she could get some physical sensations sent through to her brain during intercourse, they weren't enough to satisfy her. Around that same time, she had learned about the concept of having a mental orgasm, allowing her to experience the pleasure of having sex.

And now that was exactly what was about to happen. Jefferson got back on to the bed and positioned himself over Monique. She took a deep breath and looked at him with longing.

Chapter 30

Their passionate whirlwind behind them, Jefferson and Monique lay on her bed, catching their breath. Monique's hair was matted to her head and the little makeup she'd applied earlier was now nicely smeared across her face.

"You still there?" Jefferson asked, still breathing heavily.

"Yeah," Monique replied. "Where would I go? Why would I have any reason to go anywhere?"

"I was just making sure. You've been pretty quiet."

"I have to catch my breath."

* * *

A sudden noise startled Monique awake. She looked around her bedroom but saw nothing, not that there was much to see in the dark. She thought the noise could have come from another part of the apartment. Maybe it was Presley. They'd left the bedroom door open, and the dog was nowhere in sight.

Monique looked back at her bed and saw the spot next to her where Jefferson fell asleep was now empty. In fact, it looked like no one had ever slept there to begin with, the sheets being neat and flat and the pillow remaining undented.

"Jefferson?!" Monique called, but there was no answer.

Feeling angry and hurt by the possibility that he had snuck out while she was still sleeping, Monique checked the time and saw it was 3:15 in the morning. Why go through the trouble of sleeping with me? she wondered furiously.

She then heard the noise again. It was definitely coming from somewhere in her apartment. Monique got out of bed and, still naked, walked over to the closet and pulled out her bathrobe. She put it on and headed for her bedroom door.

As she stepped out into the main room of her apartment, Monique heard the noise for a third time. This time, it was clearer, and she was sure it was coming from her kitchen.

"Jefferson?!" she called again, cautiously moving forward. "What are you doing? You scared me half to death."

She stepped into the kitchen and gasped, coming face-to-face with a figure dressed in black. Immediately recognizing this intruder, she tried to scream but no noise came. Nevertheless, the intruder pulled out a revolver and pointed it straight at Monique's chest.

"No!" Monique cried, her legs frozen in place, leaving her unable to run away. "Please don't!"

A shot rang out and Monique heard a blood-curdling scream as she fell to the floor as a large red spot spread across her chest.

Monique's eyes snapped open. She realized she was sweating, breathing heavily again, and her heart was racing. But she was alive and lying in her own bed.

Was that a dream? she wondered, patting herself down to check for bullet holes. She decided to try and move her leg, but nothing happened. Monique let out a long breath. It had been a bad dream. Somehow, her brain remembered the sensations she had had when she was able to walk as a little girl and had incorporated them into her subconscious, combining them with a nightmare she'd had so often before.

Still shaken from how real the dream had felt, Monique turned her head and propped herself up on her elbows to see the figure sleeping next to her. Wanting to make sure, she reached out with one hand and touched his arm.

This move startled Jefferson awake and he turned to look at her. Despite the limited light in the room, she could make out his face.

"You okay?" he asked. "What's up?"

"Sorry ..." Monique said, embarrassed over her own stupidity. "I didn't mean to ... it was an accident."

"Are you all right?"

Monique took a deep breath.

"What's wrong?" Jefferson asked, moving closer.

"It's nothing ..." Monique said. "it was nothing ... just a bad dream ..."

"Tell me," Jefferson insisted, pulling her against him.

"I woke up to a strange noise," Monique began. She recounted the rest of the dream, speaking in a shaky voice throughout.

"That sounds like more than just a bad dream," Jefferson remarked when she'd finished.

Monique said nothing.

"But it was just a dream," Jefferson reminded her. "You're safe. You're okay."

Monique shook her head.

"I've had it before," she told him. "Or others like it. I've had them every so often ever since someone robbed my store."

"You ever tell anyone about this?" Jefferson asked.

Monique shook her head again.

"You're the first," she admitted. "I usually sleep alone, so no one sees me when I wake up in the middle of the night."

"You've gotta talk to someone about this," Jefferson insisted. "Someone like a therapist. Obviously keeping this bottled up isn't doing you any favors."

Monique let out a long low moan.

"Can I have my water bottle?" she asked. "It's on my nightstand."

Jefferson grabbed it and she took a long sip from the straw.

"It'll be all right," Jefferson said, still holding her as she quietly breathed in and out, trembling every so often. "You're okay. It'll be all right."

* * *

Monique's alarm rang at 6:00 as usual. She reached for it and hit the SNOOZE button. Next to her, Jefferson stirred.

"Morning," he said, kissing her.

"Morning," Monique replied. "Listen, you've got about half an hour to get out of here if you want to disappear before Joan shows up. Trust me, you'll never leave if she runs into you. The shower's all yours and there's a spare towel on the right side of the towel rack you can use. My shower chair should be folded up against the back wall, so it won't be in your way."

As Jefferson headed into the bathroom, running his fingertips along the wall to orient himself, Monique reflected on the previous night. Thankfully, her nightmare was now a dim memory, while her sexual experience with Jefferson was fresh in her mind. Monique smiled as she rested her head against her pillow and replayed it. For a while time felt fluid.

This fluidity stopped with the shower being turned off. Jefferson emerged from the bathroom a few minutes later.

"Hey you," Monique said to Jefferson.

Jefferson came over and kissed her again. He then got dressed, Monique directing him on where his clothes had landed. He also helped her put on some pajamas, Monique's argument being it was better for her to be wearing something when Joan arrived.

"She's not gonna buy it," Jefferson countered.

"I'd rather try anyway," Monique replied. She also had him drive her wheelchair into the bedroom so he could help her get into it.

"Hey," she said, following him out of the bedroom and watching as he put Presley back into her guide dog harness. "Thank you for last night … for everything."

"It was nothing," Jefferson remarked. "It was fun."

Monique laughed. Jefferson soon left and she stayed strapped in her chair until Joan arrived a few minutes later.

* * *

Jefferson first picked the girls up from their school's indoor camping trip and then headed home to find Matthew and Anya already up and about. All three kids were interested in what he had been up to since they last saw him.

"My business," he told them. "Grown-up business."

They persisted in getting an answer for a little while longer, but when he still wouldn't tell them anything, they gave up. Anya didn't ask him anything, but he knew she was perceptive to deduce what had gone on.

* * *

Needing to stay late and submit midterm grades for his summer class, Jefferson was in his office at the law school, working on his computer. A knock on the door got his attention.

"Come in," he said.

He was surprised to suddenly hear the motor of a wheelchair coming into the office.

"What are you doing here?" he asked, not that he wasn't happy that Monique had made the trip.

"I wanted to see you," Monique explained innocently. "It's been three days and we've only talked on the phone."

"Sorry," Jefferson said. "I've been busy."

"That's why I came here. Plus, it gives me an opportunity to see where you work."

She looked around the office, which, unfortunately, wasn't big enough for her to move forward any further.

"Well," Jefferson said, "if you give me a minute, I could grab a quick bite with you on my way home."

"Sure," Monique agreed.

She then heard a noise behind her and looked back to see a woman standing in the doorway.

"Good," Gloria Lawson said. "I caught you before you left."

It took all the energy Jefferson possessed to withhold a groan.

"I just wanted to inform you that a formal custody hearing has been set for August 14th. You'll be receiving the official notice in the mail in the coming days."

Jefferson was certain this was not why she was here. And, sure enough, Gloria Lawson didn't move. She occasionally glanced at Monique, but her glare held contempt for the woman. Monique tried her best to ignore this.

"Is there anything else?" Jefferson asked.

"Yes," Gloria Lawson said. "I just wanted to see what was going on here. You said you were teaching a class during the summer, but I come here to see you socializing."

"Monique just got here. Monique Vasquez … Gloria Lawson."

"Nice to meet you," Monique said. She thought about holding out her hand to shake, but Gloria Lawson clearly wasn't even considering such a gesture.

"Well," the woman said instead, "just make sure that when you're here at work, you're working."

She then left.

"I'm sorry about that," Monique said when she was sure they were alone again. "I didn't mean to cause any trouble."

"Don't worry about it," Jefferson said. "She would have found some other ridiculous accusation without you here."

"She's that sweet, huh?"

Jefferson nodded.

"We're still on for our 4th of July dinner next week, right?" Monique asked.

"Yeah," Jefferson assured her. "I just have this block party out on Long Island that one of my colleagues invited me to, but I should be back on my way to the city around five. I'll definitely see you at 7:30."

"Sounds great."

"Come on," Jefferson said, shutting down his computer and grabbing his briefcase. "Let's go get that bite to eat. I could use a not-so-bite-sized drink with it."

* * *

"Do we have to?" Abigail asked.

"If you want to play under the sprinklers, you do," Jefferson told her.

With that argument, Abigail gave in. She hadn't been against the idea of wearing a bathing suit. She had been against the idea of wearing one during the drive out to Long Island.

"Hurry up and finish getting ready," Jefferson told her. "We're leaving in fifteen minutes.

* * *

Sure enough, Eric arrived with his minivan fifteen minutes later. He and Jefferson loaded up the three kids and their stuff plus Presley and they were ready to go. Anya bid them farewell as they drove away. She would be meeting up with Virginia and they were going up to Connecticut for a night for the holiday. Apparently, one of their friends had a boat up there.

Eric had to make a small detour in Queens to meet up with Amy and their sons. Since there wasn't enough room for everyone in the minivan, they were taking a separate car.

The drive out to Long Island took about forty minutes. Eric's and Jefferson's colleague, Dawn Shay, and her husband, Brian, were taking part in hosting a 4th of July block party their neighborhood put together. Dawn had invited several of her law school colleagues and their families.

* * *

Eric parked the minivan along the side of the street with Amy pulling the family's sedan up right behind him. The group walked the final block, passing several more parked cars, until they reached the wooden sawhorse barricading the area where the party was underway.

Dawn Shay made her way through the crowd and met them as they were walking around the barricade. Having met Abigail, Taylor, and Matthew only once before, she didn't remember them right away. Jefferson reintroduced everyone.

"Abigail?" Dawn queried, looking at the girl. "Anybody ever call you 'Abby'?"

"Yeah," Abigail replied. "but I don't like it."

"All right. I'll just call you Abigail."

"Okay."

Dawn's husband, Brian, came over.

"Anybody hungry?" he asked. "We've got burgers, chicken, and sausages on the grill and plenty of fries, salads, and beer to go around."

"Where are the sprinklers?" Matthew asked, excited.

"Right over there," Brian said, pointing out a nearby home's front yard, where several kids were already playing. "Enjoy."

, Jefferson helped the kids discard the clothes they were wearing over their swimsuits. While Taylor's suit was a one-piece with dolphins adorning it, Abigail's was a two-piece with a flower pattern printed across it. Matthew's swim trunks were plain dark blue with a white Nike swish.

With their uncle watching their clothes, they ran under the sprinklers, laughing and having fun with the other kids.

"The things that make a child happy," Eric commented, giving Jefferson a beer, his own sons having run off somewhere else.

* * *

Holding a Coke, he watched the three newcomers join the other kids under the sprinklers. The two redheads caught his attention. He smiled as he made sure his admiring glances stayed subtle as to not arouse suspicion.

* * *

"Hey," Frank said, coming over to Monique. "You've got another big date tonight, right?"

Kathy and Samuel, the latter manning the register, both looked up. Though it was the 4th of July, they were keeping the store open for a few hours, planning to close around two, when everyone was sure to be on their way to parties and barbecues.

"I do," Monique said, deciding not to deny it. "So?"

"Nothing," Frank said. "I'm happy for you. He seems like a nice guy."

* * *

"Uncle Jeff," Abigail said, approaching him, Brian, and Eric. "I have to go to the bathroom."

They'd been at the party for just under two hours and she was the first of the three to make this statement.

"There are some Porta-Potties two houses away from us," Brian said. "Direct line of sight from here."

"You can use those," Jefferson said. "Come back this way afterwards."

"There's a line," Abigail complained, seeing three or four people standing by the tall, narrow, blue-and-white structures.

"You can come in our house and use that bathroom," Dawn offered, walking by and overhearing. "Come on. I'll take you."

"You sure?" Jefferson asked.

"It's no problem. I have to get more ice anyway."

"All right then," Jefferson told Abigail. "Go with Mrs. Shay. Don't make a mess."

"Thank you," Abigail said as she walked off with Dawn.

* * *

Seeing one of the redheads walking away with Mrs. Shay, he devoured the remainder of his hot dog and followed, weaving through the party in a deliberate manner to not alert anyone that he was following Mrs. Shay and the girl.

* * *

"There you go," Dawn said, pointing out a nearby door. "The bathroom's right through there. You know your way back outside?"

Abigail nodded and hurried off through the door.

Dawn retrieved another bucket of ice from the freezer and headed back out the front door, greeting one of her neighbors, a teenager named Aaron Chesterfield, along the way. She kept walking, not noticing Aaron slip into her house.

Once inside, Aaron moved slowly, taking his time and keeping one hand in his pocket. He turned into the hallway adjacent to the kitchen just as Abigail was coming out of the bathroom. She stopped when she saw him.

"Hey there," Aaron said with a grin.

"Hello," Abigail said, returning his smile.

Aaron moved forward slowly. Abigail began walking forward again as well, intending to pass him and go back outside. But he blocked her path, his hand still in his pocket.

"What are you doing?" she asked.

Aaron said nothing.

"I want to go back outside," Abigail insisted, no longer sounding cheerful.

She tried to get around him, but he grabbed her shoulder and pushed her against the wall. She stumbled and fell, crying out.

"Let me go," She demanded, now scared.

Aaron crouched down in front of her, a lecherous grin on his face.

"Let's have some fun," he said, running his finger along the trim of her swimsuit.

"I'll tell," Abigail whimpered.

Aaron smiled as he pulled his hand out of his pocket, a pocketknife grasped in his fingers. He flipped open the blade, his grin growing wider.

"Now let's have some real fun," he said, moving even closer.

Chapter 31

Abigail burst out of the house, screaming at the top of her lungs while running as fast as she could. Several people looked up as she streaked across the front yard, making a beeline toward Jefferson, who had been talking with Eric and Brian again. She crashed into his legs and clung to them, whimpering.

"Abigail?!" Jefferson asked in alarm. "Abigail, what's wrong?"

Abigail kept clinging to his leg, continuing to whimper. She was causing Jefferson to lose his Balance and Eric quickly grabbed his friend's arm to steady him.

"Abigail!" Amy said, having come over to see what was going on. "Abigail, you're bleeding."

She pulled out a pack of tissues while barking at Brian to go find Dawn and a first-aid kit. She examined the cut on the side of Abigail's neck. Abigail flinched and whimpered as she worked.

"It's not bad," she assured Jefferson. "It looks more like a scrape than anything else."

Jefferson wasn't listening to her. He finally managed to separate Abigail from his legs and crouched down to be at eye-level with the blubbering child.

"Abigail," he said as calmly as he could despite knowing his niece was on the verge of tears with a bloody wound on her neck. "Abigail, what happened?"

"The boy …" Abigail cried.

"What boy? Abigail, please tell me."

"The boy …" Abigail repeated, tears welling up in her eyes, "in the house …"

Dawn, who was coming with the first-aid kit, heard this and gasped. Taylor and Matthew were also coming over and Eric moved to intercept them.

"What happened?" Jefferson asked. "Abigail, you have to tell me. What happened with the boy?"

Abigail began to cry.

* * *

With help from Amy and Dawn, Jefferson persuaded Abigail to somewhat describe what happened, but it was more than enough for them. While Dawn went to call the police, Eric and Brian led a search party to find Aaron Chesterfield. That didn't take long, as he was in his parents' kitchen just down the street, bandaging a bloody finger. He denied Abigail's allegations, but they wouldn't hear any of it. They could see her bite marks on his knuckle.

"Girl's got razor blades in her mouth," Brian commented. "Good for her."

The Nassau County Police soon arrived and took Aaron Chesterfield away for questioning while an officer drove Jefferson and Abigail to the hospital to get her checked out. Despite Abigail saying the boy had only touched her and she'd scraped the side of her neck on his knife blade when she managed to escape, Jefferson wouldn't have it any other way.

* * *

Monique finished up the paperwork in her office and headed up front to make sure the front door was locked. With that confirmed, she headed up to her apartment and straight towards the closet in her bedroom. Though Joan wouldn't be there to help her for a little while, it didn't hurt to already look. Monique wanted to dress up tonight.

* * *

"She was very lucky," the nurse said. "The cut on her neck is the worse injury, and the blade barely broke the skin. He didn't get a chance to do worse, though according to her story, it was not for a lack of trying."

Nassau County Police Detectives Roy Nolan and Seth Burton nodded. When the report of the suspected sex crime came in, they were assigned to the case. Now, they were in the Oyster Bay Medical Center, waiting to interview the victim, Abigail Thomas.

"The doctor will let you know when she's ready to talk," the nurse finished.

Both detectives nodded and thanked her. They then waited, not saying anything to one another. Detective Nolan had been investigating sex crimes for the past five years. Detective Burton had been doing it for three. Still, neither of them was ever truly ready to deal with the children. In their minds, no one that young deserved this.

Abigail's attending physician soon came into the waiting area. She repeated the nurse's summary, adding they could speak with Abigail now. The detectives followed her directions to the hospital room.

Abigail was sitting on a stretcher, her feet hanging over the side. She wore tan shorts, a purple t-shirt, and flip-flops. A white bandage was visible on the side of her neck. Her uncle, Jefferson, was sitting next to the bed. They both looked up at the detectives, as did Jefferson's guide dog.

"Hello, Abigail," Detective Nolan said. "You mind if we talk to you for a little while?"

"Okay," Abigail said in a small voice.

Jefferson looked ready to completely break down.

"Mr. Thomas," Detective Burton said, "Could we speak outside while my partner talks to Abigail?"

Jefferson didn't move from his seat.

"Come on," Detective Burton insisted, gently pulling him up. "We're just gonna go talk outside."

He carefully led Jefferson and the dog out of the room. Detective Nolan sat down in the chair next to the stretcher.

"Abigail," he said, showing her his badge. "I'm a police officer. I wanna know what that boy did to you so I can help you. Do you understand that?"

"Uh-huh," Abigail said, nodding her head but not meeting the detective's eyes.

"We're gonna talk for just a little while. Any time you wanna stop, you just say so and we'll stop, understand?"

Abigail nodded.

"Can you tell me what the boy did to you?" Detective Nolan prompted. "Start from the beginning."

Abigail recounted how Aaron Chesterfield had cornered her in the hallway outside the bathroom in the Shay home. She described how he'd pushed her down and how he took out his knife and pressed it against her neck to keep her from screaming, threatening to cut her if she made a sound.

He had then started touching her through her swimsuit. At this point, Abigail had been too scared to even move. Then, Aaron suddenly pulled the knife away from her neck, scraping her skin in the process, because he needed to hold his hand up to his nose for an oncoming sneeze. It came and Abigail managed to wriggle away from him. Getting her feet under her, she'd run as fast as she could towards the front door, screaming. Aaron had tried to stop her, but she whirled around and sank her teeth into one of his fingers. She then kept running.

Detective Nolan couldn't resist a slight smile as he heard about the bite.

* * *

"This is all my fault," Jefferson said, unsteady on his feet as he and Detective Burton stood in the hospital corridor. "I should have gone with her. I should have been there. I shouldn't have brought her to the party. I should have …"

"You can't dwell on what you could have or should have done," Detective Burton told him. "You gotta focus on what you're gonna do next to help your niece get past this."

"I don't know what to do next," Jefferson protested, tears welling up in his eyes.

"You'll figure that out. Listen to me. It'll take time and you have to be patient, but you will both move forward."

Jefferson couldn't think of anything to say. Detective Burton's cell phone rang and he stepped away just as Detective Nolan stuck his head out of Abigail's room.

"You can come back in," he reported. "We're done."

"Good," Jefferson said. "I just wanna get her home."

"That's probably the best thing for her. Hopefully, it'll give her a sense of safety. I'll go track down her doctor so you can get the discharge paperwork done."

* * *

Half an hour later, Abigail walked out of the hospital with Jefferson, Presley, and the detectives. Dawn was waiting with her car.

Detective Nolan shook his head as he and his partner watched the group drive out of the hospital's parking lot. It made no sense. How could anyone be sexually attracted to a seven-year-old?

"Let's go do the paperwork on this," he muttered.

* * *

Jefferson quietly entered his house with Abigail, Presley, and Dawn. Amy was waiting for them. While Eric had taken their sons home, she had taken charge of Taylor and Matthew, bringing them back to Manhattan and staying with them.

"Where are they now?" Jefferson asked.

"Sleeping," Amy replied. "I don't think they entirely believed my assurances that everything was okay."

Her voice shook as she spoke.

"Go get ready for bed," Jefferson told Abigail. "I'll come check on you in a couple minutes."

"I gave the other two dinner," Amy said as Abigail headed up the stairs. "I found the food Anya left in the fridge."

Jefferson nodded. Abigail had eaten a sandwich at the hospital and proclaimed not to be hungry anymore during the drive home.

"Jefferson," Dawn said when Abigail was definitely out of earshot, "I don't know what to say ... I am so sorry."

The drive from Long Island had been pretty quiet, but things weren't any better now that one of them was speaking.

"It wasn't your fault," Jefferson said. "Thanks for the ride."

"Sure," Dawn replied.

"We'd better go," Amy said. "You call if you need absolutely anything. I'll probably be awake and worrying anyway, so don't feel bad."

Jefferson nodded and the women left. He fed Presley and headed upstairs to check on Abigail.

* * *

Her styled hair starting to droop, Monique repetitively made a fist before relaxing her fingers again. The fireworks were lighting up the sky through the windows behind her, but she ignored them. She was fuming.

She had been sitting at Jefferson's reserved table for an hour and a half, getting plenty of looks from the staff and other customers along the way. She had tried Jefferson's home and cell numbers several times, but he wasn't answering. By now, Monique felt effectively stood up.

* * *

Jefferson was lying in bed, unable to sleep. It was 11:40 at night and he had been tossing and turning for the last two hours. He couldn't forget what had happened just a few hours ago and he had no idea what to do next.

Abigail had gone to sleep much easier than he had, but she was a child. She was being resilient. He, on the other hand, was losing his mind. He had been replaying the afternoon over and over again in his mind, trying to figure out what he could have done different. So far, he was coming up empty.

A noise outside his door startled him and, thinking it was Abigail, Jefferson immediately got up to investigate. To his surprise, the noisemaker turned out to be Taylor.

"What's wrong?" Jefferson asked.

"Abigail had a bad dream," Taylor said. "She's crying in our room."

Jefferson couldn't withhold a groan.

"Okay," he said. "Here's what I want you to do. You're gonna spend the rest of the night up here in my bed, all right?"

"Okay," Taylor said, sounding enthusiastic about this idea.

"All right. Go back to sleep."

Taylor darted past him and climbed into the large bed and under the covers.

Jefferson headed downstairs towards the girls' bedroom. He could soon hear Abigail crying. He quietly entered the room and found her curled up on her own bed. She pulled back when he first touched her, but upon seeing who it was, she let him hug her tightly as she continued to cry into his t-shirt.

"What's wrong?" Jefferson asked.

"The boy," Abigail said between sobs. "I was sleeping. I woke up and he was in here. He had his knife."

She began to cry again. Jefferson could feel tears welling up in his own eyes.

"It's okay," he said, still holding her tight and stroking her hair with one hand. "It's okay."

Chapter 32

Jefferson was sitting on the couch in his den, his eyes red from sleep deprivation. He'd managed to get Abigail back to bed and wound up spending the rest of the night on the floor of the twins' room, letting Taylor stay upstairs in his bed. He had still been unable to sleep and he instead reverted to the same thoughts he had prior to Taylor coming up to his bedroom.

Jefferson wasn't sure what to do next. He knew he had to get Abigail into therapy. True, she slept through the rest of the night and she seemed to be okay now, but she was being quiet, which was unusual for her. Plus, more nightmares were sure to come. She needed professional help.

Anya hadn't gotten back from Connecticut yet. Jefferson had no idea how he'd explain to her what had happened.

Suddenly, there was a thud. Startled, Jefferson looked around. More sounds followed and he realized someone was knocking on the rear sliding glass door. Not knowing what to expect and bracing himself for an ambush, he moved towards the door.

"Hey," Monique snarled when he slid the door open.

Surprised, it took Jefferson a moment to organize his thoughts.

"Oh God," he said. "We were supposed to … last night …"

He'd remembered to cancel the baby-sitter, but he'd forgotten to cancel the actual date.

"Oh, so you do remember," Monique said angrily. "Tell me something … do you still know how to answer phones? Because I called every number I have for you repeatedly and never got an answer. I waited at that restaurant for two hours before I used my better judgment and gave up."

Jefferson couldn't come up with anything to say.

"Do you have any idea how embarrassing that was for me?" Monique asked. "I am sitting there at that table, dressed up for you, and everyone keeps looking at me, wondering what I'm doing there by myself, in a wheelchair no less. I thought you were better, but you've obviously proven me wrong. Tell me something … was it ever real? Did I ever matter?"

"Monique ..." Jefferson stammered. "I ... I do care about you. It's just ... I ..."

He turned and, on unsteady legs, walked back to the couch and sat down. Monique followed him. Having lashed out and burned some adrenalin, she was able to focus again. She could now tell he was upset about something else than missing their date. Her anger began to soften.

"Jefferson," She demanded. "What's going on? Talk to me."

Jefferson looked at her and she could see tears welling up in his eyes. He swallowed many times before he seemed to be able to speak again.

"Abigail ..." he said in a choked voice, "Abigail ... at the party ... some kid groped and cut her."

"What?!" Monique asked, her anger now completely replaced by immeasurable shock.

The revelation seemed to have been the final straw for Jefferson, who broke down crying. Monique reached out and put her arms on his shoulders, looping her hands around the back of his neck. She wanted so badly to ask, but she was now also having trouble finding words.

"Was she ..." she began, "I mean, did he ..."

Catching her meaning, Jefferson shook his head.

"No, she's okay," he replied. "not that he didn't try."

"My God, Jefferson," Monique said. "What happened?"

She was sure it was painful for him, but they were far past the point of letting this go. She needed to know.

"It happened yesterday afternoon," Jefferson said. "At the block party."

He went on to recount the previous day's events. Monique listened quietly while looking into his eyes, noticing he probably hadn't been able to sleep since then.

"Where's Abigail?" she asked when he finished.

"Upstairs," Jefferson replied. "She's been up there all morning."

"How's she sleeping?"

Jefferson told her about Abigail's nightmare.

"Is she eating?" Monique asked, not knowing what else to say.

"She had some cereal this morning," Jefferson replied. "God ... yesterday she was such a happy kid, greeting everyone. Today, she's barely speaking ... all because of what that animal tried to do to her."

He clenched his fists.

"Jefferson, don't," Monique said, noticing this. "You have to be the clear-headed one now. Abigail's confused and scared. You have to show her everything's gonna be okay. You have to show her she has you."

"How am I supposed to do that?" Jefferson asked. "Gloria Lawson is going to be all over this. I'll be lucky if Abigail or any of them are even allowed to live here anymore."

"You can't think that way. It's gonna be okay. I'm going to help you guys get through this. It'll be okay."

"I don't wanna lose them," Jefferson whimpered.

"I know."

Monique moved one hand back to her chair and undid the straps holding her shoulders up against the seat. Her upper torso now free, she pulled Jefferson close to her, using him as a prop to hold herself up at the same time. She wrapped her arms around him and held him there, comforting him as he cried.

"You have to pull yourself together," she told him when he had calmed down a bit. "There is a little girl upstairs who needs you to be her rock. I know you and I know you can do that for her."

"I wanna make it right," Jefferson said.

"You can't. You can't do that. You can only help her recover and move on. They're all gonna need you now more than ever."

Jefferson took a few deep breaths. He looked at Monique and she knew she'd officially adopted the role of being his rock in this.

"Listen to me," she said. "You're not gonna do anything just yet. You're gonna use today to calm down and just keep everyone else calm. Then, tomorrow, you start with the next step. I'll be here for you … I promise."

She planted a soft kiss on his forehead.

"Thank you," Jefferson said, leaning his head against her shoulder.

"Don't worry," Monique told him.

Jefferson managed a weak chuckle.

"You missed out on being a shrink," he remarked. "You study this or something?"

"Only as a minor at Syracuse," Monique replied.

They shared a laugh.

"I've gotta hit the head," Jefferson said.

"Sure," Monique said, using her arms to push herself up against her wheelchair again. "Go ahead. I'll hold down things out here."

Thankfully, there wasn't anything to really "hold down" right then.

Jefferson got up helped Monique strap herself back into her wheelchair. Seconds after he left the den, Abigail came down the stairs.

"Hey kiddo," Monique said. "Hi."

Abigail was startled, having clearly not expected to find Monique in the den. She came over, taking slow, deliberate steps.

"Where's Uncle Jeff?" she asked, stopping a couple feet from the wheelchair.

"He went to the bathroom," Monique assured her. "He'll be right back. Do you need something?"

Abigail shook her head. Monique noticed the cautious stare she was giving her and realized she didn't fully trust her either. She felt a surge of anger at this. She then noticed the hospital bracelet Abigail was wearing. She figured Jefferson had forgotten to cut it off, or maybe he hadn't dared to try.

"You want me to help you get that off?" Monique asked, gesturing at the bracelet.

Abigail looked at it and then back at Monique, making no other movements.

"Come on," Monique encouraged. "I'll help you."

Abigail hesitated before following Monique into the kitchen. Monique looked through a few drawers before finding a pair of scissors.

"Hold out your wrist," she prompted.

Abigail definitely seemed to be battling with her inner demons about this idea. Monique set the scissors on the counter and waited, saying nothing.

Finally, Abigail slowly raised her wrist with the bracelet on it. Monique carefully retrieved the scissors and encircled the plastic bracelet with the blades.

"Hold still," she said.

Abigail nonetheless flinched as the bracelet was cut, even though she wasn't touched. She seemed to realize this a second later as Monique was throwing the bracelet in the trash.

"Thanks," she said quietly.

"Sure thing," Monique replied as she put the scissors away.

She moved closer to Abigail, who didn't move at all, reached out, and lightly grazed the girl's hair with her fingertips. Abigail seemed to be about to move away, but she stood still, looking up at Monique.

"I miss my mom and dad," she said in a soft voice.

"I know," Monique said.

She took a deep breath.

"My dad died when I was young," she said. "I wasn't much older than you."

She was seventeen when the heart attack struck, but she wasn't about to bring numbers into this.

Abigail stared at Monique, seeming to process this revelation.

"Do you miss him?" she asked.

"Yeah," Monique said. "He taught me so much about running a bookstore. I miss him every day."

She remembered coming home from school one day and being told by her grandmother how her father went to the grocery store and collapsed in the dairy aisle. He was dead before the paramedics arrived.

Monique imagined this little girl and her siblings being home with a babysitter and suddenly learning their parents weren't coming home from dinner as planned. Tears welled up in her eyes.

Without thinking, Monique draped her arm around Abigail's shoulders. The girl flinched again but then allowed herself to be nudged closer to the wheelchair.

* * *

Jefferson came back from the bathroom to find Monique and Abigail in the den. The three of them decided to play UNO and when Matthew and Taylor came down a bit later, they joined in as well.

Abigail didn't talk much during the game, but she was nevertheless actively participating. Monique watched Jefferson as he kept an eye on his niece, in the process not keeping an eye on how she was holding her cards. This resulted in her losing her grip and dropping them on the floor, something which amused all three kids.

"You find that funny, huh?" Monique asked with a slight smile as Jefferson went to retrieve her cards. "Take a more careful look at those cards. I would have had you all beat."

She was pleased to see Abigail smile at this.

* * *

The doorbell rang. Jefferson got up to answer it. Monique, who had been looking at a drawing of horses that Taylor had made, glanced his way before returning her attention to the drawing. Abigail was reading on the couch while Matthew was playing with his blocks.

Monique became alarmed when she heard the doorbell again, where it was then rung repetitively, similar to how she'd knocked on the sliding door earlier. She wondered who else needed to talk to Jefferson so urgently.

The ringing stopped when Jefferson greeted whoever was at the door. Things became anything but pleasant when the woman began yelling. Monique looked at the three kids.

"Why don't you guys go up to your rooms for a little while," she suggested as calmly as she could.

"Who's that?" Taylor asked, having obviously heard the yelling. Abigail and Matthew also looked up.

"I don't know," Monique replied. "Just go upstairs and your uncle will take care of it … please."

"But my castle," Matthew said, pointing at the structure he had been building. "I don't want it to get wrecked."

"We'll make sure it won't get wrecked," Monique promised, becoming anxious as whoever was at the door kept yelling. "Just go on upstairs."

The three kids abandoned their activities and headed up the steps. Thankfully, they were out of sight just as Gloria Lawson pushed her way into the den. She scowled at Monique.

"Where are they?" she demanded, turning on Jefferson, who'd followed her in. "I want to see them."

"They're upstairs …" Monique began as calmly as she could.

"I want to see them," Gloria Lawson demanded. "I don't know what kind of freak show you're running here, but I am putting a stop to it now."

She paused to catch her breath, but she definitely was not finished.

"First, I hear that you let one of the girls become a victim of sexual abuse," She continued. "And now you and your girlfriend are stonewalling me."

"We're not trying to stonewall you," Jefferson said while Monique decided to keep quiet. "Just calm down. I don't wanna worry them. They've been through enough already."

"Yeah. Ever since they came here, there have been problems. Well, I am putting a stop to it now. I should have said something from the start. What was I thinking? No blind person can handle kids, especially if he's got a paralyzed squeeze to deal with on the side."

Jefferson said nothing, clearly unsure of how to respond.

"Get them down here now!" Gloria Lawson demanded. "I'm taking them with me now!"

Monique could see Jefferson's worst nightmare becoming a reality. He was speechless. Gloria Lawson was too busy mumbling angrily to notice this. She walked across the room, kicking Matthew's half-finished castle and sending the wooden blocks flying off in all directions.

"Bring them down now or I'm calling the police," she snapped at Jefferson, who hadn't moved yet. "I'll have you arrested for obstruction and reckless endangerment, and I'll have them take your girlfriend here as well …"

"Now wait just a minute," Monique said, unable to stay silent any longer. "Lady, you are out of control. Think about what you're doing and what this would do to those kids."

"Who are you to tell me anything?" Gloria Lawson asked. "I didn't ask for your opinion and I certainly don't want it."

"I'm someone who has watched this family grow closer almost from the beginning. And you know what I've seen? I've seen a guy stepping up to take on the responsibility of three kids who have suffered a loss no child should ever have to experience. He has worked hard to make them as comfortable and as happy and well-adjusted as he could. And on top of that, he's got one heck of a support system from his friends and family … one that you folks should use as a model for others to live up to."

"I doubt that. I'm now here because a little girl was almost raped."

"The only one you can blame for that is a disgusting snot-nosed punk who will hopefully never see the light of day again. And if you're going to use this against Jefferson, know that I will not sit back quietly while you try to rip his family apart."

"Oh really?" Gloria Lawson asked. "And what are you gonna do?"

"I'll call your bosses and tell them about your perceived notion that blind people aren't fit to raise children, which you've had fixed into your brain from the beginning," Monique replied. "And then I will call everyone I know who can back me up. I'll have them call your bosses. Just think about it … your colleagues … other children … their parents … all of them calling in about you. That's probably not the best kind of feedback."

She was tempted to add, "I've got a bookstore's worth of customers and I'm not afraid to use them" but decided to forgo this cliché. Besides, she could tell this was having an effect on Gloria Lawson. The woman was stepping back and seemed to be considering whether or not to take this threat seriously. Monique looked at her with an expression of confidence and determination.

"Jefferson loves those kids," she said. "He'd do anything for them. The only reason he's not saying something is because he's too stunned from you threatening to take them away from him. That's his worst nightmare right there."

Gloria Lawson looked at Monique and then at Jefferson, studying each of them for a couple seconds. She turned around and left without another word. Jefferson seemed to regain control of himself and silently went to lock the front door. Coming back, he went over to Monique, and hugged and kissed her.

"You are amazing," he said.

"Thanks," Monique said, smiling. "I thought you needed some backup."

"Thank you."

They kissed and held each other for a few minutes before finally breaking apart.

"I wonder if you've seen the last of her though," Monique pondered. She could tell from the expression on Jefferson's face that he didn't want to think about that right now. The last twenty-four hours had taken their toll on him.

"Tell me something," he said. "Were you serious about what you said earlier?"

"Of course," Monique said. "I'd do it in a heartbeat. I've got a bookstore's worth of customers and I'm not afraid to use them."

"How?"

"When you run a bookstore and have a love for the kids who come in, you get to know a few foster kids along the way. Sometimes you wind up meeting their case workers. You build relationships that way. I think you lawyers call it 'networking'."

"Wow. You really are amazing."

Monique smiled.

"I know," she said. "It's nice to hear though."

"Hey Uncle Jeff!" Taylor called from upstairs. "Is it okay to come down?!"

"Yeah, sure!" Jefferson said. "Come on down!"

All three kids returned to the den. They stood in a huddle, looking at Monique and Jefferson. They all wore apprehensive expressions on their faces.

"Why was Miss Lawson yelling?" Abigail asked.

"Don't worry about that," Jefferson replied. "It's taken care of."

"She said she wanted to take us with her," Taylor said but seemed unsure of how to continue with that thought.

"Don't worry about it. It's taken care of. You guys aren't going anywhere."

All three kids looked relieved. Matthew's eyes then fell on his destroyed castle.

"It's ruined!" he wailed. "It's ruined! You promised and it's still ruined!"

He looked directly at Monique.

"I'm sorry," Monique said. "I couldn't stop her …"

Her voice trailed off. She wasn't sure if it was right to paint Gloria Lawson as the bad guy in the kids' eyes. As mixed up as her beliefs were, she was still just trying to do her job and keep them safe. She was just doing it in completely the wrong way.

"Come on Champ," Jefferson said. "I'll help you fix it."

"It has to be just like it was before," Matthew insisted. "It has to be just right."

"We'll figure it out. Don't worry."

* * *

Anya came home from Connecticut about an hour later. While Monique entertained the kids out in the backyard, Jefferson sat her down and told her everything, from the party right up to Gloria Lawson's visit. Anya was silent, shocked by the whole thing.

"Are you all right?" she finally asked.

"I'm working on it," Jefferson replied.

"And Abigail?" Anya asked, seeing the girl through the sliding glass door. "Is she all right?"

"We're working on it," Jefferson replied.

"I am here for you," Anya said as though this needed to be made absolutely clear. "I am here for all of you."

She got up and headed out to the backyard. A minute or so later, Monique came back into the house to find Jefferson sitting on the couch with his head in his hands.

Chapter 33

"Hey man," Eric said, coming into Jefferson's office at the law school, followed by Amy.

Surprised, Jefferson looked up towards them.

"What are you two doing here?" he inquired.

"We came by to see how you were doing," Amy explained. "Everything okay?"

"We're hanging in there. I've gotten Abigail into more therapy and Anya's been great with helping to keep her upbeat at home."

This was his first day back at work since the 4th of July party. Abigail was coming around, but she still wasn't the same happy child with too much energy. The therapist explained that, since a stranger had attacked and abused her, she would seek to trust Jefferson even more in the hopes he would protect her. So far, he had been reluctant to let her out of his sight when they weren't at home.

Jefferson was also starting to come around. While he'd not yet accepted what happened, he now understood he had to move forward and, more importantly, he had to help Abigail move forward. He also had to somehow make Taylor and Matthew understand what happened to their sister. He hoped it would help them in the long run.

Abigail had endured two more nightmares, but she was working past those. Jefferson was thankful he didn't have to spend any more nights on the floor in her room, as he was just starting to sleep again himself.

"Do you need anything?" Amy asked.

"No, I'm fine," Jefferson told her. "Thanks."

Studying her, he realized he was seeing her differently. His passionate longing for her had diminished, even if it was still in the back of his mind. This was his friend, and his best friend's wife. He had a woman he was in love with, someone he saw a future with.

Despite everything, Jefferson managed a smile. Maybe Amy was also his best friend, even if she wasn't on par with the likes of Eric.

"How's Dawn doing?" Eric asked. "I haven't had a chance to speak to her."

"She still feels guilty," Jefferson said. "She's called me a number of times to apologize. I've told her it wasn't her fault, but still ..."

"Do us all a favor," Amy said. "Tell yourself that. It wasn't your fault either."

Jefferson nodded.

"Par Angusta ad augusta," he said. "Through trial to triumph, right?"

"Yeah," Amy confirmed with a chuckle.

"Wait," Eric said. "You're actually retaining this stuff?"

* * *

Monique moved her wheelchair up to the sliding glass door of Jefferson's house and knocked. He soon answered it and, upon learning who was there, invited her in.

"Do you have someone you trust who could watch the kids?" Monique asked.

"Why?" Jefferson asked.

"I wanna get you out of town. You need to take care of yourself as much as you need to take care of them right now. I want to take you to this cabin down in Pasadena, Maryland, by the Patapsco River. Some friends of my mother own it and I snagged it for us for a weekend. No cost. They do a lot of wine-tasting in the area."

"That's your solution? You, me, and alcohol?"

"Makes me feel better."

Jefferson hesitated.

"I don't know ..." he said.

"So, don't answer now," Monique offered. "Think about it. I made the arrangements for two and a half weeks from now. So think about it."

Jefferson nodded.

* * *

Eventually Jefferson gave in to Monique's suggestion. He decided to take the kids down to Charlottesville to stay with their grandparents while he went a little further back north for the weekend. Anya would get the weekend off like when he and Linda went away together.

Thrilled with his agreement, Monique confirmed her reservation. The only catch to the plan was that Joan wouldn't be coming along, meaning Jefferson would have to help Monique out more than usual. When she brought this up, He said he would, so the trip was set.

* * *

The doorbell rang and was followed almost immediately by a series of brisk knocks. Jefferson went to answer it while the kids, who were playing in the den, looked up with some interest. Anya poked her head out of the kitchen, where she was cleaning the counters.

"Yes?" Jefferson asked as he answered the door.

"Jefferson Thomas?" a man asked in a brisk, business-like tone of voice which matched his precise knocks.

"That's me," Jefferson confirmed.

"Hi," the man said, injecting some emotion into his voice. "Nice to meet you. Jason Greene from Children's Protective Services. I've been reassigned to your case. I've got my hand out in front of you here."

"I've been working with Gloria Lawson," Jefferson said as they shook hands. He wasn't unhappy about the change, but he was curious.

"What happened to her?" he asked.

"She's asked to be taken off," Jason Greene explained. "She said she couldn't be objective. The bosses agreed and moved some things around. So now I'm here."

He was speaking rather quickly.

"Okay," Jefferson said. "Come on in."

Jason Greene did just that, walking almost as quickly as he spoke.

"We're on a bit of a time crunch here," he said. "The courts aren't giving us an extension on your hearing, so I'll just have to make a lot of surprise visits between now and August 14th. That's about five weeks. If we can work together through this, we should have no problem. Where are the kids?"

"In here," Jefferson said, leading the way into the den. He introduced the twins and Matthew to Jason Greene, who greeted them each enthusiastically.

"You guys like staying here with your uncle?" he asked. "Is he feeding you right."

All three of them nodded but didn't say anything, somewhat put off by this stranger's energy.

"Well listen," Jason Greene said. "Your uncle and I are gonna chat in the kitchen for a little while and then I wanna see your rooms. That sound good?"

"Okay," Abigail said while the other two remained silent.

Jefferson led Jason Greene back into the kitchen and offered him some water. While doing so, he introduced the social worker to Anya, who excused herself to go do some laundry.

"Miss," Jason Greene said before she could leave. "I'd like to speak with you before I leave today."

"Okay," Anya said. "I will come back."

Jason Greene nodded as Jefferson brought the water.

"Before we begin," Jason Greene said, taking the plastic cup and sitting down, "off the record but on the issue … I know you had some problems with Gloria Lawson. She had certain … opinions which impaired her objectivity."

Jefferson nodded.

"I'm here with an open mind," Jason Greene continued. "I'll use her notes here and there, but I wanna learn about you on my own. So, the more straight-forward you are with me, the easier it is on everyone. There are gonna be problems … there have been problems, but there are solutions. My guess is that some of the problems are resolved already. Essentially, you've got a clean slate with me, but not a lot of time. I have to submit my report to the judge by the 12th. So, we've got about five weeks."

"Okay," Jefferson agreed.

"I'll start with the most serious incident I've got," Jason Greene went on.

* * *

Jason Greene left about an hour and a half later. Jefferson definitely felt better than he had at any time during his supervision by Gloria Lawson. This time, there was a social worker who was clearly on his side.

After the two men spoke, Jason talked to the kids some more. As promised, he went upstairs to see their bedrooms. He found nothing to alarm him. He did ask Jefferson to be allowed to look at Abigail's psychological records, but his tone made it clear this too was a matter of routine. He also spoke to Anya, being interested in her qualifications as a nanny, and seemed to approve of her. He ended the visit by promising to be back soon and left.

"A professional," Anya remarked after the front door was closed, "but he did look at me the way so many men do."

Jefferson would not comment.

* * *

The Amtrak train pulled into the station in Charlottesville. William and Beth were already waiting on the platform when Jefferson, Presley, and the kids disembarked. The kids immediately ran over to their grandparents, leaving Jefferson to deal with the luggage. William soon came over to help.

"Thanks for watching them for the weekend," Jefferson said when they rejoined the rest of the group.

"It's no problem," Beth assured him. "We've been wanting to have them over for so long."

"You just saw them early last month."

"We're grandparents," William retorted. "We could never get enough of our grandchildren."

He ruffled Matthew's brown hair as he said this.

"But you can get enough of your son," Jefferson remarked.

"You have your own life to worry about this weekend," Beth replied. "Let us just be concerned with spoiling our grandchildren."

"Don't spoil them too much. I don't wanna find twenty additional pounds on each one on Sunday."

Beth seemed to be ignoring him.

Jefferson helped get the kids' overnight bags out to William's car. He then said, "goodbye" to the twins and Matthew and waved as they rode away with their grandparents before returning to the station.

* * *

Strapped into her wheelchair with a roller bag being pulled along behind her, Monique moved across the small platform. She found a spot where she wouldn't block the foot traffic and waited.

Soon enough, Jefferson's train from Charlottesville arrived and she was able to get his attention and direct him towards her.

"Hey," she said after he kissed her. "I met your new social worker yesterday."

"Really?" Jefferson asked.

"He came by the store. Apparently, you mentioned me?"

"You came up in our conversation."

"He seems like a nice guy. I'd say he's better than Gloria Lawson, but there's no contest there. You seem to be in good hands this time around."

* * *

Jefferson couldn't remember the last time he hadn't been in charge of making the arrangements for a vacation. It felt refreshing.

Not only had Monique ensured the cabin would be theirs for the weekend, but she had also signed up for the Anne Arundel County paratransit service. Since she was a client of New York City's Access-A-Ride, she could sign up as a limited-time guest with any equivalent service in the United States.

A small bus picked them up at the train station and, making two stops to pick up other passengers, dropped them off at the end of the long drive leading towards the cabin. Jefferson set one foot on the drive and realized it was made of gravel.

"Your chair going to be okay on this?" he asked. They normally didn't concern themselves with the needs of their disabilities, but there were exceptions. For one thing, Manhattan's streets and sidewalks didn't have gravel.

They made it up the drive and Monique used her key to unlock the front door, describing the cabin for Jefferson's benefit as they entered.

"It's a ranch-style house," she elucidated. "It's got two bedrooms and the sofa in the main room is also a bed. Then, there's one and a half bathrooms. The kitchen is to your right."

She led the way into the master bedroom. Jefferson could smell the cleaning materials which had been recently used. Touching The bed, he realized it had been made.

"Good service," he remarked.

"It's a close friend of my family," Monique replied.

"Guess they want you to have a good weekend."

Monique smiled.

"I'm sure," she said. "I'm even more sure we can accomplish that."

She glanced towards the nearby bathroom door.

"You got the lecture from Joan about how I need help to use the toilet here," she said. "You ready to apply it? I haven't had a chance to relieve myself since leaving Manhattan."

Jefferson nodded, giving Presley a toy.

* * *

William stood over the barbecue while Beth watched Matthew and the twins playing tag in the backyard. They were certainly making use of the extra space this much-larger yard provided.

As William and Beth watched their grandchildren play, they reflected on the loss they still felt. True, Stan and Maggie had been

292

dead for about four months, but the pain was as prominent as ever. They figured Jefferson maybe felt it a little less because his life was now occupied with the kids, but the semi-retired William and Beth had free time to grieve.

Watching their grandchildren, the couple wasn't opposed to the arrangement of them living in Manhattan with their uncle. If anything, they'd get to see them more now. But what a trade-off this was. Losing Stan and Maggie was too high a price.

* * *

Jefferson leaned in close and kissed Monique. She reciprocated, wrapping her arms around his neck and pulling his body against hers, the two of them sinking slightly into the mattress.

"Sure wish we could have left the curtains open," she commented when he had pulled away again. "It might have added a romantic touch to have that view of the bay at night while we made love."

"Or it might have given others a clear show of what we were doing," Jefferson suggested. "Any boat could have come by."

Despite his wealth, he'd never stayed anywhere so close to the water. The cabin's back door was less than a hundred yards from the Chesapeake's shoreline, a gentle downwards slope protecting the property from potential flooding.

"Maybe I'm an exhibitionist," Monique cracked.

Jefferson kissed her again, running one hand across her bare chest.

* * *

"You're out of your mind," Jefferson said, staying only somewhat quiet. "I'm serious. This is more complicated than the arrangements we have to make before we can have sex."

Blushing, Monique dearly wished to have the ability to kick him underneath the table. But thankfully, no one else seemed to have heard the remark as they were all listening to the woman running the wine-tasting.

"They don't want me mixing the wines," she told Jefferson. "I don't have enough tumblers and straws with me to do it myself. Just hold the glass up to my lips, tilt it slightly, and I'll take care of taking a sip."

"And you don't even want to try doing it yourself?" Jefferson asked.

"With the few glasses I have at home ... maybe. But these ... no way. They're practically designed for me to drop and break."

"Fine," Jefferson said, giving in.

As he held the glass, Monique grabbed his wrist and guided it up to her lips.

"Cheers," Jefferson remarked as she took a sip.

Monique's idea having worked, they continued participating in the wine-tasting, getting the occasional glances and outright stares from some of the other people there. They ignored this.

* * *

Abigail sat at the kitchen table, watching Beth make a potato salad, Taylor was in the den, showing off her reading skills to William, and Matthew was also in the kitchen, playing with some refrigerator magnets. So far, he had thankfully not tried to put any of them in his mouth.

"I don't like ..." Abigail said, beginning her recitation of the foods she wouldn't eat for the third time.

"Why do you not like these foods?" Beth queried. "So many of them are delicious."

"They're yucky," Abigail replied, making a face.

Beth gave up and continued working on dinner. Let Jefferson work with this child on that, she thought. After, he and Stan went through their own picky-eating phases. At some point, all those boys would eat was plain pasta.

* * *

With Jefferson's help, Monique had moved onto the couch in the cabin's main room. Jefferson sat next to her while Presley was sprawled out on the large carpet in front of them.

"I've been thinking about something you once said to me," Monique said, "and I think you were right."

"Okay," Jefferson said, somewhat confused, "I've said a number of things to you since we've met. Could you be more specific?"

Monique shook her head.

"No," she said. "All you need to know is that you were right."

"I guess I can live with that," Jefferson remarked with a smirk.

Chapter 34

"Oh," Monique commented, squeezing Jefferson's hand, "I wish you were coming back with me."

"I've gotta pick up the kids in Charlottesville," Jefferson pointed out as Monique's train pulled into the station with a blast of its horn and the accompanying bell. "You're welcome to come with me."

"As much as I love you, I think I'll take the direct route. Thanks."

Jefferson kissed her one more time before making sure her roller bag was securely fastened to the back of her wheelchair. Monique knew she had to board now and moved forward. She was able to get on to the train just fine and gave Jefferson one final wave before the doors slid shut.

Jefferson's train to Charlottesville arrived about twenty minutes later. The ride wasn't long and the kids were already waiting for him when he arrived, William and Beth standing on the platform with them.

"Hey, you guys," Jefferson said, hugging them each. "Did you have fun with Grandma and Grandpa?"

The kids' responses seemed to indicate they did.

"We missed you," Abigail said.

"I missed you too," Jefferson said, smiling as he turned to speak to his parents.

* * *

Dr. Wade Abbens sat at his desk, reviewing one of his patient's files while taking an occasional sip of water. The patient had just left, and he was seeing what updates he had to add before putting the file away. He knew he still had a few minutes until his next appointment, a new patient, was due to arrive.

Dr. Abbens added his notes from the day's session to the file and found that nothing else needed to be updated. He stored the file away in a cabinet and stood up to stretch, thinking about who was coming in next. He didn't know much more about this patient than her name and the fact she was having recurring nightmares based on a bad experience she recently endured.

Dr. Abbens was sitting down again and taking another drink of water when someone knocked on the door.

"Come in," he said.

He was surprised when a woman entered, strapped into an elaborate-looking wheelchair. Pulling out the file, he saw no notes or other mention of the chair in the intake paperwork she'd submitted online.

"Monique Vasquez?" he asked.

The woman nodded. Dr. Abbens noticed she was operating her wheelchair with a joystick. He figured she could shake hands and stuck out his own. Monique shook it.

"Would you like to get out of that chair?" the doctor asked, gesturing towards his couch.

"No," Monique said. "I'm fine."

Dr. Abbens didn't push the matter and instead offered her some water. Monique took it in her tumbler. He sat back behind his desk, asking why she was seeking therapy.

"You were a bit vague on the intake form you completed," he pointed out. "I'd like to understand more about these nightmares you're having."

Monique took a deep breath.

"A few months ago," she began, "my store was robbed …"

* * *

The phone rang just as Jason Greene was leaving, having completed one of his surprise visits to Jefferson's house. He encouraged Jefferson to answer it.

"I can let myself out," he added.

Anya nonetheless followed him in order to lock the front door. Jefferson pulled his iPhone out of his pocket.

"Hello?" Jefferson asked.

"Jefferson," a female voice said. "Hi. It's Cassandra Kingman."

Jefferson couldn't believe it. He'd spoken to Cassandra a couple times since leaving Berlin, but it had been a while since their last conversation.

"Oh hey," Jefferson said. "How are you?"

"I'm good," Cassandra said. "But more importantly, how are you? How is everyone?"

"We're good. Everyone's healthy, happy, and so on."

"That's good. Listen, we're coming to New York for a few days to see my parents on Long Island, and we were wondering if we could come see you as well. Would that be possible?"

Jefferson smiled.

"Sure," he agreed. "Come on by. When's your trip?"

* * *

Though Ellen O'Bryan and her friends were generally a great source to find a baby-sitter, they were all busy one day, leaving Jefferson to search for an alternative solution. That solution turned out to be Monique. After the two of them brain-stormed how she could supervise the three kids while Jefferson was teaching and Anya was seeing a doctor regarding a possible ear infection, she agreed to do it.

Monique was knocking on the sliding glass door at 10:00 one morning, waiting to be let inside. Opening the door, Taylor was happy to see her.

"What are you doing here?" she inquired.

"I'm baby-sitting you guys today," Monique told her, coming into the house.

The look on Taylor's face suggested Jefferson had shared this bit of information with her at one point or another but she had forgotten about it until now.

Jefferson came downstairs, briefcase in hand. He greeted Monique and then called for all three kids to come down as he put Presley in her guide dog harness. They came, curious about what he wanted.

"Okay guys," Jefferson said. "We talked about this. Monique's gonna watch you today while I'm at work. You're gonna listen to what she tells you and you are absolutely not going to go upstairs. She can't get up there, so if something happens to you, she can't help you. Got that?"

All three kids nodded.

"Okay then," Jefferson said. "Be good,"

He reminded Monique where the emergency numbers were kept.

"We'll be fine," Monique assured him.

Jefferson nodded and left with Presley. Monique turned to the kids.

* * *

Jefferson arrived to find Jason Greene talking with Amy and Eric outside his office. Apparently, he had run into them while looking for Jefferson.

"Ah," he said as a greeting. "Your friends were just telling me some nice things about you. Some of the attributes are being shared in Latin, but I think I get the point."

"I'm sure," Jefferson said. "What can I do for you?"

"I just wanted to make sure you were okay. We're a week out from the custody hearing and I've seen plenty of parents and guardians get nervous as it gets closer."

"I'm okay. I mean, I'm a bit nervous, but I'm okay."

Jason Greene nodded.

"Yes, you lawyers don't show fear right before the battle," he said. "Don't forget that you've gotta have all your paperwork in the judge's hands by the twelfth, including any testimonials from friends and family."

"I'm helping him with that," Eric chimed in. "I'm his lawyer."

"Then I'll see you around."

Jason Greene bid the group a good day and left.

"I think I actually like this guy," Eric commented when he was gone. "And I've dealt with my fair share of social workers."

"What are you two doing here anyway?" Jefferson asked.

"Eric had to come in to take care of a few things for the hearing," Amy explained. "Then we're going to lunch."

"If you didn't have to teach, we'd invite you," Eric remarked. "Though you'd have to be okay with us going to a hotel room for a while afterwards."

Jefferson heard Amy emit a slight, embarrassed gasp. He was amused as he pictured the possible faces she was making right then.

"I tell you," Eric said, "I've got letters coming in left and right. Everyone's behind you on this."

This was true. Colleagues and students alike wrote letters of support for Jefferson, dropping them off with Eric or e-mailing them to him. He'd deliver everything to the judge.

"I'm gonna need a truck for that," he commented. "Then there's the e-mails."

Jefferson nodded.

"I got one from your parents as well," Eric went on. "I know Monique is still working on hers, and I got one from Germany … someone named Cassandra."

Jefferson nodded again.

"Your nanny dropped one off yesterday," Eric said.

"Isn't that biased?" Amy asked.

"Still couldn't hurt," Jefferson said, shrugging. He was thankful Anya had taken the time to do this.

"We're gonna blow that judge away," Eric said enthusiastically. "Everyone, including the law, is on our side on this."

* * *

"Monique?" Taylor asked. "Can we play outside?"

She was pointing at the backyard, which she could see through the sliding glass door that led out onto the small patio.

"Sure," Monique said. She followed the three kids over to the door, which Abigail unlocked and pushed open, and headed outside.

Monique stayed on the cement patio while the kids started up a game of tag on the lawn. Since the yard was small, there wasn't much space for them to run and they were often cornered and tagged "it" pretty quickly.

"You can't run inside," Monique said when the twins tried to enter the house to evade Matthew.

Thankfully, they listened. Then, when Abigail was "it", she decided to come over and tag Monique.

"You're it," she declared.

"I think you guys could all outrun me pretty easily," Monique remarked with a chuckle.

* * *

Eric sat in his office, working. Amy had found a couch out in the hallway, where she sat and read a magazine while he updated some things for Jefferson's case. He promised they'd be done soon, and they would then go on their lunch date.

However, Amy soon changed her mind about waiting and instead burst into Eric's office, seeming to hold some important information. Eric stared at her.

"Fugiendum, et absconderis," she said.

"What?" Eric asked.

"Run and hide. I just saw Paula Franks coming this way."

"I thought she graduated," Eric said with a groan. "What does she want?"

Just then, Paula Franks entered the office. Amy sprang away from Eric's desk, hoping to be able to sneak out. But Paula Franks wasn't paying attention to her to begin with, instead focusing solely on Eric. He looked back at her but said nothing.

"Relax," the former student said. "I won't stay long."

"Then why are you here?" Eric asked.

"I just wanted to drop this off. I hear you're collecting them."

She put an envelope on his desk. Eric reached for it and read the name written across the front. He looked back up at Paula Franks, confused.

"Jefferson's a good man," Paula Franks stated. "Those kids are lucky."

"Does this mean you'll stop pursuing him?" Eric asked, daring to hope for his friend.

Paula Franks didn't answer, but Eric could tell she wouldn't.

"For what it's worth," he said, "thanks. You are a good person."

Paula Franks gave him a single nod and left. Both Eric and Amy stared at each other and then at the envelope.

"Are you actually gonna give that to the judge?" Amy finally asked.

* * *

"Hey Monique?" Taylor asked, coming up next to the wheelchair.

"What's up?" Monique asked, turning her head to look at her.

"You have to sit in that chair because you can't walk, right?"

"That's right."

It had started to drizzle, so they were all back in the den.

"Why can't you walk?" Taylor asked.

Monique took a deep breath.

"Well," she said, choosing her words carefully. "when I was a little girl, I got very sick. I had to stay in bed for a long time and I had to see a lot of doctors. They were finally able to give me the right medicine to make me better, but my backbone didn't work properly anymore, so I couldn't walk anymore after that."

"Oh," Taylor said thoughtfully. "Could that happen to me?"

"I don't think so. You look pretty healthy to me. Plus, I was a lot younger than you when I got sick. It usually only happens to really little kids."

Taylor seemed satisfied with this and went off to play again.

"Don't go upstairs," Monique reminded her.

Jefferson returned home around 3:30 in the afternoon, shortly behind Anya, who was complaining about the medicine she had to take for her now-diagnosed ear infection. The woman definitely didn't like doctors.

"Listen to these possible side effects," she said, studying the small bottle. "A temporary burning or stinging sensation in the ear ... redness. ... swelling in or around the ears ... can I just keep the ear infection?

"Not on my health plan," Jefferson replied.

All three kids greeted their uncle enthusiastically, asking if Monique could baby-sit again. Monique was still in the den, waiting for the greetings to die down. Jefferson was eventually able to come see her.

"So," he asked. "things went well?"

"Yeah," Monique said. "we had fun."

"I'm glad."

He figured this was a good omen for their future.

"How are you doing?" Monique queried. She could tell he looked nervous, and she was sure she knew why.

"I'm okay," Jefferson said. "Though I think I need a drink. You want anything?"

Monique asked for water and watched as he headed off to the kitchen. She then dug out her cell phone and dialed a number.

"Hey Joan ..." she said when the nurse answered, "I'm gonna cancel our appointment tonight ... no, I'm not gonna be home tonight ... Yeah, I'll be okay ... it's important ... thanks."

Looking at the nearby staircase, she thought back to hers and Jefferson's weekend at the cabin. She figured she might as well spring this on him.

* * *

That evening, Monique borrowed one of Jefferson's button-down shirts to sleep in and got him to help her into his bed. It had taken some coaxing, but she finally got him to allow her to spend the night. Neither of them had sex in mind, but she wanted to be there for him.

Apart from offering to help get Monique up the two flights of steps, Anya kept out of this. She simply bid them a good night before going to her room to give herself another round of ear medication.

"I figured I could get you to bring me up here sooner or later," Monique cracked, surveying his bedroom.

Jefferson didn't smile. Clearly his earlier drink hadn't helped. Monique reached out and rubbed his arm.

"Come here," she encouraged, wanting to hold him close to her.

Jefferson didn't move.

"Look," Monique said, trying to withhold a sigh, "two-thirds of my body is dead weight. I can't get over to you. So, stop being stubborn and let me make you feel better."

She tugged at his arm and Jefferson finally gave in, allowing her to hug him.

"You'll be fine," Monique said as she embraced him. "You're good to them. There's no reason a judge should see otherwise."

* * *

Strapped into her chair, Monique made her way down the corridor, checking the names on the doors. She finally found the office she was looking for and knocked.

"Come in!" a voice called.

Monique got the door open and moved inside. Eric looked up from the paperwork he was reading. He smiled when he saw who it was.

"What brings you to law school?" he queried. "Looking to apply?"

"I just wanted to drop this off," Monique said, handing him the envelope containing her testimonial for the family court judge.

"Thank you," Eric said, taking the letter and adding it to a pile on the corner of his desk.

"I've gotta run," Monique said and turned to leave again.

"Hang on a second," Eric said, stopping her.

"What's up?"

"I just wanted to tell you something. Ever since he's met you, I've noticed a real change in Jefferson … for the better. Thank you."

Monique smiled.

"No problem," she said. "He brings out the best in me."

* * *

"Hey Uncle Jeff," Abigail said, finding him cleaning up in the kitchen. "Can we watch one of our home movies that Mom and Dad made with us?"

"Sure," Jefferson said, deciding it was about time he watched one of those. "You wanna join us, Anya?"

"No, thank you," Anya replied, carrying a clean stack of laundry up the stairs.

Jefferson headed up to his office with Abigail in tow. He retrieved the DVDs from his desk. Taylor and Matthew had also seemed interested in this idea, but they decided to wait downstairs.

"Okay," Jefferson said, setting the DVD cases down on the coffee table. "Which one do you guys wanna see?"

He almost immediately wished he hadn't asked as he got about two dozen different requests. Deciding to ignore the kids, he began looking through the choices himself.

"How about this one?" he suggested. "Family vacation 2018. That'll include all of you guys."

"Dad won't be in it very much," Taylor commented. "He was always holding the camera."

"Well, I'm sure he's in here somewhere," Jefferson told her as he inserted the disc into the DVD player.

As the movie began, he sat on the couch with the three kids around him.

It opened on what seemed to be footage of the family on the beach. Jefferson vaguely recalled his brother once talking about a trip to somewhere in the Mediterranean, but he couldn't remember it now. Still, the sounds of waves and birds made the general location clear.

One of the twins seemed to be building a sandcastle and Maggie was helping while Stan handled the camera and made occasional comments.

"You need to fortify your structure on he north side," he was saying.

Jefferson guessed Maggie was wearing some sort of bathing suit and he flashed back to his one-night-stand with her. To this day, he wondered how it had happened, but like with Amy, no clear answer came to him. He just had to make his peace with that.

"Hey!" Matthew exclaimed. "There's me."

Sure enough, Matthew could soon be seen running around the beach, occasionally getting his feet wet, while his parents reminded him to be careful. Abigail could also be seen here and there. She was pretending to look grown up and was spread out on a beach blanket, apparently getting a tan. As though for Jefferson's benefit, Stan also commented on this from behind the camera.

"Don't grow up too fast there," he remarked. "I'm not ready to chase the boys away from you."

As he listened, Jefferson couldn't help thinking that this was a family. There were the parents, the daughters, and a son. They were a family. Now, Stan and Maggie were dead, and he was left to raise Abigail, Taylor, and Matthew. What a world, Jefferson thought as Taylor climbed into his lap. What a world.

Chapter 35

"Abigail!" Beth called up the stairs. "Abigail, sweetie! Come on down!"

Abigail came downstairs, wearing a green and white dress. Beth began to fuss with her hair, which had been washed and brushed earlier, causing the girl to complain loudly.

"You have to look nice," Beth told her. "It's an important day,"

This didn't seem to convince Abigail, who was now trying to escape.

"You know," William remarked, "lawyers have to always dress nicely when they go to court. Your uncle does the few times he actually goes."

"I'm never becoming a lawyer!" Abigail shrieked and Anya couldn't resist laughing.

Beth eventually let her go and she went over to her grandfather, who surely wouldn't dare touch her hair.

Taylor came down soon after, wearing a similar blue-and-white dress. Though she complained, she didn't make as big a fuss when Beth put the finishing touches on her hair.

Matthew was the easiest. He wore a child's size suit, complete with a clip-on tie. His hair was combed, and Beth quickly found there was no more she could do to it.

Eric and Amy soon arrived. The kids were loaded into their minivan with Amy and Beth while Jefferson, Presley, Eric, Anya, and William drove to the courthouse in William's rented sedan.

* * *

Monique steered her wheelchair down the corridor. Following the directions a court officer stationed by the metal detector gave her, she found the elevators. One arrived upon being summoned and she entered it. As she was selecting the sixth floor, she heard someone call out.

"Hold that elevator, please!" the man was saying as the doors began sliding shut.

Monique managed to stick her hand out and the doors stopped closing. Jason Greene slid in next to her.

"Miss Vasquez," he said, recognizing who he was with. "How are you? How's the book business?"

"It's good," Monique replied as the doors slid shut and the elevator began its ascent.

"And now you're here to support Jefferson and the kids. Very good. It's always nice to have someone in your corner when you do this sort of thing."

Monique nodded.

"What are the chances that Jefferson will get the kids permanently?" she asked.

"I'd say it's about fifty-fifty right now," Jason Greene replied after thinking it over for a moment. "I mean, there's a good case, but any little thing could cause a judge to go the other way. It all comes down to what they think is in the children's best interests."

Monique nodded and swallowed a lump in her throat as the elevator doors opened on the sixth floor. What did "the other way" mean?

"Here we go," Jason Greene said, leading the way.

"Here we go, Monique agreed.

* * *

While Jefferson, Presley, and Eric sat at the petitioner's table, Abigail, Taylor, Matthew, William, Beth, Anya, and Amy took up the first row of the courtroom's gallery. Several more people who had come to show their support sat in the rows directly behind them. A lawyer for Children's Protective Services sat at the other table. Eric said he knew her and didn't expect trouble.

"She just has to be here," he whispered to his friend and client, not even bothering to share the woman's name.

Monique pulled her chair up along the far side of the gallery where she wouldn't be in the way. Because of traffic, she had barely made it on time and had not had a chance to wish Jefferson luck. And of course, she felt a bit unnerved by what Jason Greene had said in the elevator. The man was nice, but he had been brutally honest. Monique kind of wished he hadn't.

At 9:00, the bailiff called for everyone to rise for the Honorable Judge Maurice Battles. The judge strode in, followed by his clerk, and took his seat at the bench.

"Be seated," he instructed.

He waited another minute for the clerk to get set up and then asked her to call the case, which she promptly did.

"This hearing is to determine if the minors Abigail Thomas, Taylor Thomas, and Matthew Thomas are to remain in the sole, permanent custody of their uncle, Jefferson Thomas," Judge Battles said. He took a moment to sort through some papers in front of him. "Are the parties ready to begin?"

Eric and the attorney from Children's Protective Services affirmed they were.

"Are the minors here today?" Judge Battles asked.

"Yes, Your Honor," Eric said, pointing out the twins and Matthew for the judge's benefit. "Right there."

Judge Battles nodded.

"I will say that I have received many letters of support for Mr. Thomas," he said. "I have also reviewed all other documentation regarding the minors, including a report by Jason Greene of Children's Protective Services. Is Mr. Greene present today?"

"Yes," the attorney from Children's Protective Services said, pointing out the social worker.

"Mr. Greene, please step forward and give your final recommendation to this court."

Jason Greene rose and stepped through the gate separating the gallery from the tables and the judge's bench. He gave Jefferson and Eric a quick glance before turning his attention to Judge Battles.

"Your Honor," he said, speaking slightly more slowly than usual. "You've read my report. I haven't left anything out. In the short time that I've known Jefferson Thomas and his nieces and nephew, I have seen a family being formed out of a tragedy. Jefferson shows genuine love and affection for these kids, who reciprocate. True, there have been bumps in the road, but this man has a support system that I have rarely come across before in my eleven years of doing this job. As you have seen for yourself through the letters you have read, not only has Jefferson Thomas stepped up to a responsibility that he had committed to years ago, but others have come to his aide in order for him to be successful at it. Friends, family, colleagues, and students … they are all behind Jefferson on this. In my opinion, this is a model that the rest of us should live up to. Jefferson Thomas is a smart man, and he knows to ask for help when he needs it. Therefore, it is my recommendation that Abigail, Matthew, and Taylor stay right where they are, as stated in my report."

He stood there, waiting silently.

"Thank you, Mr. Greene," Judge Battles said. "You may sit down."

Jason Greene did so, and Judge Battles looked at Jefferson and Eric.

"Does the petitioner have anything else before I give my ruling?" he asked.

"Your Honor," Eric said. "My client would like to make a statement."

"Very well. The floor is yours, Mr. Thomas,"

Jefferson rose. Despite having not made many court appearances, he knew where the bench was. Some things were consistent, no matter which courtroom served as the venue.

"Five years ago, my brother and his wife were working on updating their will," Jefferson said. "They asked me to sign the agreement that stated that I would be the guardian of their three kids if anything ever happened to them. I agreed and I admit that at the time, I never believed it would ever be necessary. How many times do you actually know such a thing will happen? Then, five months ago, I got a phone call. My brother and sister-in-law were killed in a car accident and it was time for me to stick to my commitment. Knowing how serious this was, I didn't give it a second thought and brought the kids here to live with me. And over the past few months, I got to know them … and honestly, I now could not imagine my life without them. Your Honor, I made a promise to my brother and my sister … please let me keep it."

He sat down again.

The courtroom was quiet except for the occasional whisper as Judge Battles made some notes. Matthew began fidgeting in his seat and Beth settled him down. Abigail whispered something to Taylor, who giggled, but neither of them seemed to be inclined to share their funny secret.

"I'm prepared to make my ruling," Judge Battles said.

Everyone's attention immediately turned back to him.

"Mr. Thomas," the judge said, "it is abundantly clear to me that you love your nieces and nephew. However, such a love is not enough to persuade me to grant you custody."

Jefferson was about to react when Eric grabbed his arm and squeezed it, signaling him to wait.

"Such a responsibility requires more," Judge Battles continued. "It requires humility and a willingness to ask for and accept assistance from those around you who might know better. It requires you to understand and accept that mistakes will happen. It requires you to not dwell on these mistakes but rather to learn from them and use this knowledge to your benefit in the future as you move ahead."

Monique thought Jefferson already knew all this. What was this judge getting at?

"The life of a child is something that must be handled with care," Judge Battles said. "My job is to make sure that each of my decisions is in the best interest of the child ... not their parent and not their guardian."

Eric wished he would get to the point.

"Therefore, Judge Battles said, "it is my decision that you meet the criteria and I hereby award full, permanent custody of Abigail Thomas, Taylor Thomas, and Matthew Thomas to their uncle and guardian, Jefferson Thomas."

A murmur erupted through the courtroom. Jefferson, whose heart had been racing all morning, now felt like it had stopped. Eric was grinning. From his seat in the gallery, Jason Greene was smiling. Monique could feel tears coming on. Amy and Beth were both crying.

"Order!" Judge Battles called, banging his gavel. "Order! Order!"

The noise slowly died down again.

"I would like to add a personal note for the record," Judge Battles said. "I have to agree with what Mr. Greene said. The system of support that has surrounded Jefferson Thomas over the past few months is indeed a model for the rest of us to look up to and to implement in our own lives. It is my hope that this system does not falter as the children continue to grow."

He looked at Jefferson.

"Mr. Thomas," he said. "Please be aware that your two-year probation period does continue. A social worker will continue to monitor your home during this time and will submit periodic reports to me. I still hold the authorization to revoke custody."

"I understand, Your Honor," Jefferson said.

In the gallery, Jason Greene nodded.

"Very well," Judge Battles said. "We'll have a five-minute recess before the next matter."

He banged his gavel again.

Everyone began rising from their seats. Jefferson, Presley, and Eric made their way into the gallery and met up with Anya, William, Beth, Amy, Taylor, Matthew, and Abigail. All three kids looked at Jefferson.

"Does this mean we still get to live with you?" Taylor asked.

"That's right," Jefferson said. "You guys aren't going anywhere."

"Yea!" the kids cheered.

Jefferson smiled.

"Congratulations," Anya said.

* * *

Monique took out a tissue and wiped her moist eyes. A sense of relief was washing over her. Jefferson now had full custody of the kids. True, Children's Services was still going to be watching him, but she felt there was nothing to worry about now. Jason Greene seemed honest and trustworthy.

She considered going over to Jefferson to congratulate him. But he was surrounded by a lot of other people, including Jason Greene, who spoke to him briefly before leaving the courtroom. Monique decided to just go home. She could call Jefferson later.

She turned around and headed for the exit.

"Monique!"

She stopped and turned to see Jefferson working to make his way over with Presley, they having extracted themselves from the crowd of family and friends who wanted to offer their congratulations. Eric was saying something as Jefferson got closer to Monique.

"Hey," Jefferson said, reaching her. "Sorry we didn't speak earlier."

"That's okay," Monique assured him. "I barely made it in time. Traffic was a nightmare."

She reached out and manage to grab hold of Jefferson's hand. She clasped it in both of her own.

"Congratulations," she said. "You did it."

"Thanks," Jefferson said, beaming. The judge's ruling still seemed to be sinking in and he was silent for a moment.

"Hey," he said, "we're all going out for lunch to celebrate. You should come with us."

"Okay," Monique said. "Sure."

"And you'll finally get to meet my parents," Jefferson added as they went to rejoin the others. "You won't be able to bug me about that anymore."

Monique laughed and beamed.

* * *

The doorbell rang.

"I'll get it!" Abigail announced as she ran towards the foyer.

Jefferson wasn't far behind her and Anya came downstairs to see what was going on.

The visitors turned out to be Cassandra Kingman, her husband, Darren, and their daughter, Tiffany, who were coming by for lunch.

Remembering her, Abigail, Taylor, and Matthew greeted Cassandra enthusiastically.

"Hey you guys," Cassandra said. "How are you doing? I've missed you."

All three kids answered at once, each trying to recap their own exciting adventures in New York.

"Hey guys," Jefferson said. "Easy, easy. Let her breathe."

The kids quieted down and scattered, seemingly off to find something they wanted to show their guests. Cassandra turned to Jefferson.

"So," she said. "You've had full custody for a week now. Congratulations."

"Thanks," Jefferson said and introduced the Kingmans to Anya.

"Sorry we couldn't be there for the hearing. I couldn't get off work in time."

Jefferson nodded.

"And I hear you have a new lady in your life," Cassandra said. "How is she?"

"She's great," Jefferson said, wondering how she knew that. "I'm pretty lucky."

"That's good. I'm glad."

Jefferson thanked her and turned to Darren.

"I believe I owe you a beer," he said.

Chapter 36

"I've got cookies!" Kathy announced, holding up a large plastic Tupperware as she entered the store following her lunch break.

"Wait, are we your grandchildren now?" Frank asked.

"You're never too old for my peanut butter chocolate chip cookies," Kathy insisted, pushing one into his hand.

Monique didn't hear him argue further.

"Hey," she asked, eyeing the large number of cookies and getting an idea. "Can I have a bunch of those?"

She knew it'd be about one and a half weeks too late, but she could still tell Jefferson it was a present for officially getting full custody of the kids.

* * *

The cab pulled up to the curb. Nancy Caliban paid the fare and got out, adjusting her purse strap as she went. She walked up to Jefferson's front door. Fishing through her purse, she located the key he had given her so long ago and used it to unlock the front door.

"Jefferson!" she called. "Jefferson! Sweetie, it's me! It's Nancy! Are you home?!"

She got no reply and decided to wait. She set her purse on the coffee table in the den and sat down on the couch. It wasn't long before she had her compact out and was checking her makeup. She then took the opportunity to survey her immediate surroundings, noting that not much had changed since the last time she had been here. True, there were some children's toys around, most of them sitting in a plastic crate in one corner, but those could easily be tucked out of sight.

Eventually, she got up and went to the kitchen for some water. As she was walking back to the couch with her glass, she heard knocking. Looking around, Nancy saw a woman in an elaborate-looking wheelchair on the back patio, knocking on the glass sliding door while holding a bag in her hand. She stopped knocking and stared as Nancy came closer.

"Who are you?" Nancy asked, opening the door.

"I'm Monique," the woman said. "Who are you? Where's Jefferson?"

"He should be back soon. I just let myself in with my key."

As she spoke, she stared at Monique and her wheelchair.

"Okay," Monique said, confused. "Who are you?"

"I'm Nancy," she said. "Jefferson's girlfriend."

Monique was stunned, her jaw going slack and her eyes widening.

"I can tell Jefferson you stopped by when he gets back," Nancy offered. "If you want to leave something ..."

She eyed the bag in Monique's hand.

Monique was still unable to speak. Nancy finally had enough and shut the door in her face. She then went back to the couch, turning her back to the door.

* * *

Left outside alone, Monique's face finally showed signs of life as she began sobbing. While covering her face with one hand, she clumsily steered her wheelchair back across the patio and out through the gate, not bothering to close it behind her. She maneuvered the chair back to the front of the house, where her cab was waiting.

Tears still rolling down her cheeks, Monique stared at the house, trying to make sense of everything that just happened. How could she have been so stupid? Jefferson had slept with married women. Who was to say he wouldn't have had another relationship she didn't know about? Sure, he claimed he never cheated on his partners, but that was obviously not true.

She knew about it now. She tightened her grip on the bag of cookies and, with all the strength and control she could muster, hurled it at the house, sending the contents flying everywhere. She then got into the cab and left, crying again. Her lone spark of luck came when the driver didn't ask any questions.

* * *

Nancy was still sitting on the couch when she heard the key in the lock of the front door. She could also hear voices on the other side, one of which she recognized as Jefferson's. She rose to meet him.

"But why not?" Abigail was asking as she led the way through the door.

"Because you do not eat cookies that you find lying on the sidewalk," Jefferson told her as he freed Presley from her harness. "They're dirty."

"What if we washed them?"

"No," Jefferson said as he hung the harness and leash on a hook in the foyer closet.

He was expecting a response from Abigail, but the girl said nothing. Neither did Matthew or Taylor. Something was definitely up. Even Presley wasn't scampering around like she usually did when let out of her harness.

"Hello Jefferson," Nancy said with a smile.

Jefferson immediately recognized her voice and his face darkened.

"Who are you?" Abigail inquired.

Taylor and Matthew were still silent, apparently driven to their usual shyness around strangers.

"I'm Nancy," she explained. "I'm a friend of your uncle's."

"How come we never met you before?" Abigail asked, some suspicion evident in her tone.

Nancy seemed to be about to answer when Jefferson stepped in.

"Guys," he said. "Go upstairs to your rooms and play. This lady and I need to talk."

Deciding he wasn't going to be more informative about this strange visitor, the kids headed upstairs with Presley following them. Jefferson could soon hear doors being closed above him.

"You've got a good handle on them," Nancy observed.

"What are you doing here?" Jefferson asked, ignoring her statement. He knew it was an empty compliment.

"I'm here to see you, Silly," Nancy said. "Where were you for so long? You're usually home around this time."

"I took the kids to the park," Jefferson replied. "Why is that any of your business?"

"I care about you, sweetie."

"We broke up five months ago. You remember that? I definitely do."

"That was a fight," Nancy said in an innocent tone. "Couples fight, then they make up. I've done a lot of soul-searching, and I'm ready to give us another shot."

"Nancy," Jefferson said, "there is no 'us' anymore. We're over. We've been over since my brother was killed."

"You were upset," Nancy said, stepping towards him. "Your judgment was clouded. I can understand that and forgive you for it."

She set her plastic cup down on the small table in the foyer.

"Forgive me?" Jefferson asked, stepping away from her.

* * *

Abigail quietly opened the door of hers and Taylor's bedroom. The two girls crept out and down the hallway to retrieve Matthew.

"Come on," Abigail whispered. "Be very quiet."

Matthew didn't ask what they were doing. He followed his sisters, excited about this adventure.

They snuck over to the staircase and around to the set that led up to Jefferson's bedroom and office. They scampered up a few steps and stayed there. This hiding place allowed them to easily hear everything being said downstairs while remaining out of sight. They listened intently while Presley settled at the bottom of the steps, watching them with interest.

* * *

"Come on," Nancy said. "Let's go out ... just you and me."

"Nancy," Jefferson said, "I don't know if you remember this, but I walked in here with three young children about a minute or so ago. I can't just leave them."

"So?" Nancy asked. "Hire a baby-sitter."

"It's more complicated than that. How do you think they'll react if I suddenly tell them you're my girlfriend? It's not a change a child readily accepts."

"They'll get over it. Besides, what happened to me being the most important thing in your life?"

"That ended with our relationship. You refused to accept that things had to change."

Jefferson couldn't believe he was having this conversation. What on Earth even prompted Nancy to come back?

"I didn't want the change," Nancy said, sounding angry for the first time. "You threw those brats in my face."

"I did no such thing," Jefferson corrected. "I never asked you to help me with them, just to accept them."

"You never asked me about any of it!"

"I asked you when my brother and his wife asked me to become the kids' guardian if anything ever happened," Jefferson said, working to stay somewhat calm while she was losing her cool. "You didn't have a problem with it then."

"How was I supposed to know anything would happen? How often do these things happen anyway?"

Jefferson knew she had a point. He'd said the same thing years ago. But Nancy didn't need to know this. He seriously hoped that, whatever the kids were doing, they couldn't hear any of this. He did not want them coming downstairs to investigate. He kicked himself for not having sent them all the way up to his own room, where they definitely couldn't hear anything.

"And," Nancy went on, "as I recall, you never wanted kids to begin with. I know because we talked about it and agreed on that a long time ago. You can't go back on that now!"

Jefferson was silent. Nancy was right and she knew it. They had had that very conversation four years ago. Only now, things were different.

"So, what's it gonna be?" Nancy challenged. "Me or those three twerps?"

Jefferson didn't have to think about it.

"Leave," he told her. "Leave … and don't ever come back."

Nancy gasped, having clearly not expected that answer. She had thought that giving Jefferson the ultimatum would force him to see things her way.

"You … you're kicking me out?" she asked, shocked.

"Yeah," Jefferson said. "Out of my house … and out of my life. There's no place for you here."

"W … why? We have so much history. We've always been good together. You wanna throw it all away?"

Jefferson nodded with certainty.

"Yeah," he said. "I think I made that pretty clear last time. I've got those three kids now. They've already suffered once. I'm gonna make sure they never feel that kind of pain again. You were never able to accept that."

"Well, who would?" Nancy asked.

"A great woman. Someone really special. And being with her makes me realize we never had anything. I'm just sorry I took five years to figure that out."

Nancy began to laugh.

"A special woman?" she asked. "You mean that prop dummy with the talking head who can't even sit up straight on her own?"

Jefferson stopped short, his facial expression giving away his question.

"Yeah, she was here earlier," Nancy confirmed with a sense of glee. "She seemed pretty dumbstruck when she saw me. Probably would have fallen right out of her chair if the straps weren't holding her in place."

"Get out," Jefferson hissed.

"Fine," Nancy said, resigned to the facts in front of her. "Fine, have it your way. But don't ever expect to get me back."

"I won't hold my breath. You know the way out."

"Have fun with your three orphans and your half a vegetable," Nancy remarked as she grabbed her purse and headed for the front door, laughing at her own joke.

"Hold up just one second," Jefferson said. "I want my key back."

"Oh really?" Nancy asked.

She pulled the key off her key ring and tossed it across the room.

"Good luck finding it," she said with a final laugh as she left the house.

When she was gone, Jefferson locked the front door. He'd find the key later. The important thing was it was in the house and Nancy no longer had it. Too bad he'd forgotten to get it from her the first time around. Maybe he'd change the locks just to be sure this time.

With everything settled down, Jefferson let out a long breath. He sighed with relief as he headed for the kitchen, in serious need of a drink.

Then, he heard the sound of a door being slammed shut upstairs, followed by a second identical sound. Great, He thought as he changed course and headed for the stairs.

He now knew that, during his argument with Nancy, the kids had left their rooms without him realizing it. He wondered how much they heard.

Presley was waiting for him in the hallway on the second floor, where both bedroom doors were closed. Jefferson decided to check the girls' room first. The immediate silence told him they were either hiding or trying to not make any noise.

However, despite their efforts, the girls couldn't fool Presley, who went straight to the large closet and began sniffing at the crack beneath the door. Taking the hint, Jefferson came over as well and pulled the door open.

Taylor and Abigail were sitting close to one another on the floor, their backs against the wall. They both looked up at Jefferson and he could tell from the way they were breathing that they were on the verge of tears.

"Hey," he told them. "it's all clear now. She's gone."

"Who was that?" Taylor asked.

"I'll explain in a minute. First, we have to get your brother. Come on."

"Was she telling the truth?" Abigail demanded. "Did you really not want kids?"

Jefferson let out a long sigh.

"You guys heard all that, huh?" he asked. "Guess I've got a lot of explaining to do. Come on and I'll tell you everything."

They headed over to Matthew's room, where they found him hiding under his bed. With some similar coaxing from Jefferson, he too came out.

Jefferson took the three kids up to his room, where he had them sit on his large bed. Presley followed them and rested her chin on the edge of the mattress as Abigail absent-mindedly petted her.

"Okay," Jefferson said, also sitting on the bed and facing his audience. "I'm just gonna assume you guys overheard pretty much everything."

"Who was that lady?" Taylor asked.

"That lady used to be my girlfriend. That was before you guys came to live with me and before I met Monique."

"Why isn't she your girlfriend now?" Matthew asked.

"That's complicated. You see, when I got the call to come and get you guys, she was upset because things were going to change. We had a fight and I told her to leave."

"Was she telling the truth?" Abigail pressed. "Did you really not want kids?"

Jefferson knew this question was coming, and now he had to answer it. He took a deep breath.

"Yeah," he said. "That's what we were fighting about."

hearing movement, he managed to reach out, find, and grab Taylor's arm before she could get off the bed. That had to be the luckiest grab in human history.

"Hold on a second," Jefferson said as Taylor tried to pull her arm free. "Let me finish."

Taylor seemed ready to protest but stopped. She sat back down on the bed and looked at her uncle, as did Abigail and Matthew.

"I thought I didn't ever want kids," Jefferson said. "But, when I heard what happened to your parents and that you guys needed a home, that was the last thing on my mind. You guys are my family and you needed help. That was all that mattered. And you know what? Having you here has been pretty fun, so I was wrong about not wanting kids. I have you three and I wouldn't want to change that. I love you guys."

The three kids looked at him for a long time. None of them were sniffling anymore but they were still quiet.

"Come over here," Jefferson encouraged.

It took an eternal ten seconds before Matthew became the first to move. Abigail quickly followed while Taylor waited another couple seconds before also moving. they scrambled forward to hug him, pushing his back against the headboard in the process. Presley bounced around next to the bed, waiting for someone to be close enough to reach with her tongue.

"I love you guys," Jefferson said as he hugged all three kids at once. "And you don't have to worry. You guys aren't going anywhere, and that lady is not coming back ... ever."

"We love you too Uncle Jeff," Taylor said.

Her siblings echoed this sentiment.

They finally broke apart and the kids looked at him, wondering what would happen now.

"Hello!" someone called from downstairs.

For one heart-stopping moment, Jefferson thought Nancy was back again. Then, he realized it was Anya, back from the grocery store. Boy had she missed something.

"We'll be right down!" Jefferson called, turning back to the kids. "Go wash up. I've got to make a phone call and then we'll figure out what we'll have for dinner."

The kids got off the bed, finally giving Presley the much-anticipated opportunity to lick their faces. As they all headed out of the bedroom, Jefferson went over to his office, intending to make this important call in private.

He shut and locked his office door and sat down behind his desk. He picked up the receiver and dialed the number.

His heart raced in his chest. Monique came over while he wasn't there and met Nancy. He didn't even want to think about what the latter had said in that meeting, but he knew he had to talk to Monique.

"Hey," the recording for Monique's answering machine said after several rings, "it's Monique. I'm not in right now, so just go ahead and leave a message and I'll get back to you soon."

She sounded so cheerful on that recording. There was a beep and Jefferson began speaking quickly.

"Monique," he said. "It's me. Listen, we need to talk. Something happened today and I need to explain ..."

Chapter 37

"You haven't heard from her?" Eric asked.

"Not for the last two days," Jefferson said. "She's not answering her phone and she won't return my calls."

They were drinking beers in Jefferson's kitchen. The kids were playing with Presley out in the backyard and Anya was supervising them while she cleaned up in the den.

"She was so upset, she left the side gate open," Jefferson described. "I'm lucky Matthew caught that or Presley would have taken off on a tour of Manhattan."

"And you think Nancy's really gone for good this time?" Eric asked.

"Yeah. I'm pretty sure she is. She definitely can't get back into the house."

"Good. I'm glad."

* * *

Monique was in her office, angrily drumming her fingers on her desk. She didn't really have anything she needed to do, but she did not want to be around anyone right then.

What had once been the phone on Monique's desk now lay smashed on the floor next to her desk, its cord having been yanked out of the wall. Monique hadn't let anyone clean it up yet, as it gave her some satisfaction to roll over it with her chair every so often. Jefferson was still calling her home and cell phones, but she'd calmed down enough not to destroy those as well. After all, other people still needed to reach her. She was already working to replace the office phone.

Jefferson was also sending the occasional e-mail. Monique ignored these as well. She did not want to speak to him and if she had the misfortune to run into him again someday, she'd probably kill him.

She was still kicking herself for being so stupid. Jefferson had just fed her some sob story about his girlfriend. She knew that his brother's death was the real deal, as was the origin of the twins and Matthew, but everything else was a lie. How could she have fallen for it? Monique did not have an answer for that one.

* * *

"Hey Uncle Jeff?" Taylor asked. "Where's Monique been? She never comes here anymore."

Jefferson, who had been sitting on the edge of his bed, looked at her for a long time before answering. It'd been about a week, but he supposed that seemed longer to a child. It certainly felt like forever for him.

"I'm not sure," he said, deciding the truth was too complicated.

"That's too bad," Taylor commented. "You were always so happy when she was here."

Seemingly finished sharing her thought and unaware of the maturity of her observation, she walked away while Jefferson stared at the ceiling.

"She is right," Anya said, having passed by the bedroom door and now turning to come in. "You were happy."

Jefferson still didn't say anything.

* * *

Monique was in her apartment, waiting for Joan. The nurse was running late because one of her other patients was having some sort of crisis which she needed to tend to. She'd called a few minutes ago, saying she was now on her way over. So, Monique sat there and waited.

The phone rang again and she went to answer it, working to handle the receiver with her hands.

"Hello?" she asked when she finally got the correct end up to her ear.

"Monique," a male voice said. "It's Jefferson. Look, please don't hang up ..."

"I have nothing to say to you. Don't call me ever again. Goodbye!"

She tried to slam the receiver down in its cradle but missed and hit the counter instead. Further enraged, she grabbed the phone and sent the whole thing towards the ground, yanking its cable out of the wall in the process. That definitely ended the call.

Monique was still breathing heavily when Joan arrived a couple minutes later. It didn't take much guesswork on the nurse's part to figure out what had happened.

"He called again," she concluded.

Monique didn't reply.

"Forget about him," Joan encouraged.

She took Monique into the bedroom and got her ready for bed, offering a mild sedative to help her sleep. An idea coming to her, Monique declined.

"I'll be fine," she insisted.

Joan was hesitant but decided to obey her patient's wishes.

"Good night," she said and left.

Monique lay alone in the dark, contemplating her idea. For anyone else, it might not be so radical, but in her case, the detours she'd have to make with her chair made it an extreme action. But Monique was set on it. It was the only way to start over.

* * *

The doorbell rang. Jefferson went to answer it and found the Kingmans standing on his front steps.

"Hi," Cassandra said. "We thought we'd stop by and say our farewells before we leave tomorrow."

"Sure," Jefferson said. "Come on in."

They entered and greeted Anya as she worked in the kitchen.

"Everything okay?" Cassandra asked, noticing the pained expression on Jefferson's face. "You look like someone just died."

Jefferson didn't respond as the twins and Matthew came into the room. It was at that moment that he decided exactly what he needed to do. He quietly took Cassandra aside into the kitchen.

"Do you guys have any plans for this afternoon?" he asked.

"Not really," Cassandra replied. "Why?"

"Could you stay here and watch the kids for about an hour? I've gotta go take care of something."

"Sure. No problem."

"Thanks so much," Jefferson said.

They headed into the den, where the others had now congregated.

"Guys," Jefferson said to the kids. "The Kingmans are gonna watch you for a little while. I'll be back soon."

He walked into the foyer and pulled Presley's harness on over her head. As he pulled on his shoes, Anya came into the foyer.

"I am here," she protested. "I can watch them …"

"I need you to do something else," Jefferson interrupted. "I need a sighted guide. I don't know what's gonna happen or where I'll end up. I need you to help me with this."

Anya hesitated only for a second.

"I am right behind you," she agreed.

She hurried back to her room to retrieve her shoes and purse. As they were heading for the front door, Darren Kingman poked his head out of the den.

"Hey," he said, "go get your girl."

* * *

Jefferson entered the bookstore to find Kathy working behind the register.

"Good afternoon," she said.

The tone in her greeting suggested she'd rather stick an ice pick into his chest. Jefferson decided to ignore that for the time being.

"Where's Monique?" he asked.

Instead of getting a reply, he felt a sharp blow on the back of his head and stumbled forward. He did manage to remain standing with Anya's help.

"You've got a lot of nerve coming here," Frank said, standing behind Jefferson with a broom in his hand. "and even more to be asking to see Monique."

He and Kathy glared at Jefferson while Samuel stood nearby, confused about how involved he should get in this.

"Look," Jefferson said, rubbing the back of his head. "I just wanna talk to Monique."

Anya decided it was best if she didn't say anything right at this moment.

"After what you did?" Frank asked incredulously. "That is not gonna happen."

"It was a misunderstanding," Jefferson said quickly. "Nothing …"

He received another blow, this time to the side of his head, before Anya could warn him. Again, she grabbed his arm to help him stay on his feet.

"Don't you dare make excuses," Kathy hissed. "Monique knows what she saw."

"I don't have to explain myself to you," Jefferson said. "I just wanna talk to Monique. Where is she?"

"She's not here," Frank said.

"What do you mean? Where is she?"

"She went to visit her mom in Pennsylvania. She needed to get away from the city for a while so she could clear her head and figure things out. She asked us to watch the store while she was gone. And that's what we're doing. So, get out."

Eager not to get hit a third time, Jefferson left with Anya right behind him. Once out on the street, he stopped to think. Monique was going to Pennsylvania. It was doubtful that she would fly, as flying required too many arrangements for her to pull off at the last minute. He knew of flights from New York to parts of Pennsylvania, but the routes were either convoluted or super-short. Either option required those complicated logistics. There had to be only one other way Monique was taking this trip, and Jefferson hoped he was in time to stop her.

"Where do we go now?" Anya asked.

"We need a ride," Jefferson told her, pulling out his iPhone.

* * *

Monique bought her ticket and pulled away from the counter. She didn't have much luggage, just a small overnight bag. but that didn't matter. Her mother could help her get some things when she got to her home in Marshal. Pittsburg wasn't far away. All that mattered for Monique was getting out of New York as soon as possible.

Checking her ticket, Monique turned in the direction of the waiting area to await her train.

* * *

The Uber arrived at Grand Central Station. Jefferson paid the driver on his phone as he, Presley, and Anya climbed out, including a big tip. They descended the stairs and made their way over to the ticket counter.

"Was there a woman in a wheelchair here earlier?" Jefferson asked the man on the other side of the window. "Probably to somewhere in or near Pittsburg?"

Thankfully, the woman working behind the neighboring window remembered Monique.

"Her train's coming in on Track 16," she said.

"Thank you," Jefferson said.

"Someone in her condition shouldn't be traveling so far alone."

Ignoring this statement, Jefferson followed Anya to the Information Board, where she studied a map of the station.

"It is down this way," she reported, guiding him.

They reached the platform for Track 16 and moved through the throng of people. The train was already there and Jefferson prayed she hadn't boarded yet.

"I do not see her," Anya reported. "It will be tough to see her over all these people since she is sitting."

Jefferson nodded. He was beginning to think they had missed her when he heard the faint sound of a motor, filling a gap in the conversation occurring in front of him.

"Forward," he told Presley. "Find a way."

They made their way around the group of people.

"Monique!" Jefferson called.

The continuing sound of the motor told him she was there but choosing to ignore him.

"You can't just run," Jefferson said while Anya fought her way through the crowd to stay with him. "I'll follow you to Pennsylvania and beyond if I have to!"

The sound stopped.

"Just give it up," Monique said. "Go home and be with your girlfriend."

"But you're here," Jefferson said, catching up to her. "You're the woman I love."

Monique was about to say something, but he wouldn't let her. Anya joined them.

"I will give the two of you a few minutes," she said and stepped away.

Jefferson and Monique looked at one another.

"You've had affairs with married women," Monique said. "Multiple times. You've admitted that. I'm supposed to believe I wasn't some side dish for you?"

"Nancy showed up," Jefferson explained. "I had taken the kids to the park when you came by and met her. She thought we could just pick up where we left off. I told her it was over and kicked her out."

Monique said nothing.

"She wanted me to cast the kids aside in favor of her," Jefferson continued. "She insulted you. I'm sorry that happened to you."

"How can I believe it's really over?" Monique asked. "What's to stop me from finding some other woman, or even her, at your house another day?"

"Because I wouldn't do that to you," Jefferson said. "Monique, I've talked to you ... held you ... kissed you ... made love to you ... that all meant something to me. I wouldn't want to do anything to lose you. You're not a side dish."

Monique again said nothing.

"If you want proof that Nancy's really out of my life, come back to the house," Jefferson offered. "Help me find the key she threw across the room as I kicked her out."

Monique still didn't speak.

"I was never sure I wanted to have kids," Jefferson continued. "When I was with Nancy, we sort of agreed to never have any. But when my brother died, I immediately took in his kids. Now I wouldn't want my life to be anything else. That includes you. I want you in my life."

Monique began to soften. She looked at Jefferson for a long time and he seemed genuine to her. His explanation made sense. She thought about if she should take a chance again.

"Monique," Jefferson said. "Please don't go."

He reached to take her hand but missed. Monique looked at him, her eyes moist with tears.

Chapter 38

Monique looked up from her computer as Samuel stepped into the office. She waited for him to speak, knowing that being the one to start this conversation wasn't the best idea.

"Everything's cleaned up," Samuel reported. "Frank and Kathy already left."

"I hope they said 'goodbye'," Monique remarked.

"They did."

"Good. When do you leave for Boston?"

"I'm driving up tomorrow. That'll give me about a week before classes start."

Monique nodded.

"Well, I have your parents' address in the Bronx and I'll mail your last paycheck to that," she said. "It's your responsibility from there."

Samuel nodded.

"You'll be missed here," Monique told him.

Samuel smiled.

"Thanks for everything," he said. "I learned a lot."

He gave her wheelchair a quick nod and Monique nodded back.

"You'll do just fine in Boston," she said. "They're lucky to have you."

"Thanks," Samuel said. "I'd better get going."

"Hold on," Monique said, stopping him. "You're not leaving just yet. Come here."

She motioned for him to come around the desk. Samuel did so and she pulled him down for a hug. He hesitated at first and then hugged her back.

"I probably crossed some kind of line there," Monique said, "but I'll live."

They laughed.

"All right," Monique said. "Get out of here before I decide to keep you from leaving. Good luck."

Samuel gave her one last smile and left. Monique sighed and pinched the bridge of her nose. With Samuel having been accepted to a graduate business program at Boston College, she once again had an opening on her staff, and she would have to go to the public to fill it.

Plus, it was only a matter of time before Frank and Kathy moved on as well. But they were still here for the time being, so Monique didn't dwell on that. Nevertheless, she'd have to find a replacement for Samuel and break them in like before. And, as her memory served, that would not be an easy task.

* * *

Jefferson was in his home office, catching up on organizing some papers and deciding what could be thrown out after being scanned in and reviewed on his computer. So far, he wasn't making much progress in lessening the overload which plagued his desk. How was so much printed material still being produced in 2019?

He came across an envelope addressed to Stan and Maggie. Opening it and skimming its contents on his computer, he realized it was a bill. But since all their affairs had been set in order long ago, he knew it was no longer needed and shredded the document.

Finding more items with the couple's names on them, Jefferson realized this bundle had to have come from one of their pieces of furniture which he'd cleaned out and sold so long ago. He figured he got busy elsewhere and therefore never got around to actually going through these papers. Deciding there was no time like the present, he set to work.

The papers seemed to be mostly bills and junk mail. Judging by the dates, Jefferson figured Stan or Maggie had brought in the mail but never got a chance to look at it. Every document was dated within a week or two of the accident.

Jefferson then came across a plain-looking envelope with his name on it. Concluding he was finished going through his dead relatives' mail, he went back to going through his own things. He wondered how he had never opened this envelope before. He usually went through all new mail within twenty-four hours of its arrival.

There was no return address or stamp, so he wondered how he'd even received it. Nevertheless, he tore it open and scanned the contents into his computer.

Inside the envelope was a single sheet of paper which looked like it had come from a standard household printer. As he waited for it to scan, Jefferson dumped some magazines into his wastepaper basket. Why did he even bother to keep those?

His computer began reading the document and Jefferson paid attention, his curiosity peaked.

Jefferson,

Please understand that I have battled with myself for nearly a year on whether or not to tell you what I'm about to tell you. It's been agonizing ever since I found out.

When we were together almost five years ago, I thought it started and ended between us that very same night. But a horrible truth about that night has recently hit me. When we were together, we made a child. Jefferson, Matthew is you're son.

At first, I didn't suspect anything when Matthew was born, assuming that the protection we used had worked and that Stan was my son's father, as it should be. But as he was growing, my mother's intuition was nagging at me and I finally felt compelled to secretly run a DNA paternity test last year. That was when I learned the truth.

Ever since then, I have been unsure of whether or not to tell you what I have learned. Of course, I have not told Stan, allowing him to believe that Matthew is his flesh and blood. He is my husband and the man with whom I chose to be with and love. That fact has never changed during all the years of our marriage, which is why our night together didn't mean anything. I just felt you ought to know the truth. And I must have started a thousand letters to convey this truth to you without success. I hope this one makes it into the mail.

I don't care what you do with this information. Whether you'd like to be more involved in Matthew's life or not is entirely your decision. I know we can find a way to make it work. All I ask is that Stan never finds out. I do not want to destroy what we have. And please know how sorry I am for letting any of this ever happen.

I hope you can forgive me and that we can talk about all this in person sometime soon.

My best wishes,

Margret

Jefferson sat in his chair, feeling as though he had just been punched in the stomach.

There was no need to reread Maggie's letter. He had heard it perfectly clear the first time.

"My God," he wondered. "Was she going to send it?"

He paused, listening. The silence told him no one had heard his unattended uttering of that question. Even if someone had heard, they probably couldn't decipher the full context of his utterance. Still, Jefferson was glad to have been alone at this moment.

He now knew that he had not been finished going through the papers from Stan and Maggie's desk. Apparently, Maggie had written it, printed it, and put it in an envelope with his address on it, which she then sealed. But she never got around to putting her own address or a stamp on it. Would she have put her address on it at all? When had she written the letter, or this version of it? Would she have mailed this one?

Jefferson couldn't help wondering what had happened to the previous letters and how far she had gotten with those. Had Stan stumbled on any of them? Maggie had her own laptop, but that didn't guarantee him remaining oblivious.

But the most dominant thought on his mind right then was what the letter had disclosed. Jefferson couldn't believe his beloved nephew was actually his own flesh and blood.

"How do you explain that to a kid?" he wondered and chastised himself for thinking out loud again. Pausing again, he still heard no one.

Maintaining more control over himself, he then wondered if he should even tell Matthew at all. This is just crazy, He thought. What difference would it make now?

"Uncle Jeff!"

The cacophony of thoughts catapulting around within Jefferson's skull were interrupted by someone coming up the stairs, calling his name. He quickly deleted the document from his computer screen just as Abigail entered his office.

"What's up?" he asked, trying to keep a straight face.

"Monique's here," Abigail announced. "Come on Uncle Jeff. Let's go to the barbecue."

"Give me a minute. I'll be right down."

Abigail hurried back downstairs as Jefferson pulled Maggie's letter out of the scanner. After thinking for a moment, he sent the sheet of paper through the shredder. He then got up and headed down the hall to his bathroom. He splashed cold water on his face in an attempt to clear his head. He could hear Abigail insistently calling for him from downstairs.

"Come on, Uncle Jeff!" she demanded.

Ignoring her for the time being, Jefferson wiped his face with a towel. He took more deep breaths and descended the staircase.

On the second floor, he ran into Matthew.

"What are you up to, Champ?" he asked.

"I was washing my hands," Matthew told him.

"That's good. Did you already change into your swim trunks?"

"No."

"Come on," Jefferson said, heading towards Matthew's room. "I'll help you find them."

He quickly located the trunks in the closet and left Matthew to change, continuing down the next flight of stairs.

"Finally," Abigail said in an annoyed tone. "It's not nice to keep a lady waiting."

"I'll remember that," Jefferson said.

"She's right, you know," Monique commented, moving her chair forward slightly.

"Great. I'm getting romantic advice from a seven-year-old."

He figured Anya had let Monique in. Setting this thought aside, he came over and kissed her.

"EW!" Abigail exclaimed, making a gagging noise. "Yuck! Gross!"

"Go outside and play with your sister," Jefferson said while Monique laughed. "I'll get the sprinkler set up in a minute."

Seeming All too glad to go, Abigail scampered away while Monique looked at Jefferson.

"What kept you?" she asked.

"I had to take care of some stuff upstairs," Jefferson said. "Help Matthew find his swim trunks and the like."

He felt a pang as Maggie's words replayed in his head.

"Okay," Monique said. "Now, be a gentleman and take this bowl of potato salad off my lap. I'm pretty sure it shouldn't be staying there."

"You made potato salad?" Jefferson asked with a raised eyebrow as he found and lifted the large bowl off her lap.

"Joan helped. I mean, who do I look like? Ann Davis?"

"You be whomever you wanna be. For now, you can head on out back. I'll grab the burgers and be right there."

"Don't take so long this time," Monique advised as she headed for the open back door.

Jefferson rolled his eyes as she headed outside.

Handing the potato salad to Anya, He retrieved the plate of burgers from the kitchen just as Matthew was coming down.

"Everyone's already out back," Jefferson told him. "Go join them."

"Okay," Matthew said and hurried through the den.

My God, Jefferson thought, that is my son.

He knew it had to be the case. Maggie wouldn't lie about something like that. Plus, she hadn't planned on dying shortly after writing that letter. She was working up the courage to deal with this situation but never got the chance.

Grasping the plate of burgers, Jefferson headed outside into the backyard to find Monique telling the kids that, despite seeming capable of anything in their eyes, she could not set up the sprinkler for them to play under. He set the burgers down on the patio table, next to the potato salad, making sure it was far enough from the edge as Presley was nearby. She wouldn't steal anything, but, if something were to fall …

"Come on," he said, trying to redirect the dog's attention from the food.

He led the way to the side of the house and dragged the sprinkler across the patio to the grass. He turned it on and received squeals of delight for his efforts as the water sprayed over the yard.

The kids' desires satisfied, he went back inside to retrieve a plate of sausages and a bottle of wine for himself and Monique, having already set out the water and juice. Anya followed him, carrying the Caesar salad she had made. She accepted some wine from Jefferson and watched as the kids played.

"An 89 Loraine," Monique commented, eyeing the bottle as Jefferson poured, a small device hanging over the cup's rim telling him when it was almost full via a series of beeps. "Available at any convenience store. You really went all out."

"Perfect for a backyard picnic," Jefferson told her, pouring some into the tumbler attached to her chair.

He went over to his small barbecue and began putting burgers and sausages on it. As he worked, he listened to the kids playing under the sprinkler, Presley joining them. His thoughts drifted back to the block party and he found comfort in this smaller, more controllable environment. Everyone was having a good time while enclosed by the seven-foot-fence.

When everything was cooking, he came back and sat down next to Monique. For a few minutes, they drank and silently watched the kids play.

"Relax," Monique said, sensing something was up. "You're doing great with them. Under the circumstances, they couldn't be any luckier."

"Thanks," Jefferson said, supposing the best circumstances would be the kids still having their parents with them. "You want some more?"

He indicated the wine bottle.

"Sure," Monique said. "You trying to get me drunk or something?"

"Maybe," Jefferson said, pouring more wine into her tumbler. "We could have some fun after I get the kids to bed tonight."

"Hey," Monique asked with a smile. "How long are you planning on keeping me around here?"

"As long as you wanna stick around here," Jefferson replied, returning her smile.

The End!

Author's Note

I've been writing and revising this book since 2008, when I was a student at Loyola University. A variety of inspirations helped form this plot, some fiction and some drawn from my own experience. Here's a hint: the wilder a moment in the story sounds, the more likely it happened. Case in point: Abigail's grabbing Jefferson's dangling earphone to listen to his computer is taken from something I encountered in an Atlanta airport.

To be clear, I have had no family members die in a drunk driving accidents. For one thing, I don't even have a brother. I do have a guide dog, whom I have taken to Germany to visit relatives.

Over the years, I edited this tale to flush out the characters and the world they live in. In the original, much-shorter draft, there was no explanation of how a law professor can afford a Manhattan brownstone. Amy's role in the tale was also much simpler, leaving too many plot holes. Hopefully, my putting the manuscript away every so often and then looking it again a while later filled them. After twelve years of revising, I finally decided to put the work out there for readers like yourself to peruse. Time will tell how that goes, though I have my fingers crossed.

While this is my debut novel, my name is already floating around out there. You can find my short stories, <u>Red Bear</u> and <u>Hardwick and Carter</u>, on Amazon. Other pieces can be found on the online publications 101Words and Flash Fiction Magazine, as well as in the Calling All Writers anthologies. And, I promise you, <u>Par Angusta Ad Augusta</u>, won't be my last full-blown work ... not even close.

I'd like to thank my family, friends, and guide dogs. They've always supported my writing and inspired some of the best attributes in these characters. My mother's suggestion also inspired a much better title from the original "Reset". This also inspired some of Amy's background and a fun recurring gag, even if the related research wasn't as fun. My friends who've read this or other drafts of mine taught me more about writing than any class could, though some classes also helped. My guide dogs have been with me for a combined total of fifteen years, helping me navigate to work, school, activities, and writing sessions. They also slept relatively quietly as I wrote and rewrote.

Finally, a special thanks to Lauren. As I've taken what I think is best about me to create Jefferson, she has definitely inspired the best about Monique. Don't worry ... there are differences between us and them, and our stories will continue to diverge on their individual paths. I look forward to how it goes.

And, I hope you, dear readers, will join me on the beginning of what I hope is a long, creative journey in developing characters, settings, and plots that combine to tell unique, intense, and satisfying stories. Thank you for picking up <u>Par Angusta Ad Augusta</u> and look forward to the future.

WITHDRAWN

Made in the USA
Middletown, DE
03 January 2022

57583883R00201